THIS

SHALL BE

a

HOUSE

of

PEACE

THIS
SHALL BE
a
HOUSE
of
PEACE

PHIL HALTON

DUNDURN
TORONTO

Cover image: istock.com/Isfahan
Printer: Webcom, a division of Marquis Book Printing Inc.

Library and Archives Canada Cataloguing in Publication

Halton, Phil, author
This shall be a house of peace / Phil Halton.

Issued in print and electronic formats.
ISBN 978-1-4597-4223-9 (softcover).--ISBN 978-1-4597-4224-6
(PDF).--ISBN 978-1-4597-4225-3 (EPUB)

I. Title.

PS8615.A396T55 2019   C813'.6   C2018-902664-2
                                           C2018-902665-0

1 2 3 4 5   23 22 21 20 19

 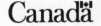  

We acknowledge the support of the **Canada Council for the Arts**, which last year invested $153 million to bring the arts to Canadians throughout the country, and the **Ontario Arts Council** for our publishing program. We also acknowledge the financial support of the **Government of Ontario**, through the **Ontario Book Publishing Tax Credit** and **Ontario Creates**, and the **Government of Canada**.

Nous remercions le **Conseil des arts du Canada** de son soutien. L'an dernier, le Conseil a investi 153 millions de dollars pour mettre de l'art dans la vie des Canadiennes et des Canadiens de tout le pays.

Care has been taken to trace the ownership of copyright material used in this book. The author and the publisher welcome any information enabling them to rectify any references or credits in subsequent editions. —*J. Kirk Howard, President*

VISIT US AT

dundurn.com | @dundurnpress | dundurnpress | dundurnpress

Dundurn
3 Church Street, Suite 500
Toronto, Ontario, Canada
M5E 1M2

To Lily and Leif

If leadership rests inside the lion's jaw,
so be it. Go snatch it from him.
Your lot shall be greatness, prestige, honour and glory.
And if all else fails, face death like a man.

— HANZALA OF BADGHIS, NINTH-CENTURY AFGHAN POET

PART ONE

PART ONE

CHAPTER 1

The sun hung behind the distant mountains, seemingly suspended in place below the horizon. Only a thin line of light outlined the far-off peaks. Swirling unseen in the darkness were clouds of dust, rolling over the landscape. As the sky began to lighten, the wind died and the dust settled over the countryside like a shroud. The air became heavy and still.

The sun's first harsh light fell upon a tiny village of a half-dozen abandoned mud-brick houses perched atop a rocky plateau. Their design was unchanged since ancient times; they squatted silently within the thick walls of the courtyard. Although the walls were solid, their surfaces were like lace, the plaster pockmarked with bullet holes and scarred by blasts, revealing the bricks underneath. The brown, terraced fields surrounding the village were untended and grew nothing but short clumps of grass. A disused track led up from a thin ribbon of asphalt that stretched across the valley below. A slight breeze blew ripples of dust between the houses, but all else was still in the heat of the new day.

In the centre of the abandoned village was the madrassa, its white paint barely visible under a thick coat of dust. In its courtyard, an old tarp was tied between the main building and one of the outer walls. A teenage boy with a wispy beard, perhaps fourteen years old, stood in the shade of the tarp, stirring a large pot of daal that bubbled over a small open fire. Set well into the ground near the pot was a large earthen jug that served as his tandoor.

A young boy no more than eleven years old played nearby, hitting a ball made from tightly tied plastic bags and scraps of cloth against the wall with an old cricket bat. "Tell me the story again," said Amin.

His brother's voice was wearier than it should have been for a boy his age. "But I have told you the story a thousand times."

Amin stopped hitting the ball and turned to him. "Please, Wasif. The smell of the daal always reminds me of it."

Wasif scowled, in the way that he had seen adults do. "I should be making you do your job and helping to prepare the meal." Even as he scolded his brother, he did not stop the rhythmic motion of the thick-handled spoon that kept the daal from burning to the sides of the pot. Amin had turned away and was contemplating the ball in his hand in silence, and so after a moment, Wasif relented and began to tell the story. "There once was a rich and powerful man with seven sons. One day, he summoned them all together and told them to sit with him. Once they were seated, he asked each of them, 'How much do you love me?'"

Amin continued to hit and chase the ball, but in his mind he saw himself seated with the other sons, preparing his reply to his father. His feet kicked up a roll of dust as he ran after the ball, quickly dissipating across the courtyard.

Wasif continued to tell the story, his mind drifting, stirring the daal rhythmically as he spoke. He had not yet reached the end when he decided that the meal was ready.

Amin implored his brother, "Aren't you going to finish?"

"You know how it ends. You could tell the story yourself in your sleep."

"That's not the point," said Amin.

Wasif gestured toward the pot and held out the spoon as he pulled a bag of yesterday's bread out of the crate that held their food. Amin put down his bat and ball, and took the spoon from him, quickly tasting the daal before beginning to stir it vigorously as his brother had done.

Wasif quietly approached the doorway of the madrassa, sliding off his sandals and standing just inside the door, waiting patiently. Young boys ranging in age from five to fourteen years old sat in rows that filled the spartan room. Other than a few ragged pillows and threadbare carpets, the only furniture was a small wooden bookstand on a low table at the front of the room.

The Mullah stood in front of the class, the boys — each one an orphan — watching him in attentive silence. Everything about him was plain and unadorned, from his thick, black beard, to his black turban and the homespun shalwar kamiz he wore. He was stocky through the shoulders and chest, and in his powerful hands was a well-worn Quran. He glanced at Wasif and gave him a brief nod before surveying the boys again in silence. They waited expectantly for him to speak, hardly moving. After a long moment of waiting, the Mullah pointed to one boy, smaller than the rest, in the middle row.

"You are truly blessed," said the Mullah. "Indeed, you are rich almost beyond belief. Do you know why?"

The small boy shuffled uncomfortably, thinking for a moment before answering earnestly in a thin voice. "Have you found my parents? Are they rich?"

An older student sitting at the front of the class shot a look of annoyance at the small boy. "Yes, we have! Your father is the

Amir! You will be going now to the palace and we all hope to find positions there working as your servants."

The class burst into laughter. The Mullah held up his hand for silence, and the boys froze. "Enough! I will accept no mockery here." In an instant, he was standing over the boy who had teased the other, his hand raised as if to strike him, but then stopped himself. He took a breath, and reassured the small boy. "No, we have not found your parents, though we are your family now and are as good as any that can be had."

The Mullah held up the Quran, its polished leather surface shining like nothing else in the dusty classroom. "All knowledge required by humankind is to be found in this book, praise God. It is the mother of all books, and it contains the solution to every human problem, no matter how complex. And here you will learn it by heart. This knowledge will be the source of your wealth, a pool of riches beyond belief."

The boys sat in complete stillness, transfixed by their teacher's voice as he spoke to them. He held their attention for a moment longer before releasing it with a wave of his hand. "But first, let us eat."

The boys were on their feet in an instant and stormed out of the room, digging through the pile of sandals on the other side of the door to find their own. The Mullah carefully placed his Quran onto the small wooden stand, and took a well-worn string of blue prayer beads off the table. The Mullah clicked his prayer beads mindlessly, as if they were a loose extension of his own fingers. Glancing around the room and satisfied that all was correct, he followed the boys outside, Wasif trailing close behind.

Hearing the boys as they rushed out of the madrassa, Amin put down his bat and went back to stand beside the pot of daal. He stirred it in earnest, hoping that it had not burned while he had been playing. The boys chattered as they lined up, from youngest to oldest, and passed pieces of stale bread back along the line.

The Mullah's voice filled the yard. "May you have your meal with gladness and health!"

The boys replied as one: "Allah yahaneek!"

They then shuffled forward to receive their food, Amin spooning daal into the middle of each boy's bread. They then made their way to a dusty carpet laid out in the shade of the compound walls. When all the boys had sat down and begun to eat, Amin spoke to the Mullah in a quiet voice. "Ma'alim, we have used the last of the cooking oil to make this meal."

The Mullah frowned. "Are you sure?"

Amin pointed to the old crate where they stored their food supplies. The contents were meagre. A sack of lentils, a smaller one of flour. A paper box of salt. A bag of tea. And two empty jugs of oil. The Mullah reached into his breast pocket and pulled out a few thin, sweaty bills, which he handed to Amin.

"Go down to the shop and buy some oil once you have eaten."

"Yes, Ma'alim."

Wasif looked down at his brother and plucked the bills out of Amin's hand. "Ma'alim, I will go to the shop. Amin, you can come with me if you like."

The Mullah pulled the money sharply out of Wasif's grasp and handed it back to Amin. "I did not ask your opinion, Wasif. You have a more important task to attend to, with me. We will eat later."

Amin tucked the money into his shirt pocket and spooned some daal onto a piece of bread for himself. Wasif's shoulders sank. He gave a longing look at the little food left in the pot as he waited to follow his teacher. The Mullah picked up a battered teapot and a glass, and with a gesture of his head led Wasif back inside.

Wasif took a seat at the head of the classroom as the Mullah
sat facing him, the familiar positions of teacher and student
reversed. The Mullah poured a glass of tea for himself and set
the pot down with a small air of ceremony. His hand reached
up to adjust his turban over the zebiba that prominently marked
his forehead. When he spoke, his voice was hard.

"Are you ready to practise?"

"Yes, Ma'alim." Wasif hesitated. "But I have a question first."

A flash of annoyance passed over the Mullah's face and was
gone. Wasif saw it and his voice faltered. "It is no matter, Ma'alim.
I am ready."

The Mullah's face darkened further. "Out with it, boy. Don't
say one thing and then change it for another."

Wasif looked crestfallen. "It is just that … I wanted to know
if you thought I would ever truly become a hafiz?"

The Mullah sighed. His hand moved toward the boy's shoulder, but he stopped himself, resting it on his own knee instead.
His words were thick in his mouth for a moment, until he managed to ask, "Tell me, why do you want to do this?"

Wasif twisted the tails of his shirt in his hand. He was sure
that his answer was wrong, and so he said nothing.

The Mullah spoke for the boy instead. "There are many reasons why one would want to memorize the entirety of the holy
Quran. Some people do so to make money from public recita-
tions. Others focus on the promise of acceptance into heaven for
all who become hafiz. There are many reasons why one would
want to do this. Which one is yours?"

When Wasif spoke, the words came out in a quick tumble.
"To please God, and so that I will have something of great value
that no man can ever take from me."

A smile broke across the Mullah's hard face. "All good things
begin with sincerity in the heart of the doer, Wasif. These are

good reasons to want to become a hafiz. I have no doubt that you will succeed. Now, let us begin."

Wasif cleared his throat. "All praise belongs to God, Lord of the Universe, the Beneficent, the Merciful, and Master of the Day of Judgment, You alone we do worship ..."

Wasif continued to recite the Quran by heart, pushing down the feelings of hunger that rose from inside his empty belly. The Mullah sat, eyes half-closed, clicking prayer beads through his fingers and reciting silently along with him.

Amin stepped out of the school compound, closing the thick wooden door behind him with a clang. It could only be barred from the inside, and so he left it unlocked. In any case, no visitors or even strangers ever came to the madrassa. Walking toward the track that led to the narrow highway at the bottom of the valley, he carried the cricket bat over one shoulder, from time to time swinging it at the countless rocks on the ground. In his mind, he was one of the Amir's seven sons, leading a hunting party through the wastes.

It took Amin over half an hour to descend the heights where the abandoned village and madrassa sat and reach the larger village nestled alongside the road at the bottom of the valley. As he left the outskirts of the upper village, he walked through small terraced fields dotted with the charred stumps of olive trees. The Mullah had said that the trees, all gone now, had dated from the time of Timur-e Lang, which Amin knew to be before the Russians. As Amin descended farther, the fields were instead filled with the wreckage of wooden frames, now grey and brittle like old bones, that had once supported grapevines. The last terraced fields were filled with rutted, dusty earth that gave no clue as to what had once grown there.

Amin kept moving, past the fields, to where the path turned very narrow and began to zigzag though a series of switchbacks down to the highway. By the time he reached his destination, the small ramshackle chai khana, his eyes were red and blurry from the blowing dust. The building sat strategically at the point where the rocky valley narrowed, forcing travellers to pass nearby even before there was a road. Set back from the broken asphalt were two dozen houses in a cluster that formed the lower village. The houses roughly followed the line of the shallow river running parallel to the road, and they were surrounded by drab winter fields that would become productive again in the spring.

The chai khana itself was a simple, low structure made from rough-hewn wood, scrap metal, and plastic sheets. A blanket hung over the doorway in a futile attempt to keep the dust from over-taking the interior. Next door was a large, green metal box that was once the closed rear structure of a ZIL army truck, abandoned by the Russians years before. Nearby were a few parked vehicles belonging to travellers who had stopped for a rest. Amin watched as a battered old bus bounced along the asphalt toward the village, avoiding none of the potholes, trailing a cloud of black smoke from its engine.

The bus stopped near the ZIL, its progress halted by a chain that had been strung across the road. A young boy, wearing a sequined black vest and a matching prayer cap perched on the back of his head, emerged from the door of the ZIL and took up a position by the chain. The boy stared at the bus like a hawk who had found his prey. Amin was certain that none of this — not the chain nor the strange boy — had been here the last time he had visited the shop a few weeks ago. The Mullah's oft-repeated words echoed in his mind: *Be pious in all things and mind one's own business.* Sloping his cricket bat over his shoulder, he flitted past the checkpoint and did his best to ignore it and the boy.

With his back to the stopped bus, Amin approached a market stall built against the side of the chai khana. The boy in the vest stared at him for a moment. Having sized up Amin, he returned his attention to the bus.

The stall had a wooden door, propped up high with a stick to form a sign reading *Dry Goods*. With this stick, the door could be pulled down to secure the stall at the first sign of danger. Amin caught sight of the shopkeeper sitting in his tiny space, hemmed in by all manner of packaged goods. The shopkeeper was focusing all his attention on the bus and had not noticed the boy approaching.

"Haji, I am here for a jug of cooking oil."

Amin's voice startled the shopkeeper. When Amin saw this, he lowered his voice mid-sentence.

The shopkeeper managed a tight smile. "What does a boy want with cooking oil, when he could be buying sweets?"

Amin persisted. "It is for the Ma'alim, to feed the boys in the madrassa. I have never asked for sweets, Haji."

"The other boy told me of your madrassa when he came to buy food. And he bought a sweet."

"That was my older brother, Haji." Amin imagined with a mix of admiration and disappointment how Wasif would have haggled for a piece of candy to be included in the price of whatever he had bought for the Mullah.

The shopkeeper stuck a finger under his turban and scratched at his forehead. "I have never seen this Ma'alim that you both speak of. Other than you and your brother, I've never seen anyone from your madrassa at all. Where do you say it is?"

Amin pointed at the top of the hills overlooking the highway and gave him the same answer as before. "In that village, Haji."

The shopkeeper scowled as he gazed up the slope. "That's no village — no one either goes to or comes from there. It has been deserted for years. Since the Russians."

"As you say, Haji. But in it is a madrassa, full of boys for whom I must buy cooking oil."

The shopkeeper snorted. "That is a place for djinn, not young boys. Why have I not seen more of you?"

Amin repeated the words that he had heard the Mullah use before. "Our needs are small, and God provides." The shopkeeper looked skeptical, but Amin continued. "I am sure that the Ma'alim would welcome visitors."

The shopkeeper laughed. "Travel up there to a deserted village, full of djinn and Russian land mines? Never." He took a furtive glance over the boy's shoulder. "We have problems enough of our own." The shopkeeper forced a smile back onto his face. "And so a boy appears from nowhere to buy oil. Wonders never cease. How much money do you have?"

Amin held up the bills given to him by the Mullah, spreading them apart slightly so that they could be counted. The shopkeeper frowned and covered the bills with a henna-stained hand, so that they could not be seen by others. He reached behind himself and lifted a very small plastic jug of oil. "This is what you can afford."

"So little? I thought it would be twice as much."

The shopkeeper picked up the jug again and placed it back inside his shop. "I can sell you twice as much for twice as much money. But the price is the price." The shopkeeper flashed his eyes toward the checkpoint. "In the past weeks, we have begun to pay high taxes."

Amin glanced over his shoulder toward the bus, still waiting on the road by the chain. He could not see anyone, not even the boy in the vest, so he turned back to the shopkeeper. Handing over his thin paper bills, he held out his other hand for the half portion of oil. Amin tightened the cap until it was snug, wiping his hands on his shirttail. With his cricket bat over his shoulder, he turned to walk back the way he had come, dangling the oil jug.

The shopkeeper reached out and yanked on his sleeve. "Not that way," he said, and gestured around the back of the chai khana. "Give a wide berth to what goes on here, and hide that oil."

Amin tucked the jug under his arm and did as he was told. He walked behind the chai khana, stepping gingerly through a pile of garbage whose stench made his eyes water. Reaching the other side of the ramshackle building, he peeked around the corner. The bus still sat in the middle of the road. Seeing no one, he darted across the road.

As he did so, two men carrying rifles stepped off of the bus. Amin had never seen men like these before. His heart quickened a little, but he kept his head down and lengthened his stride, taking only side glances at the men as he went. Bandits. One was tall, with a scar across his whole face that left his nose looking ragged, like a thick handful of torn paper. He clutched a small wad of bills that he pushed into his shirt pocket. The other was shorter and fat, with long greasy hair that hung limp around his face. Both glanced at Amin, but neither paid any attention to a boy who was not worth robbing. The fat bandit unhooked the chain so that it dropped down to the asphalt. He lazily waved the bus onward. The taller man stretched, holding his rifle high above his head in both his hands.

Amin glanced over his shoulder again, back toward the bandits, just as the boy in the sequined vest stepped out of the ZIL. He noticed Amin and shouted at him. "You! What have you got there?"

Amin did not want to stop, but he knew what was expected when strangers met. He turned to face them, but lost his nerve and looked down at the ground, avoiding eye contact with any of them. "Only cooking oil, to feed the students at the madrassa," he said, hoping that even the most desperate bandit would not stoop to steal food from religious students.

The tall bandit spoke to the boy in the vest in mock serious-ness. "Young cousin, you should go with him to the madrassa. You could become a learned man!"

Amin hesitated. Perhaps he had misjudged them. If he was serious, it would be a sin to turn the boy away. He spoke cautiously. "Our Ma'alim teaches the Quran and the Hadith to all who wish to learn."

The boy in the vest spat toward the taller bandit and marched over to the side of the road where the chain was tied. The tall bandit took a half step toward him, but the other laid a restraining hand against his chest. "Ignore it," said the fat bandit.

"Our young cousin needs a lesson. Our fathers would not have stood for this," said the tall bandit through clenched teeth.

"Our fathers are dead," replied the fat bandit, "and so the world turns upside down. The lesson to be learned is to do what one needs to do to survive."

Amin watched as the boy in the vest pulled an automatic pistol from a holster hanging on the post that supported the chain. Amin froze with fear as the boy walked straight at him. The boy kept coming and mimed shooting at Amin with the pistol held high over his head. He pressed the barrel against Amin's chest, pushing hard into his flesh. "I will teach you a lesson in respect," he spat. Amin stood still, holding his breath.

The boy shoved him, both hands gripping the pistol, but he was too small to push Amin off his feet. Finally, he shouted in frustration at the bandits, his voice shrill and angry. "I've had enough of this stupid boy. Beat him! Teach him a lesson! Beat him until your arms are tired and I am bored of it."

Amin stood his ground, unsure what would happen if he ran. His grip tightened on the cricket bat that hung at his side, but as the bandits came closer he did not dare use it on the boy. Instead, he looked at the men and pleaded, "I've done you no harm."

The taller bandit glared at a few men who were leaning out the door of the chai khana to see what was going on. They ducked back inside, the blanket door swaying in the dusty air.

"As you wish, young cousin," said the fat bandit.

His partner then grabbed Amin roughly by the collar of his shirt, ripping it as he twisted it in his fist. With his free hand he took the bat and tossed it to the side of the road. His first blow knocked Amin sideways to the ground. He dropped onto Amin's chest, grinding his knees hard into the boy's ribs before rolling him over onto his belly. Amin strained to look up, helpless as the shorter bandit squatted down by his head. As he leaned down low, his greasy hair brushed against Amin's face. "This is your first lesson."

Amin cried out in shock as the bandit hit him across his shoulders with a bundle of long antennas broken off of cars that they had robbed. As each blow fell, Amin screamed again, until it became one continuous sound. He turned his head to the chai khana, knowing in his heart that someone would help him. *No good person would let this happen*, he thought. As each blow struck his shoulders, his eyes darted back and forth all around him, but no one came. The universe shrank and time slowed down, until all Amin's thoughts were encompassed in the pain in his side and his shoulders and his head.

Towering above him, the boy in the vest looked on with cruel eyes and laughed.

CHAPTER 2

U p above the valley, the madrassa was filled with Wasif's reedy voice. "And obey Allah and His Messenger. And fall into no disputes, lest ye lose heart and your power depart; and be patient and persevering ..."

As Wasif chanted the sacred verses, the Mullah swirled the tea in his cup. He did not take his eyes off of him, anticipating the poetic words of the Quran in his own head as the boy recited them.

"For Allah is with those ..."

Wasif's voice trailed off at the sound of others shouting in alarm in the courtyard, breaking the rhythm of the Quran in his mind. The Mullah leapt from his seat and moved toward the door, where he was checked by a rush of young boys storming into the room. In their midst was Amin, staggering and trying to swallow his tears. His head and shoulders were covered in blood, his kamiz torn into fine strips revealing his lacerated back. His hands were empty and his expression was full of pain, but even more it was full of shame that the others were seeing him in such a state.

Amin collapsed onto his knees in front of the Mullah. "Forgive me, Ma'alim."

The young boys stood in a tight clutch around Amin, speaking over each other as they tried to make sense of what they were seeing. Wasif felt shame well up in his own face as he saw his brother's pain laid bare for all to see. He tried to herd the other boys back through the door and away from his brother. His throat was thick. "Get out! All of you!"

"Wasif," said the Mullah, "be still. Everyone, be quiet."

Wasif went to his brother's side, kneeling with him and taking one of his hands in his own. He kept his eyes low, not looking at his brother, worried that he would begin to cry, as well. The Mullah gestured for Amin to sit on a cushion and then took a seat. "Give him room," the Mullah commanded. Amin struggled to the cushion, supported by his brother. The boys all backed away and stood in a cluster behind the Mullah, fidgeting and pulling at their shirts. The Mullah's actions were slow and measured. He poured fresh tea from the pot into his cup, giving it a quick swish. He stood and moved to the doorway, flicking the liquid out of the cup onto the dust outside. Taking his seat again, he refilled the cup and handed it to Amin.

"Drink this, and then tell me what happened."

Amin told him in between gasps. He left out no details, even of his own humiliation. Wasif turned redder and redder as the story unfolded, feeling every bit of pain and shame as if it were his own. When Amin finished, he could barely force his words out between sobs. "They only stopped ... when a truck pulled up ... at the checkpoint. They would have ... killed me ... I am sure."

The Mullah listened in silence until the story was finished. He appeared deep in thought as next he examined Amin's back and head. His hands were rough, but he examined the boy's wounds gently and thoroughly. He tore the remnants of the boy's kamiz, leaving him bare from the waist up. "Wasif. Bring me the ewer and bowl."

Wasif let go of his brother's hand and did as he was asked, setting the bowl down behind Amin and holding out the ewer. The Mullah took it and very carefully poured water on Amin's back, using a balled-up piece of the boy's shirt to help wipe the blood away so that he could see the wounds underneath. Amin's back was swollen and covered in lacerations, and the boy shuddered every time the Mullah touched him.

"These are not so deep," said the Mullah. "These cuts will heal quickly, I am sure." Wasif reached for his brother's hand, but Amin had tucked both of his arms tightly around himself, eyes closed, as he tried to master his feelings again.

The Mullah, satisfied that he had washed most of the blood off Amin's back, tore the cleanest parts of the ripped shirt into long strips, which he wrapped around the boy's chest and back, tying them off on one side. As he tightened the bandages, Amin began to sob again, making a sound like a wounded animal.

"Enough, boy," said the Mullah. "During the war, mujahideen suffered much worse than this in silence. A man would not cry because of a wound such as this."

Amin shoved a fist into his mouth, breathing through sobs and flared nostrils. Eventually his breathing became calmer and he opened his eyes, looking over toward his brother. Wasif patted his leg and gave his hand a gentle squeeze.

Satisfied with the bandages, the Mullah stood and held out his hands. Wasif understood the gesture, and poured the remaining water from the ewer over them so that the Mullah could wash the blood from between his fingers. His hands moved in a quick and familiar rhythm, but Wasif could see the tension in his hands. The Mullah clenched his jaw, and

Wasif knew that he was angry. Angrier than he had ever seen anyone before.

When the Mullah was finished, he shook his hands dry and addressed Wasif. "Find a shirt for Amin. Then ensure that the other boys finish their practice and their chores." Before Wasif could ask him any questions, the Mullah turned and strode out of the madrassa.

Wasif followed the Mullah outside to the compound door. The Mullah paused for a moment as he stepped over the high threshold. "Bar this behind me." And without another word, he was gone.

Wasif pushed the door open so that he could watch the Mullah, his hands clutching both sides of the door frame. The boys of the school pressed close behind him, straining to see what he was looking at, but also careful not to touch him. Wasif turned to look for his brother amongst the boys, spying him sitting on the outside step of the classroom wearing a mismatched kamiz. "Brother, I'm going with the Ma'alim," said Wasif. "You must stay here with the others and rest."

Amin brushed the tears from his eyes with a dirty sleeve. "I wish to go where you go, just as it was before we came to the madrassa."

For once, Wasif didn't chastise his brother for disagreeing with him. "Brother, you can't walk back down to the highway. Rest and get strong."

Amin looked away, tears welling up in his eyes again. Wasif turned away from his brother and headed after the Mullah. As he stepped over the threshold, he repeated the Mullah's instruction to one of the other boys: "Bar this door behind me." The younger boys looked at him with wide eyes.

As Wasif reached the edge of the village, he could see that the Mullah was already striding down the switchbacks below the terraced fields. In the large and desolate landscape, he seemed impossibly small, easily swallowed up by the height of the mountains or the expanse of the desert at their foot. Wasif quickened his pace and reached the point where the path became thinner and descended the mountain. Looking back over his shoulder, he saw that the other boys from the madrassa had followed him, hanging back a little in vain hope that he would not see them.

"Get back in the madrassa," shouted Wasif, trying to summon authority to his voice. "You have chores to attend to."

None of the boys answered, but neither did they turn back toward the madrassa. They stood in a tight cluster on the pathway, simply watching. Wasif shouted again, pointing at them with his whole arm in the way that the Mullah did when he was angry. "Do as I say!"

When the boys remained standing where they were, Wasif gave up and headed down the path to catch up with the Mullah. The pack of boys began to follow him again, this time much closer than before. Wasif tried to outpace them, half running down the hill, at times sliding down the slope between the switchbacks, creating balls of dust that rolled down the hill ahead of him. Wasif stopped at the last turn on the path before it flattened out, still a hundred yards from the highway itself. He turned around to see the boys stopped in a group just behind him, unsure whether to approach any closer. Then he turned again to face the highway. In the heat of midday, there were no cars at the checkpoint. The chain was pulled taut across the road again, and he guessed that the bandits and the boy in the vest that Amin had described were lounging in the shade inside the ZIL. Through the doorway of the shop he could see the shopkeeper rearranging his wares. Everything else around the chai khana was still except for the eddying dust clouds.

Wasif watched as the Mullah slowly approached the checkpoint. He stopped often, standing still and raising his head to listen before moving closer again. Wasif moved a little closer, as well, sheltering in the meagre shade of some rocks along the side of the trail. The younger boys now crowded in with him, craning their necks over the rocks to see what was happening.

In time, the Mullah reached the highway itself, planting his feet firmly on the hot, grey asphalt, facing the ZIL. The shopkeeper was looking at him from his tiny stall, unsure who this stranger was. The Mullah stared back until the shopkeeper pulled the door of the stall shut, locking himself inside. Then the Mullah spoke loudly: "Show yourselves, thieves and blasphemers."

Wasif held his breath as the Mullah waited a long moment. There was no sound from inside the ZIL, no reaction at all that Wasif could see. Dust swirled around the Mullah's feet, pausing only for a moment before it continued down the highway to Kandahar. All of the boys were on their feet now, jostling each other to see what the Mullah would do next. Wasif moved a little closer to the highway, finding a spot where he could crouch behind a pile of dry brush. The other boys followed, unwilling to be left behind.

The Mullah drew himself taller and spoke much louder this time: "Show yourselves, thieves and blasphemers!" A head poked out from behind the blanket of the chai khana to look at him before disappearing again.

This time there was the sound of movement from inside the ZIL. The tall bandit staggered out through the door in a cloud of blue smoke, his eyes bloodshot and rimmed with red. The sound of the metal door striking the side of the ZIL caused the boys to startle, but the Mullah did not flinch. The bandit's kalash hung loosely in one hand, barrel pointing down at the ground, as he stared at the Mullah. Next out the door came the boy in the vest, whose skinny legs were bare under his long shirt. The last to leave the ZIL was the shorter bandit, who was hitching up his loose pants as he stepped through the doorway. A kalash was slung across his shoulder with a dirty piece of rope. His hands pulled at the drawstring of his shalwar and his fingers fumbled as he tried to tie a knot in the string. When he had secured his pants in place and his hands were finally free, he swung the rifle off his shoulder into both hands, gripping it tightly and pointing it at the Mullah.

The Mullah did not move from where he stood on the asphalt. When he spoke, his voice was firm and unyielding. "Give back what you have stolen and win the blessing of God."

The bandits' laughter sounded like the short barks of wild dogs. The tall bandit moved to the left while the shorter one moved to the right, approaching the Mullah from both sides as if they were a pack, circling their prey. The short bandit made a stabbing gesture toward the Mullah with his kalash, punctuating each of his words. "Enough of your noise."

"Give us whatever you have or you'll ask God for His blessing in person," added the tall bandit.

The Mullah looked straight ahead and did not move. He held his hands out to his side, showing that they were empty. "You threaten a religious man with a gun? And by blaspheming?"

The boy in the sequined vest spat on the ground and glared at the Mullah. The short bandit stepped closer to him and lifted the kalash in an overhand grip, high over his own head. Staring at the Mullah, he then drilled it slowly downward until the muzzle just touched the Mullah's forehead. He and the Mullah locked eyes, the bandit snarling to try to frighten the Mullah. The Mullah kept his head up, and it was the bandit who looked away first.

Wasif watched in horror as the other bandit charged forward and hit the Mullah in the chest with the butt of his rifle. The Mullah staggered, but remained on his feet. Both bandits shouted in his face. "Kneel!"

As Wasif lifted himself out of a crouch to better see what was going on, Amin crouched down beside him. Wasif looked at his brother, eyes wide. Amin's new kamiz was stained with blood across the back, and the boy's face was tight and stained with tears.

"You should have stayed in the madrassa," whispered Wasif.

"I don't want to be apart from you again," croaked Amin through his tears.

Wasif hissed into his ear. "Choke it back, brother. Act like a man. The Mullah will make this right." Wasif wiped his brother's face with his own sleeve, but Amin pushed him away. Wasif saw that his sleeve was red with blood. Amin wiped his tears away with his own sleeve and tried to harden the expression on his face, staring down at the road away from where the Mullah still stood with bandits on his right and on his left.

Wasif saw that the Mullah had closed his eyes. His right hand clenched and reopened, his thumb and forefinger clicking with purpose through the prayer beads that dangled from his fist. Other than his hand and his lips, which were moving slightly, he remained perfectly still. The bandits stared at him, confused by this man who showed no fear.

Amin kept his eyes fixed on the bandits, but spoke quietly to his brother. "We have to help the Mullah."

Wasif's voice wavered with doubt. "Amin, what can we do? I've already seen how well you fared against them." Amin's face recoiled as if he had been stung. Wasif took his hand again, but Amin pulled it away. "I didn't mean that, Amin. Any one of us would have …" Wasif didn't have the words to continue.

The Mullah, who had been whispering to himself, began to speak louder, his words growing in strength, tumbling out of his mouth. "As for the thieves, amputate their hands in recompense for what they have committed, as a punishment from Allah, for He is exalted in might and wise."

The bandit pressed the muzzle hard against the Mullah's forehead, trying to push him to the ground. "I said kneel!" he shouted. The Mullah's body bent backwards at the waist under the pressure from the gun, but his feet did not move. His fingers gripped the prayer beads in his hand so tightly that he snapped the string that held them together. The beads scattered at his feet.

Amin gripped his brother's arm. "We have to do something." When Wasif did not reply, he gripped his arm even tighter. "We have to do something *right now*."

Wasif picked up a stone off the ground and ran a short distance until he was in range of the bandits. He drew his arm back and threw the stone as hard as he could. His first throw fell short, but he grabbed another jagged rock from the ground and threw it even harder. It struck the short bandit on the arm, causing him to turn to see where it had come from. Another boy who had followed Wasif threw a stone of his own that struck the taller bandit in the chest. Soon all the young boys were pelting the bandits with a steady hail of rocks. The bandits turned and pointed their rifles at the boys, but neither fired.

"We'll kill you all if you don't stop," shouted the short bandit. The boy in the vest hid behind the taller bandit, clutching the man's legs with both hands.

The Mullah opened his eyes and looked around. Seeing the boys, he stepped back from the bandits, out of the way of the hail of rocks. The boys redoubled their efforts, raining down a torrent of stones that struck the bandits again and again. The Mullah pointed an angry finger at his tormentors and once again began to recite scripture: "But whoever repents after his wrongdoing and reforms, indeed, Allah will turn to him in forgiveness."

Under the barrage of rocks, the bandits contorted their faces in frustration. They pointed their rifles at the boys and shouted curses. A sharp stone struck the short bandit in the face, staggering him and drawing blood. The bandits began to wither under the hail of stones and the Mullah's shouted sermon. Then both bandits covered their heads and faces with their arms and shrank away from the Mullah and the volley of stones. The boy in the vest, who had been struck in the head, lay in a fetal position on the dark grey asphalt strip, his arms shielding his face. The short bandit peered through his fingers in fear at the Mullah, who seemed to tower over them now, roaring out the judgment of God.

"Indeed, Allah is Forgiving and Merciful," the Mullah shouted, waving with one hand in a gesture for the boys to stop. They had moved even farther forward as the bandits' power waned, and they now stood in a loose line behind the Mullah, still gripping rocks in their hands.

The boy in the vest squirmed on the ground in pain but reserved all his spite for the Mullah. "Kill him!" he whined to the bandits. "Get up and kill him! Or Tarak will hear of it!"

Amin, holding onto his brother's shoulder for support, pointed at the writhing boy. "He's the one who ordered them to beat me."

The Mullah was incredulous. "Are you sure? These men listen to that boy?"

The short bandit regained his wits and grabbed the boy by the wrist, pulling him to his feet. He was met by a sudden shower of rocks from the boys. The bandit scuttled away from the Mullah and the students, pulling the boy with him along the road. As he went, he called out to the Mullah: "You don't understand. This one is Tarak's favourite."

The boy hissed and spat but could not break free of the bandit's grip. The taller bandit disappeared behind the ZIL, quickly reappearing atop a battered motorcycle, his kalash balanced across the handlebars. A few of the boys threw rocks at the rolling target, but they all missed, their missiles clanging off the metal sides of the ZIL. The bandit kick-started the bike and tore off down the highway, stopping by his two companions.

The taller bandit handed his kalash to the other one, who mounted the bike and lay the weapon with his own across his knees. The boy, who had turned toward the Mullah, shouted at him: "Tarak will know of you!"

Wasif threw another stone that struck the boy full in the face, staggering him. The short bandit reached behind himself to pull the boy onto the motorcycle seat, and was hit by another hail of stones. The motorcycle began to pull away, and with both hands on the boy the bandit lost his grip on the two kalashes, which clattered to the ground.

As he sped off, the taller bandit shouted back at the Mullah, "Nothing happens here without our say-so! We'll be back." The boy sat sideways behind the two older bandits, holding on to the underside of the seat, staring malevolently at the Mullah as they peeled away into the distance in a churn of dust.

The smallest boy from the madrassa threw one last rock that fell well short of the retreating bandits. The Mullah shook his head in disbelief. "Imagine! Bandits ordered around by a bacha bereesh!"

Wasif was puzzled by the unfamiliar word. "I don't understand, Ma'alim."

The Mullah's answer was curt. "Be glad that you don't." The boys had gathered around him in a tight knot, seeking his protective nearness.

"Ma'alim, you won't let them come back?" asked Amin, forcing his voice to be firm.

"Insh'allah, they will not return."

Amin persisted. "But if they do?"

The Mullah turned, an expression of irritation showing on his face as he looked above Amin's head over at the chai khana. "Then we will do what is right."

The shopkeeper raised the door to his stall, and at the same time a small crowd of men approached the Mullah cautiously from the chai khana. At their head was the tea shop's owner, a heavy-set old man named Faizal, with few teeth and some grey hairs cut close to the scalp showing under a greasy, green turban. He waddled toward the Mullah, holding his hand at his forehead in a vague, obsequious gesture and looking down at the ground.

"Haji, I was just coming out to assure you that I can pay you for protection, as I paid the last, er, police at the checkpoint."

The Mullah scanned the faces in the crowd, looking to see someone laugh at what sounded to him like a joke. "Police?"

Faizal looked nervous as he explained. "These were Tarak Sagwan's men. He is calling himself the chief of police for the district." Faizal broke into a wide gap-toothed grin. "But this cannot be news to you, Haji. You must all know each other's doings ..." His voice trailed off as the Mullah's face turned even more grim.

"Perhaps all bandits do know each other's doings. I know little of this Tarak Sagwan."

Faizal bowed and shuffled his feet as the men behind him began to murmur, wondering who this man really was, with his crowd of boys. "Of course. Of course, I did not mean to imply anything of the sort. A thousand apologies."

The Mullah scanned the crowd again, but no one else stepped forward to speak. Weary of the interaction, he ended it. "Now we will return to the madrassa and leave you to your business."

When the Mullah mentioned the madrassa, the villagers' faces relaxed and their voices became louder. Faizal's smile broadened and he gestured at the orphans with a dirty finger. "Ah, Haji Mullah! I see that you have students, but where is this madrassa?"

"In the village on the plateau," replied the Mullah. "We will be returning now, after Amin retrieves the oil that was stolen from him." Amin understood and nodded. He and Wasif began looking for the oil among the many pieces of loot strewn around the checkpoint. All the other boys soon joined in.

"That village has been deserted for years," continued Faizal.

"Was deserted," said the Mullah. "I moved into my uncle's home three months ago."

Faizal wrung his hands and let his jaw drop in confusion. "But how is it that we have never seen you in all that time?"

The Mullah looked Faizal square in the eye. "Hospitality, though a duty, is onerous. The boys come to market. I make my own tea." The Mullah seemed distracted by a sudden thought, and turned to address the boys. "It is time for us to return."

Faizal raised both hands in a loose gesture of prayer. "Praise be to the Righteous! Let me at least feed you to say thanks."

The Mullah spoke curtly. "As I have said, we will not be staying." He turned his back to the crowd, supervising the boys, who were still searching the checkpoint.

When it was clear to Faizal that he had been dismissed, he returned to the chai khana, the crowd following him inside, abuzz with conversation. The Mullah saw that none of the boys had picked up the two rifles that lay on the asphalt, although they eyed them with interest.

Before he touched the weapons, the Mullah first gathered up the scattered bits and broken string from his prayer beads. Satisfied that he had found all of the beads, he put them into a pocket to be restrung later. He picked up the first rifle, the butt covered in layers of blue tape to hold it together where the wood had split. The Mullah's hands flowed over the worn and familiar parts of the weapon. He pulled the action partway back to expose, to his surprise, an empty chamber. He looked and saw that the magazine was empty, as well. He set the first weapon aside and inspected the second rifle in the same way. It, too, had only an empty magazine.

The Mullah glanced up to see that all the boys had stopped what they had been doing and were squatting on their haunches in front of him, watching as he handled the weapons. Their eyes followed every move of his hands, drinking it all in.

He put the second rifle down in the dust at his feet and gave a sparse laugh. Neither kalash had been loaded! Looking at the boys, the Mullah repeated something that his own father had often said. "An unloaded gun makes two people afraid." The boys looked baffled. Instead of explaining, he asked them, "Did you find the oil?"

Amin looked uncomfortable as he answered. "Not yet, Ma'alim."

The Mullah nodded at Wasif. "Get the boys into two lines and count them to see that they are all here. We will leave in a few minutes." When he saw Wasif start pushing the boys into line, he focused his attention on the ZIL. He took a few steps in its direction, pushed aside the door covering, and stepped inside. The boys watched him enter the ZIL, wondering what he might find in it.

Wasif finished manhandling the boys into line, counting them twice to be sure that they were all there. He put Amin at the end of the second line and told another boy to support him. Amin was tired and in pain, but he complained bitterly. "Brother, you could for once put me at the front of the line."

Wasif went to give him a playful swat, but stopped when Amin winced before he even touched him. "Brother, it is not from spite that I put you here. I will be at the head of the line. With you at the end, we will be sure to shepherd all the boys home."

Amin was embarrassed at his own complaint and said nothing more.

Before long the boys became rowdy, pushing and wrestling each other on the asphalt as they waited for the Mullah. Wasif's thin authority could not to keep them in line — the group risked descending into chaos. Just then, the Mullah reappeared in the doorway. An automatic pistol, stuffed in a leather holster, hung from a belt slung over one shoulder. In one fist the Mullah held a hand grenade that had lost so much of its olive drab paint it was now nearly silver; his thumb was hooked around the jug of cooking oil. In his other hand was a small tin cigarette box stuffed with so many bills the lid would not close.

The Mullah set the pistol and grenade down beside the rifles and handed the oil to Amin, who held it gingerly. He looked at the boys, who had now moved back into an approximation of two lines. "Amin, you will take the boys back to the madrassa. I will join you shortly. Wasif, you will wait here with me."

Amin thought to complain and be the one to stay with the Mullah, but he saw from the Mullah's expression that he should simply obey. The boys began to stream back up the mountainside, and Amin left his place at the rear of the line to lead them, setting a slow pace up the steep track. Silent at first, they became more excited the farther they left the highway behind. Their chattering reached Wasif and the Mullah back at the checkpoint.

"Wasif, watch these weapons until I return. I will only be a moment."

Wasif answered as he'd been taught. "Yes, Ma'alim."

The Mullah nodded, and taking the cigarette tin in his hand, approached the shopkeeper in the stall beside the chai khana. Wasif positioned himself close enough to hear them speak. The shopkeeper seemed nervous but greeted the Mullah politely enough. The Mullah skipped over the usual pleasantries in his irritation at this day spent in the unwanted company of others.

"How much did they take from you?"

The shopkeeper's hands rested possessively on his few wares. "They always left enough so that I would survive."

The Mullah shook his head. "Survive to be robbed again, that is." He pulled a fraction of the dirty bills from the tin and gave them to him. "Take this, then. Some of it was probably yours to begin with."

The shopkeeper stuffed the bills into a deep pocket hidden under his kamiz. "And what do you expect from me in return?"

The Mullah's next words came easily to his lips. "Only that you honour God, pray daily, fast during Ramadan, strive to make the hajj in your lifetime, and give zakat to the poor."

The shopkeeper sat up straighter and leaned out toward the Mullah, straining against the confines of his tiny stall. "Jazak'allah! May God reward you!" He thought for a moment and then rummaged around in a jumble of stock behind him and pulled out a small waxed-paper package, wrapped and tied tightly, which he handed to the Mullah. "A gift for a gift. You'll need these more than I will."

The Mullah weighed the package in his hand without opening it and grunted his thanks. After a short glance at Wasif, he walked around the front of the chai khana.

Wasif called out to the Mullah. "Ma'alim, should I come with you?"

"This is no business for children," replied the Mullah. "You will.wait there." Pulling the blanket that covered the doorway aside, the Mullah disappeared inside.

Wasif watched him go. The shopkeeper climbed out of his stall and lowered the swing door over it, sealing it shut with an ancient iron padlock. He did not look at Wasif as he walked to his home. Wasif looked around, alone in the landscape. He could hear muffled voices in the chai khana but could not make out what was being said. He walked out to the middle of the highway, straining to see as far as he could in each direction. He thought he could perhaps see the minarets of Kandahar in the distance. But he was not entirely sure what they might look like even if he could see them.

The afternoon wore on as Wasif waited by the road, gazing anxiously in each direction. He had nearly given up looking when an indistinct bump appeared at the distant end of the highway. As he squinted and shaded his eyes with his hand, he could just make out two hazy shapes travelling along the highway toward him, sunlight flashing off their windshields. As they began to close on the checkpoint, Wasif turned toward the chai khana to warn the Mullah, but stopped himself. The two kalashes lay nearby, and the slack chain still stretched across the road. He did not stop to reconsider the idea that had come to him, but instead did as the Mullah did and acted with conviction.

He tightened the chain and tied it back in place on the short post. Then he picked up one of the rifles, huge and heavy in his hands, and held it in the same manner that the Mullah did. Looking down the highway, he waited.

The distant shapes resolved into two vehicles, travelling one behind the other. A battered minibus piled high with bundled luggage was followed by a taxi so dirty that Wasif could not make out its colour. Wasif waited until he could clearly see the driver of the bus through the windshield, and then he waved for the vehicles to stop. He clutched the kalash across his chest, his arm aching with the effort of holding it.

The minibus slowed and came to a stop just before reaching the chain. It was packed with people sitting and standing, and Wasif could see them passing money hand to hand toward the driver. The man behind the wheel hastily rolled down his window and held out a small wad of the bills in Wasif's direction without looking him in the eye.

Wasif's voice cracked as he barked at the driver. "Cousin, keep your money. I am only stopping you to wish you safe travels. And to tell you to be careful! There are bandits around here."

The driver looked at him for the first time, and only then realized how young he was. He looked around for other bandits, but seeing none, spoke to Wasif. "Is this a joke?"

Wasif shook his head. "No joke, cousin. No taxes here. Do you see that little village up above? Our madrassa is there. We're students, not thieves. I am here to keep you safe, not to rob you."

The driver hung partway out of his window to gesture with both arms. "This is a joke. There are twelve checkpoints on the highway from here to Kandahar City. This road costs more in bribes than it does in gasoline."

Wasif untied the chain and let it fall, and waved the minibus through. "Go in peace, cousin," he said as the minibus pulled away.

The taxi, playing loud Bollywood music on a tinny radio, pulled to a stop in front of Wasif. The driver wore Russian sunglasses and was smoking a cigarette. "I heard all that," he said. "If there are no taxes, let me pay zakat instead. For the school." The driver put a few bills into Wasif's pocket.

"Thank you, cousin," said Wasif, beaming with pleasure. "But why pay zakat like a pious man while listening to that sexy music? If you're going to be pious, be pious in all things." He pulled the bills from his pocket and shook them at the driver and his radio. "This little bit won't make up for all that." Wasif was serious, but the taxi driver laughed and pulled away with a honk and a wave.

Wasif stood in the middle of the road alone again, looking toward Kandahar in hopes of catching a glimpse of another car. He squinted and shaded his eyes, positive that through the swirls of distant dust and heat shimmer from the road he could see all the way to the outskirts of the city. He was not certain what the city would be like, but imagined great mosques and madrassas full of students in perfectly white clothing.

The Mullah's voice behind him brought him back into the present. "What are you doing, boy?"

Wasif turned around quickly, and blushed. "Nothing, Ma'alim. Just warning the cars about the bandits."

The Mullah didn't speak, but snatched the kalash from Wasif and tucked it under his own arm. He spotted the money peeking out of Wasif's pocket and drove a finger toward it as he questioned the boy. "And this? What is this?" The Mullah's voice rose a little. "Are you now a bandit?"

Wasif's eyes welled up, but he tightened his face and held back the tears. He could feel the Mullah's disappointment washing over him. He stammered out an answer, holding the money in his fingertips and offering it to the Mullah. "No, Ma'alim. Never. It was given to me. Zakat, for the madrassa."

The Mullah pulled the money from Wasif's fingers and tucked it in his pocket with the cigarette tin. He chewed on his words for a moment before speaking. "Wasif." He was unsure how to say what he was thinking. Instead, he scolded the boy. "What did I tell you about an unloaded gun?"

Wasif didn't look up. "I wasn't afraid, Ma'alim."

"Then you are a fool," said the Mullah.

Wasif deflated. "Ma'alim, if I was taught how to use a kalash —"

The Mullah's voice was hard. "Enough!" he snapped. "This is not a game."

Wasif stood still and did not speak as the Mullah gathered everything of interest at the checkpoint into a pile at his feet. Their silence was broken by the approach of Faizal, who showered them with greetings as he walked the short distance from the chai khana. He carried two pieces of naan bread wrapped around bits of kebab. He handed the food first to Wasif, with a flourish. He then extended his hand with the second kebab to the Mullah. "As promised, and with my gratitude," said Faizal.

The smell of the spicy lamb and the fresh bread filled Wasif's nostrils and made his stomach groan. He began to devour his kebab without thinking, grease running down one of his hands and onto his sleeve, not noticing that the Mullah had raised his hands to refuse the offered gift. He stopped, the dripping remains of his kebab in his hands.

A quick scowl crossed the Mullah's face, gone again in an instant as he saw that Wasif had lost his composure. He spoke to Faizal in measured tones. "Your thanks are appreciated. But they are not necessary. We have only done what is right. We do not seek or deserve a reward."

Faizal stood awkwardly holding the greasy kebab half-extended toward the Mullah. "And if they come back?"

"Insh'allah, they will not. If they do, God will provide."

Faizal backed away, unsure of what to say. "In any case, you have my thanks."

Wasif set his kebab down on a stone by the side of the road. The Mullah bent down to put the grenade in a pocket and sling the pistol belt over one shoulder before picking up the rifles. He cradled them in the crook of his arm, resting much of the weight against his chest. He did not look at Wasif as he turned in the direction of the madrassa, but simply began to trek back up the mountainside, glancing down at the kebab as he passed. "Now that you've begun, it is haram to waste it," he snapped at the boy. Wasif scooped it up off the ground and shoved it in his mouth, trying to dispose of the evidence of his sin. His mouth full, he took a few steps and stopped to snatch up his brother's cricket bat, which he saw lying on the roadside. Then he ran until he caught up to his teacher. Once he was close behind him he slowed his pace, carrying the bat in his arms just as the Mullah carried the kalashes.

The setting sun, low against the horizon, cast a pair of long shadows across the valley, obliterating the distinction between the grown man and the mere boy. Both shadows looked like giants striding across the land.

Wasif lay wrapped in a patu, a candle stub burning down beside him. Amin lay at his side, the cricket bat between them. All around them, filling the madrassa, they could hear the breathing of sleeping boys. Wasif lifted his head, careful not to make any noise, and surveyed the room to see if any of the boys were still awake. Once he was convinced that they were all sleeping soundly, he put his head down again and rubbed his forehead furiously on the rough wool of his patu. He rubbed it back and forth until it burned. His fingers touched the skin an inch above the bridge of his nose. He wasn't certain, but he thought that it was beginning to toughen into a zebiba, like the Mullah's.

He lay down and rolled onto his back, thumbing through a well-worn notebook into which he'd copied poetry, songs, and passages from the Hadith. He had yet to write anything of his own. He went to one of his favourite poems, one that he'd heard the Mullah reciting one evening not long ago. The Mullah had said that it was by an ancient poet called Mawlana.

> *Consider the difference*
> *in our actions and God's actions.*
> *We do act, and yet everything we do*
> *is God's creative action.*
>
> *Ignorance is God's prison.*
> *Knowing is God's palace.*
> *We sleep in God's unconsciousness.*

44

We wake in God's open hand.

Fighting and peacefulness
both take place within God.
Who are we then
in this complicated world-tangle,
that is really just the single, straight
line down at the beginning of the name of Allah?

Nothing.

We are
emptiness.

Wasif read the poem to himself, again and again, filling his mind with its words to block out the day's events. Looking over at his brother's swollen back and scarred head, he knew that he had failed Amin. If he had been better at his studies he would not have needed the tutoring from the Mullah, and then he would have been the one to go to the market instead. Wasif doubted that he would have fared any better against the bandits, but at least he would have taken his younger brother's place. He knew that he had failed Amin. And the Mullah. And himself.

But Wasif also remembered how it felt to see the bandits retreating on their motorcycle, their faces bloody from the boys' stones. The Mullah had talked before about the temptation caused by the sin of pride, but Wasif had not really understood what he had meant. Until perhaps today. Wasif felt pride well up in himself each time one of their stones struck a bandit. Each time a bandit flinched. Each time he saw blood.

He pushed these prideful thoughts from his mind and instead repeated the poem silently, until he eventually fell asleep.

CHAPTER 3

The bandit leader Tarak's ancient compound sat atop a low hill that dominated the flat terrain all around it. Once a large and magnificent garden of the Amir's court, it was now overgrown and neglected. The surrounding landscape was a patchwork of farms and villages; nothing moved among them except under the watchful eyes of those who lived in the garden.

A few of the buildings inside the compound were originally part of the royal garden, but more had been added in recent years. Unlike the ancient ones, the new buildings were roughly made and laid out haphazardly in what had been the symmetrical garden. The newer structures had ill-fitting doors that sat askew on their hinges, letting light stream out into the night. One whole side of the garden had been converted into dog kennels made from wire fencing and scrap wood. Pacing back and forth inside their cages, the dogs bayed and barked, day and night.

The two bandits and the boy from the checkpoint raced up the road leading in to the garden, all three astride the motorcycle. The gates stayed closed as they rolled to a halt in front of them.

"Open up!" shouted the tall bandit. "We have news for Tarak!"

A man peered at them over the compound wall, pushing a dirty turban up his forehead with one hand while scratching himself with another. Satisfied that he knew them, he dropped off of his perch and lifted the locking bar from the metal compound gates. He had barely opened one of the doors when the motorcycle pushed through and into the garden.

The dogs began to bay and howl louder than before. The pack worked itself into a frenzy. The gatekeeper threw a heavy stick at the kennel and it bounced off the fencing. Those dogs closest to where it struck were silent for a moment, but quickly rejoined the barking.

Before the motorcycle had even stopped, the boy leapt off the back. His skinny bare legs dripped with blood under his filthy kamiz. He ran straight through the blanketed door of the central building, yelling: "Tarak! Tarak!"

The two bandits looked nervously after him. Both were hesitant and remained mounted on the motorcycle. The tall bandit spoke first.

"Maybe coming back here was a mistake."

"If we had kept the boy with us, Tarak would have been sure to track us down."

"Maybe now that we have delivered the boy, we should just leave."

"Don't fool yourself." The short bandit spat into the dust. "When he hears what the boy tells him, he will come and find us."

"We should never have sold the bullets. Eventually, we'd have been paid."

"I have a story. He'll believe us over a bacha bereesh."

"I'm not so sure. It would have been better to tell him our story first."

Neither of the men were eager to face Tarak, but they knew staying on the motorcycle would help nothing. They dismounted and followed the boy, out of the darkness and into the harsh light of the central building.

The moon hung over the madrassa, its whitewashed walls glowing dully in the night. The interior was filled with the soft noises of young boys sleeping soundly on the floor. Their bodies were strewn in messy rows, each wrapped tightly in a patu, which doubled as jackets for them in cold weather. Wasif and Amin slept near each other, almost touching, at the front of the classroom.

Outside the madrassa, the Mullah sat alone in the yard, cross-legged. Beside him was a battered kerosene lamp turned down very low to conserve fuel. There was a chill in the night air, and so he wore a patu loose over his shoulders. Laid out on a second blanket, stretched flat in front of him, were the pistol and the two kalashes taken from the bandits. Each weapon was fieldstripped, the parts laid out in careful order. The Mullah's expert hands rubbed each piece with an old rag, leaving a very light coating of oil. He applied just enough oil to lubricate the parts, but not enough to attract dust that would gum them up.

Once he finished cleaning and reassembling the weapons, he took out the gift he had received from the shopkeeper. The Mullah untied the knotted string that held the waxed-paper package together. Inside the paper wrapping were a few dozen tarnished rifle and pistol bullets held together with rubber bands. The Mullah separated them and poured them into his upturned turban. His mind wandered while his hands repeated their task like machines. He then plucked each bullet from his turban, one by one, and pressed them firmly into the empty magazines.

A banging on the compound door brought him to his feet. The Mullah pulled one side of the patu over the guns to conceal them and flipped his turban back onto his head, tightening and adjusting it as he rose. He picked up the lamp by its misshapen handle and went to stand by the thick wooden door. Whoever was on the other side had heard his footsteps as he approached, and called out to him.

"Haji Mullah, I need your help. You must come with me."

The Mullah recognized the voice of the chai khana owner, and without responding, unlatched the wooden door. Faizal stepped through into the dim light of the lantern. Before the Mullah could speak, Faizal recited a phrase that he had learnt by rote as a child. "Whosoever relieves from a believer some grief pertaining to this world ..."

The Mullah finished the quote for him, his voice hardening. "... Allah will relieve from him some grief pertaining to the Hereafter. Chaiwallah, you are not here to quote the Quran to me. What is it you want at this late hour?"

Faizal wrung his hands as he spoke. "It is too terrible to say with words. I do need your help, but pray let me show you rather than tell you."

The Mullah glanced back at the madrassa and all it contained. "Is it far?"

Faizal's eyes followed his gaze. "Not far. Perhaps an hour's walk. And the more hands we have, the better."

The Mullah bade Faizal to wait with a hand gesture, and went into the building. He stepped over the sleeping boys until he found Wasif and Amin, and shook them awake. "Both of you. Come with me."

The boys stood up groggily, pulling their patus tightly over their heads and shoulders as they followed the Mullah out of the building. Faizal stood by the door, anxious to leave. The Mullah sat Amin down by the lantern. The boy's movements were slow and painful, though his cuts had scabbed well and did not seem infected. Lifting one kalash in his hand, the

Mullah snapped a magazine into it and cocked the action. Both boys' eyes opened wide as the Mullah set the kalash down beside Amin.

"Bar the door behind us, and watch over the other boys until I get back. Don't touch the rifle unless you must. It's loaded and off safe. If there is any trouble, point it in the air and pull the trigger. I will hear the shots and be back in an instant. Do you understand?"

Amin nodded, his mind still foggy with sleep, but his back was straight and his hands reached out to touch the rifle before he remembered his instructions and clasped them tightly in his lap instead. The Mullah turned so that Faizal would not see what he was about to do, and reached down to pull the pistol out from under the fold of the blanket. He hesitated for a moment, looking at the weapon. The pistol fit easily but felt heavy in his hand. Changing his mind, he slid it back out of sight. "Wasif, you will come with me."

The two men and the boy walked together away from the madrassa and out into the night. Faizal's face was set in a grim mask as he thought about the unmentionable task for which he had enlisted the Mullah. Wasif's thin body was shaking in the cold, and he pulled the patu over his head to try to stave off the chill night air. The Mullah carried the battered lantern, unlit. The only light came from the moon, casting stark shadows over the grey landscape. Not one of them spoke.

Wasif's mind was racing, trying to work out what Faizal could possibly want of them in this desolate waste. He kept close on the heels of the two men, despite having to take several steps for every one of the Mullah's. Faizal's movements were stilted; his limbs seemed cramped and tight. In contrast, Wasif could see that the Mullah moved with a loose, long gait that made it seem as if he were gliding over the rough ground.

Their path rose above them, rocky and forbidding. They climbed for under an hour, Faizal's breath coming in short gasps as he struggled up the rocky ground. In time they reached a high plateau, dotted with boulders and covered in tough, scrubby grass. A small herd of sheep slept in heaps all around the pasture. Watching them was a young shepherd who sat by a low fire, wrapped against the night air in two enormous brown patus.

The shepherd raised a hand in greeting and rose from his seat as the three figures approached. He did not speak, but lay his hand across his heart when they reached the fire, a gesture that Faizal and the Mullah repeated back to him. Neither the shepherd nor Faizal looked at the Mullah; instead, both stared at the low fire, at a loss for words. Wasif stood as close to the fire as he could, trying to warm his feet without making it obvious that he was cold. The Mullah looked expectantly at Faizal and the shepherd in turn. He waited. Their breath, visible in the night air, hung like unsaid words between them.

Finally, the Mullah broke the silence. "You've brought me to see sheep?" The shepherd looked up nervously, but his expression was vacant. The Mullah realized that the shepherd was simple, and would not be able to give him the explanation he was waiting for. He turned to Faizal. "Out with it, chaiwallah."

Faizal adjusted his turban with both hands, pulling it down on his head as he spoke. "This boy visits me when he brings sheep down to the village to sell. He came down the mountain earlier tonight and insisted that I follow him. It was so unusual for him to come to me like this. ... He brought me here to show me something."

Faizal made the boy understand what he wanted with gestures and looks, and the shepherd led them over to a run of rocks and debris. It spilled down from the edge of a narrow path leading far below to the populated part of the valley, the chai khana just visible in the moonlight.

The boy pointed down the hill to where the loose rocks had spread out in the shape of a fan. The Mullah lit his lantern, turning the wick up until the lantern shone brightly. He held it high above his head and aimed it down the tumble of rocks. At the bottom, half covered in brush and dirt, were two bodies. An old man lay on his back, hands thrown over his head as if in surrender. Beside him lay a young girl, her dress and chador pulled up and askew, covering her face and torso. The pool of blood stretching between them made the gravel look black outside the light of the lamp.

The Mullah glanced over at Wasif, who was transfixed by the sight of the bodies. He gestured at the shepherd. "He did this?"

Faizal raised his hands defensively. "I don't think so. I saw this old man at the checkpoint, pleading with the bandits, perhaps three days ago. I suspect that they had a hand in this."

"Pleading about what?" asked the Mullah.

"It often pays to mind one's business," Faizal tutted. "So I don't know, but I'd never seen him before, nor have I since, until tonight."

Wasif turned away from the bodies and watched the Mullah instead. He followed the light as the Mullah panned the lantern across the scrub around them, searching for something. He angled the light to shine down the rough dirt path that led from the plateau to the highway. A single motorcycle track cut across the dust and dirt, obscured in places by the footsteps of the shepherd.

As there was nothing more to see, the Mullah extinguished his lamp, leaving them bathed in grey moonlight again. "Chaiwallah, why bring me into this?"

"Mullah, I didn't know what to do," pleaded Faizal. "They can't be left here." Faizal looked around, as if unseen threats lurked over his shoulder. The Mullah felt the man's fear. "There are wild dogs. And worse. No one is going to come up here to bring a dead old man and a raped girl down to be buried."

The Mullah grunted in reply, but said nothing. He looked past the two bodies to the village behind the chai khana. Faizal did not let him brood for long before speaking again. "You said before that you did the things that you do because they are right."

"Do you have a donkey?" asked the Mullah.

Faizal exhaled in relief. "Praise be! I do not, but I can get one."

The sun's light burned through the morning haze, heating the ground, the chill night air a fading memory.

The Mullah, Wasif, and Faizal were weary after their night's work. They now stood in silence at the edge of the village; the donkey Faizal had brought was laden with two bodies bundled in coarse sacking.

As he tied the donkey's lead to a post outside the chai khana, the Mullah spoke. "Chaiwallah, I need water, some clean cloth, and a shovel."

"As you wish," said Faizal, hurrying off.

Wasif wiped his dusty hands on his patu and stood wearily beside the Mullah. A small crowd of men spilled out through the doorway of the chai khana. Most of them were villagers who had gathered in the early morning to swap gossip with any travellers who had spent the night. Their mood was already ugly: the stove was cold, there was no tea, and Faizal was nowhere to be found.

The men stood in a tight knot facing the Mullah and Wasif. The donkey pulled at the rope tied to his halter as he tried to back away, but the Mullah held him fast. A rough-looking man stood at the front of the crowd, his clothes dishevelled. Dark hair peeked out under a filthy prayer cap. He pointed at the donkey. "What have you there, cousin?"

The Mullah had his back turned to the men as he adjusted the donkey's rope halter. The donkey settled and started pulling at some dry grass with his teeth. "Two Muslims, gone to Paradise, insh'allah."

"I can see that. Who are they?" asked the man.

"Their names are known unto God, though not to me," said the Mullah.

Faizal reappeared from the back of the chai khana with two old blankets and a shovel. He eyed the impatient crowd nervously. "There is water for washing around back, Mullah."

The rough man rounded on the chaiwallah as an easier mark. "Faizal, who are these two?"

Faizal looked at the Mullah before answering. "A young girl and an old man, killed by the bandits." The mood of the crowd was hard to judge. Faizal lowered his voice. "They dishonoured the girl before they killed her."

The rough man's voice became louder, his tone bolder, when he heard this. "Take that whore away, then. You can't plant her here."

Wasif was shocked, and spoke up. "But why not?" The Mullah gave him a warning glance, and Wasif shut his mouth.

The rough man ignored Wasif and spoke to the crowd instead. "This cemetery is for our village. Our people — not nameless whores."

The Mullah turned to face the village men, one hand still resting on the donkey to keep it settled. He ignored the man who had been speaking and addressed the crowd instead. "This man and this girl must be put to rest. Does this village have no honour? Any Muslim, nameless or otherwise, is owed the decency of a burial."

"This whore and this man have nothing to do with us or our honour," retorted the rough man.

The crowd of villagers had encircled the Mullah, and were blocking his way in all directions. Wasif began to pull on the rope to lead the donkey through them toward the village cemetery, but the Mullah held fast to the halter and the donkey did not move. He gave Wasif a subtle shake of the head, and the boy stopped pulling.

The Mullah looked from face to face in the crowd. Wasif heard his voice come out louder than before. "I will not try to force this village to be pious. I will take them up there to be buried." The Mullah pointed toward the madrassa. Then he took the donkey's lead from Wasif and turned to lead him away.

The rough man stepped forward. Smiling, he grabbed the donkey's halter. "Do what you want with your old man and your whore, but first get them off my donkey."

Wasif turned to Faizal. "His donkey?"

Faizal looked back and forth from the boy to the Mullah. "I'm sorry, Mullah …"

The rough man loosened the fastenings and tipped the bodies off of the donkey and into the dust. The girl's face, covered in blood and dirt, appeared through a gap in the sacking. Wasif saw her clearly for the first time and realized that she must have been about his age. Her one open eye stared unseeing up at the men standing around her; the scene was enough to send most of them filing back inside the chai khana.

The rough man led the donkey away and tied it up by the shopkeeper's stall, turning defiantly to face the Mullah and make sure he was watching. As he pulled the blanket aside to go back into the chai khana, he shouted back over his shoulder at Faizal: "Chaiwallah, live up to your name and fetch us tea!"

Faizal stood outside the doorway of his ramshackle business, torn between the Mullah and his customers, uncertain of what to do or say. Only one man from the crowd had remained outside. He was short and slight, with a neatly trimmed beard and fastidiously clean clothes. He watched the Mullah with curiosity. Wasif thought he had noticed the man regarding the others with contempt.

The Mullah stood in silence for a moment, looking down at the bodies in the dust. He paused to compose himself, stooping to cover the girl's face with the sackcloth wrap, his movements sparse and controlled. When he finally addressed Faizal, his voice sounded grim, as if he was using all of his strength to grip something inside of himself. "Chaiwallah, I ask nothing more of you." Faizal ducked inside the chai khana to return to his post at the hibachi.

The Mullah set straight to work. He had Wasif help him straighten the two bodies out on the ground, securing their rough shrouds around them again. Looking out toward the eastern horizon, he saw that the dawn had turned to sunrise.

"Wasif, we will attend to this business after we fulfill our obligations."

He snapped the patu off of his shoulders and laid it out on the ground with the sun behind him, his shadow stretching out toward Mecca. Wasif went to do the same behind him, but the Mullah gestured him forward so that they were shoulder to shoulder. The Mullah knelt down on the blanket and began to ritually wash himself, using nothing more than sand. Wasif followed suit, his small hands caked in dust and stained with blood.

The small man watched the Mullah as he began his prayers. Wasif looked up at him, realizing from his manner that he was a stranger even to the villagers. Unlike all the other men here, he wore no turban, only a clean but greying prayer cap that fit tightly over his shaved head. Throughout the altercation between the Mullah and the village men, Wasif recalled, the stranger had stood apart from the others.

The stranger disappeared through the doorway of the chai khana, returning after several minutes with a few things borrowed from Faizal — a small prayer rug for himself, a large plastic bowl, and an ewer of water. He lay the carpet down beside the Mullah and offered him the bowl. The Mullah ignored him, continuing with his spartan preparations for prayer. The man cleared his throat and spoke words that he knew the Mullah could not ignore. "Asalaam aleikum."

The Mullah merely glanced up at him for a moment as he replied, but his words were sincere. "Wa aleikum salaam."

The stranger did not relent, continuing to speak the words used in greeting between men who meet as equals. "I hope that you are well. I hope that your house is strong. May you not be tired. I hope that your family is well. May you be strong. I hope that your livestock are well. May your health be ever good." He continued with the steady stream of questions and statements that run in a seemingly endless flow whenever village men meet.

The Mullah listened for a moment in silence and then relented, standing to face the stranger and raising Wasif to his feet with a gesture, as well. He began to speak his own litany of questions and statements. "And I hope that you, too, are well. May your house be strong. May you not be tired." He continued, speaking over the stranger — neither really heard the other nor replied to the other as they both recited the greeting. As their questions came to an end, the Mullah gave Wasif a nod and turned to begin his prayers again, but the man reached out to gently grasp his hand.

"Mullah, my name is Umar, son of Umar." He gestured at the bodies lying on the ground nearby. "I am not like these others who are blind to what is right. I will help you carry these fellow Muslims up to the cemetery. Once we finish praying."

The Mullah did not introduce himself in return. Instead he looked at Umar, his eyes searching the man for longer than was polite or comfortable. Umar grew nervous, imagining that the Mullah was reading the ledger of his life, outlining all of his deeds for good and evil. Umar felt naked and uneasy. The Mullah stopped his examination as abruptly as it had begun. He said nothing, but simply knelt down and positioned the washbowl between them. Without needing to be asked, Wasif lifted the ewer to pour its water for the Mullah, but the Mullah gestured toward Umar. Wasif poured it for him instead. The two men did not hurry, methodically purifying themselves with the water, finding comfort in the routine of washing. Once they were done, the Mullah poured the ewer for Wasif, who washed quickly and self-consciously. The three then adjusted the prayer rug and their blankets, standing with their backs to the sun, and began to pray, their shadows stretching out in front of them into the fields surrounding the village.

The sun was a quarter of the way across the sky by the time the Mullah, Wasif, and Umar had struggled up the rugged path to the madrassa. Wasif led the way, his patu draped low across his back. Umar carried the old man bundled over his shoulder while the Mullah carried the girl.

As they approached the top of the hill, Amin came limping down to meet them, shouting as he came. In his arms he cradled the kalash. The Mullah eyed the rifle, but said nothing.

"Mullah, the others woke up and you hadn't come back yet! I didn't know what to do!"

"Did you pray with the boys and then feed them?"

Amin stopped in his tracks. "Of course, Ma'alim."

"Then you knew exactly what to do."

Umar smiled, and Amin had nothing else to say. He was very curious about the stranger and the bundles that the two men carried, but knew not to ask the Mullah too many questions.

As Wasif approached him, he whispered to his brother instead. "Wasif, what is this?"

Wasif walked past Amin, his shoulders held high. "Righteous work. Men's work." Amin fell in behind him and followed, hoping the Mullah would explain everything in time. The little group trudged up the remainder of the hill in silence.

In between the derelict houses that surrounded the madrassa was an open space where a common well had been dug by hand. A large, flattish rock dominated the patch of common ground. The Mullah laid the girl down beside it. Umar laid his bundle directly on the rock. Amin squatted off to one side in a patch of shade formed by one of the compound walls, but Wasif stood by the bundles in hope of being asked to do something useful. Amin stayed silent so that he would not be noticed and sent away. He clutched the rifle awkwardly in both hands, balancing it on his knees.

The Mullah first unwrapped the cloth from around the old man, revealing his thin frame and filthy clothes. He carefully undressed him, pausing only to protect his modesty with a small piece of the sacking. The back of the man's head was a tangle of matted hair, mixed with blood and dirt. Wasif saw that his arms and legs were like skinny, gnarled branches from an old fruit tree.

Umar pulled the wooden cover off the simple well, lifting water from it using a battered bucket and rope. He brought the bucket to the Mullah, and together they washed the man's body. The Mullah took his time, carefully washing every inch until the old man's skin was clean. Umar helped roll the man onto his side, and the Mullah washed his back, as well.

Wasif held the bucket for the two men, trying not to look too closely at the dead man. His skin was mottled and grey. Wasif thought that he looked more like a rock or a dried stick than a man. Although he had often watched the Mullah perform mundane chores, he did not think that he had ever seen the Mullah work as methodically as this before. Once the Mullah was satisfied that his work was done, he and Umar wrapped the man in the threadbare blanket that Faizal had given them. Umar knotted it securely at the head and feet.

The Mullah turned to Wasif. "Leave the bucket here, then take your brother and bring us shovels from the yard." He glanced over at Amin. "And you put that rifle back where you found it."

Amin stood, trying to hold the rifle in the same way that he had seen the Mullah carry it. "Yes, Ma'alim."

"And when that is done, you are to both go back and watch over the other boys."

Wasif gripped the bucket tightly as he spoke. "But, Ma'alim, I want to help you. I'm old enough to be a man, not a boy."

The Mullah's voice was cold. "Which is why *you* are to watch over *them*, and not the other way around. Now go. I will not ask again."

Wasif was crestfallen, but he obeyed. Amin followed his brother, still struggling to mimic the way that the Mullah moved with a rifle in his hands.

Umar gestured at the girl, still bundled tightly in the sack-cloth. "What about her?"

"There is no one here to wash her. She will go to God as she is."

Umar was surprised. "There are no women in any of these houses?"

"There is no one in these houses at all."

"Did they run from the bandits?"

The Mullah shook his head. "It has been like this for several years. Because of the war, and also the drought. When I returned here, after the Russians had left, there was no one."

The Mullah ended the conversation by hoisting the old man over his shoulder with a grunt. He carried him out of the deserted village to a small graveyard on the edge of the hilltop, squeezed in between the empty fields. Umar followed with the girl slung over his shoulder.

Tattered prayer flags, looking more like rags, fluttered listlessly above the cemetery. Two dozen grave mounds sat inside a low, circular wall of dry-fitted stones. The Mullah and Umar set down the old man and the girl by the wall and waited for the boys to bring them shovels. The Mullah did not speak, but instead looked off into the distance around them. Umar followed his gaze, but could see nothing that the Mullah might be looking at other than the point at each horizon where the asphalt road disappeared.

Wasif and Amin arrived with the shovels. A crowd of students had followed them from the madrassa, buzzing with questions. Wasif waved his arm at them and tried in vain to keep them quiet. When he caught sight of the Mullah watching him, he turned around abruptly, shaking the head of the shovel at the boys. "Enough! This is no time for chatter." The boys finally quieted down, hanging back from entering the cemetery, their thin necks stretching to see what was going on.

The Mullah ignored the boys, content to let them squat silently in whatever shade they could find. He took a shovel from Wasif and began to dig the first grave. The soil was loose and dry, and would have been easy to dig if not for all of the stones that he had to lift out of the hole. These he placed off to the side in a little mound separate from the pile of dirt. As Wasif watched in silence, Umar worked beside the Mullah. Umar was clumsy with the shovel; twice he laid it down to examine blisters rising on his hands. But he worked hard, and Wasif saw that the handle of the shovel soon became streaked with his blood.

When they had finished digging the graves, Umar turned to the Mullah. "Will you lead us in the salat al janazah?"

The Mullah grunted. "As is our obligation."

Wasif herded the boys into rows, all facing toward the Mullah. Umar fell in line with the boys, as well, standing at the head of the front row. Wasif straightened up to his full height when he realized that he was nearly as tall as Umar.

The Mullah raised his hands alongside his head, and spoke. His voice took on a deep and rich quality that it did not have in normal conversation. His words flowed now in rhythmic, almost musical tones. "Allah-u akbar!"

The boys repeated the takbir.

The Mullah placed his arms across his chest and continued. "In the name of Allah, the Most Gracious, the Most Merciful! O Allah, let Your Peace come upon Muhammad and the family and followers of Muhammad, as you have brought peace to Ibrahim and his family and followers. Truly, You are Praiseworthy and Glorious."

The older boys recited the prayer, as did Umar. The others listened in silence, unable to follow along from memory. The Mullah's next words were his own, spoken from the heart.

"O God, if this man and this girl were doers of good, then increase their good deeds. If they were wrongdoers, then over-look their bad deeds. O God, forgive them and give to them, and to all of us, the steadiness to see and know and do the right thing."

The wind picked up and began to blow a fine layer of dust over everyone and everything in the immense valley that stretched across the province between the mountains in the north and the desert to the south.

The Mullah's voice rose again. "O Allah, we seek refuge with you from sin." The Mullah turned his head right and left, twice repeating the taslim: "May the peace and blessings of Allah be upon you."

Umar and the boys turned their heads and repeated the taslim, as well. The prayer finished, they stood blinking in the dusty wind.

The Mullah and Umar lifted the bodies one at a time and placed each one into its grave. The Mullah carefully turned each body onto its right side so that it faced toward Mecca. The soil was too dry to be formed into balls, as was the custom, and so the Mullah placed stones under the head, the chin, and the shoulders of the old man and the girl, supporting their gaze toward the west.

The Mullah gestured to the boys, who lined up to face him again. Clutching a handful of dry earth, he recited a passage of the Quran from memory, slowly releasing a stream of dust from his fist, pouring three handfuls into each of the two graves. "We created you from it, and return you into it, and from it we will raise you a second time."

One by one, first Umar and then each of the boys stepped forward and added dirt to the graves, repeating the words that the Mullah had said. When they were done, the Mullah and Umar again took up their shovels and filled in the graves completely. All the boys gathered around to pat down the earth with their hands and form a smooth, rounded mound over each grave. Nothing was placed to mark the graves other than a stone on each end.

As the boys finished shaping the mounds, the Mullah spoke to Umar. "Thank you for your assistance. If I had anything material to offer you in thanks, I would, but I do not."

Umar smiled. "Mullah, it is clear that you have much to offer. But now that these two people have been buried, do you think that the outside world has finished with you? That I will simply walk back down to the highway, and the world will go back to passing you by?"

The Mullah spoke without irony. "That is my sincere wish. Go with my thanks."

The Mullah turned away and began to direct the boys back to the madrassa. "Wasif, the boys will wash and prepare for prayers."

Wasif jumped up from where he had been crouching. "Yes, Ma'alim." He looked around at the boys and pointed across the fields at the madrassa. With as much of his newfound authority as he could muster, he gave them a command: "Get moving." He himself hung back, however, listening to the Mullah and Umar speak.

The Mullah went to pick up the shovels, but Umar lifted one before he could reach it. "Since yesterday when you chased the bandits away from the chai khana, no one there has talked of anything else."

Wasif saw the Mullah's face harden. "Little has it done for their piety."

Umar shook his head. "They are afraid, Mullah, which I know to you is inexcusable. They are not content to place their lives in the hands of God, as you do so easily. But they also have something new. They have hope. They have had the smallest whiff of peace, of not being robbed or beaten or abused at the whim of degenerates. And they want to hold onto it."

The Mullah was dismissive. "Then I suggest that they do."

"They are decent people. They will ask for your help," said Umar.

The Mullah's eyes burned brightly. "And when I sought their help?"

Umar shook his head. "To their shame, you did what was right even without their help. They will look to you as a leader now that they have seen you for what you are. Simple people fear the unknown, and they were almost as frightened of you as of the bandits."

"I have no desire to be their leader."

Umar was shocked. "But who else, if not you? Bandits still prowl, and the people of the village will suffer if no one helps them. They want justice after what has been done to them, but they do not even know where to start."

"Justice is from God, not from men. It is our place to live pious lives, nothing more. Justice will come in time."

Umar held out his hands plaintively. "Despite what happened this morning, the villagers are planning to ask you for help. I have listened to them talk while they waited for Faizal to make tea. None of them believed that the bandits would ever leave, and they saw how easily you chased them off. When they ask you to meet them at the chai khana, come and hear what they have to say. If you don't want to help them, at least tell them yourself."

The Mullah looked down at the ground for a moment, thinking. Umar had learned, in his short time with him, that it was best to wait for him to speak. Wasif, too, waited uncertainly for his teacher's reaction.

After a long moment, the Mullah spoke. He would meet with the villagers if they asked.

CHAPTER 4

The inside of the chai khana was filled with low wooden platforms covered in old, almost impossibly dirty carpets. The furniture was arranged around a huge, central samovar full of brownish tea, served in short glasses. A hibachi near the back smoked heavily, and the air was thick with the smell of lamb fat. Faizal stood enveloped in a cloud of greasy smoke, fanning the grill madly with a scorched piece of cardboard, the kebabs nearly ready to be served on a stack of naan bread peeking out of a pink plastic bag nearby.

A scruffy young boy slipped past the blanket that hung over the doorway. He stood still for a moment, his eyes adjusting to the room's low light, before Faizal noticed him. "For the last time, get out! No more charity!" Faizal stepped out from behind the hibachi to shoo the boy away, but in doing so left him an opening. The boy dodged past the old chaiwallah's outstretched arm, raced over the edge of one of the platforms, and scooped a skewer of meat up off the grill in each hand. He ran straight out the back door of the chai khana before anyone could react. The room erupted in laughter as Faizal twisted around, trying hopelessly to catch the boy.

The local men and the few travellers who filled the chai khana were in good spirits. They sat in loose rows facing the wall farthest from the main door, along which sat the most respected men of the district. A few of the oldest spingiri sat close to the bokhari instead, soaking up the wood stove's meagre heat, though no one else thought it cold. At the centre of the group of elders was the Mullah, with Umar sitting in the front row close by.

The chaotic discussion had already lasted for hours, and had ranged over many subjects: plans for crops, predictions for the weather, thoughts on bartering produce locally or trying to take it to the city to sell. When they had exhausted these topics, their talk turned to the problem of the bandits. The Mullah had not yet spoken; he was still listening to the others.

Unnoticed by the men, who were deep in discussion, Wasif and Amin crawled under the blanket door and sat on the floor just inside the doorway. The boys stared with wide eyes at the crowd of men, bewildered by speakers talking over each other while the listeners called out comments as they saw fit. Amin tugged on his brother's sleeve. "Is this truly how men conduct themselves in a jirga?"

A thin man with a cloudy eye was speaking loudly as some of the others muttered in agreement. "Tarak Sagwan has been a plague on this village for weeks. No traveller on the road is safe while his men are about. And there is not a man in the village who has not had something stolen from him by these men."

The Mullah looked from man to man in the crowd as each spoke his thoughts on the bandits, adding to the growing litany of complaints.

"The women have to keep our children silent for fear that his men will kidnap them."

"I had an old car, from Iran, that we used to drive to market. As soon as Tarak's men heard about it, they found me and beat me until I turned it over to them."

"We all assumed that when the Russians were gone we would have peace again, but we've had nothing but robbery, murder, and chaos."

"We don't just need peace, we need justice. For all of the crimes that we have suffered."

"For the murders of innocents committed in our very midst."

When the last man had spoken, there was silence. The men looked at the Mullah expectantly. Faizal spoke up, entreating him to speak. "Mullah, we know all these things to be true. The village needs a man like you. Will you help us?"

The Mullah pondered this for a moment, swishing the tea in his glass as he composed his thoughts. Before he was done, another man spoke up. "It is only a matter of time until Tarak Sagwan retaliates. Not just against you, Mullah, but against all of us. It is only right that you help us."

A ripple of fear passed through the room. When the Mullah finally spoke, his voice was harsh. "Until yesterday, you did not know I existed. Now I am essential?" He looked around the room, trying to meet each man's eye. "I am also needed in the madrassa, and I only have time to do the bidding of God."

"Perhaps leading the people of the village *is* the bidding of God," offered Umar.

The voices of the village men erupted again as each tried to talk over the other's arguments. Umar strained to hear each argument, but the Mullah sat in silence, scowling at the chaos.

Umar finally stood, waving his hands to quiet the crowd. One by one, the men fell silent. Umar looked to the Mullah, hoping that he would speak again. The Mullah clicked his prayer beads through the fingers of his right hand, staring silently at the door.

Umar tried a different approach. "Let there be order, where every man listens and weighs the words of the others on their merit. Perhaps we can hear now from someone who has not yet spoken?" His eyes scanned the crowd.

The men stared in surprise as Wasif stood up to speak. "My brother and I will protect the village."

Amin stood up beside his brother. "We're already old enough to leave school."

The men in the chai khana laughed. The two boys were too young to speak in the jirga, much less to protect the village. A flash of anger crossed the Mullah's face. He clenched the prayer beads in his fist. "I left you to watch over the madrassa, and this is what you do? You abandon your duties and demand a higher one? Stop this foolishness at once, and go back to where I left you."

"But, Ma'alim, we just want —"

The Mullah leapt to his feet. "You will leave this place at once or I will carry you back to the madrassa! And let there be no more disobedience!"

Tears filled Amin's eyes as he reached out to take his brother's hand. Wasif hesitated for a moment, his mouth hanging open as words formed on his lips, but he did not speak again. He led his brother out of the room, the blanket swinging back into place after they had left.

The Mullah took his seat again. The room sat in stunned silence. Faizal stood and muttered something about the need for more tea. Men sorted through the raisins with their fingers, but no one raised a hand to his mouth to eat. The discussion had come to an end, it appeared. Only then did one of the younger men in the room break the tension. "Mullah, we are mostly farmers, and have little knowledge of anything but tending our fields. If we formed a lashkar, we would only lose to these bandits. We do not have enough guns, and we do not know how to fight."

The men in the room mulled this over, their pride arguing in their minds against what they knew to be true. The young man continued, "But what if we found volunteers to protect the village? Men who know fighting, or who can learn. Together we could feed and house such men, I am sure."

Quiet sounds of agreement could be heard amongst the men, but none dared speak to the Mullah directly. Umar turned to look at the Mullah expectantly, hoping that he would reply.

The Mullah's eyes drilled into the young man until he turned away in discomfort. "And where will we find these men? What kind of man would defend a village that refuses to defend itself?"

The room went quiet again. Umar swished tea in his glass, his wrist turning round and round, before he spoke. He, too, did not look at the Mullah, and his words came carefully as he picked each one with care. "As all here know, I am not from this village. My father was Uzbek, as am I, though my mother was Hotaki, like many here. This business with the bandits, by rights, is not my own. But I can see a righteous cause as clearly as anyone else. I will volunteer to protect this place, insh'allah."

The Mullah looked at Umar incredulously and snorted. "Is foolishness contagious? You take the idea of a boy and make it your own?"

Umar looked up, his voice firmer now. "I merely take an idea that is right, and make it my own. And I ask that you lead us in the defence of the village, but if you do not, then I will take on that task, as well."

The Mullah said nothing as he stared at Umar. The village men watched in silence until Faizal broke the tension, passing from man to man, filling their glasses from a battered teapot. As he went, he asked, "Who else? There must be others."

Umar singled him out. "What about you, Faizal?"

"I'm an old man," said Faizal. "My place is here. But I will feed all of the volunteers at my own expense, as best I can."

Umar stood and surveyed the crowd. Most of the men avoided his gaze. "So, who else?"

A quiet man in the back of the crowd stood up. He had not yet spoken, and seemed like a stranger to all. His clothes were threadbare, though reasonably clean. He held his turban in one hand as his other brushed over the stubble on his closely shaven head. The man pushed the turban back onto his head and gazed downward. "I am called Rashid. I will help, if you will have me." He sat down again without waiting for an answer.

A light began to shine behind Umar's eyes. "That makes five of us now, Mullah — though only if you permit the boys to help us, and you become our leader." Umar ignored the Mullah's angry glare and continued. "Say that you will. I am sure that others will volunteer if you do, as well."

The Mullah stood up, his face showing irritation. "Do you understand what this means? When something like this is started? Once you begin, you can never go back to how it was. You must stay the course until it is finished, for good or for ill."

He gazed around the room to look every man in the eye. Most met his gaze, although only shyly. The young man spoke up again. "Insh'allah, we will never go back."

The Mullah took the measure of the men in the room. He could see them measuring him in return. For a long moment, the only sound was the compulsive clicking of prayer beads between his fingers. Finally, he let out a deep sigh. The Mullah raised his hands alongside his head, palms facing forward as if in prayer. He closed his eyes and spoke an oath that he meant to fulfill if it cost him his life. "Then, in the name of Allah, the Most Gracious, the Most Merciful, I pledge to lead these men, to protect this place, and to live in the light of Islam."

Umar stood, smiling, and grasped him by the hand. "Bismillah!"

The Mullah looked around at the others in the jirga. "There can be no justice in a community until it is safe, and for that we will need more men than we have."

The men looked at each other, but not one of them volunteered. Umar turned to the Mullah and took his hand as he spoke. "Insh'allah, we will find them, if it is truly justice that these people want."

"Insh'allah," replied the Mullah.

"How old were you when you joined the jihad against the Russians?" asked Umar.

The Mullah thought for a moment. "My uncles took me with them for the first time when I had barely three hairs on my chin."

Umar jumped on this. "Then why not allow us to do the same with these two boys here?" He tensed as he waited for the Mullah to reply. "This new jihad is no less important than the one we fought. It is perhaps even greater."

The Mullah did not speak at first, looking intently at Umar as if to divine his purpose. Searching his heart, he nodded. "Perhaps you are right. I will speak to them, but there will have to be limits."

Umar smiled in agreement, watching as the jirga began to break up. Men stood and stretched after many hours in the cramped chai khana. Some left, stopping first to shake hands with the Mullah, while others remained in small knots of conversation. Faizal spoke to Umar and gestured toward the rear of the chai khana. "I may have someone else for you. A volunteer, of sorts." He leaned over to explain, whispering into Umar's ear.

The quiet man who had volunteered still sat alone at the back of the chai khana. The Mullah threaded through the remaining men to the other side of the room to speak to him. "Rashid, did you say your name was?" The man merely nodded. "Tell me, why have you volunteered to help?"

Umar joined them to hear what the man would say. Rashid looked at the Mullah for a moment, thinking. "The world is a place of inequality and hardships that need not be. You are taking steps to address this. That is why."

Umar shook Rashid's hand and embraced him, as was the custom. Rashid turned and embraced the Mullah, as well, who merely stood stiffly until he was released.

Umar called back over his shoulder, "And now, chaiwallah, show us your volunteer."

Faizal led the men out the back entrance to a small, cluttered yard filled with garbage and broken things. It was enclosed by sheets of plastic strung from spindly branches stuck in the ground. Stacked up against the back wall of the building was a pile of small pieces of scrap wood, cut very short to fit in the hibachi and the samovar.

A scrawny, long-haired man was chopping up odd pieces of wood with a hatchet. He held it awkwardly, like a man unaccustomed to manual labour. His light blue shalwar kamiz, once fancy, was now soiled and stained. The collar was ripped and had been badly mended, leaving a lump of cloth on his shoulder that pulled awkwardly as he moved. The long-haired man glanced at them briefly, and then ignored them as he continued his work. The men observed him for a few minutes, during which time he split only one piece of wood into usable fragments. Umar spoke under his breath. "It's a wonder he hasn't chopped off his hand. This is the volunteer?"

Faizal smiled and called the man over. "This is the one. Isa, these men would like to speak with you."

Isa made no sign that he noticed, carrying on with his work.

The Mullah glanced at Umar, who took this as his signal to deal with the stranger. When he spoke, he did so formally. "Asalaam aleikum. I hope you are well. May you not be tired. May

PHIL HALTON

you ..." Umar's greeting faded into silence as the scrawny man failed to take notice. He finally addressed the man directly. "The chaiwallah tells me that you need employment."

Isa took another wild swing at the wood, barely missing his other hand. "No, I do this because I'm a mad sheikh. As soon as I have finished chopping this pile, I'll be going back to my palace in Dubai."

Umar's voice was severe. "He also tells me you owe him money and never admitted you could not pay for your purchases."

Isa stopped what he was doing, letting the hatchet dangle loosely in one hand. He had the dangerous look of a man at rock bottom. "And what is all of this to you?"

Faizal stepped forward, hands raised in a conciliatory gesture. "What if I offered to forgive your debts and provide free room and board from now on?"

"I'd tell you that you were trying to trick me," replied Isa.

Umar interceded again. "No trick. We're offering work."

"What does it pay?" asked Isa.

"A clean slate. Plus room and board. That's all."

Isa looked at each man's face, trying to find the angle. The grim-faced Mullah stared back at him. With a sudden move, he tossed the hatchet to the ground.

"I'll take it," said Isa.

Faizal seemed confused. "But aren't you going to finish chopping?"

Isa sneered. "No, I have an important job now, remember?"

"But you haven't even asked what it is."

Isa brushed past the three men to walk back into the chai khana. "I'm not planning to excel at it in any case," he said. He stopped in the doorway long enough to shout back over his shoulder. "And chaiwallah! Bring me tea!"

The sun set over the distant hills as the day came to a close. A reddish glow seeped across the land toward the checkpoint.

Umar and Rashid stood guard, each carrying one of the rifles captured from the bandits. Umar cradled his rifle with both arms, shifting its position often. Rashid held his loosely in one hand, grasping it at the forestock where it balanced naturally, resting against his body. He limped as he walked over to the ZIL, moving one leg stiffly, his pace slow.

Isa stood a little distance away. He carried Amin's cricket bat instead of a rifle and used it to hit stones out into the distance. With nighttime approaching, there were no more cars on the road.

A noise came from the loose gravel behind them. Rashid swung his rifle up parallel with the ground as he turned, no trace of his limp in this fluid motion. The young thief from the chai khana stepped out of the scrub brush that covered the bottom slope of the valley, where he had been watching from a safe distance.

"He's been circling us all day," said Rashid, as he lowered his rifle.

"He's like a jackal," said Umar. "It's as if he is waiting to pick the flesh from our bones."

Rashid smiled. "He can no longer taste the kebabs he stole." He walked slowly toward the scruffy boy, speaking as one might to a wild animal. "What is it you want? We have nothing for you."

The boy's eyes flashed as he held a stick up in the air like a rifle. He yelled, "I am as tough as any of you. Just give me a kalash and I will show you!" The boy's expression was dead serious, but the sight of him made the men smile. He looked to be no more than ten years old, and he was filthy. He had tied a rag around his head in an attempt at a turban.

Umar spoke to him in reasonable tones. "Go back home before it is nighttime."

"My home is wherever I am," shouted the boy again. "When my family died, I went to fight the Russians. When I defeated them, I had no home left to go to."

Rashid laughed from deep inside his chest. "When you defeated the Russians?"

The boy's face hardened. "I fought them." He beat his chest with a small fist. "And do you see any Russians around here now?"

Rashid shook his head slowly, laughing even harder. Umar kept a straight face and tried to reason with the boy again. "If you're an orphan, we'll take you to the madrassa. You should be in school."

"I don't need any school. I know everything I need to know already."

Isa, listening in frustration, batted a rock at the boy, narrowly missing his head. The boy ducked and looked ready to run away. Isa batted a second rock past the boy as he spoke. "I'm tired of this already. If you want to go, go. If you want to stay, stay. If you do, you get fed like the rest of us, you do shifts like the rest of us, and your job is to get tea for the rest of us. And I don't care what your name is, I'm calling you Lala Chai."

The boy approached the men slowly, still clutching his stick. As he drew closer, Isa threw an old copper teapot at the boy, hitting him in the chest. "Go get us some tea before we change our minds."

Lala Chai grabbed the teapot off the ground and scrambled off to the chai khana to fill it. As he went, he called over his shoulder at the men. "I'm still better with a kalash than any of you!"

"The heart of a lion in the body of a mouse," proclaimed Umar. Rashid chuckled as he lowered himself heavily onto a wooden crate, rubbing his leg. The others sat down nearby to await their tea, the day almost at an end.

Umar stood again and climbed atop the ZIL. He caught sight of Amin and Wasif, who were descending the hill from the madrassa to the checkpoint. Umar sang out the takbir in a deep and slow voice, cupping his hands around his mouth. "Allah-u akbar!" He paused and took a deep breath before singing louder. "Allah-u akbar!"

He drew out the words as he repeated them, turning the adhan into sonorous music. People across the village peered over the walls surrounding their homes toward the source of the sound. Rashid stood looking up at him, transfixed, as Umar slowly sang.

"I bear witness that there is no God but Allah!

I bear witness that Muhammad is the
Messenger of Allah!

Hasten to worship!

Hasten to success!

Allah-u akbar!

There is no God but Allah!"

Amin and Wasif lengthened their strides and arrived just as Umar was finishing the adhan. A few men from the village came to join them for prayer, as well. Amin went straight to Rashid, hand outstretched to take the rifle from him. "I could hardly study," said Amin. "I've been thinking about nothing but our shift on the checkpoint all day."

Rashid handed him the rifle. "Do you remember what we showed you?"

Amin frowned. "Of course I do."

"And what did the Mullah say to you about your duties here?"

Wasif broke into the conversation, answering for his brother. "When we are not here at the checkpoint, we must study."

"Or help the other boys to study," added Amin.

"We're the only ones in the madrassa who are allowed to do this," said Wasif.

Umar handed his rifle to Wasif. "Well, you are the oldest. And soon to be men."

Wasif smiled at the thought, holding the heavy rifle in both hands.

As the last sliver of red sun disappeared along the distant sky-line, Umar climbed down from his perch and picked up one of the prayer rugs that were now kept at the checkpoint. He touched Amin on the shoulder gently. "Prayer first. Your other duties after that."

As the men and boys lined up to pray, Isa stole away from the gathering toward the chai khana. Amin and Wasif watched him in surprise.

"What is he doing?" asked Wasif.

"His stomach has not been well," said Rashid. "He'll pray in a moment, I'm sure."

Wasif didn't understand. "Is he some kind of ..." He struggled for the word. "Apostate?"

Rashid glanced in the direction where Isa had gone. "For now, judge him by his heart's intentions rather than his words or deeds."

They turned away from where Isa had disappeared and shuffled into line in order to begin their prayer.

The next morning, the landscape was hidden by a haze of dust, the dry earth lifted into the air by the wind. The abandoned village was still, covered in a thick, brown, swirling shroud. Inside the madrassa it was calm, the air clear. The Mullah stood in front of his students, as solid and unmoving as ever, while the boys sat in ragged rows, their voices reciting a passage from the Quran in unison. Wasif and Amin, bleary eyed, were at the head of the class. They mumbled the half-remembered words, their minds foggy after a long night at the checkpoint. The Mullah frowned at their performance.

As the boys' voices continued reciting, Faizal appeared in the doorway. Standing behind him was a worried-looking man, dressed in the dirt-stained clothes of a farmer. When the Mullah noticed them, he spoke sharply. "Wasif!"

The boy's head snapped up with a start. He looked around to try to intuit what the Mullah wanted of him. The Mullah gestured to where he stood at the front of the class, and Wasif scrambled to his feet and took the teacher's place. The Mullah stepped out of the classroom into the bright sun of the courtyard where Faizal and the other man stood waiting for him.

The compound was empty except for the three men. The ever-present dust swirled around them, causing Faizal and the farmer to pull the tails of their turbans around their mouths and noses. The Mullah stood unmoved.

"We've had quite enough interruption lately," said the Mullah.

Faizal looked down at the ground. "Mullah, this man was looking for you."

The man kept his eyes low and spoke softly. "My name is Pahzman, as is my father's. When I heard what you had done here to help the village and to aid strangers, I hoped that you would help me, as well."

Faizal interjected. "And I said that you almost certainly would."

Pahzman continued. "It is Tarak Sagwan. He is marrying my daughter."

The Mullah gave a dismissive nod. "Blessings upon them. I have no time to conduct weddings." He began to turn to leave.

The two supplicants interrupted him, talking over each other.

"Not willingly," said Faizal. "You know that Tarak is an animal."

"I did not agree to give my daughter to him," said Pahzman. "He will force me to pay a dowry, and then he will do what he has done to others. He will keep her for a week, and then he will divorce her and throw her out."

Faizal continued. "He has done this a dozen times already. People fear to even speak of their daughters in case he overhears and comes for them."

The Mullah turned back to face the two men. "And how does Tarak even know of your daughter? Do you not keep purdah in your home?"

Pahzman pulled his scarf tighter over his face. "Of course! But she must leave it sometimes, to do the washing, to work in the fields at harvest time."

"But if she is so precious to you, do you not keep her covered? Away from jealous eyes?"

Pahzman's eyes were red and wet. "Please, Haji. I am a good man. A pious man. But I am poor, and cannot afford for her to stay within my house and not work."

The Mullah appraised the man with his eyes for a long time. The silence grew around them.

He finally spoke. "What would you have me do?"

"When I heard that you have stood up to his thugs already, I thought —"

Faizal interceded again. "Haji, you can't blame this man for having hope, or for having faith in you."

The Mullah shook his head. "I doubt that there is much that we can do."

Pahzman took the Mullah's hands in his own, looking up at him. "Please, Haji. I beg of you. I have no sons left, only a daughter. He will come for her in a few days. And if she is not there, he will kill us."

The Mullah hesitated.

"You've sworn to protect us," said Faizal.

The Mullah dropped Pahzman's hands and pointed at Faizal. "And if we are off threatening bandit leaders then we will not be able to do so."

Pahzman began to cry. He let his scarf fall loose. His mouth trembled. Streaks appeared in the dust caking his cheeks. "I have nowhere else to go."

The Mullah sighed heavily. "I promise ..."

Pahzman looked up hopefully.

"... to discuss this with the others. We will decide what to do as a group."

At the checkpoint below, the mid-morning sun burned through the dusty haze. Umar and Rashid had stopped a few cars, and they had waved each one through, most voluntarily paying a small amount of money as zakat. Isa wandered up to the checkpoint, swinging the cricket bat through the air as he walked, singing to himself.

"He was dirty and lousy, his head full of fleas
But he had his women by twos and by threes ..."

Rashid snickered at the song, but Umar shook his head. "Isa, are you ever serious?"

Isa's face broke into a wide smile, his eyes shining. "I am serious about making you laugh one day, brother." He was about to say something more, when he turned his head and squinted down the road. Rashid followed his gaze. A taxi had stopped short and was trying to turn around on the narrow strip of asphalt. Isa shouted. "Don't worry, cousin, we are not going to rob you!"

The taxi driver ignored the shout. He got out of the taxi and went to the trunk. He hefted a large wooden ammunition box down to the road and waved to the men at the checkpoint. When he knew that he had their attention he cupped his hands to his mouth. "I had no choice!"

He quickly got back into the taxi and drove off in a belch of black smoke. Rashid and the others approached the box cautiously. There was a letter affixed to the lid with a nail, which Rashid pulled off. He stared at it blankly until Umar became impatient.

"Well, what does it say?" asked Umar.

Rashid looked away. "There is dust in my eyes, I can't quite make it out."

Umar took the note from him and examined it. "This is a shabnamah. Threats from Tarak." He read aloud. "'Eject those men who have wronged me, and when I arrive at your village again I may be moved to show mercy.'"

Umar flipped open the lid of the box. The shorter of the two bandits who had fled from the checkpoint looked up at him. Inside the box were his head, hands, and feet, and nailed to the bandit's forehead was another note. Umar turned and retched on the ground. Regaining control over his stomach, he wiped his mouth with his sleeve and read the second note aloud to the others. "'These hands failed to grip their weapon. These feet ran from my enemies. This tongue lied to me.'"

Rashid looked for a moment at the dead bandit and began to walk up to the madrassa. "I'll get the Mullah."

Umar stood alone at the checkpoint, mostly looking off into the distant darkness, deep in thought. He had remained at his post throughout the day. When Rashid had returned with the Mullah shortly before noon, the Mullah looked briefly inside the box before taking it away to bury it in the cemetery — one more fresh grave. The boys were due to relieve Umar soon. He didn't mind his time spent alone, as it gave him time to think.

Umar took in a long breath of the cool night air through his nose. Despite the dust and smoke from the chai khana, the air smelled clean. Cleaner than he could remember it smelling for a long time.

Umar had travelled over much of the country, had lived in Iran, and had been planning to go to Pakistan. He had studied in famous madrassas, and in simple ones, but not one had ever held his attention for more than a few months. None of them had ever felt like home.

But it was more than that — it was that none of the teachers had ever seemed wholly worthy. Each teacher had his flaws, some large, some small. But once Umar saw the flaws, he could hardly focus on anything else. Umar knew that he had flaws himself — maybe even more so than others — and so he did not despise his teachers for their failings. But even still, he kept moving, kept seeking something … greater. Something unlike what one often found in the everyday world.

Like this Mullah. He was different. He lived almost apart from the world that everyone else inhabited, living a life like the Prophet himself, peace be upon him. He lived a simple life, unconcerned with anything but the word of God, and like the Prophet, he had begun to attract followers worthy of the teacher.

I am not a man like the Mullah, thought Umar. *But I can strive to be. I can live my life as an example to others and help to build something here that is greater than what we already have. Much*

greater than what anyone has. This village could be just the start.
He could feel it — this was where he was meant to be. He had
found his home.

Umar realized that he didn't need to travel anymore, looking
for a place to learn Islam. He could simply stay here and live it.

CHAPTER 5

The chai khana was mostly empty, the samovar bubbling and belching noisily in the centre of the room. The Mullah sat rigidly in the middle of the others, patu pulled over his shoulders, listening in silence as the heated discussion swirled around him. At the back of the room, Faizal and Pahzman squatted anxiously, listening. Faizal rose regularly to fill cups of tea before going back to his position on the outside of the circle.

Isa, sweaty and agitated, spoke with anger. "It's his daughter, but it's our necks if we try to stop this wedding."

Pahzman interrupted the discussion to plead with them. "Please, Mullah. There is no other way for me to save her."

The Mullah sat impassively, still listening. Looking to him for approval, Wasif spoke next. "This is not just about his daughter. It is about the dignity of all the women in this valley."

Amin snorted. "What do you know about the 'women of this valley'?"

Wasif snapped back. "I know everything I need to know from the Hadith."

"Then I know as much as you do, if not more."

With one hand, the Mullah gestured for the boys to be quiet.
"It's suicide to try to fight Tarak directly," Rashid muttered.
"He has two or three dozen men."

Isa stood up, frustrated, and began pacing around the room.
"We've seen what he's capable of."

The Mullah looked to Umar for his thoughts, as when the
discussion began it was he who had first argued in favour of getting involved. Umar spoke with confidence. "We need to help this
man, or the rest of the community will lose faith in us."

Standing, the Mullah held up his hands for silence. His
voice rang clear when he spoke, causing even the samovar to
resonate subtly. "I have a solution. If we all agree, I will go
and speak to Tarak Sagwan myself. I will ask him to leave this
girl alone."

The men sat in silence. Wasif and Amin looked at each other
in alarm. Not one of them could formulate a reply before Rashid
managed to say what they all were thinking. "Forget the girl for a
moment, Ma'alim. He'll kill you just for having chased away his
men from the checkpoint." Rashid looked around at the others,
who nodded in agreement. "I'm surprised it took him this long
to send that box."

"And we still need you at the madrassa," pleaded Amin.

Wasif looked around at the others, looking to see if one of the
other men would try to dissuade the Mullah from his plan. When
they did not speak, he said, "Let me come with you, Ma'alim. Let
us all come, to protect you."

The Mullah shook his head. "A man only needs to be surrounded by guns if he has something to fear. I trust myself to God,
and so fear nothing." The Mullah looked around at the others,
who stared in surprise at what they had just heard. "And if he
refuses to listen to reason, we will call a jirga."

"If talking fails, then we talk more?" Isa scoffed.

The Mullah looked at him in silence. Isa met his gaze, defiant. As the moment lengthened, Isa began to twirl his glass of tea in one hand on the floor, until he finally lowered his eyes.

"Justice stems directly from God Himself," said the Mullah. "The universe strives toward it. Should we doubt its existence so quickly? Even Tarak Sagwan has a family, a clan, a tribe. If he won't listen to reason, then a jirga with the elders of his tribe will make him do so."

"How are you so sure that he won't just kill you?" asked Rashid.

The Mullah gave a rare smile, cupping his hands together. "Faith, brother. I rest in the hands of God."

"He's right," said Umar. "But let's also have Pahzman bring his daughter and the rest of his family here for safekeeping."

The Mullah looked around and saw that no one had any further objections. He raised his hands, as if in prayer. "Bismillah. Then we are agreed."

The road between the village and Kandahar was a potholed ribbon of asphalt cutting through the desolate landscape. By midday the earth would be scorched by the sun, though now it was merely warm. Tiny villages and dry fields the colour of milky tea dotted the countryside on either side of the highway, filling every habitable niche in the rocks and sand.

The Mullah walked along the side of the road. He carried little: just a thin plastic bag with two pieces of naan and a scented stick he used as a toothbrush. No cars could be seen in any direction.

By now the heat was beginning to distort the air, obscuring his view of the road as it led off into the distance. The Mullah squinted at the horizon. The distant shimmer was broken by a heavily laden motorcycle swerving toward him, dodging holes in the road almost lazily as it approached. He could see that it carried two riders, one behind the other. The Mullah ignored it, and continued walking.

As the motorcycle drew closer, the passenger slid backwards off the seat, running to stay on his feet. He unslung a kalash from across his back as he gained his footing, and began to swagger toward the Mullah. The motorcycle, free of its extra burden, raced past and circled back at him from behind.

The two bandits wore filthy old police uniforms hanging like rags from their skinny bodies. Their hair hung long and loose about their faces. The Mullah ignored them both and kept walking at a steady pace. The man with the kalash in his hands spoke first.

"Where are you going?"

The Mullah gestured with his hand in the direction that he was walking. "This way."

The man planted his feet and fired a few shots into the road beside the Mullah. The loud cracks of the shots were followed by the sound of the bullets ricocheting off the asphalt and into the distance. "Don't toy with me, you fool! Answer the question."

The motorcycle came to a stop behind the Mullah, and the rider leaned forward wearily on the handlebars, already tired of this encounter. "If he's going to be trouble, let's kill him before we rob him."

The Mullah stopped walking. "I have nothing of any value that can be stolen." He held up the plastic bag for them to see.

"He's probably right," said the man on the motorcycle. "So just shoot him and let's get back."

The Mullah pointed up the road. "I am walking this way to meet with Tarak Sagwan." Upon hearing this, the two bandits sized him up more closely. This new information made the encounter more interesting.

"And why would you do that?" asked the man on the motorcycle.

The Mullah said nothing in response.

"And what makes you think that he wants to meet with you?" asked the other.

The Mullah stood still, waiting.

"I say let's take him."

"Why not just shoot him?"

"What if Tarak does want to see him? Are you going to tell Tarak that you shot him?"

"You're right, you're right." The bandit on the motorcycle looked the Mullah up and down again. "We can always shoot him later." He laughed at his own joke, looking around as if for someone else to join in. When no one did, he stopped.

The rider pulled the motorcycle up beside the Mullah. "You're lucky that we're not interested in you," he said. The Mullah climbed onto the seat behind the driver, while the other bandit slung his rifle across his back and sat behind him. Once they were all aboard, the motorcycle began to weave slowly back up the road from where it came.

The sun was not yet at its hottest as Pahzman led two women along behind him. His wife was dressed in a tattered blue chador, while his daughter merely had a large scarf draped completely over herself to conceal her face and hair. The girl could not see where she was going and held onto her mother's hand as they walked.

Pahzman stopped just outside of the door of the madrassa. They set down their burdens, dirty bundles of cloth tied with string that held all their portable belongings. Inside the bundles were a few pots and pans, a teapot and metal cups, some moth-eaten wool blankets, and a cheap Chinese alarm clock. Pahzman knocked on the madrassa's wooden door. After a short pause, it opened a crack and Umar's face appeared.

"I spent my last rupees on this chador to cover my wife," said Pahzman, pointing at the older of the women. "We have brought everything we could carry."

"All of these houses are abandoned," said Umar, stepping through the doorway. "You can take your pick."

"Where are the owners?"

"There aren't any left," Umar smiled ruefully. When he saw Pahzman's panicked look, he reached out and squeezed his shoulder. "Don't worry, you are safe here now."

The derelict garden of Tarak Sagwan's compound was filled with shouting men. Carpets that had been dragged out of the buildings formed a rough semicircle in the centre of the open space. Three dozen men sat on the carpets drinking tea and arguing. Tarak himself, a short, young man with broad shoulders and an impressive girth, sat alone on a carpet in the centre of the group. His hands were rough, his face pinched in an endless scowl, and his shalwar kamiz, finely made, strained across his belly. He was watching the spectacle in front of him intently.

Two dog handlers strained with heavy leashes to keep their animals apart, their feet digging into the ground as they tried to hold their position. The fighting dogs leaned toward each other, their snarling muzzles only inches apart, the veins in their necks like steel cables. Tarak gestured at the larger of the two dogs, indicating his approval. "One lakh rupees on this one."

The dogs continued to strain against their handlers, pulling up onto their hind legs. They frothed and made strangled noises deep in their throats, straining to reach each other. With Tarak's decision finalized, a small flurry of final wagers concluded the general betting on the dogs. Tarak raised his hand and then dropped it violently. The handlers loosened the leashes just enough that the dogs could finally get at each other.

The dogs closed the last few inches that separated them in a snarling frenzy. They spun around in a swirl of matted fur and teeth, trying to gain advantage, each seeking the other's throat. Time and again the larger dog would try to push the other one to the ground, using its size and strength. But every time it spun into position to put its weight on the other's shoulders, the smaller dog would slide out from under it, snapping at the larger dog's face. The standoff continued for several minutes, the baying from the nearby kennels nearly drowning out the sound of the men shouting encouragement.

The larger dog soon learned to anticipate the other's strategy, feinting at it and then diving to one side to snap its jaws in place on the other dog's shoulder. The smaller dog pulled away with a yelp, spinning out of the way again, injured but not out. Blood and gristle filled the mouth of the larger dog, whose yellow eyes shone brightly. It sensed that victory was near.

The smaller dog had begun to tire, its back slick with its own blood. Its head hung low on its short, powerful neck as it growled a low warning. The larger dog hung back for a moment. The men in the crowd were on their feet, screaming. Tarak was beating the ground with his hand, yelling at the dog he had selected as the winner to finish the fight. The bigger dog coiled back on its hind legs and launched itself at its fading opponent, its jaws spread wide, its eyes slitted and shining.

It realized that something was wrong only as it landed on the other dog.

The smaller dog, its stance low, had locked its jaws around the larger dog's neck from below. The weight and momentum of the larger dog carried it over, pivoting on the smaller dog, whose jaws remained clamped on its neck, until the larger dog found itself on its back. Tarak's pick wriggled and tossed and tried to break free, but to no avail. The more the larger dog struggled, the more blood drenched the ground.

The larger dog went limp in submission, yelping in pain. The match was over. The two handlers pulled the dogs apart, heaving on the leashes with all of their strength. Each handler carefully examined his dog's wounds, washing away the blood with cups of water, searching for cuts that would need stitches. The smaller dog had lost half an ear. Its handler carefully opened its mouth and noticed a missing tooth that was probably still lodged in the coat of its opponent. The larger dog was mostly unhurt, despite all the blood it had shed, with just superficial punctures and cuts on the loose skin around its throat.

Winners and losers exchanged money. Tarak threw the thick stack of rupees he had lost into the dirt in disgust, where it was gingerly picked up by the man who kept the book. Tarak stood up and looked around as if seeking an object to kick.

A sound came from just outside the compound. The men stopped talking and one by one turned to face the entrance, where they saw one of the motorcycle riders push the Mullah through the doorway.

"We found him walking on the road," the bandit said.

The Mullah stumbled as he was pushed, but quickly regained his footing. He looked closely at the men gathered in the court-yard. Ripples of fear rolled across the crowd, but one man stood seething and furious at its centre. *That man must be Tarak*, the Mullah thought. The Mullah walked toward him and began to greet him in the formal way of their people. "Asalaam aleikum. How is your family? Is your house strong? How is your health? May you never be tired …"

Tarak glanced at him briefly, his face full of contempt for this dusty stranger. When he did not reply, the Mullah stopped speaking and stared at Tarak, silent, waiting.

Tarak stood and took the leash of the losing dog from the handler and began to speak, mostly to himself. His men watched in silence. "When a dog loses like that, it will never win another fight again, even once it has healed. This dog gave up. And he lived. He'll always believe that he can give up, and that someone will come and save him."

Tarak reach under his shirt and pulled out a pistol. "From now on, he'll never be any good for anything but losing." Without any hesitation he fired, driving the dog's head down into the dirt with a single shot. He threw the leash to the ground and turned to the Mullah. "And so, dear guest, what are you good for? Winning or losing?"

"I am called —" began the Mullah.

Tarak cut him off with a wave of his hand. "I don't care who you are, stranger. What do you want?"

The Mullah remained composed with great difficulty. "I've come to discuss your bride."

Men began dragging the dog carcass out of the fighting ring. Fresh dirt was spread over the bloody ground, making it ready for the next fight. Tarak stood by the carnage and spread his arms out wide, encompassing his world. "Which bride do you mean? Standing in my home, can't you see that I am a rich man, and can have as many brides as I like?"

His men laughed at this, but the Mullah was undeterred. "The one that you intend to marry next. Against her father's wishes."

"Ah, yes — now I know the one. What? Do you want her for yourself?" Tarak looked around at the others. "She's only twelve, and they say that already she has tits like fresh melons." He gestured with his hands, playing to his men.

The crowd all laughed again. The Mullah stood rigidly, his arms held close to his sides. The fingers of his right hand twitched as they counted his prayer beads. "I have no stake in this," said the Mullah firmly. "Other than as a Muslim, as a Hotak, and as an honest man. I've come simply to speak."

The crowd was suddenly still as the men waited to see Tarak's reaction. His face was inscrutable, his voice tight. "You've come to speak, cousin, then speak."

"You must find this girl bewitching," teased the Mullah, "for a rich man to forget his duties and to neglect to offer a glass of tea to a traveller."

Tarak stared at the Mullah silently.

The Mullah raised his hands in the customary gesture. "Melmastia, Tarak Sagwan."

Tarak spat on the ground. "Keep your Pashtunwali." He stared at the Mullah. The men around Tarak waited, watching for what Tarak would do next. Soon, all around the bandit king was still, except for the scuffling of the dogs in their kennel. The Mullah stood with the appearance of perfect calm, awaiting Tarak's reaction.

Tarak turned his cruel gaze to those around him, looking over the faces of his men, deliberately drawing out the tension. When he finally stepped forward, his face broke into a wide smile. He placed his arms around the Mullah in a gusty embrace, and the men around him laughed along with his clownish expressions. "Melmastia, stranger. Sit, be my guest, and perhaps I can name you a price for me to forget about this girl." He turned to look at his men again. "Though it will be more than the dowry that was promised." He pulled his shirt open to bare his chest to the crowd. "Because you'll have to pay for my broken heart, as well."

The bandits laughed at their leader's humour and began to settle down to listen while Tarak and the Mullah seated themselves on a single rug at the centre of the crowd. The Mullah waved away a small glass of tea, while Tarak took two.

"This girl —" began the Mullah.

"My bride," corrected Tarak.

"Her family do not approve of this marriage. They say that they have been forced, and that you will ..." he paused as he searched for the word, "misuse her."

"Then let them come and tell me themselves," said Tarak. "Are they not free men, with honour?"

"You know well why they do not," said the Mullah, gesturing at the pack of rough men who surrounded them. "If this was merely a dispute between you and this one family, perhaps they would be right not to worry. But the number of families who feel wronged is growing."

"Then it is their shame that they still do not dare to speak to me themselves," mocked Tarak. "I am a free man, and I will do as I wish."

"You may not see any troubles that need bother you now, but they are gathering just beyond the horizon. As you well know, these debts of honour will not disappear. Even after a hundred years, these families may seek revenge."

"May I live to see them do so," said Tarak, provoking laughter among his men. "Stranger, your thoughts are those of a man who lived in our grandfathers' time." Tarak looked around at his men, speaking more loudly. "That world is dead. The truth is that our world is ruled by the sword, and the strongest arm that swings it. This girl has been promised to me, and I will take her."

The Mullah bristled. "This world is truly not as you describe," he said. "In the name of Allah, the Most Merciful, and on behalf of her family and her people, you must leave this girl alone."

The bandits were silent for a moment, uncertain that they had heard him correctly, but then they roared with laughter at the Mullah's audacity. Tarak was stunned. He mockingly leaned back as if swooning and in shock. "In the name of Allah?" he asked. "You come here alone, unarmed, not to ask me something, or beg me for something, but to *tell* me your will?"

One of the bandits who'd pushed the Mullah into the compound turned to the other, smiling. "I knew this wouldn't be boring."

"I serve only as a reminder of God's will." The Mullah looked around at the armed men in the crowd. "One way to measure a man's fear is by the number of guns that he keeps. You would appear to have much to be afraid of." The Mullah held his empty hands out in front of him. "I, however, am unarmed, as I trust in God, and therefore have no fear."

The men around them had grown quiet again, waiting to see how their leader would respond. Tarak's eyes bulged as he tried to find the right words, but then he burst out in braying laughter. His men joined in, but the Mullah was silent. Tarak had tears in his eyes when he regained his composure. "I've not had a surprise like this one you've brought me in years," he said. Tarak leaned toward him conspiratorially, "You say that you are not interested in the girl. Maybe this will be to your taste." Tarak waved his hand, and a man pressed *play* on a blocky Soviet-made tape recorder.

Tinny music crackled from its speakers. The bandits craned their necks toward the doorway of a nearby building to see the entertainment begin. From behind a curtain emerged a young dancer, dressed in the clothes of a girl, with heavily rouged cheeks and bells tied around his wrists and ankles. The dancer moved slowly backwards toward the crowd, swaying suggestively until he came to a stop in the centre of the semicircle. He made a slow and dramatic turn to face Tarak. As he turned, it was the Mullah's face he spied.

With incredible speed, the boy launched himself forward, howling and scrambling at the air with his hands. He landed on the Mullah, trying desperately to tear out the man's eyes with his fingernails. Before the Mullah could turn his head he found himself looking into the eyes of the boy from the checkpoint. The crowd of men leapt to their feet and moved back in confusion; the dogs in their cages went wild. The Mullah grabbed the boy by the wrists, quickly gaining control of him. He pinned the boy's arms to his sides and lifted him off the ground. Before the boy could break free, the Mullah managed to toss him roughly onto the bloody soil.

The boy's eyes were wet with tears of frustration as he got back to his feet. He turned to Tarak and shouted: "Kill him! I want him killed!"

Tarak stood up and moved toward the boy, putting a protective arm around him. His face was dark, his voice low. "Ah, now I understand. You're the one from the checkpoint."

"Yes," said the Mullah.

"Didn't you receive my gift?" asked Tarak. "I boxed it up carefully for you."

The boy, his face smeared with makeup and tears, began to plead with Tarak. He reached up to the bandit chief and stroked his beard with his small hand. "Please, please, let me kill him. He hurt me. I want to kill him."

Tarak's face remained dark, and he jabbed a short finger at the Mullah. "Stranger, whoever you are, go back to your fly-shit village."

The boy punched Tarak ineffectively in the stomach and stormed off, crying.

"And tell the villagers that once I am married again, I will be coming back for them," said Tarak. "And that they will pay for your insolence."

"We will call a jirga to settle this," said the Mullah. "You will be fighting against the world."

"To hell with your Pashtunwali."

The Mullah's jaw clenched, but he managed to spit out one word: "Insh'allah."

Tarak turned away from him in contempt. "And if I ever see you again, I will let the boy kill you. And then I will feed your body to my dogs." Tarak walked away, disappearing inside one of the buildings.

The crowd stood facing the stranger, their mood ugly, but not one of them dared to touch him now that Tarak had told him to bring a message back to the village. They knew that this was how Tarak worked. Fear was better business, sometimes, than killing. The Mullah surveyed them for a moment before giving a slight nod and turning his steps toward the doorway of the compound.

The Mullah placed each foot with a purpose, lengthening his gait to get away from the corruption of the place as quickly as he could without running. The metal gates of the compound slammed shut behind him with a clang, but he did not turn around. He saw now that this stretch of the road was littered with shell casings, a scattered carpet of tarnished brass and steel. Once he was out of sight of the garden walls he stopped. Looking up at the sun and judging the time, he swallowed his feelings and took a few deep breaths. Certain that the intention in his heart was pure, he began to prepare himself to pray.

Tarak lay back on one of the doshaks that had been rolled out on the floor of his room. He could hear the slow and steady breathing of the boy nearby in the darkness. The air was hot, almost stifling, and he could not sleep.

Picking up a kalash from the floor, Tarak went outside. A few men sat by the gate, supposedly on sentry but mostly smoking from a chelam. The water pipe bubbled noisily as each man drew deeply on the sweet smoke before passing the hose to his right. The bandits rose to their wobbly feet as Tarak approached. He asked for a few coals from the chelam for his own pipe, but they insisted he take the whole thing; they would prepare themselves another. He accepted the obsequious behaviour for what it was, and grabbed the tall chelam around the neck with his free hand.

Tarak went back to his own building and climbed a rough wooden ladder to the roof. Positioned so that it would catch the cool breeze was a bed made from ropes strung over a wooden frame. He lay down and took a long pull on the chelam. As he had suspected, it was chars, not tobacco, that they had been smoking.

Tarak imagined the slight body of the boy sleeping below, his smooth skin free of scars and blemishes. Had his own skin ever looked that way? Certainly not now, after two decades of war, or whatever this was. Survival. Life. He blinked.

The day had started well. But then came the loss of his favourite dog. And the arrival of the Mullah. Pashtunwali be damned, he should have killed him on the spot. Elders and preachers had always tried to tell young men what to do, claiming it was about honour or some damned thing. *Most of those men are dead now*, he thought. *The only thing that gives you the right to do what you want, and to tell others what to do, is force. Some people will say that it is money, but force can get you money, while money alone won't give you the strength to overcome those who want to take it from you.*

Tarak thought back to what his father had often said: You can't buy a man, you only rent him for a time. And men get big ideas that have to be cut down before they grow too big. Dogs are easier to manage, but men are handled just the same. Use one hand to feed them, and one hand to hit them. Show them both from time to time. Keep them hungry enough. And never show fear.

Tarak saw that the Mullah didn't show fear, either. That made him dangerous. But not for much longer.

CHAPTER 6

The Mullah walked along the side of the road, a fine shower of dust blowing over him as he strode, head down. He looked up and squinted at the distant horizon. A motorcycle was approaching, moving fast. The Mullah stopped and planted his feet firmly on the earth, readying himself for whatever might come.

The motorcycle stopped a short distance from him, and the rider unwound his scarf to reveal his face. He looked young and pampered, his face soft and a little puffy. "I'm looking for the mullah who fights bandits," he said. "Travellers in the chai khana down the highway said that he had gone this way."

"I've seen no holy men fighting bandits," said the Mullah.

The young man looked doubtful. "My uncle wishes to speak to this mullah. Are you this man, by chance?"

"Who is your uncle?" asked the Mullah.

"Nasir Khan," said the young man. "He's at a wedding in a village near here."

The Mullah frowned. "Nasir Khan? The famous mujahid?"

"The same," said the rider. "Are you the mullah or not?"

"Forgive me," said the Mullah. "I am he. I am less trusting of others, as of late."

"We mean you no harm," said the rider. "My uncle is an admirer of yours and wishes only to speak with you. I have been sent to find you and take you to him."

Seeing him more closely, it was now clear to the Mullah that he was barely a man. His beard was wispy and his hands and face were soft, like someone unaccustomed to work. The Mullah climbed on the back of the motorcycle and the young man drove it in a slow circle, bringing it around to face the other way and then quickly accelerating.

"Where exactly are we going?" shouted the Mullah into the youth's ear.

"It's not far," he shouted back, swerving a little as he turned his face toward the Mullah so that he could be heard.

Rashid carried a few pieces of naan in one hand and two glasses of tea in the other as he walked back to the checkpoint. "Breakfast," he said simply, handing Umar some bread and one of the glasses.

"They're late again," said Umar, watching the boys' distant figures walking down the mountainside.

"They likely had trouble organizing the younger ones again," said Rashid with a shrug.

"I need to revise the schedule once more," sighed Umar. "Perhaps if we split the shifts?"

Rashid said nothing, having heard Umar's concerns many times already. He focused instead on his breakfast, softening the days-old bread in his mouth before trying to chew it. The tea was fresh, at least, and he savoured each slightly bitter sip, content to be alive and fed for another day.

Umar stood facing the track up the mountainside and shouted when the boys came within earshot: "You're late again!"

Wasif and Amin increased their pace, covering the last part of the distance to the checkpoint at a jog. Amin sat down almost immediately after he arrived, his legs sore from the walk down the mountain. He eyed the bread that Umar and Rashid were eating enviously.

"You're late," repeated Umar.

"We had to feed the boys, and there was no wood for the fire," said Wasif, shooting a reproachful look at his brother.

"I didn't collect any wood because I was here at the checkpoint," said Amin quickly.

"Have you already eaten?" asked Umar.

Wasif's face reddened. "We used the last of the beans to make daal, and there was not enough for everyone."

"You're both here now," said Rashid, "which is what matters." He picked up his rifle and handed it to Wasif, pulling the action back a little to show the boy that it was loaded. "I'll bring some more bread and tea for you, and then the checkpoint is yours while we sleep."

"Has the Mullah returned yet?" asked Wasif.

"Not that we have seen," said Umar.

Both Wasif and Amin glanced down the empty road.

A few minutes later, with bread and tea starting to fill their bellies, the boys were seated comfortably within the shade of the low stone wall of the checkpoint. Neither Umar nor Rashid had left yet, and talk returned to the subject of the Mullah.

"It has been two days since he left," said Wasif. "We have to follow him and find out what has happened."

"That will leave us even weaker here in the village," cautioned Rashid. "It is not yet time to panic."

"But what if he needs us?" asked Amin, his mouth full of bread.

"You are not yet such a man as to be indispensable to him," chided Umar. "He will return, and our focus should be on ensuring that all is in order when he does."

"Like what?" asked Amin.

"Like ensuring that someone supervises the boys, and that I get some rest," said Umar as he stood and stretched. "I will walk up to the madrassa now," he said, looking to Rashid to see that he concurred.

"I will meet you there later this morning," said Rashid.

Umar took his time leaving the shade at the checkpoint, the heat of the sun already making exertion unpleasant. Rashid sat with the boys, shifting his position to take advantage of the diminishing shade.

"There is much to do, and few of us to do it," said Rashid. "Why didn't you bring Isa down from the madrassa?"

"He's not there," said Wasif. "Wasn't he on shift with you last night?"

Rashid slapped his leg. "I've not seen him since yesterday," he said. "The last thing we need is to be another man short."

"Maybe he ran away," said Wasif. "He hates work."

"He does little enough of it," said Rashid, "so I don't think the tasks we put on him would have driven him away just yet."

Amin sat silently, his fingers twisting the tail of his shirt, ignoring the conversation about Isa. Rashid watched him for a moment before asking, "Amin, have you seen where Isa goes when he is not here?"

Amin's head snapped up and his face reddened. He began to stammer out a reply before he was cut off by his brother.

"Do you know something about this that you didn't tell me?" demanded Wasif.

Amin looked back and forth between Rashid and his brother, uncertain what to say.

Rashid put a hand on the boy's shoulder. "You can tell me what you know, my friend. I'm sure that it didn't seem significant until now."

Amin nodded, giving a sidelong glance at his brother. "I saw him visit the house on the edge of the village once."

"That's all?" asked Wasif.

"That's all," said Amin.

"Well, it's worth asking if he is there," said Rashid. "Wasif, stay here with the rifles. We'll be back in a few minutes."

Wasif nodded, hefting one of the kalashes up into his arms. Rashid stood, bent down quickly to knead the muscles in his left leg, and then gestured for Amin to lead the way. Wasif watched them go for a moment before walking out into the middle of the road, alert for any cars that might approach.

Amin led Rashid down a rutted pathway along the side of a field, heading toward the village houses inside their heavily walled compounds. When they reached the last house, set slightly apart from the others, he stopped, gesturing at a green wooden door set into the mud-brick wall. It hung slightly askew on its hinges, but was firmly barred shut.

"This house is the one that I saw him visit," said Amin.

Rashid stepped past him and struck the door heavily with his fist. He waited for a moment, listening, but hearing no sound of movement inside, he pounded on the door again.

"We are looking for our friend Isa," he called out, hoping that someone inside would hear him.

"Wait, wait," replied a man's voice from inside the compound. They could hear something heavy being dragged across the yard, and finally a man's head appeared over the top of the wall. He was young, but with a heavy beard that grew so thickly on his face that it started just below his eyes, and Rashid recognized him as one of the local farmers who frequented the chai

104

khana. "What do you want?" the farmer asked.

"Salaam," began Rashid, "and my apologies for disturbing you, cousin, but we are seeking our friend Isa."

The bearded farmer looked at him doubtfully and said nothing in reply.

"He's a skinny man with long hair," said Rashid.

"And he talks too much when you don't want and not at all when you do," added Amin. Rashid hushed him with a wave of his hand.

The farmer looked uncertainly at the boy and then back at Rashid.

Rashid held up his hands to show that they were empty. "As I said, we come in peace, and only to find our friend."

The farmer gestured off to one side with his head as he climbed off the ladder behind the wall. "Go to the door of the hujra, over there."

Rashid and Amin walked around the corner of the compound where there was another door, this one much older and thicker. They could hear the sound of a rusty bolt being slid aside, and a rustling noise as whatever else that was barring the door was pulled away. When it swung open, it revealed a tiny courtyard, shaded by an old sheet.

"Come in," said the farmer, pulling the door open.

Rashid stepped over the high lintel and ducked at the same time, followed quickly by Amin. Inside, they saw that the courtyard had a small sitting platform covered in carpets and round, threadbare pillows. Stretched out on a heavily embroidered mattress was Isa, eyes shut, fast asleep.

"Wake up, brother," said Rashid. "It is past time to be awake! The day is slipping by!"

He stepped up onto the platform to give the unresponsive Isa a shake. His hand hesitated in midair, and instead of shaking

Isa awake, he turned to face the farmer, his expression dour.

"How long has he been here?" he asked.

The farmer looked panicked. "Only since last night," he said.

"And how often has he been here before?"

"Four, perhaps five times," he said.

Rashid reached over Isa, lifting a ceramic plate off the carpet with both hands. On the plate was a short glass lantern and a thick wooden pipe with a large metal bowl. He slipped something off the plate into his pocket, and then passed the plate to the farmer, who took it in his hands without looking Rashid in the eye. "Put this away where he won't see it," said Rashid.

The farmer ducked through an interior door to some other part of the house, returning quickly without the plate.

"What is that?" asked Amin.

"Upym," replied Rashid. "This explains much about our friend Isa. We need to get him up to the madrassa where he can rest." Rashid lifted his friend up by the shoulders, Isa's head lolling to one side, and tried to pull him to his feet. "Lend a hand, Amin," he said, struggling with Isa's dead weight.

Amin grabbed Isa by the arm, trying to support him enough for Rashid to raise him higher, but Isa's limp body resisted them. "Enough," said Rashid, "place him back down again."

Amin's face was serious. "Is he dead?" he asked.

"No," said Rashid, "just in a deep stupor." He turned to the farmer, who squatted in the shade by the interior door. "How much has he smoked?"

The farmer looked at the plate that sat on the ground beside him. "Nearly two tulees since yesterday."

Rashid looked surprised. "No wonder he is like a stone."

"Should we leave him here for now?" asked Amin.

"He would be best among friends," said Rashid. He turned to the farmer. "Help us carry him up to the madrassa."

The farmer looked doubtful, and turned his head to one side to spit onto the ground. "He hasn't even paid me for the tulees. He said he would collect the money today."

"Collect the money?" asked Rashid.

"From the cars, he said," explained the farmer.

Amin's eyes widened. "He buys upym with the zakat?"

"Don't judge what you have never known," explained Rashid. "He would only do such things when he is ill, I am sure."

"In any case, it is only fair that I be paid," said the farmer.

"There are no thieves here," said Rashid. "You will be paid. Help me bring him to the madrassa, and I will see that the money you are owed is given to you."

The farmer acquiesced, taking Isa's arm from Amin and, together with Rashid, lifted him to his feet. The narrow doorway confounded them for a moment, until they lifted Isa off the ground entirely and carried him through it as one would a bundle of firewood. Once they were through, they went back to supporting him under each arm, half carrying and half dragging him back to the highway, with Amin trailing behind them.

When they reached the checkpoint, Wasif was still on his feet in the sun, watching for cars approaching. Seeing Isa, he rushed over.

"Is he injured?" asked Wasif.

"Not as you might think," said Rashid. "Amin, stay here with your brother, and our cousin and I will bring him the rest of the way."

Wasif looked at Amin for an explanation, but his brother merely shook his head. Certain that his instruction would be followed, Rashid continued to the path up the mountainside. The farmer, looking up, protested. "He would be better off resting in the chai khana."

"If you want to be paid, you'll take him to the top with me, and be thankful that he's not some fat merchant," said Rashid.

Moving slowly, in just over an hour they had reached the outskirts of the upper village. As they approached the first house along the trail, they were met by Umar, walking back down.

"Is he ill?" asked Umar, puzzled to see Isa hanging in their grip.

"In a way," said Rashid. "I think we've discovered why he behaves as he does."

"Some sort of fever that makes one lazy?" asked Umar.

Rashid smiled, grim faced. "Of a sort. Upym."

Umar's face fell. "Here? Under our noses? Where does he get it?"

The farmer broke into the conversation. "He has taken it from me, without yet paying me for what he has smoked." He looked over at Rashid. "I've been promised money when we reach the madrassa."

Umar struck the farmer across the side of the head with his open hand, knocking the farmer to the ground. Rashid, off balance, dropped Isa on top of him. When Isa landed, he let out a long groan and rolled off to one side.

"Poisoner, you will be paid what you deserve!" shouted Umar.

Rashid stood over the man, both hands raised defensively. "He did not start Isa's habit, he has merely given him what he demanded."

His fists clenched, Umar looked ready to strike Rashid next. "This man sells poison, no matter whether his customers ask for it by name. What he is doing is haram!" He looked at the farmer with disgust, kicking him in the ribs as Rashid tried to keep him back.

"It is not as simple as that," said Rashid.

"Please, Haji," said the farmer, "this upym is all I have of value. Last year, when the crops failed, my family would have starved. I took it as payment for twenty jeribs of land that I sold. I couldn't take cash — our rupees have become worthless."

Umar jabbed a finger at him. "It is against Islam."

"I have only sold what I need to buy seeds this year. My family will starve otherwise. I am not an evil man."

Umar spat on the ground, looking at Rashid. "His family deserves to starve."

Rashid spoke quietly, still holding his hands up to ward off Umar if necessary. "Brother, no one's family deserves to starve."

"Do they deserve to live by poisoning others?"

The farmer held his hands together in supplication. "What would you have me do?"

"Upym is haram," said Umar, "but providing for your family is a duty."

"Will we feed them from the zakat, then?" asked Rashid.

"If we fed every family that grows this poison from the zakat, there would be money for nothing else," countered Umar.

"Didn't I tell you — this is not a simple problem," said Rashid.

"We will lock them both up until the Mullah returns," said Umar.

"But where?"

"Follow me," said Umar grimly.

The kishmesh khana sat fortress-like on the edge of the upper village, surrounded by low mud walls dividing the fields. Its own thick walls were pierced, checkerboard-like, with holes to let air circulate around the grapes drying into raisins. Most of the holes were clogged with debris, as the building had sat unused for many years. A rough wooden door was set in one end of the squat building, with a massive ancient padlock sealing it shut.

The early morning sun had begun to warm the outside of the thick mud structure, but the inside remained cool.

After a long and sleepless night, Isa lay slumped in a puddle of his own filth against the mud-brick wall of the kishmesh khana. Both his hands and feet were wrapped with chains that were secured through the holes in the walls, and they had been left too short to allow him to lie down flat. He looked across the room at the bearded farmer, who was also chained to the wall, although they had left his bonds just long enough that he could lie down. The man was still asleep, noted Isa with more than a little jealousy.

He heard the sound of movement outside. The door swung open on rusty hinges. He shielded his eyes from the sun that shone in through the doorway, recoiling back from the dark figure that stepped inside.

"Brother, are you awake?" asked Rashid in a gentle voice.

"Loosen my chains, please," pleaded Isa. "Just for a little while."

Rashid shook his head. "It is Umar who has the key." He took a piece of bread from his pocket and wrapped it around the stub of the tulee that he had hidden in his pocket at the farmer's house the day before. "Eat half of this now, and half tonight. You will have to suffer eventually, but this will push that a bit farther out into the future."

He offered it to Isa, who snatched it from his hand like an animal. "I need more than this," said Isa.

Rashid shook his head. "There will be no more. And eat the bread, as well; you will need your strength."

Isa pulled on his chains angrily. "I can't even look at food. I just want out!"

The farmer was awake now, staring at Rashid. "My family will not forget this harm you have done," he said.

"Fuck your whole family," said Isa.

"They'll fuck you," said the farmer.

"Enough," said Rashid, passing the farmer a piece of bread, as well. "This will all be fixed when the Mullah returns. I'll come back tonight for your bucket," he added, "and with fresh water."

Isa pulled on his chains, over and over, until his wrists and ankles were bloody. He screamed and yelled until his throat was raw.

The farmer eventually closed his eyes and turned away.

The temperature in the prison began to drop as the sun set. Isa was silent now, and had little to do but think. The filthy building was far different from what he had once been used to.

Life as a mujahid, he thought — *what a joke.* When he thought about his old life, he realized that although they called themselves holy warriors of Islam they had lived as if they were already in Paradise. Whatever good life was to be had in Peshawar, and later Jalalabad, they lived it. Women, boys, drugs, alcohol — they had it all.

It was not how he had intended to live his life. He had wanted to fight the Russians and free his homeland. But by the time he was old enough, the Russians were gone. He still joined the men who called themselves mujahideen, but the only people they ever fought were others like themselves. And rather than fight, they mostly lived as best they could off of whatever they were given from the zakat, or wherever else they could find money.

And while the others had passed him an upym pipe one night without even telling him what it contained, he needed no one to trick him into trying poder soon afterwards. He had never even had a needle from the doctor — the idea frightened him. But he saw the men who used this stronger drug, and he had never seen such joy on their faces as when that needle slid into their arms. Who wouldn't have tried it? Wasn't it true that whenever a smart man found a source of joy, he grabbed it and held on tight? People talked about the good days, years ago, but even with the Russians gone one had to wonder how those good days could ever return.

Isa sipped the last of the water from his plastic bowl, drawing it slowly and painfully across his chapped lips. He swallowed the last piece of the tulee and then shuddered, knowing that the real pain was yet to come. He'd seen others try to kick their habits, bodies wracked until they inevitably went back to using the drug just to stop the suffering. He looked around his prison and asked himself again: *How is it that my life has brought me here, chained to a wall by my friends?* He could shout for them, but he knew that they would not come.

As he sat in the building that was once used to shrivel grapes into raisins for sale in the market, a thought flashed across his mind: *What is the human equivalent of a raisin?*

CHAPTER 7

They had been riding for just over an hour, mostly at slow speeds on pitted tracks away from the highway. The motorcycle slowed down even more as they turned toward a small farming village. They passed the rusting hulk of a destroyed Russian vehicle that had swerved off the road and come to a halt against a low wall that surrounded a field. It was blackened from the fire that had destroyed it, a ragged hole ripped through one side, with a smaller hole through the other. The Mullah merely glanced at the wreck as they passed it, focusing instead on the village that they now approached. It looked poor, but nothing seemed out of the ordinary. There were a few crops growing in the fields, and sheep grazed in the bare patches between them.

Men's voices could be heard from one of the walled compounds, and women's voices came from another. The Mullah and the young man had just pulled up into the alley between the walls of the houses when a man stepped out through an ancient wooden door to greet them. He was beardless, but with a drooping moustache that concealed part of a scar that ran from his jaw over his nose and forehead. The Mullah thought that he knew him, but he didn't think the man he remembered had such a scar, and so he hesitated. Looking away from the man, he saw that all around were armed men, lounging in concealment between the houses.

"Asalaam aleikum," said the scarred man.

"Wa aleikum salaam," replied the Mullah. "May your family be strong. May your livestock be well." The men both recited a long greeting, looking at each other closely and speaking over each other, until they had nothing more to add. The Mullah then stated the purpose of his visit. "I am here to meet with Haji Nasir Khan. I was told he is attending a wedding."

"My uncle has summoned him," spoke the young man on the motorcycle.

A moment passed while the Mullah, still sitting on the back of the motorcycle, and the scarred man watched each other. At last the scarred man nodded. "Today is a day of peace."

The Mullah relaxed and showed his open hands, his prayer beads hanging from his right thumb. "Then I am here on the right day," he said.

"Come, you are welcome," said the scarred man. The armed men who had been watching the new arrival closely went back to resting in the shade of the compound walls.

As the Mullah dismounted from the motorcycle, he suddenly realized who the scarred man was. "Ghulam Zia, old friend! Is it you?"

Ghulam Zia embraced the Mullah stiffly. "It has been many years," he said. "Since the Russian days."

"But I don't recall the Russians doing this to you," said the Mullah as he gestured at the scar across Ghulam Zia's face.

Ghulam Zia scowled, with only one side of his face moving. "No," he said, "that came after." He said nothing more, turning from the Mullah to look out over the fields.

After a moment, the Mullah asked, "How does it come to pass that you are here?"

"I am Nasir Khan's man now," said Ghulam Zia. "As are many others from our jihadi days. Anyone who is to get close to Nasir Khan must come through me."

The Mullah looked around at the armed men who filled the alleys of the village. "What does Nasir Khan need so many men for?"

"For protection, of course," said Ghulam Zia. "We live in an age where everyone must be able to protect what is his. Almost every day we must defend ourselves against the corrupt militias of men like Ustaz Abdul Haleem or Haji Ahmad."

The Mullah frowned, "But these men are mujahideen."

"*Were* mujahideen," corrected Ghulam Zia. "Now they are nothing more than bandits. One controls the western approaches to the city and the airport, though it is little more than a heap of ruins and wreckage. The other has blocked the highway to Chaman, and takes half the cargo in taxes from any truck that uses the road."

"How can good men come to this?" asked the Mullah.

Ghulam Zia gave a short, barking laugh. "In the end, men are just men, neither good nor bad."

The Mullah shook his head. "I cannot believe that is true," he said.

The nephew, who had parked the motorcycle off to the side of the alley between the houses, led the Mullah into the small compound that was used as the village's hujra. He noted that it was in good repair, having been recently plastered and painted. Even the fact that such a house existed, not to mention that it was well maintained, spoke volumes about the village's honour.

Long lines of carpets had been laid out in the garden, and sitting on them were all the men of the wedding party. Seemingly never-ending tea flowed into glasses as large communal plates of qabuli pilau were served. Sitting at the head of the carpets was a well-dressed young man with a pockmarked face whom the Mullah took to be the groom. Beside him sat a small, older man whose shalwar kamiz was a delicate creamy colour and whose back was ramrod straight. No introduction was needed for the Mullah to know that this was Nasir Khan. In the darkest days under the Russians, when many mujahideen were being killed, Nasir Khan led a band of men who not only avoided capture, but attacked the offices of KHAD itself in Kandahar City. No mujahid in the province was more famous than Nasir Khan. His grey beard was neatly trimmed, and his clothes were expensive. His turban was made of silk, a deep green, and the tails of it hung low on his shoulder, as befitted an elder. Ghulam Zia took up a standing position behind him, where he could survey the men around his master.

Nasir Khan spoke, and the crowd fell silent. "And so that our tribe continues to grow, and be strong, I give you this gift," he said. Nasir Khan handed the groom a thick envelope, pressing it firmly into the young man's hands.

"Thank you, Haji," said the groom. "Your generosity is only overshadowed by your wisdom and strength."

The men in the garden all clapped appreciatively. The groom's father, seeing that the Mullah was a new guest, leaned in to speak to him. "My son is marrying my brother's daughter. It keeps the dowry in the family."

The Mullah nodded his approval. "It is good for a young man to get married."

Nasir Khan spied the Mullah and sprung to his feet, walking quickly between the rows of guests to greet him. He took the Mullah by the hands, a melodious greeting flowing from his lips and spilling over the Mullah's own brief words. When they finished, Nasir Khan smiled and squeezed the Mullah's hands.

"I'm very pleased that you have come," he said.

"And I am surprised that you know me at all, Haji," said the Mullah.

Nasir Khan laughed, and looked around to include others in the conversation. "I remember you from the jihadi days," he said. "And now I am hearing even more stories. A mullah who chases and threatens bandits? And who controls a checkpoint? Such a mullah is destined to be famous indeed. What are we to make of you, exactly?" Nasir Khan's eyes twinkled as he spoke, though the Mullah could see that his words were carefully chosen.

The Mullah paused to compose his reply. When he spoke, his words were slow and equally deliberate, and he looked Nasir Khan in the eye in a way that other men did not. "Our country has become a complicated place," said the Mullah. "It is far simpler in my madrassa, which is where I wish to remain."

"And so you are still a religious man?"

"That is for others to judge," said the Mullah. "I strive in that direction."

Nasir Khan put one arm around the Mullah, who stood stiffly. He spoke in lower tones, bringing the Mullah into his confidence. "To be frank, I am very impressed by what you have done. Our people need strong and pious men." The Mullah regarded him in silence. Nasir Khan continued. "I sponsor a large madrassa near Quetta. It has need of a man such as yourself — I would like for you to become its leader. Your salary will be paid by me, and I will find positions for all of your friends, as well."

The Mullah was surprised by the offer. "That is much too generous, Haji."

"Surely not too generous to accept?" asked Nasir Khan.

"My skills would not be up to the task," replied the Mullah. "I am struggling with the tiny madrassa that I have. I know my part in the scheme of God, and it is a small one."

A flash of irritation passed over Nasir Khan's face, unaccustomed as he was to being refused. "My offer remains open should God decide for your part in his plans to change," he said.

The groom's father interrupted the exchange, tugging on the Mullah's elbow. "You must sit and eat with us as our guest." Nasir Khan smiled again and gestured for the Mullah to join the celebration. Nasir Khan did not take his seat again, but began circulating among the guests, talking intimately with each and every man. Ghulam Zia followed him at a discreet distance, watching the guests with cold eyes.

Inside the chai khana, the mood was sombre as the men awaited the Mullah's return. Umar stepped out to look down the road, but the sun had set and the landscape was blanketed in darkness. He stepped back inside. Pahzman sat despondently in the corner, swirling cold tea in his glass. Rashid lay on his back, eyes closed, deep in thought. Faizal and Lala Chai sat next to each other, a bowl containing tiny cubes of stringy meat between them, carefully sliding the pieces onto metal skewers. No one spoke.

The night wore on, and the candles that Faizal was using to light the chai khana had burned down to stubs. Suddenly, Amin burst through the blanket hanging in the doorway, rifle in hand. "Praise God," he said, "he's alive and has returned."

All the men were on their feet as the Mullah stepped into the room, covered head to toe in dust. The room filled with a sudden energy. Lala Chai leapt up from where he sat and brought a washbowl and an ewer of water to the Mullah. Without speaking or looking at anyone, the Mullah took a seat and began to wash. As Lala Chai poured a stream of water, the Mullah began by washing his face three times. Everyone watched him anxiously, waiting to find out what had happened.

Umar signalled to them to be patient, but Pahzman broke the silence. "Will my daughter be safe?" he asked.

The Mullah continued with his washing. "Have you given the salat-e-isha yet?"

"We have," said Umar.

"I have not," said the Mullah. "First I will pray. Outside, where the example can be seen and heard by others."

Pahzman was distraught. "But my daughter?"

"There is a rhythm to all things in life that must not be denied," said the Mullah.

"Patience," said Umar.

Having finished washing, the Mullah stood up and walked outside again. Umar herded the others outside. They lined up to follow his example. The Mullah went to stand in the middle of the road and rolled out a prayer carpet from a stack kept by the checkpoint. The others began to take up positions behind him, all facing westward. The Mullah nodded at each man who came to join him, checking to see that all were present.

"Where are Wasif and Isa?" he asked.

Amin answered, placing his carpet directly behind the Mullah's. "Wasif is back at the madrassa already, watching the boys, Ma'alim."

The men all looked at Umar to supply the remainder of the answer, who looked suddenly uncomfortable. "We must speak of Isa later," he said to the Mullah.

The Mullah looked at Umar for a moment but did not pursue the matter any further. Satisfied that everyone was in position, the Mullah turned and closed his eyes briefly, considering his intentions toward this prayer and toward life. Certain that his motives were pure, he raised his hands and began.

"Allah-u akbar!" he intoned. The others repeated his words in unison and began to pray.

All the doubts of the preceding days faded away as the men prayed together in the middle of the road. The darkness that surrounded them retreated a little, and the cool night air smelled fresher than before.

When he finished his prayer, the Mullah remained kneeling, enjoying the clarity of thought that he often felt after going through the familiar ritual. Pahzman stood behind him for a few moments, waiting for the Mullah to stand, but when he did not, he forced himself to interrupt him. "Mullah, what news of my daughter's marriage? Please tell me if we are safe to remain here."

The Mullah remained calm and focused. He stood and took the man by the shoulders. "Come and sit inside where we can speak."

The men assembled back inside the chai khana and took up seats facing each other in a small circle. Lala Chai poured short glasses of tea from the samovar, and handed them first to the Mullah and then to the others.

"Please," repeated Pahzman, "I must know if we are safe to stay here."

"You are safe here with us," said the Mullah.

"But what of Tarak Sagwan?" asked Pahzman.

"He still intends to marry your daughter. He said that he let me live to carry his threats back here to the village," replied the Mullah.

Pahzman began to rock back and forth, consumed with fear. The Mullah raised a single finger and leaned in to speak to him. "Be still. Rest easily in my hands, just as we all rest in God's."

Pahzman heaved a great sigh, very close to tears, but tried to produce a thankful smile. It twisted into more of a grimace as he choked out a reply. "Like any other small man in this world, what other choice do I have?"

Umar looked at the Mullah with concern. "And so it will come to a fight?"

"Insh'allah, no," said the Mullah. "We will call a jirga. Tarak Sagwan is a Hotak, as am I. No Pashtun stands alone — he is not just one man, but a part of a family, a clan, and a tribe. We will call the elders of our tribe and his clan, along with those of this district, and we will agree together on what he can and cannot do." The Mullah looked around at the others, who appeared doubtful. "Our elders have grey in their beards not just from age, but from war, pain, and turmoil. They will do what is right. We will send out word in the morning."

Pahzman took the Mullah's hand in his own. "Thank you, Haji."

The Mullah gave him an irritated look. "No thanks are required for merely doing what is right."

Inside the madrassa, the Mullah carefully swept the floor, which gathered small dunes of dust every day. The sound of boys playing outside was muted by the mud-brick walls and by the Mullah's intense concentration. He moved the broom back and forth meditatively, with a long, slow rhythm, carefully covering every inch of the floor. His concentration was broken by Umar, who hesitated at the door of the room.

"I thought that I would find you here," said Umar.

"Not as often as one used to," replied the Mullah.

"Or as often as you would like?"

The Mullah stopped sweeping and ran his fingers through his beard. His next words were uncharacteristic. "I'm not sure."

Umar was rocked onto the heels of his feet. "I have never heard you say that before."

The Mullah put down the broom and gestured toward some pillows that he had stacked in one corner. Umar entered the room, carrying a small sack, and the two sat down facing each other.

121

"Tell me what has become of Isa," asked the Mullah. "Neither of the boys would say."

"He is an addict," said Umar bluntly.

"How do you know?" asked the Mullah.

"He was caught using drugs, which he bought from a local farmer with money from the zakat," said Umar indignantly.

The Mullah sucked air through his teeth at the mention of the zakat. "And what has become of him?"

"I've locked him in the kishmesh khana, knowing that you would want to deal with him," said Umar. "The farmer who sold him the upym is there, as well."

The Mullah thought for a moment. "Intoxicants are haram, as you know. We will not allow them here."

Umar nodded eagerly in agreement.

"Upym," continued the Mullah, "is used only by kafirs and not by Muslims, and so its trade will be permitted. The chars, however, is used by Afghans and must be destroyed."

Umar nearly disagreed, but decided against it. "And what of our prisoners?" he asked.

"Release the farmer. Owning upym is not a crime; using it is. Isa can remain where he is for now."

"Will there be a trial?" asked Umar.

"I think not," said the Mullah. "Let God's will take its course."

Umar chose his words carefully. "If we allow the sale of upym between traders, we should at least collect ushr on it."

The Mullah nodded. "As long as when we do so we ensure that it is being sold outside of our lands." The Mullah saw Umar's doubt. "There is no virtue in taking a man's livelihood or savings," he said.

Umar conceded the point. "Life has been hard for our people," he said.

"When we were fighting the Russians," said the Mullah, "we thought that times could get no more difficult than they were. I did not see my family for many months at a time. Then, when I was with the tanzim, I heard that they were dead, though I still do not know how. I don't know where their graves are, or if they even have graves."

"Are you saying that you regret fighting the Russians?" asked Umar.

"Not at all," said the Mullah. "Even though life was hard, I *knew*. I knew that everything I did brought us closer to defeating them. And once they were defeated, that all would be well again. That we would have peace."

Umar gave him a sad look of sudden understanding. "Not yet, it seems."

"Not yet," replied the Mullah. "Nowhere today is there peace. It is worse now than when the Russians were here, and people grow more desperate every day. This madrassa is full of boys without families whom I collected around me on my journey here. I thought that I was moving back to the village of my ancestors, but truly, this is nothing more than a village of ghosts."

"So what is the answer, then?" asked Umar.

The Mullah's eyes began to shine a little more brightly again. "When we fought the Russians we called it jihad. We struggled against the unbelievers who defiled our country and I was a different man. I hated the Russians as one hates the Devil himself."

"You were not the only one to think that way," said Umar.

"But since that time," said the Mullah, "I have come to know one thing. That we were wrong. The real struggle was not against the Russians, it is within ourselves. It is against all inside each of us that is less than perfect. Everything within us that is made in less than the very image of God."

"You have been teaching here since the end of the war," said Umar. "What fault is there to be found in that?"

"I decided to live a religious life, free from disturbance," agreed the Mullah. "But now I wonder if this is enough."

"What we have all chosen to do here is surely pleasing to God," said Umar.

The Mullah shook his head. "We are as His slaves," he said. "We do not choose how we must serve; we merely act out the parts that we are given."

CHAPTER 8

W
asif stood guard at the roadside checkpoint, his rifle
leaning against the metal side of the ZIL. He waved
cars through the checkpoint cheerfully, taking zakat
with thanks when it was offered. A clutch of younger boys from
the madrassa squatted in the shade of some rocks on the other
side of the road. They were not speaking, but watched his every
move with interest. Wasif had been ignoring them for over an
hour before he finally turned to them and waved them away. "Get
back up the hill! You should be studying!"

One of the boys leaned down behind another's back so that
his face couldn't be seen and shouted back at Wasif. "Studying?
Like you and your brother?"

Wasif puffed out his chest just a little. "I've finished my studies at the madrassa. I work here, with the other men."

The boys all spoke at once, their words tumbling over each
other in confusion.

"We do study, but all day by ourselves!"

"The Mullah has other matters to attend to!"

"We'd rather be doing something exciting, like you!"

"Tell us the story about how we all drove off the bandits."

Wasif looked both ways, up and down the road, and saw no cars. "I suppose I have time for one story."

The boys surged across the road and squatted around him in the shade of the ZIL. He began again to tell the story they had heard dozens of times. The boys listened intently, even though they had all seen it themselves.

The chai khana nearby was surrounded by all manner of dusty cars and trucks, many more since this stretch of the highway had become safe again. Tucked in between the parked cars were a few horses as well, pulling with their teeth at the plastic that covered the chai khana. Many days had passed since word went out about the jirga, and now men from across the district were gathering, travelling by whatever means they could. Many old friends and distant family members were reunited over the question of Tarak Sagwan.

Inside, Umar greeted all the new arrivals that he could, wishing them a simple welcome and introducing them to the Mullah. Most had only heard of the Mullah recently and were surprised that someone so suddenly famous would also be so reserved. His reticence only seemed to add to his piety.

A very old man, blind in one eye, was practically carried by a younger relative to meet him. His voice was soft and wispy, and the Mullah had to lean forward to hear what he said. "Even my deaf ears have heard of you, Mullah. I am pleased to meet you in person."

The Mullah grunted in reply, but took the old man's hands in his own nonetheless. He muttered a blessing and followed the gaze of the man's one good eye. A tight knot of men were standing in the doorway, their eyes adjusting to the smoky dimness of the chai khana. At their centre was an old friend, Jan Farooq, flanked by a few other men the Mullah knew to be tribal elders.

Jan Farooq was tall and carried himself in a way that accentuated his height. He tossed away a cigarette that he had been smoking, leaving both hands free to raise in a vague sort of prayer. Lesser men gave way as he approached the Mullah.

They were still a few paces apart when they each began to greet the other, the two men speaking simultaneously. "Peace be upon you. And upon you. I hope you are well. May your house be strong. May you never tire. May your family grow large. May your business prosper."

The two men embraced warmly.

"Welcome, old comrade," said the Mullah.

"It is good to see you again," replied Jan Farooq.

"Indeed it is. If only it were under better circumstances."

"No matter what the reason for a jirga," said Jan Farooq as he gazed around the room at the men watching him, "it is a pleasure to see friends and trade news."

The Mullah sucked air through his teeth. "I hope that there is good news to share."

Jan Farooq smiled at the Mullah, white teeth showing, but his eyes were cold. "Give me some news about this army that you are building."

The Mullah shook his head and smiled thinly. "I am merely a teacher now."

Jan Farooq looked around as he spoke, directing his comments to others besides the Mullah. "A teacher, I hear, who controls this part of the highway with armed men and boys."

"A teacher who keeps his students safe. Nothing more."

Jan Farooq gripped the Mullah's shoulders in a friendly way. "There is no shame in leading armed men. Only in concealing it," he said. The Mullah set his lips tightly. Jan Farooq seemed ready to push the point further with another comment, but stopped. His face tightened back into a smile once again. "I know that few men have heeded your call for a jirga, but do you really intend for all of us to fit in this little chai khana?"

The Mullah shrugged. "It will do."

"One of my nephews has brought a tent. Let us find a better place to sit. Near the river perhaps," said Jan Farooq.

As the Mullah considered this, there was a crackle from inside one of Jan Farooq's vest pockets. He opened the flap and pulled out an old Russian walkie-talkie, quickly clicking the rotary switch to *off*.

"What is that for?" asked the Mullah.

"A souvenir from our old friends, the Russians. I'll tell you the story later on."

Jan Farooq took the Mullah's hand and held it as they walked together a few miles toward the spot on the river where the tent would be set up. As they went, Jan Farooq kept up a light conversation that avoided any serious matters. By the time that they had walked to the spot, Jan Farooq's men had already laid out the canvas and were arguing over how the wooden poles would be arranged. With the wind blowing a plume of dust off of the canvas as they raised it, the tent was soon visible for miles around. The sight of it acted as a focal point for all the visiting men.

The Mullah watched as the workers finished the job by rolling up the canvas sides to invite what wind there was to cool the tent. A few dozen men gathered around it, waiting for the elders of the district to seat themselves first. The men laughed and gossiped, and seemed to be enjoying the meeting as a social occasion, despite the grim reason for which it had been called. Most were farmers, and even they were dressed in their best clothes. Some had walked for several days to attend this jirga, staying in hujras or in mosques along the way. Not all the men knew each other, but all knew each other's families and could almost always trace back enough generations to know how they were related.

As Jan Farooq and the Mullah stood at the entrance to the tent, they were surrounded by the older men of the district. Jan Farooq said nothing, coolly smiling at the others, so the Mullah gestured toward the back of the tent. "After you, my friend. You are our guest in this village and should have the best seat."

"No, my friend, you are both a mullah and a guest in my tent."

"You are like my elder brother, Jan Farooq. I insist."

Rather than decline a second time, as would be polite, Jan Farooq nodded and ducked inside the tent, taking the most prominent seat for himself. The Mullah gestured to the other elder men of the district, who followed and took the seats closest to Jan Farooq. The Mullah entered just ahead of the general press of men from across the district. He seated himself near the other men, but not at the focal point of the space.

The men settled in, sitting in tight semicircles radiating from where Jan Farooq sat. Lala Chai had brought a heavy pot of tea from the chai khana and was passing between the rows of men, pouring short glasses of strong black liquid. As he rounded a corner between rows, the heavy pot got the better of him, and he stumbled, spilling a few drops of scalding tea on a heavy-set man in a dark shalwar kamiz.

The man drew back his hand to strike him. "Watch what you are doing, little fool."

Lala Chai put down the teapot and raised his fists. "I will show you who is the fool, fatty."

The man stood up and grabbed for Lala Chai's neck. No longer burdened by the teapot, the boy skipped quickly backwards, out of reach. Rashid and Umar waded through the other men from where they had been sitting at the edge of the tent, quickly positioning themselves between the man and Lala Chai. Rashid placed a warning hand on the man's chest. "Our little brother apologizes, cousin."

"No need for this to get out of hand," said Umar. The man brought his hands down to his sides, sizing up Lala Chai's protectors.

"Enough," said Jan Farooq, irritated by the delay. "Sit down, and let us begin. You can fight the tea boy later, cousin." The crowd laughed, and the man sat down, red-faced. Jan Farooq beckoned for the Mullah to move forward and sit beside him. Room was made, and the Mullah picked his way through the seated crowd of curious men watching him closely. As the Mullah was taking his seat, Jan Farooq stood up and took control of the noisy meeting.

"Cousins, cousins!" The crowd quieted down. "We Hotaki are here today for a serious purpose. We are here to build peace within our tribe."

The Mullah did not stand to speak, but his voice carried weight nonetheless. "Cousins, we are here to discuss wrongs done against the people of this village, but also against our whole community."

"To reach agreement is the way of our people," said Jan Farooq.

The Mullah then stood and addressed the crowd more emphatically. "Tarak Sagwan has lost his way. He threatens families so that he can marry their daughters. When he marries, he does not pay a mahr. When he is done with the girls, he divorces them and gives them nothing. His men rape and rob and terrorize this district. He drapes their actions in a dark cloak by calling them a police force."

Jan Farooq regarded the Mullah coolly. "These are serious allegations, my friend, not yet proven. But we will come to the truth of the matter and agree on what must be done."

The Mullah continued, ignoring Jan Farooq's comments. "Tarak must be brought to heel. Every one of you who is a true Muslim knows that this is the case."

Jan Farooq smiled and calmly took a seat. He left the Mullah standing awkwardly, alone in his passionate display. Jan Farooq's voice was melodious, reasonable. "My friend, let us hear from others in the community, as well. Truth, like a river, is made drop by drop."

The Mullah nodded his assent and sat down. Everyone began speaking at once. Eventually, one man had enough listeners to establish himself as the speaker. He stood, and everyone listened. "Like many of you, I was a mujahid. I fought alongside many of these men who now control the roads. It is no longer possible to make an honest living, I tell you ..."

As the man spoke, Rashid quietly slipped out the back of the tent and began walking back to the checkpoint. By the time he reached the highway, his limp had become pronounced. He paused for a moment to rest, surveying the countryside around him, breathing deeply. After a few minutes he moved off again, giving a wave to Wasif and Amin as he approached the checkpoint.

Wasif called out to him. "Is the jirga over already?"

"It has barely started," said Rashid.

"Don't you want to be there to help make the decisions?"

Rashid squatted down beside the boys and picked up a handful of sand from the roadside. "Make the decisions?" Rashid's tone was weary and discouraged. "Our men scurry around, talking, making decisions as if we were in charge. And then the hand of God sweeps them all away as if they had never existed." As Rashid spoke, he blew the sand from his hand. "Once gone, it is as if they were never there."

Amin refused to be discouraged. "Jan Farooq is a powerful man. They say that he and the Mullah fought the Russians together. And nearly every man in the district is there in that tent right now."

Rashid shook his head. "We're all just fooling ourselves." He smiled faintly at the boys, but with nothing more to say, he walked away and headed back to the madrassa.

"What does he mean by that?" asked Wasif.

"He's just tired," said Amin.

The two boys fell again into silence, tightly gripping their rifles.

Inside the jirga, the day wore on, the men talking over each other endlessly. They variously argued as well as agreed, the jirga providing entertainment and diversion for all the men there. As darkness began to fall, some of Jan Farooq's men hung lanterns along the edges of the tent, casting a meagre light on the meeting. It was only as daylight turned to dusk and Faizal admitted that he had run out of tea that the crowd became restless, the discussion even more disjointed and rowdy.

The Mullah rose again, gesturing with his hands for silence. When he spoke, it was with an authority that had grown over the course of the day. "Friends. Cousins. Brothers. Like many righteous men here, I, too, fought the Russians to protect our homes. After many years of war, do we not all now deserve to live in peace and security, free from the terrorizing of bandits?"

Jan Farooq cleared his throat. "Tarak Sagwan is also a mujahid. And did not the Russians then call all of us mujahideen 'dushmen'? Is he not deserving of respect also?"

The Mullah did not reply to him, but addressed the crowd. "It is enough for now, then. The day is coming to a close."

Jan Farooq spoke loudly, his voice sounding slightly rough after a day with much talk. "This has been a good day. We have much yet to talk about, but we will resume again in the morning, insh'allah."

"And so to bring blessings upon this gathering and this day, let us all pray together," said the Mullah.

Jan Farooq smiled, baring his teeth, and his voice dripped like honey. "Of course, Mullah, of course."

The men began to head outside to wash, using water drawn from the stream in buckets by Faizal and Lala Chai. Each man poured water from an ewer over the other's hands, taking turns.

Once each man had completed his ablutions, they lined up in rows to pray. The Mullah took a position at the front of the crowd, and all eyes turned to him for the signal to begin. He raised his hands to the sides of head, cleared his mind, and focused on the prayer he was about to offer. When he spoke, his voice was deeper and more melodious than the men recalled it having been during the jirga.

"Allah-u akbar."

The Mullah led the men through the prayer. To finish, he turned his head to the right and left, speaking the words of the taslim with deep sincerity. "May the peace and blessings of Allah be upon you."

As each man completed the prayer, he stood and looked around him. The crowd began to dissolve into little knots of friends and relatives. Jan Farooq approached the Mullah. "Where can I find you tonight? I have a few men I wish to speak with, and then I would like to speak with you alone."

The Mullah stood and stretched his legs. "I will be sleeping in the madrassa, as always."

Jan Farooq smiled and embraced the Mullah, who stood stiffly, arms at his side, until he was released. "Very good, my friend. Until later." Jan Farooq wandered a short way off and joined a small group of other elders, who turned toward him respectfully as he approached. He took the eldest man by the hands, and leaned in to speak to them all in quiet tones. He said something the Mullah could not hear; the old men laughed. They followed Jan Farooq as he moved on to speak to other men in the crowd.

The Mullah and Umar began to walk back to the checkpoint. Umar reached out and held the Mullah's hand. Umar had two prayer mats over his shoulder, steadying them with his free hand. "Is this what you expected from the jirga?"

The Mullah was distracted. "What do you mean?"

Umar sighed. "Everyone gossiping and ignoring the problem at hand. Insisting on having the opportunity to speak and then saying the same things that had already been said. Every man talking over the other, and no one agreeing to anything."

The Mullah gave a short, dry laugh that was uncharacteristic of him. "Is that how you see us Hotaki? As endless arguers?"

"Your words, Ma'alim, not mine," said Umar.

"On the first day of a jirga, everyone wants to be heard," explained the Mullah. "No one wants to reveal what he will agree to or not agree to. In this case, though, the eventual outcome is clear."

Umar was surprised. "Truly?"

"No one will support Tarak. Not if they are true Muslims. They are just maintaining their dignity. It would appear weak to give in and agree on the first day."

"So tomorrow, then?"

The Mullah shook his head. "Get your rest. If not tomorrow, then the day after. Perhaps the day after that."

As the two reached the checkpoint, Amin and Wasif greeted each in turn. Umar briefly embraced each of them, but the Mullah stood apart, gazing up the mountainside.

"I shall stay here with the boys for a while, Mullah. Will you join us?"

"I have things to ponder," said the Mullah, and he turned from them and began to walk uphill to the madrassa.

Umar watched him for a moment, thinking, before turning back to the boys.

"What was decided?" asked Wasif.

"To meet tomorrow," said Umar.

The boys looked confused. Umar smiled and sat down on one of the crates that they used as seats. "I will tell you all about it."

———

Jan Farooq sat sullenly in the passenger seat of his rusty GAZ. He picked from a few pistachio nuts that he held cupped in one hand, spitting out the shells after peeling them apart with his teeth. *That jirga seemed to last forever,* he thought.

People trumpeted about the equality of all men under the Pashtunwali. Every man in the jirga was entitled to speak, and honour could be held by all in equal measure. He let out a laugh. *Nonsense. The equality of men has never been true, not since the beginning of time.*

As they say, the five fingers are brothers, but they are not equal. Why God chose that it would be so is a matter for others to debate, but it is clear from birth that not all men are equal. Some are stronger than others. More eloquent than others. Richer than others. More powerful than others. Even the biggest fools can see it plainly, if only they care to look.

Jan Farooq lit a cigarette and stared out the window.

The jirga was not a place for men to be equal, but a place to provide an equal footing for men to demonstrate their power. It was an arena for the powerful to duel, and the remainder to watch. Jan Farooq believed this with every fibre of his being.

The Mullah did well today, he thought. Although he was until recently unknown to the others, his speech was simple and convincing. He made men blush at the thought of their own lack of piety. He was the holiest man that any of them had ever met, and he was there, in their own village, asking them to deal with Tarak Sagwan. It felt to these men like an epic poem in the making.

But what the Mullah hadn't counted on was something that almost all men knew. Fear. The village men feared the wrath of Tarak Sagwan more than the holiness of the Mullah. Jan Farooq had seen that when the jirga ended for the day and word began to circulate that Tarak knew who had gathered and what they had said, the group began to dissolve. The jirga was only binding once consensus was reached — for now, every man but the Mullah could leave without having opposed Tarak and with his own petty honour intact.

Jan Farooq smiled. Not one of these farmers had the imagination to consider what they could gain from this conflict. He bid his driver to start the engine, and cursed his people for being fools. The driver looked doubtfully up toward the top of the hill where the madrassa sat.

"Am I to take you up there to speak with the Mullah?" he asked.

Jan Farooq scowled. "We're done here."

The GAZ drove off from the village, the tent used at the jirga already folded up in the back. Jan Farooq spat out the window again.

"I've had enough of this place," he said, "and this Mullah, as well."

CHAPTER 9

The evening air had begun to cool. Rashid walked through the scrub along the ridge overlooking the highway, avoiding the path that was being worn along the straightest route from the checkpoint to the madrassa. As much as he felt at home with the Mullah and the others, he valued time alone, to walk and to think. He thought through the events of the day, eyes scanning his surroundings as a matter of habit. A slight movement where there should not have been any caught his eye.

He stopped and crouched down low in a small fold in the ground. His eyes focused in on a particular rock in the distance. Rashid looked slightly away from his target, as he had learned long ago, to better see in low light. In the growing quiet of the early night, he waited, watching. After a few minutes he saw the movement again. A figure left the cover of a large rock, moving farther along the side of the slope, to a position overlooking the checkpoint. The figure settled in there, stretching out under a brown patu the colour of the surrounding dust.

Rashid carefully moved out of the fold in the ground and picked his way back and farther up the slope of the hill. All pain in his leg forgotten, he slowly worked his way around the watching figure until he approached him from behind. Carefully choosing where to place his foot at every step, Rashid made slow but silent progress toward the man watching the checkpoint. When he was ten yards away, he stopped.

He could see the man more clearly now, legs and sandals just poking out from the back of the patu. Rashid crept closer, ready should the man hear him and startle. He paused as the man began to inch backwards away from where he could best see the checkpoint. As the man started to raise himself, Rashid pounced.

The blow knocked the man sideways, away from the short rifle that had lain unseen beside him on the ground. Rashid pinned him down, knees on his back and neck. The man grunted in pain and surprise, but Rashid did not yet let him up. His hands expertly ran over the man's back and sides, searching for weapons. Finding nothing, he shifted his weight onto the man's neck one last time before rolling back onto his feet, snatching the rifle off the ground as he rose.

The man rolled over and gasped, hands held up to his face. "I mean you no harm."

Rashid paused, recognizing the man as the taller of the two bandits from the checkpoint. Although he was not proud of it, he had paid taxes then just like everyone else. Rashid pushed those thoughts away and held the bandit's rifle at the low ready, pointed straight at the man's chest. "We'll see what the Mullah decides to do with you. Now get up. Slowly."

The bandit stood and raised both his hands in surrender. Rashid gestured with the rifle and marched him down the slope toward the checkpoint. Both slipped and skidded on the loose earth, but Rashid was careful to stay behind the man and to stay upright, rifle at the ready. By the time Amin and Wasif saw them approaching along the road, Rashid was limping badly.

As they reached the checkpoint itself, Rashid hit the bandit in the small of the back with the butt of the rifle, driving him down to the ground. The bandit cried out like a wounded animal, tucking his arms and legs in to form a ball as he lay on the highway. Umar appeared at the door of the ZIL, his eyes blurry with sleep. Rashid gave the bandit a kick in the ribs. "Look who I found scouting our position."

The bandit rolled over onto his back to face his captors, and held his hands up to protect his face. "A fair warning to you. Run away now. All of you," he said.

Umar walked over to where the bandit lay, looking down at him with contempt. Without warning, he kicked him, hard, his toe catching him under the ribs. The man curled up in pain again, gasping for breath. Umar stood over the man, watching him intently. "Why should we run away? Surely not from you?"

The bandit spoke through gritted teeth, his body tensed in expectation of another blow. "Fools. Tarak told your mullah that he would be back. Right now, he is preparing to attack you, and when he does, you will all die."

Umar squatted down beside the man, looking at him with dull eyes. "Will it matter to you if you are already dead? If it's even true?"

Rashid picked up a bayonet that the bandits had left behind in the ZIL, and squatted down on the other side of the prone man. He looked at Umar. "What do we need to know from him?"

Umar shook his head at Rashid and addressed the boys. "Amin, quickly, run to the madrassa and wake the Mullah. He needs to hear of this. Wasif, wake the elders and the men of the jirga down by the river. They will need to hear this, as well."

As the two boys ran off in opposite directions, the bandit swore at them under his breath. "You are all fools."

Amin reached the madrassa faster than he ever remembered having scaled the hill before. He rushed in through the door and straight into the classroom. The entire floor of the class was covered with sleeping boys. The Mullah slept off to one side, breathing deeply and wrapped in his woolen patu. Amin went straight to his side to wake him. "Haji, Haji! Rashid has captured a bandit! He says we are going to be attacked!"

The Mullah turned over with a start and woke quickly. He stood, already dressed, and pulled the pistol from the pile of belongings next to where he had lain. He checked that it was loaded and handed it grip-first to Amin. "Take this, and stay here. I trust you to watch over the other boys."

Amin nodded, unsure of what to say. The Mullah looked him in the eye and hesitated, words caught in his mouth. He quickly turned away and left the madrassa.

The other students had begun to wake, and they turned to Amin for answers. The only thing truly distinguishing him from the others was the pistol that he held in both of his small hands. "Go back to sleep, brothers," said Amin. "The Mullah is not here, but I will watch over you." He settled the other boys as best he could and found a place to sit near the front of the classroom, facing the entrance. A blanket pulled tightly around his narrow shoulders, he began to recite the Quran under his breath, eyes fixed on the doorway, the pistol held out in front of him.

The Mullah hurried down the hill and straight to the checkpoint, where the lantern that customarily burned at night had already been extinguished. Rashid and Umar stood alert in the darkness, gripping their kalashes, and straining to see or hear any movement around them. The bandit had his hands tied behind his back and was now lying face down on the ground on one side of the road. Rashid did not turn to greet the Mullah as he arrived, focusing on the task of scanning the countryside in all directions for the approach of the bandits. Umar walked up to the Mullah and held out the newly captured rifle for him to take, but the Mullah waved it away.

Without turning away from where he was looking, Rashid gestured at the bandit with one hand. "I found him watching the checkpoint from up on the hillside. You already know him."

The Mullah crouched near the bandit's head, recognizing him in the pale moonlight. He spoke in a reasonable tone: "Why are you back?"

The bandit did not lift or turn his head other than to keep his mouth out of the dirt as he spoke. "Tarak told you he'd be back."

"Where is Tarak now?" asked the Mullah.

The bandit gave a short laugh. "You'll find out soon enough."

Umar gave the bandit another hard kick, this time from behind, deep in the groin. The bandit squirmed and dry-heaved in pain, but said no more. Umar drew his foot back to kick him again, but the Mullah waved at him to stop. His tone once again was reasonable, even conciliatory, as he questioned the bandit: "Tell me. How does he plan to attack?"

The bandit answered between clenched teeth. "He doesn't have a fancy plan, and he doesn't need one. He's just going to swat you aside like flies."

Umar laughed. "What, all of us? Nearly every able-bodied man in the district is here."

The bandit said nothing; he just grinned and closed his eyes. At that very moment, Wasif came running up the road, shouting. "The elders! Everyone! They're all gone! They must have left as soon as it got dark!"

"Is there anyone left?" asked Umar.

"No!" panted Wasif.

Now the bandit began to laugh at them. "I told you to run away."

Rashid muttered a curse under his breath. *"Chyort poberi!"*

The Mullah gave Rashid a sharp look on hearing the foreign sounds. He seemed about to say something, but remained silent, instead gathering everyone around him. He stayed crouched on his haunches.

Before he could speak, Umar interrupted. "This is the moment of judgment. We must place ourselves in God's hands. Our success will be a sign of his favour."

Rashid was less convinced. "And if we fail?"

"Then who are we to question it?" replied Umar.

When the Mullah spoke, the others were still. "Fighting them head-on is not necessary. There is another way. A better way."

Rashid spoke again. "No matter what you propose, we have only two kalashes and a rifle. Those are not good odds."

Umar's eyes burned brightly. "God favours the righteous."

Rashid countered. "And the clever."

The Mullah turned to face Rashid. "Hear what I propose." As he drew a diagram with one finger in the dust at their feet, the men squatted down and listened to him intently.

In a small village farther down the valley, chaos reigned. A pickup truck, flanked by three motorcycles, was parked at the edge of the village. Bandits ran riot from house to house, followed by the sounds of screaming and gunfire. Tarak stood in the centre of the village.

His face was impassive. A frightened villager, blood on his clothes, was dragged through the dust and dropped at his feet. Tarak spoke to him as he would a slow child. "Where is your neighbour and his daughter?"

The man stammered out an answer. "I don't know, they left."

"I want my bride!" shouted Tarak as he casually shot the man in the leg and walked away. The others ignored the wounded villager as he clutched his bloody thigh and rolled in pain. A walkie-talkie in Tarak's pocket crackled, the voice calling urgently. "Tarak. Tarak."

Tarak took it in his hand and answered. "Haji, this is Tarak. Did it work?"

"They are waiting for the jirga to start again, and so they are all there. You know what to do."

"How many men does he have?" asked Tarak.

"There are just a few men at the checkpoint. They have only two kalashes."

"And does this Mullah have my bride?"

There was a pause. When the voice came over the radio again, it was firm and direct. "Do as I have asked, and we will find your bride afterwards. I am well out of the way. Begin when you wish."

Tarak's eyes gleamed at the thought of the Mullah sprawled at his feet, dying slowly. "Where exactly is he now? I will go there directly." Tarak listened closely, and began to wave his free hand over his head to gather his bandits for the attack.

The Mullah, Umar, and Faizal lay behind a hastily stacked pile of rocks partway up the slope, overlooking the road. Rashid and Wasif rushed up to join them, out of breath.

Rashid handed one of the kalashes to Wasif, and picked up the old semi-automatic rifle he had taken from the bandit. He found a comfortable position to fire from, adjusting the rocks in his line of sight to make a rest.

Faizal carried a long cloth sack that had sat untouched in the back of the chai khana for years. As he settled into position behind the rock wall, he pulled out an ancient jezail, covered in oil. Its long barrel, brass fittings, and curved buttstock made to fit under a horseman's arm marked it as having come from another era. When the others saw it, they couldn't help staring at his outlandish weapon.

"It was my father's father's," said Faizal. Rashid sniggered.

Settling in behind the protection of the rocks, the men lay close together, shoulders touching, and waited. Rashid lay still, his rifle braced upon a stone rest and tucked tightly into his shoulder. Umar adjusted the position of his legs over and over, trying to get comfortable. He whispered to the others. "I don't understand. Where are the rest of the villagers? The guests in the chai khana? The men from the jirga?"

"There is no one sleeping in the chai khana. They've all evaporated into the night. No one else wants any part in this," said Faizal.

"With their help, we could easily win this fight," complained Umar bitterly.

"We will win, with or without them. These other people, they just want to survive," said the Mullah. He was unarmed, lying just above the others behind a rock pile of his own, observing the road.

The silence as they waited drew longer, making most of the men nervous. Only Rashid and the Mullah seemed unperturbed, simply waiting for what they knew must come. Each man seemed lost in his own thoughts, no one speaking, when the noise of someone scrambling through the brush behind them caused them to start.

Umar rolled over onto his back, weapon pointed at an odd angle toward the sound. Wasif did the same, though the rifle was so heavy that he had to rest the butt on the ground to do so. Rashid tucked himself into a crouch, eyes straining to see what was behind the noise. He began to slowly move along the slope, rifle at his hip.

The sound grew louder, more like a wild animal moving heedlessly across the rocky ground than a man. A few small rocks rolled down onto the road, dislodged by whatever was moving along the slope, and Rashid brought his rifle to his shoulder to fire.

Bursting out of the darkness came Lala Chai, carrying a battered pot in one hand and a stack of glasses in the other. "I've brought tea. To make you strong!" he said.

Rashid lowered his rifle and laughed.

"We might have shot you," warned Umar.

Lala Chai ignored him, looking at the others. "Where is *my* gun? I want to fight."

"Be quiet and get back to the chai khana where you belong," said Umar as he rolled back over to face down the road.

Rashid reached toward Lala Chai and tugged on the corner of his kamiz. "But first pour me a glass of that tea."

Umar shot Rashid an exasperated look as he watched him take a glass from the boy. He kept watch down the road while the others laughed quietly with Lala Chai, but when a steaming glass of tea was passed to him, he didn't refuse.

A flash of light from up the road focused their attention back on the highway. Just visible in the distance were the headlights from a truck and two motorcycles. All three sets of lights came rushing toward the checkpoint. As the headlights drew nearer, gunfire flashed from the back of the truck.

Now the men on the slope could see the bandits firing wildly into the air and hear them shouting. The Mullah's voice was calm. "Wait. They're used to intimidating their foes rather than killing them. They will not expect us to fight."

As the vehicles approached the checkpoint, they were forced to slow down and weave through piles of junk that Rashid had left in the middle of the road. The men all looked to the Mullah, awaiting his signal to fire. He did not look back at them. Instead, he remained staring down at the road. The seconds ticked by, marked by the clicking of the prayer beads in his hand. When the bandits had nearly come to a stop among a large pile of debris, the Mullah shouted: "Now!"

Everyone with a gun opened fire at once, the two kalashes pouring bullets toward the bandits on full automatic. Wasif closed his eyes and held his face in a grimace as he fired the whole magazine in one long, chattering burst. Rashid took only aimed shots, choosing each target carefully, one by one. The tight pack of men in the open back of the truck were an easy target as they scrambled over the sides of the truck to find cover. Lala Chai moved into a half crouch behind the Mullah's men, fingers jammed in his ears while he strained to get a look at the destruction below.

Wasif opened his eyes for a second, seeing the chaos on the road below where he was pointing his rifle, and shut them tightly again. He could feel the rifle pulsing in his hands as it fired each round, the impact against his shoulder causing a dull ache that got worse with each shot fired. He tried to block out the sounds, the sharp cracks all around him, the shouts of wounded men that sounded like dying animals. Grinding his teeth together, he hoped it would be over soon.

He was brought back to the moment by a sharp blow to the side of his head. The rifle was pulled from his hands, and when he looked up the Mullah was standing over him. The Mullah cleared the jammed weapon without taking his eyes from Wasif, snapping a fresh magazine in place before handing the weapon back to the boy. Wasif realized then that he had not been firing, so lost in his own thoughts that his blunder had not registered on him.

Wasif's cheeks burned with shame, driven home by the Mullah's words. "We are all counting on you to fight, boy. We are not so many or so powerful that you can fail to carry your part of the burden." He continued watching him until Wasif aimed the rifle back down to the road and began firing again. Wasif did not look over toward the Mullah, but could feel his teacher's eyes burning through his kamiz to look directly into his heart. With each shot, Wasif tried to show him that he was worthy.

Although the fire was not heavy, it was accurate enough that it brought the vehicles to a stop. Bandits pushed at each other in their rush to take cover on the side of the road away from the ambush. The ditch was soon full of wounded and confused men. One of the bandits tried to rally the others, demanding that they give him cover fire as he made a dash for the machine gun mounted behind the cab of the truck. Wild-eyed and hoarse, the bandits agreed. The alternative was to die in a ditch.

As the bandits scrambled around on the ground to find the best cover, one of them caught his foot on a tripwire made of twine. The twine pulled the pin from a grenade buried in the gravel. After a few seconds' delay the grenade detonated, along with a cooking-gas canister buried next to it, and they both exploded with a sharp crack. The explosion flipped the pickup truck over on its side, crushing the man who had climbed up to get behind the machine gun. Shrapnel from the grenade and gravel from the road peppered the bandits in the ditch. Their screams were short and pitiful. Rashid kept firing into the ditch until the Mullah signalled him to stop.

Within minutes of having started, Tarak Sagwan's attack was over.

In the ringing silence, Rashid nudged Faizal with an elbow. "Thanks for the gas canister from your chai khana, brother! That worked even better than I expected." Faizal, still staring ahead, hardly seemed to notice he was being spoken to.

Without the sound of gunfire, Wasif could tell that his ears were ringing painfully. He opened and closed his mouth, trying to get his ears to pop, though no matter what he did it made little difference. Umar clapped him on the shoulder, speaking loudly over the sound in his own ears. "You've done well, Wasif. Your first fight is not one that you'll soon forget."

Wasif smiled and looked to the Mullah for approval. His teacher was not paying attention to any of them there, but was still watching the site of the ambush intently. Rashid had been doing the same, but seeing no movement and hearing no more fire, he turned to the others as he stood up. "I am going down to finish off any survivors."

The others rose as one to follow him down to the highway, though the Mullah's long strides quickly carried him ahead of the others. When he reached the road, he stopped for a moment to take stock of the chaos that they had caused. The site of the ambush was littered with parts of the damaged vehicles and the shattered bodies of the bandits. The Mullah continued to watch as the others moved past him through the wreckage, scavenging weapons and other things of value, illuminated by the burning truck.

Rashid ignored the vehicles and went from body to body, kicking them or rolling them over with one foot to see if they were still alive. Any that gave a sign of life were dispatched with a single close-range shot. The Mullah followed him from body to body, looking each one in the face, searching for Tarak. He held his fists clenched tightly, the prayer beads hanging limply from his right hand.

Soon they had collected whatever was worth taking from the wreckage and piled it on the side of the road. Over a dozen kalashes and three times as many magazines sat as a mute tribute to their victory.

Umar was still scavenging along the side of the road. The others heard him give a shout: "I think this dushka might still work!" Wasif and Faizal came over to where he stood and helped him lift the machine gun and bring it into the circle of light cast by the burning truck. Umar searched the shadows where he had found it until he also found the tripod on which it had sat behind the cab of the truck. He called Wasif over to watch him as he began to brush the dirt from its workings.

"These machine guns are unbreakable," marvelled Umar. Wasif gazed at him blankly, until Umar gripped the boy's shoulder and said, "Much like you, young lion."

Wasif smiled weakly and asked in a thin voice, "Umar, is it always like that?"

Umar was busy with the machine gun and did not look up. "Mash'allah! This was a rare easy victory, my friend." When Wasif said nothing, Umar gave him a quick glance. "Our battles will not get easier, but you will find them easier." Wasif felt sick to his stomach. Anticipating the boy's thoughts, Umar added, "The Mullah will forgive you, Wasif, if he hasn't already. Now watch as I show you how to load this gun."

The Mullah took a moment to look around him, the scene lit by the harsh light of the fire that still burned. Rashid was calmly sorting through the magazines, separating the loaded from the empty. Faizal was seated on a rock by the side of the road, lost in thought, his ancient musket resting on his knees. Umar and Wasif were leaning close together, the boy listening intently as Umar explained the workings of the machine gun. The Mullah saw that they were good men. Righteous men. He knew that this victory was —

The sound of three quick shots interrupted his thoughts, echoing down from the distant madrassa. The Mullah's head snapped around at the sound, his eyes straining unsuccessfully to find the source. Before anyone else had moved at all, the Mullah had grabbed a rifle from the side of the road and was running up the hill, checking that it was loaded as he went. The others followed.

The Mullah covered the distance to the madrassa with long strides, keeping mostly to the well-worn path that led up the hill. His chest heaved from the exertion, but when he reached the madrassa he rushed in through the outer door without a pause. He skidded to a halt just inside the classroom, rifle held at the ready in front of him. He saw the boys all huddled in one corner around Amin, who stood stock-still, pointing the pistol straight out in front of him. Tarak Sagwan lay face down, dead, at the Mullah's feet.

The Mullah kicked his body over, revealing the short-barrelled automatic that he had been carrying and the bloody mess that the pistol rounds had made of his chest. The Mullah placed his own weapon down on the ground and slowly walked toward Amin. Approaching the boy from the side, he gently took the pistol from his small hands. The other students shuffled over to where the Mullah stood and formed a circle around him.

For the very first time, the Mullah placed his arms around Amin and held him in an embrace.

The other men barrelled through the door, stopping at Tarak's body. The Mullah turned to them, one arm still around Amin, and said, "He is a boy no longer. And we shall no longer call him simply Amin, but Asadullah Amin — the Lion of God."

Wasif went to take his brother's hand, but it remained limp, so Wasif merely stood beside him, unsure of what else to do. Umar and Rashid each took turns embracing the boy, using his new name to praise him for killing the bandit king.

Although he tried to look brave, Asadullah Amin wept uncontrollably, though secretly his heart was filled with pride.

"No tears," chided the Mullah. "Not in front of these boys. Now that you are a man, you must act like one."

Asadullah Amin wiped his eyes with his sleeve, setting his face into a mask, pushing his memory of this night away.

CHAPTER 10

The Mullah led the others as they loaded the bodies onto a trailer hitched to an old Russian tractor.

Umar quickly searched each body one last time before it was lifted onto the trailer. Each of the men now had a kalash slung across his back, won in the fight the night before. Rashid righted a damaged motorcycle and was closely examining the engine. He did not need to examine the pickup truck or the other motorcycle, as they were charred black and damaged beyond repair. "I think this one might run again," said Rashid.

"Why can't we bury them here?" asked Asadullah Amin as he helped lift one of the bandits onto the trailer.

The Mullah answered him in a tone that invited no discussion. "They should be buried near their home."

Wasif waited for his brother at the foot of the last of the bodies and turned to speak. "And it sends a message to any of Tarak's men who are left that we —"

The Mullah interrupted the two boys with a glare. "That we do what is right."

They both met the Mullah's statement with silence. With all of the bodies loaded, the men climbed aboard the trailer while Rashid started the tractor that they had borrowed from one of the villagers. It had no muffler, and it roared loudly enough to almost deafen the men.

The sun hung high in the sky as they made slow progress down the road. It was not long before all of the men had pulled scarves over their mouths and noses, though nothing they tried blocked the smell rising from their gruesome cargo. The roads they travelled were deserted; as they passed the small villages, no one came out to greet them or even to see who they were. It was as if the whole countryside had gone into hiding. Long hours passed slowly in the heat, and it was well into the afternoon before they turned off the highway and onto a track that led to their destination: Tarak's lair.

Rashid stopped the tractor well short of the compound itself, though there was no movement anywhere around it. The Mullah waved the men off of the trailer and into a loose line spreading out on either side of himself. He unslung his rifle, as did the others, holding the weapons in front of themselves at a low angle. It was unclear to any of them whether there would be another fight from the remaining bandits. At the Mullah's signal, they walked slowly up a long, low rise toward the gates of the compound.

They reached the gate without seeing any sign of life. The Mullah tried the metal doorway, which, to their surprise, swung open at his touch. As it creaked on its hinges, the compound erupted with the noise of barking dogs. The Mullah stepped through the gateway and into the compound, followed by the others.

"I'm sure that they are gone," said Umar.

The dogs' barking reached a frenzied pitch as they strained toward the strangers at the entrance. The compound was strewn with discarded belongings; the surviving bandits must have

THIS SHALL BE *a* HOUSE *of* PEACE

abandoned it in a hurry. A few fresh tire tracks cut through the dust at the gate.

Wasif looked around, frustrated. "If we find any more bandits, we should feed them to these dogs. That's what they say the bandits do to their victims."

The Mullah turned around suddenly and lunged at Wasif. He stopped himself, his face inches from the boy's and his eyes raging with intensity. "We haven't come here to imitate these sinners. There is but one judge of all human hearts. We have come to return them to Him."

Wasif's face turned crimson red and he said nothing. Asadullah Amin and Rashid walked away and looked into each of the buildings within the compound. Rashid called back to the others, "Whoever was left took everything of value when they fled."

"We have not come for spoils," said the Mullah. "All we need are blankets for shrouds."

"Come with me, Wasif," said Umar as he moved off toward the kennels. The barking intensified as he approached, the dogs leaping over each other to get out of their makeshift cages. Umar lifted his rifle and aimed at the huge, shaggy mastiff that was nearest to him. He shot it once in the head, and it was driven to the floor in a pool of gore. Both the sharp crack of the rifle and the squealing of the other dogs caused Wasif to startle and take an involuntary step backwards.

"Help me finish the rest," said Umar. Wasif hesitated, looking to the Mullah.

"They're unclean creatures," said the Mullah, nodding his assent. Wasif fired a few shots into the kennel, hoping that Umar would not see that his eyes were closed.

"Aim, boy, aim," said Umar as he continued to dispatch the dogs one by one. Over the next few minutes the yelping of the dogs reached a crescendo, and then there was silence.

The Mullah stepped out of the compound, looking around for a suitable piece of ground. A mound that might once have been a garbage heap rose up just outside the wall of the compound. It was visible from the road for a long distance in either direction, and the Mullah knew that it would do. Once they had finished searching the compound for shrouds, the Mullah had the others dig one long grave across the top of the mound. They dug sullenly in the heat, but by the end of the day the bandits were washed and shrouded and laid to rest as Muslims, as was their due. The Mullah's prayers over their graves were no more or less genuine than those he'd given for the old man and the girl.

His voice was firm and strong as he spoke. "It makes no difference whether these men were virtuous or not virtuous. Kind or unkind. Cowardly or brave. By burying them as we would our own family, we simply do what is right."

The others murmured their agreement. "What we do is for God, not for any of the dead men lying in these graves," said Umar.

The Mullah had the boys collect some long sticks pulled from structures inside the compound, to which they attached simple flags torn from coloured sheets. These he pushed into the soft earth along the head of the mass grave. Even though the poles were spindly and the flags were little more than rags, they marked the burial site for the local villagers to see. No signs were placed to distinguish the individuals from each other. Nor was Tarak buried in a position of prominence. Laid in the dust of the earth, all men are finally and truly equal.

With no time to return to the madrassa before dark, the Mullah bade the men follow him a short distance away from the compound. There they built a fire and, wrapped in blankets, prepared to pass the night under the stars.

"I will take the first watch," said Rashid. When no one replied, he lifted his rifle and moved to find a place that was well outside the circle of light cast by the fire. Shrouded in darkness and unseen, his eyes ran along the contours of the ground all around them, watching for signs of trouble. As his gaze ran back over where the others were resting, he realized that the Mullah had selected a perfect spot for the night. The group was in a slight bowl on the crest of the rise that Rashid had not seen before. It not only provided cover for the sleepers around the low fire, but the crest itself gave good views of the surrounding area. It would be hard for anyone to surprise them in this position, even without a sentry.

The position that the Mullah had selected was not random at all. He suddenly felt safe in the hands of this man, and comfortable enough to sleep deeply when his turn came. Rashid heard the others speaking softly, but he turned away from the fire, preferring the company of his own thoughts.

The others sat or lay wrapped in their patus in a small circle around the fire. Umar shook his head in disbelief. "How is it that nearly every man in the district knew that the bandits would attack before we did, and yet no one said a word to us?"

"The power of the jirga," said the Mullah, "is in building consensus. Where there is no consensus to be had, it dissolves. Then the matter is resolved through other means."

"So they never intended to bring Tarak to heel?" asked Umar.

"They came to talk and to listen," replied the Mullah. "After they heard what was said, they must not have believed that Tarak could be stopped easily. They likely knew that the lashkar would be needed to bring him to justice." The Mullah broke a twig that he had been holding in his hands and threw it into the fire. "And none of them had the stomach for it."

"And what about your old friend, Jan Farooq?" continued

Umar. "I have only ever heard him described as a brave mujahid. Is he also a coward?"

"He is no coward, of that I am certain. We fought in the same tanzim against the Russians. That was many years ago. He is a shrewd man. He chose with his head, not with his heart."

Wasif, who had been listening intently, blurted out a question. "But, Ma'alim, a man like that cannot be trusted!"

The Mullah paused, thinking for a moment, and Umar interjected. "Men like Jan Farooq can always be trusted — to do what is best for themselves."

The Mullah smiled and nodded. "Jan Farooq seeks power. That in itself is not evil, if the intentions in his heart are true."

"But what of his men? They seem too rough and heavily armed to be virtuous," said Umar.

"When a mother porcupine calls to its baby," said the Mullah, "it speaks softly, saying, 'Oh, my child of velvet.'"

Umar laughed at this proverb.

Wasif looked back and forth between the men, confused. The Mullah noticed, and said, "Jan Farooq does not look at men with the same eyes as you or I do, Wasif."

The men sat in silence for some time, watching the fire burn down to embers. In time, the Mullah turned from the others and lay down on the ground with his patu wrapped around his shoulders and head.

"Forgive me," said Umar, "but before we rest, tell us what we shall do next."

Wasif and Asadullah Amin leaned closer to hear the Mullah's quiet words.

"I intend to return to the madrassa," said the Mullah.

"But you said once we opposed Tarak we could never go back," said Asadullah Amin.

The Mullah lay still, considering his next words very carefully.

"That is true. But the madrassa and its teachings are eternal."

"And what of Isa and now the bandit, held in the village?" asked Wasif.

"The answer will become apparent in time," said the Mullah.

Umar interceded before Asadullah Amin could ask another question. "Mullah, we do not question the importance of the madrassa or its teachings. It is at the core of what we believe. But now that the bandits are defeated, what next? We have all accepted you as our leader — we wish only to know where we are being led."

The Mullah was silent again for a long time. "I wish to accomplish one thing. To bring peace to our village, under the laws of God. Nothing more."

The Mullah pulled his patu tight over his eyes, ending the conversation. Umar and the boys pondered his answer in silence. One by one they fell asleep, and the darkness of night deepened around them.

The next morning, the men woke just before dawn. As had become their custom, they lined up in a row behind the Mullah and prayed as a group.

Their first duty discharged, Rashid tried to start the tractor. As he held down the starter the engine turned over again and again, sounding weak and phlegmy. He jumped down from the metal seat and looked under the engine cover. Reaching into the dark recesses of the engine, he pulled on the stub of a broken cable that controlled the choke.

"Hold this, brother," he said to Umar. Umar clamped the wire between his fingers, and this time when Rashid tried the starter the engine caught. He jumped down again, looking at the engine as it vibrated in its mount, and clapped Umar on the shoulder. He would have said something, as well, but the noise of the tractor was deafening.

Rashid shouted at the others instead, though it was doubtful that anyone could hear him. "Forward the Tank of Islam!" The men climbed aboard the empty trailer and the tractor began its journey with a lurch.

Their return journey was as slow as the one that had taken them to Tarak's compound. Again they saw not a soul as they rattled along the track back to the highway. This part of the countryside had few people living in it, most having been driven off by the rapaciousness of Tarak's men. As they turned onto the highway again, however, they were surprised at what they saw in the distance.

At a small bridge that brought the highway across a large, dry culvert was a jumble of burnt-out vehicles. Their blackened hulls had been ploughed off of the road years before and were now heaped together at odd angles. Taking cover in the shade of the ruined vehicles was a group of armed men. With the news of Tarak's death, new nests of vipers had begun to emerge.

The noise of the tractor attracted the attention of the bandits, who stood to face down the highway. Rashid looked to the Mullah for direction, but receiving none, continued to drive forward. The tractor chugged down the road, heading toward the checkpoint. The Mullah stood up on the trailer, holding his rifle out to one side so that it could be seen. The others did the same, gripping their rifles in their hands.

The bandits remained facing down the highway toward them, spreading out into a loose line behind the cover of the car wrecks. Although the distance was still too far for accurate fire, a bandit listlessly fired a few rounds from his rifle toward the tractor. The shots whistled past harmlessly. The Mullah clapped Rashid on the shoulder and motioned with his finger across his throat for him to kill the engine. Rashid brought the machine to a halt and the Mullah stepped nimbly from the trailer, leading the others into the shelter of a ditch.

Umar looked to the Mullah. "What will we do?"

The Mullah peeked over the edge of the ditch and watched the bandits intently for a few minutes. When he was satisfied, he turned to the others and laid out a plan.

Pointing to a low hill off to the left, he said, "Wasif and Asadullah Amin will come with me to the top of that crest overlooking the bridge. Rashid and Umar, you will stay here with our tank. When you see us atop the hill, you will drive forward again. We will fire down on them as you approach."

Umar seemed perplexed by the plan, but said nothing. The Mullah did not pause to let him form a question and instead began to stride toward the hill. Wasif and Asadullah Amin fell in behind him, rifles over their shoulders. The Mullah picked up a trail that kept them largely out of sight of the bridge, hidden by the folds of the ground. The bandits watched them leave the road but strained helplessly to see where they had gone. They fired a few more rounds ineffectually in the direction of the tractor.

The Mullah led the two boys to a point behind the hill guarded by a jumble of rocks he had spied from the road. He lay down in a gap between two of the largest rocks and slithered into position, the boys close behind. Though the hill was not high, it looked down upon the bridge, a few hundred yards away.

The Mullah muttered softly, "They should have put a man here themselves."

The bandits, four in number, had retreated from the wreckage of the cars and now huddled behind a low wall of stones and mud bricks that they had built beside the road. Most of them still watched the tractor, though one scanned the ground around the hill, looking for the Mullah.

"Go back down on the far side of the hill and wave to Umar to start," the Mullah said to Wasif.

The boy slid backwards as he had seen both the Mullah and Rashid do before, and scrambled partway down the hill. Once in a position where he thought Umar could see him, he waved his arms in the air to get his attention.

Rashid spotted him first. "That's the signal."

Umar had to look hard before he spotted Wasif. Rashid mounted the tractor again and settled into the seat, while Umar stood on the step beside him, clutching the frame with one hand. Umar clenched his rifle in his fist and pumped it in the air over his head, shouting as loudly as he could: "Takbir!"

Rashid gave the reply: "Allah-u akbar!"

"Takbir!"

"Allah-u akbar!"

"Takbir!"

"Allah-u akbar!"

The two men shouted themselves hoarse. Rashid started the engine with a roar, and the tractor began to grind its way forward again. As soon as it did, the Mullah and the boys began firing down at the bandits from the hill. Bullets struck the rocks and bricks that made up their shelter and whizzed overhead, forcing the bandits to duck and press themselves against the rocks or the ground. Asadullah Amin fired as he remembered Rashid doing before, taking each shot as carefully as he could. Wasif's firing was wild — it came in long bursts that kicked the barrel up high. He didn't think of the bandits he saw in his sights as people, but as something less. Sinners. Apostates. Murderers.

Asadullah Amin called to his brother: "Slowly, brother, slowly."

"I've fought bandits, when you were hiding in the madrassa!"

he shouted, still firing wildly. His magazine ran dry, and he looked helplessly at the Mullah.

"Shoot carefully, like an instrument of God's will, not a wild animal," said the Mullah, handing him a magazine. Wasif's face reddened, and he gave his brother a poisonous look.

Soon, the bandits worked up the courage to begin firing back. First one, then another, and then all four held their rifles up over the low wall and held down the trigger without aiming or exposing themselves to return fire. Neither the firing from the hill nor the movement of the tractor slackened, and the bandits' resolve began to waver. When the tractor was about half a kilometre from the checkpoint, the bandits broke and ran.

First one scrambled away from the highway, and then the others. They fled without firing another shot, sheltering in the fields and among the houses in the area.

As the tractor rolled up to the culvert between the wrecked cars, Rashid shut down the engine. Umar stepped down, watching the fleeing bandits in amazement. "What are they doing?"

Rashid laughed. "What cowards always do. They are saving themselves."

The two men waited for the Mullah and the boys to join them at the tractor, still watching to make sure that the bandits did not turn around and come back. As the Mullah approached, he called out: "Rashid, what do you think of that?"

Rashid was surprised that his opinion was sought, but answered with a laugh. "These are not the dogs of war, but the hyenas and jackals. They fight only when they think they will win easily, and when there is something to gain."

Umar was still amazed. "But who are they?"

"Did you think that Tarak was the only bandit in the district?" asked the Mullah. "With him gone, others have taken the opportunity to replace him."

"Some of these bandits may even have been his men," said Rashid. He spat on the ground. "There must not have been anyone strong enough to hold them together."

"These men might yet come around if we show them what peace looks like," said Wasif. "Righteous lives are like a candle in the darkness."

"More like moths to a flame," said Asadullah Amin. "They will swarm around us until we kill them, or we will never be safe."

"Then why wait?" said Wasif. "If it is the right thing to do, then let us do it now. We can follow them and kill them wherever we find them."

The Mullah shook his head and scowled at the boy. "Unless we were at a disadvantage," he said, "they would only run away. They are not going to stand and die as you might like."

With a wave of his hand, the Mullah signalled everyone to climb aboard the trailer. Rashid started the engine, and they began to roll forward. As they travelled along the highway, they saw that other checkpoints had been set up as well, men quickly taking up arms to fill the vacuum left by the shattering of Tarak's gang. The noise of the tractor ensured that all of the bandits had ample warning of their approach, and no one tried to stop them. A few bandits jeered at them from a distance as they drove past, but that was all the opposition they faced.

The sun was setting by the time they reached the madrassa. They had set out the day before feeling victorious.

On their return, victory was no longer clear.

Rashid stood alone at the checkpoint, rifle grasped in one hand. His eyes scanned the familiar horizon, turning in all directions, looking for any small anomaly. As he looked he listened carefully to the soft noises around him. He heard Umar's deep breathing from inside the ZIL and the wind whistling along the rocky features above. The plastic sheets tied over the shop beside the chai khana rustled. Everything was as expected.

Everything, except for his own thoughts. Rashid exhaled deeply, his mind turning over the events of the last few days.

He had found his place here in the madrassa, of that he was sure. It was true that he did not study as the others did, but he shouldered other burdens instead. For the first time in many years he felt accepted without question. He was judged by his actions above all else. Where else could he hope to find peace?

But the last few days also worried him. He was not at all surprised that the end of Tarak solved nothing, or that new bandits manned the checkpoints again. As long as people were free to rob and murder travellers, there would always be those who chose to be criminals. This was a fact of life. He did not understand how the others around the Mullah could be surprised.

He guessed that it was because they had lived sheltered lives. As much as Umar was a good, learned man, people like him seemed detached from the reality of the world they lived in. If they expected to change society for the better, it was not enough for them to live a life steeped in Islam. All around them were chaos and mayhem. Every ounce of authority in this country, in the end, stemmed from the barrel of a gun.

It would not be easy to bring justice — true justice — to this country. Rashid worried that his companions did not understand what it would really take to do what they intended. Were they that blind?

Rashid shook his head, worried that his thoughts amounted to heresy. Did not God shape the universe according to His own will, unknowable to men? If that was the case, then the others were right. It was enough to do right, and to place one's faith in God. All would be right again, insh'allah.

His gut feeling, though, was that nothing would change unless they took action. Rashid thought about this. Perhaps he was wrong. He knew that in the past, in his darkest hours he had been buoyed up by the hands of God. He had been carried through the night when things seemed the most hopeless. The idea that anything he undertook by his own free will might influence the direction of the universe seemed laughable.

Rashid looked out at the night again, scanning the horizon. Everything seemed to be in order. Every rock, every bush, was in its place. *Best to be like those rocks*, he thought. *Best to be content and solid in one's place.*

CHAPTER II

The chai khana was filled with patrons drinking tea and eating. Faizal and Lala Chai bustled between them all, keeping their glasses full and brushing up the crumbs left on the carpet as men departed. The chatter stopped as the blanket covering the door was pulled aside and two hard-looking young men stepped in the room, scanning the crowd. Behind them stepped Jan Farooq. When he smiled, the patrons again began to talk among themselves.

"Chaiwallah! It is good to see you again," he said.

Faizal shooed a few local men out of the way to make room for the new guest and his guards. Faizal held his hand over his heart and greeted the senior man with a stream of well wishes, to which Jan Farooq replied by briefly and wordlessly touching his own chest.

"Haji, you are most welcome here. Tea? Food?" asked Faizal.

Jan Farooq nodded and took a seat cross-legged on the platform in the back of the room that Faizal had cleared for him. He took the cup of tea offered by Lala Chai and sipped at the liquid that was still too hot. The two hard young men sat on either side of him, still watching the crowd. Both waved away offers of tea.

Jan Farooq spoke loudly enough for all in the room to hear him. "Cousins, listen, I have good news."

The crowd quieted down respectfully, and the patrons all turned to face him. Now the centre of attention, Jan Farooq began. "I have seen the abandoned homes and fields atop the hill that surround the madrassa. They do no good to anyone. I have for several weeks now tried to track down the families of the original owners, who are almost all dead or missing."

The crowd murmured at this news of their ancient neighbours. Jan Farooq held up a thick sheaf of documents. "I have purchased all of the farms around the madrassa and I have signed documents to prove it. I will repair all of the homes at my own expense and will soon rent the farms out in exchange for a portion of the harvest."

Murmurs of appreciation arose across the chai khana. Jan Farooq raised his hands for silence. "I know that many, if not all of you, know the story of the village on the hill. That a wealthy man from Kandahar, hundreds of years ago, bought the land and divided it between his sons, for each of whom he built a house. As they had sons, they did the same, the village growing from two houses to twenty over the years. Although this is the history, I think of the future. And of those who would be as my own kin, to whom I can provide these homes."

One of the farmers from the village along the river called across the room to him. "Haji, what about those of us who have farms already? How will we afford seeds this year? This village has been strangled by bandits and we have no money."

Jan Farooq made an expansive gesture. "I will provide seeds to anyone who asks, also in exchange for a portion of the harvest."

This declaration was met with approval from all the farmers in the room. They stood up and waited in a loose line to shake Jan Farooq's hand and thank him for his generosity. The two men guarding him remained seated, but with dead eyes they carefully watched each man as he approached. They both fingered the short-barrelled automatics that hung on slings underneath their tunics.

While all eyes were on Jan Farooq, a dusty traveller entered through the blanketed doorway. Faizal moved to serve him. "Tea, friend? Food, perhaps?"

This man's face was dark. He spoke loudly for everyone to hear. "I come for justice."

The room went silent as everyone turned toward the man. Jan Farooq's men stood up and placed themselves between their patron and the newcomer.

Faizal held out his empty hands, confused. "Justice? This is a chai khana."

After another moment of silence, the tension broke. Quiet laughter rippled across the room and the men went back to their own business.

"I want to speak to the Mullah," demanded the traveller.

Faizal, relieved to not be the object of this man's concerns, pointed up toward the madrassa. "Then justice you will get," he said.

A ray of late-morning sunlight shot through the gap above the door of the kishmesh khana, illuminating the face of the tall bandit chained to the wall inside. He blinked, shielding his eyes with one hand, and shifted his position out of the sunlight. Across from him, still in darkness, was Isa, held upright by the chains that tied him to the wall opposite.

Accustomed to being ignored, both men started when the heavy wooden door was slammed open. Umar and Rashid, both carrying rifles, ducked low through the doorway to enter the room and stood facing the bandit. Isa's eyes were open, but his dull gaze was cast downward and away from them, the expression on his face blank. As the two men moved toward the bandit, Isa leaned back in his chains, straining to be as far from them as he could get. The bandit turned toward the wall, crying, "What are you going to do to me?"

Umar stepped to one side and aimed his rifle at the man's head.

"No! Please!" cried the bandit.

Rashid grabbed him roughly and unlocked the padlocks securing his hands and feet in the tight loops of chain. The skin underneath was red and weeping. The bandit continued pleading for his life, his words incomprehensible as he sobbed. Rashid silenced him with an open-handed blow to the back of the head.

"Shut up or I'll gag you."

Rashid tied the bandit's hands together behind his back with a rough piece of rope and pulled the man to his feet. He shoved the bandit forward, pushing his head down as he guided him through the kishmesh khana's door. Neither Rashid nor Umar acknowledged Isa as they shoved the tall bandit out into the open.

The door banged shut behind them. Isa's face fell, the tension gone, and he began to cry.

Umar and Rashid half carried the bandit across the upper fields to the madrassa, dragging him over the threshold of the door of the compound and across the yard. Dozens of sandals covered the ground outside the door into the madrassa itself. When they shoved him inside, the bandit saw that the room was filled with students and men from the village. The Mullah sat farthest from the door, facing the others. The bandit stumbled through the crowd and fell to his knees in front of the Mullah.

The bandit's voice was panicked and loud, in contrast to the sombre mood of the others. "They made me come here," he said, "to report on what you were doing before the attack. On where you were." He turned to look at the room full of boys and men. "They made me," he repeated.

The Mullah held up a hand to silence him. His voice was hard. "That is of no consequence. Tell us, what is your name, and the name of your father?"

"I am called Noor," said the bandit. "My father was named Wafa."

"Noor, son of Wafa," said the Mullah, "you are being tried for the murder of a man and the murder and rape of his daughter."

Noor was incredulous. "What? That can't be."

The bandit's reaction caused the angry traveller from the chai khana to launch himself up off the floor from where he sat in the front row. "That man was my uncle. His name was Ahwad, as was his father, my grandfather."

The Mullah waited for the man to finish, staring at him impatiently. The traveller sat down again, embarrassed.

"And you are?" asked the Mullah.

The man straightened his clothing and cleared his throat. "My name is Qasim, son of Aziz, son of Ahwad. The man that has been described, who was murdered, was my Uncle Ahwad, son of Ahwad."

"And who was the girl who was with him?" asked the Mullah.

"She was his daughter, my cousin. He was taking her to be married to a man in Lashkar Gah. They had only travelled for a day down the valley before they disappeared. They were last seen here, in the village below."

"And what was her name?" asked the Mullah.

Qasim looked flustered. He hesitated. "Zaina. Zaina, I think. What does it matter?" Qasim stood up again, pointing at the bandit. "He is a murderer!"

The Mullah waved for the man to take his seat again. He then pointed at Noor while addressing Faizal. "Is this man before us the one you saw threatening Ahwad and his daughter?"

"Yes," said Faizal. "He was one of the bandits who ran the checkpoint outside my chai khana."

The shopkeeper whose tiny stall was propped up against one wall of the chai khana spoke next. "I saw him threatening the man, and heard him make lewd comments to the girl."

The Mullah nodded at this testimony and looked around the room to find other witnesses. "Are there others who have seen or heard these things?"

A few of the other villagers called out in agreement, saying that they recognized the man as one of the bandits, as well. Noor shook his head and pleaded with the Mullah. "It's not true. I did not do these things. I don't know who you mean."

"The bodies of the man and his daughter were found dumped among some rocks, near a motorcycle track," said the Mullah.

"This bandit is the one who rode the motorcycle!" said Faizal.

"I saw him use it often!" echoed the shopkeeper.

The bandit turned to the men in the room and spoke in a strangled voice. "I have hurt no one!"

The crowd roared its disagreement. "You robbed everyone you met!" said Faizal.

"You and that evil boy stole from me every day!" said the shopkeeper.

The Mullah stood, and the room became silent again. He turned and lifted the Quran from its stand behind him, cradling it in both hands. He carried it to the tall bandit and held it out in front of him.

"An oath is a serious thing," said the Mullah. "Swearing falsely will shear you from the faith as surely as a razor shears one's hair. Understand me: you will never, ever gain forgiveness for a false oath. You will instead spend the afterlife covered in hellfire."

The bandit began to shake and cry.

The Mullah's voice was hard. "Will you swear an oath on the holy Quran that you did not harm this man or this girl?"

"I still don't know who you mean!" cried Noor.

"That you did not harm any man or any girl?" asked the Mullah.

Noor turned away from the Quran, his eyes filling with tears. The Mullah towered over him, holding the Quran directly in front of Noor's face.

"Will you swear the oath," asked the Mullah, "knowing that to lie condemns you forever?"

The bandit's body shook, his eyes closed, but he said nothing further. The Mullah asked him a third time. "Will you swear the oath?"

The bandit sobbed, but said nothing. The Mullah turned and sat down again, holding the Quran high above his head. "There are two witnesses against this man. He will not make an oath to defend himself. By reason of this, I have reached a decision."

The crowd leaned forward in anticipation.

"This man, Noor, son of Wafa, is guilty of the murders of Ahwad, son of Ahwad, and his daughter."

"No!" cried Noor, "I didn't do it! It was the man who was with me!"

The crowd roared in anger at this lie.

"I'll swear an oath!" said Noor. "I am innocent. I will swear it!"

"It is too late for that," said the Mullah, his eyes hard and empty.

A voice in the crowd called out. "And of her rape?"

The Mullah lifted his head to scan the faces of the crowd. "Is there any man here who was witness to this crime?"

The men and boys were silent.

"Then he cannot be found guilty." The Mullah looked at Noor, slumped over and weeping in front of him. "Murder is enough, in any case."

The Mullah addressed Noor again. "To make recompense, a blood price must be paid."

"I have no money," said Noor, "not a penny. Tarak stole from us, as well, and took everything I ever had."

"What about family?" asked the Mullah.

"I have no family."

Qasim the traveller leaped up from his seat and spoke angrily to the crowd. "I don't want his money. I want justice!"

The Mullah looked at him and spoke slowly. "As all well know, if the guilty cannot pay the blood price, or the victim will not accept it, then the blessed Prophet says, 'An eye for an eye, a tooth for a tooth.'"

The bandit began to panic, and struggled to work loose the ropes that were binding his hands. He filled the sudden silence in the room with pleading. "I have cousins in Iran. They will pay!"

Qasim again shouted at Noor: "I want your blood to wash the pain from my heart!"

The Mullah gestured to Rashid and Umar. "Take him outside." They yanked him to his feet and almost carried him out the door. The bandit struggled, but they held him fast. His feet dragged on the ground as they brought him to the area that the Mullah had set out for the next stage of his fate. They stopped on the edge of the graveyard, near the fresh graves of the old man and the girl. Qasim followed close behind him, leading the village men and the boys from the madrassa.

The crowd filed past Qasim, surrounding the bandit. The Mullah stepped into the loose circle, gesturing for everyone to stand back. "Umar, Rashid. Turn him. Let him face the graves of his victims."

Rashid pushed Noor down to his knees and the Mullah stood behind him. The Mullah's hands had begun to shake, and he gripped the bandit's shoulders to keep them still. His voice carried across the fields. "Believers! Equivalence is the law decreed for murder. Let the murderer die as did his victims."

The crowd roared in agreement.

"Let him suffer as they suffered!" said the Mullah.

Noor shivered and wept, his eyes squeezed tightly shut. The Mullah held him upright by the back of his collar, although Noor strained to lie flat on the ground as though he meant to prostrate himself and appeal to the crowd's pity. Rashid stepped forward at a signal from the Mullah, and drew a bayonet from under his kamiz. He handed it to Qasim, who held it uncertainly, and who for the first time appeared to hesitate.

The Mullah gestured to the graves. "Justice stems from the knife in your hand, as they are your witnesses."

Qasim took a step toward Noor and grabbed the bandit's head as one does a sheep before its slaughter. Noor's eyes opened and rolled wildly as he struggled to look over his shoulder at his executioner. The front of Noor's shalwar darkened, and Qasim's face wrinkled at the smell. The Mullah kept a hand on Noor's shoulder to hold him steady. He knew that a clean cut was necessary or the execution would turn into a bloody shambles.

Noor spoke in a small voice. "God have mercy. I did it. I killed them. But I am truly sorry, I swear it. God have mercy." The bandit who had once terrified the villagers was transformed into a pitiful creature, less than human, as he begged for his life. His executioner himself was in tears as he held the knife at his victim's throat.

The Mullah spoke gently to him. "Qasim, this is your right, and is not adjudged to be murder. But know, as well, that God blesses those who pardon sinners. Mercy is the province of God, but also of great men."

Qasim dropped the bayonet on the ground at once and turned away from Noor. "I see the terror that was in the eyes of my uncle and his daughter when I look at him. I would not slaughter a sheep in this state, much less a man. Even if it is justice."

The Mullah took his hands off of Noor's shoulders, letting the man fall to the ground. He embraced Qasim, speaking softly into his ear. "May God bless you, your kindness and your mercy."

Umar lifted the bandit up onto his feet and freed him from the rope that had bound his hands. Noor fell to his knees at the feet of the Mullah. "Mercy! Please, mercy!"

The Mullah lifted him by his arms and brought him to his feet again. "Noor, son of Wafa, you are a great sinner," said the Mullah. "But you are forgiven. Live your second life righteously, unlike your first."

Noor gave him an uncomprehending look. He stammered a reply. "I will. I will."

"You are free, Noor," said the Mullah. "Take your freedom and use it well."

Noor pushed through the crowd, who still stared at him harshly. He walked quickly through the fields surrounding the graveyard and then broke into a run. Soon he was running as fast as his legs would carry him down the hillside and away from the scene of his trial. The crowd watched as his back grew smaller in the distance.

The Mullah called for their attention. "Remember, we are not punishing men for the sake of punishing, or fighting for the sake of fighting, or even fighting just to protect ourselves. We are engaged in a struggle — all of us — to rebuild society as it once was. A society that is perfectly in line with the will of God."

The crowd murmured appreciatively and began to disperse.

Umar clasped the Mullah by the hand and spoke to him warmly. "There has been enough death," said Umar. "This feels like justice in a way that killing him would not."

The Mullah nodded and turned to look off in the distance to where Noor had run.

Noor walked along the side of the highway, anxious to get away from the village. He had no belongings beyond the dirty clothes that he wore, but this was a life that was familiar to him. As the sun went down the air began to cool. Although the coolness felt pleasant, he knew that the night would be frigid. Noor stretched out his pace and walked a little faster, although he did not know exactly where he was headed.

His mind raced over the events of the day. Now that he was forgiven, he was safe from revenge by the relatives of that old man. As for any of the others that he had robbed, or worse, that was not the case. There was safety in numbers, such as he had sought with Tarak's gang. That was all gone now. He had heard the Mullah and the others as they had carried Tarak's body out of the madrassa.

Noor's chest was tight, his breath short, but he pushed onward. As the sky darkened, he felt safer. His limbs loosened again and felt less stiff; he began to relax. The road followed the course of a mostly dry riverbed. Not having any reason to stop, even as the night deepened, he kept walking.

His mind recalled the first few lines of a song that some of the other men would sing at night. He stumbled over the words, though the tune was clear in his head.

"There is a boy across the river …
with a bum just like a peach …
But alas, I have never learned to swim."

He chuckled to himself as he sang the rest, repeating it over and over as he walked. The road rose up over a low hill, and when he reached the crest he could see down the highway toward a light that shone by a small building. Noor stepped to the side of the road and crouched. He watched and waited patiently for some time. Dark figures passed in front of the light as men moved alongside the building. He counted three men, perhaps four, all of whom were moving restlessly, at least one of them holding something that looked like a rifle. He saw that the building sat at a choke point in the rough terrain around the dry riverbed that forced travellers to stick to the road, with no possibility of finding a bypass. Noor recognized what that meant, and therefore who those men must be.

Noor walked down to the riverbed to find a place to sleep in the remaining hours of the night. Worried about how he might be received by the men near the light, he decided to approach them in the morning instead. Early, when the bandits would be slow.

PART TWO

CHAPTER 12

The evening sun was disappearing in the distance, leaving only a red smear across the horizon.

Weeks had passed since the fight along the highway. The men had settled into a simple routine. Bandits continued to rob travellers farther out in the district, but a degree of peace had settled over the valley below the madrassa.

The checkpoint on the highway had become permanent. The men had stacked heavy rocks waist-high in a ring, forming a position to fight from by the side of the road. The dushka taken from Tarak's truck was mounted behind the rocks on its salvaged tripod, the machine gun's thick barrel pointing down the road toward Kandahar.

At the changing of the shifts, all of the Mullah's men sat together inside the protective ring of stone. This evening Umar and Rashid had come down from the madrassa and prayed with Wasif and Asadullah Amin, all four kneeling on carpets laid out on the hot asphalt of the highway. Now, their duty fulfilled, they chatted. Without the Mullah present, the banter between the men was lighter. They all sat with their weapons across their laps, fingers absently running over the warm metal. Lala Chai passed among them, filling glasses with tea by lamplight.

Umar held out his glass to be filled. "You have never told us how you came to be students at the madrassa," he said.

Wasif was focused on his kalash, which he had decorated with brightly coloured plastic wrappers from the trash that blew around the checkpoint. He pulled the bits of plastic tightly around the grip and forestock of the rifle, tucking in the edges to hold them in place. He shifted uncomfortably at Umar's question, and did not look up as he answered. "The Mullah found us, up by the madrassa."

"And your family?" asked Umar.

"Our parents were killed," said Wasif in a tight voice, "working in the fields."

Asadullah Amin spoke quietly, "And our sister, too."

The men sat in silence, absorbing this. "And do you have other family? Cousins?"

Wasif shook his head, working hard to hold back a flood of tears. "We don't know. We were very young. Neither of us knew the name of our village, or even of our father. My brother is my only family. I took care of him until the Mullah found us."

"You're not from here originally?" asked Umar.

"I'm not sure where we are from, exactly," said Wasif.

"I remember that we walked a long time with nothing to eat," said Asadullah Amin.

"We had nothing but our clothes," said Wasif.

"And the chador," said Asadullah Amin.

Wasif looked embarrassed. "We carried it with us. I guess it was our mother's …"

"It is all we have of her," said Asadullah Amin.

Everyone sat in silence, deep in thought. Rashid tried to lighten the mood. "Taking care of Asadullah Amin all that time — that makes you the mother of a lion!"

Both Umar and Rashid laughed, but Wasif turned red. "At least we have family!" he said.

Rashid put a hand on the boy's shoulder. "It was only a joke, my friend," he said. "No one doubts the good you have done by caring for your brother." Asadullah Amin stood and quietly bid the men good night. Rashid watched him disappear outside the circle of lamplight.

"Tell me, Wasif, have you ever seen an Uzbek before?" asked Umar.

"Never," said Wasif. "What do they look like?"

Rashid laughed and pointed at Umar. "There is one sitting right there!"

"Truly?" asked Wasif.

"There are Uzbeks like my family in Kandahar, but only a few. My father and his father were carpet traders. We moved back and forth from the north to the south, but we are from Maimana originally."

Wasif looked puzzled, but said nothing.

"Do you know Maimana?" asked Umar.

"Is it a country?" asked Wasif.

Umar laughed. "No, it is a city in the north."

Rashid chided Wasif. "You don't even know your own country!"

"I know it well enough," said Wasif, his temper flaring.

"The mother of the lion has claws!" said Rashid. Both he and Umar laughed again, and Wasif's cheeks reddened.

Umar waved Lala Chai over to fill his glass with tea. Lala Chai glanced at the others, checking to see if they wanted more, as well. Rashid held out his glass and asked Umar a question, steering the conversation away from Wasif. "And how is it that you came to be here?"

"Much like you, I imagine," said Umar. "It wasn't really my plan."

"Honest men don't speak in riddles," said Wasif.

Umar ignored the jibe. "When I was a barely a man," began Umar, "I joined the mujahideen with my father and uncles. When my father was killed, my oldest uncle sent me to work for the leadership of the tanzim, where it would be safer. I organized logistics from Iran, and I studied Islam."

"Iran is far from here," said Wasif.

"It is," said Umar, with a touch of kindness in his voice. "But I wanted to learn, and so I made the journey. There are schools now in Herat, but the best teachers are in Pakistan. I was travelling this highway to Quetta when the Mullah asked for volunteers."

"Quetta is not so far," said Wasif.

"Perhaps not by road," said Umar, "but it is far from my heart." He looked Rashid and Wasif in the eye as he spoke. "To think that I wanted to go to school to learn Islam, when here we are actually living it."

Asadullah Amin sped up the hill toward the madrassa, hoping that no one would follow him. His mind was filled with memories of his family, growing fainter every day. He had held back the tears that now filled his eyes until the pressure had become too much. He wept silently as he walked, trying to both release his sorrow and control it, so that by the time that he reached the madrassa he could face the other boys.

As he began to walk through the terraced fields just below the village, he saw the Mullah walking down the path carrying a lantern in one hand, with a bowl and ewer tucked under his arm. He quickly wiped his face with his sleeves, hoping that his reddened eyes wouldn't betray his weakness.

The Mullah saw him approaching and stopped, lifting the lantern so that its light shone farther down the path.

"Come with me," said the Mullah. "I have a task for you to help me with."

Asadullah Amin merely nodded, keeping his face low so that the lantern wouldn't shine directly on it. If the Mullah noticed that the boy had been crying, he said nothing about it, leading him through the upper fields to the kishmesh khana.

The little building with its thick walls sat squat and forlorn amongst the dead fields. Inside, Isa sat leaning against the wall, his chains slack. His face was hollow, his skin sallow. He held his body still in the dank air of his prison.

His eyes opened at the rattling of the lock on the door. The door opened, and what little light there was in the night sky illuminated the room. The Mullah stood in the doorway while Asadullah Amin peered from behind him.

"Awake, my brother. The day is new, another gift from God."

Isa barely moved his jaw as he spoke, but he turned to look at the Mullah. "It is the middle of the night."

The Mullah ignored him, unlocking the chains wrapped around Isa's wrists and ankles. "How are you feeling?" Asadullah Amin watched as the Mullah's hands moved gently to unwrap the chains.

Isa did not answer the question directly. "What have you decided for me?"

The Mullah's eyes flashed in the reflected light as he turned his face up toward Isa. "I have not spent all this time making a decision. I spent it *listening* for a decision."

"What will you do with me?" croaked Isa.

"Isn't it obvious?" said the Mullah. "I will do what is right. The will of God. He has set us all on a path that we must accept, no matter how difficult."

Isa, now unchained, sat leaning against the wall, waiting.

"I asked how you feel," said the Mullah.

Isa sighed deeply. "Like a new lamb, just born."

The Mullah gave a rare smile. "Come then. It is time to rejoin the flock."

The Mullah lifted Isa under the arms. "Get on the other side," he said to Asadullah Amin. They limped through the doorway together and set him down against the wall. By the doorway were the ewer of water and the bowl.

"Before we go any farther, you must wash," said the Mullah.

Asadullah Amin helped him to pull the dirty kamiz over Isa's head, and then the Mullah took a cloth and dampened it, washing gently around Isa's hands and wrists, which were rubbed raw from the chains. Isa looked at the Mullah in wonder, his voice just above a whisper.

"And after I wash, we will pray together."

The conversation at the checkpoint continued after Asadullah Amin had left. Umar turned to Rashid. "And what about you, my friend? How did you come to find yourself here with us?"

Rashid deflected the question. "I'd rather hear from Lala Chai," he said. "Tell us about fighting the invaders with your teapot."

The group burst into laughter. Lala Chai was composing a retort when Isa appeared at the edge of the lamplight. The Mullah and Asadullah Amin stood beside him, helping to keep him on his feet. No one had seen him clearly in the weeks that he was chained in the darkness of the kishmesh khana, but in the light of the lamp it was clear that he was a broken man. His clothes hung off of his body like a sagging tent, and his skin appeared bloodless yet was covered in red scratches. The laughter died out immediately.

Wasif jumped to his feet. "Why is he free?"

"We don't need drug-addicted apostates among us," said Umar.

Isa stood hunched over, his filthy shalwar kamiz hanging loosely from his thin shoulders, but did not look up or reply.

"Do you think that I freed him just to hear your curses?" asked the Mullah.

Wasif picked up a stone from the road, weighing it in his hand. "He'll feel my curses, not hear them!"

Wasif cocked his arm to throw the rock. The Mullah moved closer to Isa and raised a protective hand. Wasif froze. "Rashid," asked the Mullah, "what do you think of my bringing Isa down here?"

Rashid was silent.

"He thinks the same as we do," said Umar. "That there is no place for sinners here."

The Mullah ignored Umar, and waited for Rashid to reply.

After a moment, Rashid spoke quietly. "There is a bigger sinner here than Isa."

"There are no sinners here other than Isa," spat Wasif.

"Who are you speaking of?" asked Umar.

The Mullah left Isa standing by the edge of the lamplight and stood beside Rashid, placing one hand on his shoulder. "Tell us about this sinner."

Rashid's face looked blank, almost wooden. "Unlike you," said Rashid, "I didn't fight the Russians."

"That's not a sin," said Umar.

The Mullah held up a finger, gesturing for Umar to be silent. "Go on," he said.

"I am not one of you," said Rashid.

The Mullah's face was impassive. "I have long known that," he said. "Tell us your name, and where you are from."

"My birth name," said Rashid, "was Oleg Pugachev. I was born in Leningrad, and was drafted when I was eighteen."

Wasif looked around at the others. "I don't understand."

Umar's face tightened into a knot. "I do. He's a liar."

"I haven't lied," said Rashid softly.

The Mullah's voice was also softer than normal, more conciliatory. "Everyone sit down now, and listen."

Everyone arranged themselves on the ground, leaning against the circle of rocks at the checkpoint. Rashid and Isa sat with the Mullah on one side of the shelter, while everyone else sat opposite, facing them. Rashid's face was grim, but at a signal from the Mullah he continued his story. "I was assigned to an infantry battalion based in Khost. One night, we landed by helicopter. We were ambushed right away, and I was hit through the thigh and the head. Most of the others just jumped right back on the helicopters, but I was left behind. With the dead."

Wasif's voice was filled with venom. "If the mujahideen had found you, you would be dead."

Rashid smiled thinly. "Not so. They did find me. They left the others, who were already dead, but they took me with them. I woke up the next day in a small room in a house, under careful guard. They had little medicine and no medical supplies, but even so they nursed me back to health."

"Why would they waste the effort on a Russian?" asked Wasif.

"I don't know," said Rashid. "What I do know is that I didn't want to go back to the army. So I couldn't go home. I had nothing at all, and so I began to pray, alone, asking God for guidance or a sign. Anything."

Umar spat on the ground in front of him. "And what did your God tell you?"

Rashid's face fell at the implication. "Not my God, Umar. *God*. Allah. When the men holding me realized what I was doing, they showed me how to pray the same way that they did. Soon I prayed with them. Praying together suddenly made sense to me. Everyone was looking for guidance, not just me."

Wasif, still clenching the stone in his hand, shook it at Rashid. "Your kind is not welcome here," he said. "And neither is yours, Isa."

The Mullah pulled both men closer to him, arms stretched around their shoulders. "What kind of person is that, Wasif?"

Umar answered for the boy. "You've said it yourself, Ma'alim. Sinners. Apostates. Invaders."

"I see two men here," said the Mullah. "One, born into a godless society, sent to fight far from his home." The Mullah studied Rashid's face in the lamplight. "Not only did he hear and accept the message of the Prophet, peace be upon him, he chose to remain here and join with those he had been sent to oppress. He saw a righteous cause and abandoned his own people."

Rashid mumbled in reply: "You are my people now."

The Mullah next looked at Isa, who slouched, weak as a new-born lamb. "The second man, sick and confused, forgot God and fell away from what he knew to be right. But he has fasted, he has prayed, and is now returned. What would God have us do with him?"

Isa's voice was quiet but firm as he spoke. "There is no God but Allah, and Muhammad is His Prophet."

The group looked at him doubtfully, but the Mullah continued: "In the Quran it says that Satan sows hatred and enmity amongst us, with intoxicants and false religions, so that we may not recognize or know the true faith. And so tell me, what would you do to oppose Satan and to serve God?"

Umar and the boys sat still, confused, as if in a trance. Umar's thoughts were filled with all that he had seen, all that he had done, and all that he believed in. All of those things that had led him here. Suddenly, he stood and walked toward the Mullah. Leaning down, he embraced Rashid and Isa in turn. "You are both my brothers."

Wasif and Asadullah Amin awkwardly did the same, though with less conviction. The Mullah smiled gently at them as they did so.

"Forgive my ignorance," said Umar to the Mullah. "Where I saw weakness and sin, you have shown me strength and righteousness."

They took their seats in the lamplight, and Lala Chai passed the teapot among them again. As the men resumed their conversation, Wasif bid them good night and began to walk back to the madrassa. He carried his rifle in both hands, at the ready, should bandits try to attack again. The path up to the top of the hill was becoming worn smooth by the constant traffic to and fro. His eyes could pick it out from the surrounding ground even in the darkness.

Wasif could still hear the others' laughter in his mind. *Mother of lions! What do they know?* Wasif felt certain that none of these men truly knew him. His thoughts raced back to the many nights here his brother had needed him above all others. He thought of the day when the Russians came and his parents were killed, and how he led his brother by the hand to safety. Because Amin had cried for days, that meant that Wasif could not. He knew that he had to be the strong one, the one who would find food and water, and who would make all the decisions.

He remembered that Amin kept asking, over and over, when their parents were coming to get them. That and a hundred other useless questions. And even though he had no answers, he did what he could. He made sure that his brother always ate more than half of whatever meagre food they had, and he put his arms around him to help him sleep at night.

Wasif remembered that when the Mullah first found them they were both frightened. They had been searching through the fields for anything that had been dropped or forgotten. They mostly found shrivelled grapes to eat. They had avoided people for so long that they nearly ran away at the sight of the tall man approaching them. But the Mullah stood so still, and watched them so closely, that they were transfixed. He attracted the boys in the same way that a boy attracts birds. He showed them a few pieces of naan and then lay the bread down on the ground. As he backed away, Amin ran to grab the food. Wasif first tried to stop his brother, but soon he followed. The two boys devoured every piece on the spot.

The Mullah squatted nearby, watching. As the boys finished their meal, he beckoned for them to follow him. Wasif and Amin did, but only at a distance, their hands clenched together. Wasif remembered how he had grown nervous as the Mullah led them between deserted houses, and how he was about to tell his brother that they should run, when a sound changed his mind. It was a familiar sound that they had not heard in a long, long time. Wasif thought about that sound: the voices of children, laughing and playing, coming from within the walls of a compound. The Mullah gestured for them to come in, and Wasif recalled his amazement when he saw that it was filled with young boys.

That first night, Wasif whispered to a boy he didn't know who was lying next to him on the floor, "Does he lock us in at night?"

The boy looked back at him, his head still touching the floor. "He doesn't have to," the boy whispered. "We stay because we want to."

This had never occurred to Wasif as a possibility. Soon Amin was snoring gently beside him, and Wasif was pulling the blanket tightly around himself.

Wasif remembered how that first night the Mullah had stood at the front of the room and told a story about an ancient king and his sons. He didn't hear how the story ended that night, as he was soon fast asleep.

PHIL HALTON

The night air was clear and still as Wasif finished climbing the hill to the madrassa. He rapped lightly on the door, and it was opened by a young boy left as a sentry by the Mullah. Stepping through the gate, Wasif needed no light to find his way into the classroom where he usually slept.

Lying on the floor, his kalash beside him, he felt the tension in his muscles begin to relax. Looking around at the spartan room and listening to the sound of the other boys sleeping, Wasif realized what he had accomplished.

Against all odds, he had found a home for himself and his brother.

CHAPTER 13

There were cars and trucks parked along the highway by the chai khana, and a thin line of stalls set up on the road's edge. News of the defeat of Tarak Sagwan, and the protection afforded by the Mullah and his men, had begun to spread throughout the province. New people were arriving in the village, seeking shelter from bandits and injustice.

Rashid and Isa stood at the checkpoint, each with a kalash slung over his back. Most vehicles they waved along, but Rashid stopped an old truck that caught his interest. In the back of the truck was a jumble of bicycles and broken parts, wheels and rusty frames sticking out of the cargo bed at odd angles. Seated at the window across from the driver was a woman, covered head to toe in a chador, and between them sat three small children.

Rashid approached the driver. "Are you staying or passing through?"

"We've come to stay," said the man. "To set up a shop."

Isa stood at the other window, though he looked past the woman without glancing at her. "Then you must hand over any guns that you have."

The man sputtered a reply. "Guns? Who said anything about guns?" Rashid watched him in silence. The man's face grew red, and he continued to sputter. "But what about my family? My honour?"

"Your family and your honour will be safe here," said Rashid. He gestured to a small stack of guns collected from new arrivals that sat against the low stone wall of the checkpoint.

"You'll be safe because we're the only ones with guns," said Isa.

The man got out of the truck and reluctantly pulled an old rifle out from under the seat. He passed it to Rashid, who put it with the others.

"You and your family are most welcome here," said Rashid.

The man drove through the checkpoint, past where Umar sat outside the chai khana with a group of farmers. Low seats had been built around the building to accommodate the overflow of customers. Pahzman, the farmer whose daughter they had saved from Tarak, sat beside Umar in a place of honour, respected because of his relationship with the Mullah.

An old farmer with no teeth spoke, his words hard to understand. "We used to draw water from the river at each house, brought to us by a canal. And every field had channels that ran from it."

"And what happened to the canal?" asked Umar.

"There were too few of us to keep it clear. It has filled in." The man looked around at the younger farmers accusingly. "Now people use it only for garbage and filth."

"Can we agree, then, to work together to clear the canal, and dig channels to all of the fields?" asked Umar.

"And to prevent others from filling the channels with their filth," said the old farmer.

"I can mark where the channels are to go," said Pahzman. "But I cannot prevent others from dumping their garbage."

"We will add it to the list of things that are forbidden here," said Umar. "We will ensure that no one violates this rule. And I will speak to the Mullah. This project is for the good of the whole community, and so we should be aided by the whole community."

The clutch of men broke up to go back to their farms. Pahzman and Umar finished their tea and crossed the road to climb the path to the madrassa.

The houses on top of the hill were beginning to be rebuilt, and families had moved into almost all of them. The surrounding fields, long lying brown and fallow, were being worked again. Where the grapevines in the middle terrace of fields were still intact, the new farmers cleared the broken wooden frames and bound the vines to newly cut sticks. Where the vines were dead, the farmers cleared them out to plant new crops.

"And so you will stay in the house that you chose?" asked Umar.

Pahzman nodded. "Jan Farooq is kind and asks for no rent, only a portion of the harvest. And he will provide us seeds, as well."

"Kind indeed. Though he has yet to speak to the Mullah directly since the jirga."

"Insh'allah, he will. Soon," said Pahzman.

The two men ducked through the low door of the madrassa compound and left their shoes in the pile outside the door. Inside, the boys sat in rows, practising their writing on small wood-framed slates. The Mullah passed between the rows, making corrections and giving small praise. Umar and Pahzman waited for him to see them.

When the Mullah saw the two men waiting, he moved between the rows of boys toward the door, leaving his students to their writing. Pahzman spoke first. "We've come to ask for your guidance," he said.

"In what matter?" asked the Mullah.

"Irrigation ditches," said Pahzman.

The Mullah gave Umar a quizzical look. "You need no guidance from me on such matters."

"Mullah," said Umar, "the ditches themselves are not the problem. We have need of manpower to dig them, so that the spring rains in the mountains are diverted from the river and into the fields."

"And so I thought that you might agree to use the zakat to pay for men to dig the ditches," said Pahzman, his voice anxious.

The Mullah shook his head and scowled deeply. "That is not the purpose of the zakat. We will not pay men to do work for their own benefit. The zakat is to feed and clothe those unable to fend for themselves. Destitute travellers, orphans, the sick and elderly."

"But how will we convince the men to dig an irrigation ditch?" asked Pahzman.

The Mullah raised a finger. "The men and boys of this village will volunteer their time. Without farms there would be no village. And with no village there would be no shops. I will speak with them."

"Praise be," said Umar.

"Spread the word," said the Mullah. "Men are to bring shovels tomorrow for jummah prayers. Afterwards, we will all dig."

Umar nodded and left the madrassa. The Mullah turned back to look over the students, all writing silently. He took his seat again at the head of the class, deep in thought. Lala Chai appeared in the doorway, kicking off his sandals, his hands full with a heavy teapot and a bundle of cloth. He approached the Mullah carefully, not looking at the boys in the class.

"Faizal sent me with fresh tea and bread for you," he said.

"But we have these things here at the madrassa," said the Mullah.

"Faizal said that he had tasted your tea," said Lala Chai, suddenly concerned that he had overstepped.

The Mullah's face was serious. He clapped his hands twice, and in an instant, the attention of all the boys was riveted upon him. "We will return to our practice after we take a break. Everyone outside." The students noisily got up and began to file out of the classroom, picking their sandals from the pile at the door. Lala Chai turned to leave, as well, but the Mullah stopped him, gesturing at a spot beside him on the floor. "Sit with me first," he said.

He studied Lala Chai as the boy sat down uncomfortably, still clutching the teapot and bread.

"Why don't you study at the madrassa?" asked the Mullah.

Lala Chai squirmed as he answered. "I am not worthy of it, Ma'alim."

"How so?" asked the Mullah. "How are you different than any of the rest of us?"

"I'm completely different," said Lala Chai. "I have no family, no education, and I can't read. I have accomplished nothing in my life. I make tea — that is all."

"So why do you choose to stay with us?"

Lala Chai struggled to find the words, looking down at the floor. "Because here, I am with good people. Great people. Even if I only make them tea. My life has been hard. It is hard. But here it has purpose."

The Mullah placed his hands on Lala Chai's shoulders and straightened him up. He looked at his face, reading the truth in his eyes. "All of life is a struggle," said the Mullah. "For everyone. And God rewards everyone based on their intentions."

Lala Chai began to cry.

"Small things done well are pleasing to God," said the Mullah, "but you are capable of great things, as well."

"If you will have me, I will try," said Lala Chai.

The Mullah stood. "It is settled, then. You will learn with us here in the madrassa, and if you wish, you may still help Faizal from time to time. You will be one of us in every way."

Isa and Rashid sat at the checkpoint by the dim light of a lantern, leaning against the inside of the stone wall, which gave some shelter from a breeze blowing along the floor of the valley. Isa's thin shoulders were wrapped in two blankets against the bite of the night air. Rashid was holding a Quran, slowly reading a passage aloud.

"Nothing will happen to us except what Allah has decreed for us: He is our protector. In Allah let the believers put their trust." Rashid looked up, hesitant.

"You're really getting it," said Isa.

"Thanks to you, my friend," said Rashid. He smiled. "It is hard to be an illiterate amongst scholars."

Isa nodded. "Yes, it is hard to be ..." Isa stopped, looking down at his feet.

Rashid placed a hand on his friend's shoulder. "Rest easy. Our futures are written for us. We must live our lives as they are meant to be, and worry about nothing more. Think of where I started, and where I am now. I am a universe away from the start of my life. I was wounded and left for dead. But then I was healed. I became accepted. Got married even, and had children. And then I had it all taken away by the war, only to heal and be accepted all over again."

Isa seemed to be studying the flickering lantern light, and so Rashid said nothing more. The two men sat in silence beside the deserted highway.

Like low-hanging stars, sharp points of lantern light from other checkpoints along the various roads in the district could be seen flickering in the far distance.

The morning light cast a warm glow across the fields and houses around the madrassa. Fresh masonry stood out where old broken walls had been repaired, and everywhere there was evidence of new life. Wasif and Asadullah Amin walked through the upper village, one carrying a basket and the other a battered metal jug. Both had their rifles slung tightly over their backs.

As they walked along the edge of the village, Wasif noticed movement in the cemetery. Curious, they walked closer and saw that a few women in heavy blue chadors were praying at the graves of the old man and the girl. Two flat stones had been set upright at the head and foot of the girl's grave, a piece of string tied between them. These women, and others, had tied small ribbons to the string with their prayers written on them.

Wasif gestured to the maharam, a boy about his age, who was with the women. "What are they doing?" he asked rudely.

The maharam, though a head shorter, squared up to him before replying. "What business is it of yours what my women are doing?"

"Tell us why they are praying here," said Wasif.

Asadullah Amin squinted up at the sun, too high in the sky for it to be time for prayers. "And why now?"

The women didn't speak, but stood up and moved away to the edge of the cemetery.

"They are praying to the pir for justice," said the maharam.

Wasif quickly rebuked him. "All justice comes from God," he said. Pointing at the grave, he waved his hand contemptuously. "She is no pir, just a girl."

"So you say," replied the maharam, "but she is the girl who caused the defeat of the bandit Tarak Sagwan."

Dropping the basket, Wasif unslung his rifle and held it out in front of him. "This is what defeated Tarak," he said. "Nothing else."

Asadullah Amin tugged at Wasif's sleeve. "Leave him and these women."

Wasif gave the boy one last contemptuous look before following his brother on their rounds.

"No good can come from questioning him over those women," said Asadullah Amin.

"No good can come from false idols," retorted Wasif.

The two walked on in silence until they came to the outer gate of the first of the newly occupied houses. Wasif knocked on the battered wooden door. They stood and waited. A voice called from inside the compound, but the door remained bolted shut. "What do you want?"

"Asalaam aleikum!" said Wasif.

"Wa aleikum salaam," came the reply. The voice said nothing further.

"Haji," began Wasif, "we are from the madrassa. We have come to collect food to feed the students."

"Cousin," said Asadullah Amin, "even a few pieces of naan and a scoop of dahi would be most welcome."

There was a long pause, and then the boys heard the sound of the door being unbarred. A young man stood inside the doorway and passed the boys a short stack of fresh naan. He turned and picked up a battered metal bowl, and carefully poured some of the yellowish dahi into the boys' metal jug. Wasif scowled at the paltry donation.

Asadullah Amin nodded to the man. "Our thanks."

"Allah-u akbar," replied the man as he shut the door.

The boys continued on their rounds, visiting each of the houses in the village before returning to the madrassa. In the village square was the well from which the boys often drew water. Rashid was

there, tinkering with one of the motorcycles taken from the bandits. Its back end was held up on an improvised stand, its rear hub
spinning freely.

"Salaam, Rashid," said Asadullah Amin. "What is this?" he
asked, gesturing at the contraption.

Rashid put down his tools and waved them over. "Just watch."

He pulled a length of old rubber hose tied into a loop over
the rear hub. The other end of the rubber hose was wrapped
around a second hub on a metal box with more hose running
out of both its ends. One short end lay on the ground beside the
motorcycle, while the other disappeared into the well. Rashid
reached under the motorcycle seat and pulled out the choke.
Rising up high in the air, he pushed down on the kick-starter
with one foot, dropping down again to the ground as the motor
thudded to life. The hub spun madly as he revved the engine. The
well gurgled, and after a few moments water began to flow out
of the short end of the hose and onto the dusty ground. Rashid
turned off the engine.

"Mash'allah!" said Wasif.

Rashid wiped his oily hands on the hem of his shirt. "We'll
have to dig the well deeper so that this machine doesn't run it
dry, but if we are careful there should be enough to dig irrigation
channels from here to the fields just below the village."

Wasif ran his hands over the bike's mechanism, imagining
that he was in control of the machine.

Rashid smiled. "And then this will be a growing village again."

The sun was just past its zenith in the sky, and the highway near
the checkpoint was filled with men, kneeling in rows. The Mullah
knelt in front of them, leading the community in prayer. No one
was visible in any direction who was not praying with the group.

The prayers finished as the men whispered the taslim over both of their shoulders, first right and then left: "May the peace and blessings of Allah be upon you."

The Mullah stood up and rolled his carpet tightly. He set it aside within the circular wall of the checkpoint, and picked up a shovel that he had left there. Behind him the other men were doing the same, many of them carrying simple wooden shovels.

Pahzman looked to the Mullah for his permission to begin. The Mullah nodded, and Pahzman turned to the crowd. "Follow me," he said.

The men grumbled a little among themselves but soon were streaming down from the highway to the riverbed. The water was running higher with the start of the mountain snowmelt. Only a suggestion of a canal remained, running from the river through the village fields. Pahzman walked until he stood facing this indentation in the ground, pushing the wooden blade of his crude shovel into the dry earth and making a deep wound. The other men soon went to work around him.

The Mullah worked alongside them in silence as they passed the hours digging out the canal and the channels, and shoring up the sides of each. The dusty earth turned easily at first, but became harder as they dug down. The men talked and joked quietly around him, but he took no part in their banter. His arms worked mechanically, the rhythm of his movements steady and even.

Pahzman worked silently beside the Mullah until his arms were sore with the work. Putting down his shovel, he dug into his pocket for a small bundle wrapped in a tightly tied scarf. His parcel contained a few pieces of hard, white cheese, which he offered to the Mullah.

"Mullah, there is something that I wish to discuss," said Pahzman.

The Mullah took a small piece of the cheese, which he rolled between his fingers to soften before placing it in his mouth.

"My daughter is of a certain age," began Pahzman. "You know that she is, Mullah. It is time for her to marry. Her jehez is small, but she cooks well."

The Mullah brusquely interrupted him. "I have no interest in marrying again, my friend."

Pahzman paled. "No, Mullah. I did not mean to suggest that you …"

The Mullah stared at him, watching his discomfort in silence.

"I thought perhaps the eldest of your boys …" said Pahzman. "Their ages are close, and it would be a good match."

The Mullah considered this for a moment. One day, he knew, the boys would marry. Indeed, they should marry. But now was not the time.

"I have no money for the mahr, nor the walwar," said the Mullah.

"Is there not zakat that could be used?"

The Mullah's face tightened. "The zakat is not collected for our own benefit. It is for the less fortunate."

"It is still a good match," said Pahzman. "The payments are something we could negotiate, I am sure. I have already paid a jehez to Tarak, and have little to offer now. It is no slur on my family if the walwar is small, when it comes from a man such as you and in times like these."

"It is written in the Hadith that a mahr must be paid for the marriage to be valid," said the Mullah. "Let us wait until such time as we have an appropriate sum. Then we can discuss this again."

Pahzman placed a piece of cheese in his own mouth, rolling it around with his tongue. When the Mullah turned back to his work without saying anything more, Pahzman picked up his shovel, as well, and set to work again.

The digging continued for several more hours, and the shape of the canal and channels became apparent again. A trickle of water from the river began to fill the canal as it slowly cut across the field. As the sun made its way across the sky and began to dip into the west, nearly all the men began to seek shade, sitting in small circles or short lines against the low walls dividing the fields. The Mullah sat with Umar, Isa, and Rashid, while the boys manned the checkpoint. The men were all in good spirits, and freely gave their opinions on recent events. The Mullah sat quietly, his thoughts his own.

A ripple of chatter floated across the groups of men as Jan Farooq, followed by his two usual bodyguards, walked across the field through the seated workers. His two men kept a watchful eye on the villagers as they moved between the little groups, each clutching a short-barrelled rifle barely concealed beneath his shalwar. Jan Farooq greeted every man that he passed, holding his hand over his heart and merely saying, "Salaam," rather than embracing or shaking muddy hands. He walked directly to where the Mullah was seated and spoke loudly so that all could hear.

"Salaam, my friends. Is there room at this shura for a guest?"

All the men in the field stood up and pressed closer around the Mullah to hear what the two men would say to each other.

The Mullah remained seated. "Asalaam aleikum, Haji. I hope you are well. I hope that your house is strong. May you not be tired. I hope that your family is well. May you be strong. I hope that your livestock are well. May your health be ever good."

Jan Farooq mumbled the same phrases in return, speaking over the Mullah's words. When they were finished, and the Mullah did not offer him a seat or any refreshment, he scowled. "Is it considered polite to let a guest expire from thirst?"

The Mullah replied quickly: "Is a man still a guest when he owns half the village?"

The crowd laughed quietly. Jan Farooq looked around, speaking to all the men. "I have given farms and houses to those who had none. I have given seeds when fields would have stood barren. I think not in terms of what I own, but in terms of what I may give."

There was an appreciative rumble through the crowd. Many in the village were in his debt. And unlike the Mullah with the zakat, Jan Farooq gave freely and without question.

The Mullah paused before he finally said, "Sit with us, my friend. We are resting for now, but would you give your time to help dig this canal?"

Jan Farooq took a seat beside the Mullah, and took his hand in his own. "I am too busy to do this myself, but can send some men to dig if that is what is needed."

"The digging will be complete by the time your men arrive," said the Mullah. "Though your gesture is appreciated."

Jan Farooq raised his voice when he spoke again. "I have wanted to speak to you. I want to donate land to build a proper mosque for this village, as well as a hujra to house our guests."

The men who had gathered around them to listen murmured their appreciation.

The Mullah looked him in the eye. "May God see all of your deeds and reward you appropriately."

Jan Farooq stood up, still holding the Mullah's hand. He led him a short distance away, to speak more privately. Jan Farooq's voice was low, his eyes cloudy. "I wish for only what is good to rain upon this village. And for yourself. I ask that you forgive the matter of the jirga, Mullah."

"What is it, exactly, that I am to forgive?" asked the Mullah.

Jan Farooq chose his words carefully. "My leaving the jirga before a solution was found may have set the example for others," he said. "But you must understand that it was clear to everyone that we were not going to reach a compromise."

"But did you know that Tarak would attack us?" asked the Mullah.

"I did not," answered Jan Farooq, squeezing the Mullah's hand. "But sometimes, this is the only manner to solve disputes with any degree of finality. Again, I ask your forgiveness."

The Mullah hesitated before replying. "It is in the nature of God to forgive."

Jan Farooq smiled.

Pahzman walked home alone up the path toward the madrassa, carrying his shovel over one shoulder. He had finished his small meal of cheese, and he now wore the scarf in which it had been wrapped in tied over his head and neck to ward off the sun. He walked slowly, deep in thought.

The Mullah had neither accepted nor refused the suggestion that his daughter marry one of the boys. Without money for walwar it might be considered embarrassing to marry, but few had money for the lavish gifts common in their fathers' time. No one would question the worth of his daughter because of that, he was sure. The Mullah would not allow such vindictive thoughts.

Pahzman was unwilling to return to the farm his family had left, beset with bandits and lawlessness. It would be best to put down roots here where it was safest. Having cousins, and even family by marriage, nearby would give them further stability. It made life safer, as well. Pahzman felt that his family was adrift, and he wanted to anchor them in society again. Marrying his daughter to one of the Mullah's boys would be the best way to do that.

He thought about the discussion that he had overheard between Jan Farooq and the Mullah. He had not heard all of it, no one had, but he had heard enough to feel the tension. He owed a debt to both men — a moral one to the Mullah, and half of his harvest to Jan Farooq. *When elephants fight, it is the grass that suffers*, he thought. Would that it not come to that.

CHAPTER 14

The landscape around the village had been the same for centuries. No one living there ever expected it to change, and so when dawn broke that day, the news passed from house to house in minutes.

Across the shallow river stood a black tent, its sides stretched low to the ground. Beside it lay two camels who jockeyed for position in what little shade it cast. At least a hundred sheep with dirty grey wool lay in a circle around the tent, some grazing on what grasses could be found, others wandering a short distance away to drink from the river.

Faizal sent a young man running up the hill to the madrassa with the news. He burst into the classroom, chest heaving as he fought for breath, and stumbled over the pile of sandals at the door. When he saw the Mullah he nearly shouted the news at him, only barely restraining himself. The classroom was filled with boys sitting in rows as the Mullah led them through a recitation of the Quran. The young man squatted by the doorway, fidgeting with the tails of his shirt, waiting. As the recitation finished, he pushed through the boys to reach the Mullah.

"Ma'alim, you must come. There are Kochi on the other side of the river!" he said.

The Mullah bid the boys practise writing on their slates until he returned, and followed the young man down to the highway. By the time the Mullah had reached the bottom of the hill, all the men of the village were lined up along the river. They squatted on their haunches in small groups, talking quietly and watching the Kochi. The Mullah walked past them to stand on the edge of the newly dug irrigation ditch, stepping up onto a fresh pile of earth from where he could see the entire breadth of the wide pasture on the far side of the river. In addition to the one tent he had been told about, there was now a second tent pitched farther back from the river, with the sheep of both families grazing together between them. No person could be seen among the animals, although the Mullah was certain that the Kochi were watching them closely as well.

The Mullah made an elaborate show of unwinding his patu from around his shoulders and folding it at his feet. His thin black shalwar kamiz hid no weapons. He pulled his loose pants high up about his waist and walked slowly down to the river, wading across the water in the direction of the closest tent. The water was cool, fed by the snow melting far away on the mountains.

As he reached the other side, the few sheep near him scattered, creating a ripple effect as their flight encouraged others to flee, as well. Soon, the sheep were spread out in a wide crescent around where the Mullah stood. He chose not to approach either of the tents too closely. Instead, he crouched by the riverbank where he could easily be seen, and waited.

Before long, a single shot rang out from somewhere behind the tents. The bullet whizzed harmlessly overhead; the Mullah did not react, but continued to wait. He heard the loud barking of dogs by the far tent, but again chose not to move.

Eventually, his patience was rewarded.

A young boy suddently appeared out of nowhere, dressed in rags, looking both wild and carefree. He was quite close to the Mullah — he had approached unseen until he chose to stand up and show himself. He clutched an old bolt-action rifle left behind by the British, its wooden stock polished to a high sheen and decorated with brass inlay.

The Mullah remained squatting, but held his hand over his heart as a simple greeting. "Asalaam aleikum," he said with great sincerity.

The boy repeated the gesture and replied: "Wa aleikum salaam."

"Who are you?" asked the Mullah.

"We are the Free People," said the boy.

"Of which tribe?" asked the Mullah.

The boy's eyes twinkled. "We are the sons of Barak."

The Mullah kept pressing, beyond what would be considered polite. "And who is your leader?"

"Our leaders are the sun and the moon and the stars. We follow them all, each in its time."

The Mullah's voice was tight. "Are there any men here for me to speak to?"

The boy laughed and gestured across the river. "There are more true men here than there are over there."

"Are there more of you coming?" asked the Mullah.

The boy laughed again and gestured from horizon to horizon over his shoulder. "We will fill these fields from there to there."

The Mullah grunted, and with nothing more to say, he turned to wade back across the river. The boy fired a few shots in the air out of joy, and shouted: "Come back tomorrow, if you wish, and you will find more of us to speak with!"

As the Mullah reached the other bank again, the village men gathered in a tight cluster from where they had been watching to hear what he had to say. Umar and Rashid, who had been at their post on the highway, stood at the front of the group, rifles in their hands.

"Are they Kochi?" asked Umar.

"Kochi. Powindah. Whatever word is used," said the Mullah.

Umar glanced over his shoulder at the black tents. "Should we be worried?"

The Mullah shook his head. "They are Pashtun, like us. Barakzai. These must only be the first elements of their group. I suspect that I will speak with their leader tomorrow."

One of the village men spoke fearfully. "But what of our pasture? Their animals will drink all the water."

The Mullah looked at him with amusement. "What magical sheep are these that can drink a river dry?"

The man persisted. "They cannot graze on our lands!"

The Mullah spoke loudly, and looked around at all the men to see that his message was being heard. "Everyone knows that a man's pasture extends no farther than his shout can be heard. This is our law. That grassland on the other side of the river is not ours. And God has given water for all men to drink." The Mullah clapped his hands on the man's shoulders. "They cannot steal from us what we do not own. We will settle whatever our small differences may be tomorrow."

The Mullah ended the discussion by walking back up to the highway. Umar and Rashid followed him closely. The Mullah looked back and gestured for Rashid to come closer, leaning in to speak to him. "Have one of us watching across the river at all times," he said. "And make sure he is armed. If there are any problems, come and find me."

Early the next morning, the Mullah stood at the riverbank again, making sure that he could be seen before he crossed so that he would not surprise the Kochi. Lining the near side were the men of the village, watching closely to see what he would do. On the far side of the river were dozens of black tents and countless sheep. Satisfied that he was expected, the Mullah pulled up the legs of his shalwar and waded across the river. Aside from the grazing animals, no people were in sight.

Two huge dogs, the type called jangi spai, circled around one of the tents and began to growl and bark at the Mullah as he approached. He stopped and picked up a stone, first threatening the dogs with it and then throwing it, narrowly missing one of them. The two dogs held their ground, heads low and growling as they watched him.

He backtracked away from the dogs and carefully walked along the riverbank toward one tent, no larger than the rest, which had a dozen camels resting in its shade. The dogs followed him, tracking his movement and staying between him and the rest of the tents. As he got closer, a harsh voice called out from inside the tent, stopping the dogs in their tracks. They lost interest in the Mullah and trotted back to the shade from which they had been watching their flock. The flap of the tent opened, and a man stepped out.

This man was roughly the Mullah's age, but taller and thinner. His beard was streaked with grey and coloured red with henna, and his eyes were rimmed black with kohl. The Mullah saw that the man tied his turban like any other Pashtun, its free ends running past his shoulder, and he relaxed slightly. The man stepped forward until he and the Mullah stood face to face.

"Asalaam aleikum," said the Mullah.

"Wa aleikum salaam," replied the man.

The Mullah waited for the other man to speak further.

"Sit and drink tea with me as my guest," said the man.

The Mullah nodded. The man called back to his tent, and soon two boys came out carrying a large carpet over their shoulders.

They rolled it out in front of the Mullah and quickly returned to the tent. One emerged carrying an armload of cushions, the other with a tray of food and drink. The Mullah and his host took seats on the carpet facing each other. The Mullah waited in silence again.

"I am called Gol, son of Rahman, son of Barak," said the man.

The Mullah cleared his throat. "And I am —"

Gol Kochi interrupted him, laughing. "Everyone has heard of you, Mullah. I have been looking forward to this meeting."

The two boys served the food from the tray. One spread sweet butter thinly across a piece of flat bread for each man. He then placed a bowl of sheep's milk yoghurt between them. The second boy rinsed two glasses with hot tea from a pot. Before the boy could fill the glasses, Gol Kochi took the pot by the handle and poured two glasses himself, the first for the Mullah and the other for himself, grasping it between his thumb and forefinger.

"The people of this village are concerned," said the Mullah. "They want to protect their lands from being misused."

Gol Kochi's face became serious. "Their lands? These pastures belong to no one and to everyone. And is it misuse to graze animals on grass?"

"They plan, in future, to irrigate and plant them," said the Mullah.

Gol Kochi turned away from the Mullah and spat off into the long grass. "Our ways are the ancient ones. We have travelled between the high pastures in the north and the lush river lands of the south for over a thousand years. Neither kings, nor war, nor anything else has ever stopped us."

"So you do not intend to stay?" asked the Mullah, grasping at a point of potential agreement.

Gol Kochi laughed again, this time more deeply. He held out his glass to be refilled by one of the boys, and then swirled the tea with one finger. "If you offered me the whole of Kabul,

I would never consider giving up this life. To stay in one place, for us, is to die."

"For how long will you stay, then?"

"Only to gather and water our flocks," said Gol Kochi, "and then we move north. We will spend the summer in the Hazarajat."

"But if this is an ancient way," asked the Mullah, "how is it that no one in the village has ever seen you here before?"

"As I have said, nothing in history has stopped our journey. But we are like water, and seek the simplest way to flow from here to there. A peaceful valley such as this is like sweet water to a thirsty man."

"The people here will still be concerned, even if you do not intend to stay."

"Their concern," said Gol Kochi, "is no concern of mine." He drew a small leather bag from the pocket of his vest. Untying it, he pulled out a roll of leather. He spread the leather out on the carpet in front of him, revealing worn writing inked onto the skin.

"This firman came from the Amir himself. It gives us the right to graze and water our animals in this and all the surrounding valleys on our way to and from the Hazarajat, until the end of days."

"From which Amir?" asked the Mullah.

"The Iron Amir. He gave that firman with his own hand to my father's father's father's father," said Gol Kochi.

The Mullah lifted the leather firman reverently in his hands and quickly read it. He suspected that Gol Kochi could not do so, but only knew the contents of the document by heart. As the Mullah finished reading, he could see plainly that Amir Abdur Rahman Khan had granted rights to these lands, and many others, to the Kochi sons of Barak. The Mullah was convinced that the firman was real. He gently rolled it up and returned it to Gol Kochi.

"Sons of Barak, we will greet you with an open hand. And we will govern our disputes by the ways of our people, Hotaki and Barakzai," said the Mullah.

"And let there be no disputes to govern," added Gol Kochi as he signalled to one of the boys to come forward. In the boy's hands was a small package, wrapped in cloth. Gol Kochi unwrapped it to show the Mullah. "A gift for you. Tea, matches, and sugar from Pakistan."

The Mullah took the gift in both hands. "Mash'allah," he said. "We shall have peace. You have my word."

The two men stood up, their meeting at an end. Gol Kochi stepped forward and embraced the Mullah, who accepted the gesture stiffly. He spoke in the Mullah's ear. "I trust that you can convince your people of this, as well."

As the Mullah walked back toward the river, he spied movement out of the corner of his eye. Lying behind a seated camel, hidden in the shadow of a tent, was a Kochi man with a rifle. The Mullah made no sign that he had seen the man, though he assumed that if he looked harder he would see armed Kochi hidden in every fold of ground, every shadow, all around him. He stood straight and did not look back as he waded through the cool stream of mountain water. This time, no shots were fired.

Every man in the district was crowded together in the chai khana, which Faizal had recently expanded by adding more walls made from wooden crates and plastic sheets. The men had been speaking for some time already, mostly to express their dislike and distrust of the Kochi people.

"A man's honour is tied to his land," said one. "What honour has a man with no land, or a man who cannot protect what land he has?"

"Kochi are nothing more than robbers in disguise," said another. "That is why they keep moving!"

"My grandfather said that a Kochi cannot be trusted," added a third man. "Who will say that he is wrong?"

The Mullah listened in silence for over an hour as the discussion went in circles. When he finally spoke, the room fell silent. "It is true that these Kochi are not like us. They travel great distances, moving with the seasons. They measure their wealth by their herds, not their land. But remember that they live as our own people did, a thousand years ago, perhaps more."

The men in the room accepted this grudgingly.

"But it is also true," continued the Mullah, "that these people are exactly like us. They are Pashtun. They are Muslim. They wish for peace."

This time, the Mullah's words were unwelcome, and the sounds of grumbling came from the men in the back of the room. The Mullah stood up to look at those men directly. "What is the alternative to peace? Would you start a war with them? Their tents and animals may seem unguarded, but I have been across the river. They are watching and waiting to see what we do."

One of the farmers who had grumbled the loudest stood up, arms outstretched as he appealed to the Mullah. "You drove off the bandits who threatened us, and you protect us now. We give zakat, and we feed you and your men. Protect us now from these thieves of Barak who have settled on our land. What else can you expect us to ask you to do?"

The Mullah shook his head. "These Kochi do not wish to take your lands. They are travelling north to the Hazarajat. They will rest and water their animals for a few days, a week at most, and then they will move on."

The discussion in the room became loud and heated. The Mullah continued, "They have goods to trade with us brought from Pakistan — tea, sugar, matches — things that are hard for us to find. If we keep the peace, in a few more days they will be gone."

Pahzman stood up and waited for everyone to be silent again. "We must listen to the Mullah," he said. "He not only defeated the bandits, but he brought peace to our village. The Mullah and his men will watch over and protect us, if we trust them."

The Mullah spoke loudly, "We will protect you as always."

There was muttering among the men, but no further disagreement. Pahzman sat down, and the meeting would perhaps have ended then, when Jan Farooq stepped into the room, followed by his two men and a weeping farmer.

"This man's daughter has fallen ill this morning!" declared Jan Farooq.

The Mullah responded. "This is sad news, but we speak now of the Kochi."

Jan Farooq took a prominent seat beside the Mullah, leaving the others who had come with him standing. He held up a hand for a glass of tea, waving for Faizal to hurry. "As do I, Mullah, as do I. You don't find it unusual that a healthy girl falls suddenly ill? She became sick after collecting water from the river this morning."

A man in the back called out, "What is wrong with her?"

"It is the evil eye!" declared Jan Farooq. "She has been cursed by one of these Kochi!"

The discussion in the room became heated again.

"Kochi are famous for sorcery!" shouted one man.

The Mullah quickly lost control of the discussion. The men resumed their argument about whether the Kochi could be trusted, and whether they prayed to djinn, or practised sorcery, or even if they were really Muslims at all.

The Mullah listened again for a while, but then stood. "Let me be clear. There will be peace. I have given my word. I will protect this village but I will not attack the Kochi to do so."

The Mullah walked out of the chai khana and returned to the madrassa on the hill.

Gol Kochi sat by the smoky fire in the centre of his tent. His wife and daughter sat nearby, both stitching complex patterns onto pieces of clothing. Flowers, rivers, seas of grass — these were the things they knew, and so these were the shapes they embroidered on the cloth. His daughter sang a song, softly, about a young man who longed for a girl who lived with another tribe. The lovers arranged to draw water from a communal well every day to see each other without their parents' knowledge.

He should have disciplined her for singing this song, he knew, but instead he sat silently, listening to her voice and to the sounds of the night outside as they grew louder. He heard the animals shuffling about while they looked for somewhere comfortable to rest. The camels grunted and huffed like old men as they tried to settle. He heard the occasional sound of a bird that he knew did not live in this valley — young boys calling out to each other while they tended their flocks.

Life such as this had continued for centuries.

And yet, much had changed.

The Russians had tried to make them give up their tents and live in houses. They promised schools, hospitals, jobs, all of the things of which the Kochi had none. Some went and lived in those houses, and so ceased to be Kochi. The Russians bombed the tents of those who remained, claiming that they contained dushmen. The dead women and children could not argue with them. Flocks of animals found minefields meant for men, and soon the transit from summer to winter pasture was fraught with death.

With the Russians gone, chaos reigned. The Kochi fought the Hazara to keep their pastures, fought other Pashtuns to pass through their lands, and slowly, tent by tent, his people grew fewer.

Gol Kochi reflected on the strips of wood burning in the hearth. They curled and twisted as the flames licked them, but none escaped the fire for long. In the end, all were destroyed.

His people had slipped between the cracks in society for centuries, never wielding power but always surviving. Now they had curled and twisted for almost as long as they could.

Gol Kochi took a poker and stirred the coals, making the flames shoot higher. He wondered if the Mullah would keep his word, as few men did.

No matter, he thought. *The fire consumes all men, good and evil, just the same.*

CHAPTER 15

The madrassa's yard was full of young boys playing. Some were the orphans taken in at the start by the Mullah, but increasingly they were children sent by families in the houses around the madrassa or in the village below. Asadullah Amin and Wasif now needed Lala Chai's help to prepare the midday meal. They no longer baked their own rough bread in the tandoor, relying instead on bread donated by the families, but they still cooked daal in the large round pot.

Faizal appeared in the doorway of the school compound. He quickly looked around, peering past the young boys, looking for an adult. Wasif saw him as he glanced around and walked up to greet him. "Salaam," he said, as the two embraced, repeating the many phrases of their greeting to each other as they did so.

"I need to speak to the Mullah," said Faizal.

"He is not to be disturbed," said Wasif.

"He needs to hear what I will tell him," replied Faizal.

"Do you now presume to give him advice?" asked Wasif.

Faizal's shoulders fell, and he cast his eyes down to his feet. "That is not at all what I mean. It is simply something that I have overheard …"

"Tell it to me, and I will tell him when he is finished his dhikr," said Wasif.

Faizal looked anxiously at the boy, but then he began. "It cannot wait. They are going to drive the Kochi out." When he was finished explaining, Wasif's face mirrored his own look of concern.

Inside the classroom, the Mullah sat on a small cushion with the Quran on its stand beside him. Eyes closed, he repeated a phrase in whispers, over and over again, in meditation.

"He is Allah, Who is One.

Allah, the eternal refuge, absolute.

He neither begets, nor is born.

Nor is there to Him any equivalent."

Wasif stepped quietly into the room and watched him for a moment. Seeing that he was still deep in meditation, he stepped out again. Faizal and Asadullah Amin stood waiting for him.

"Did you speak with him?" asked Faizal anxiously.

"His dhikr cannot be interrupted," said Wasif. "We can deal with this ourselves."

"Brother, you must tell the Mullah," said Asadullah Amin.

"This is serious business," said Faizal.

"Chaiwallah, this is nothing that I cannot solve with my kalash. Come with me, brother," said Wasif. He slung his rifle over his shoulder, and glancing quickly to see if Asadullah Amin would follow him, he left the madrassa. Asadullah Amin handed the wooden spoon to another of the boys and told him to stir the daal. Then he lifted his own rifle from where it leaned against the wall.

"What choice do we have now?" he asked Faizal.

For a moment Faizal considered disturbing the Mullah, but he hastened to follow the boys. When he caught up with them, Wasif began to question him.

"Who put them up to this?" asked Wasif.

"It was one of the young, hard men who travel with Jan Farooq," said Faizal, panting slightly.

"People listened to him?" asked Asadullah Amin.

Faizal shrugged. "He told them what they wanted to hear."

By the time that they had descended to the chai khana, a small crowd had already formed. The villagers were clustered around one of the men from Jan Farooq's entourage. He was shaggy, with a heavy moustache, and he spoke well, even though the language he used was simple. He carried openly the short-barrelled rifle that normally hung under his shirt. All of the village men were armed, as well, though with farming tools, heavy tent poles, or anything else they could find.

Jan Farooq's man pointed across the river. "Everyone knows that these Kochi are little more than savages who live like their animals. They are most famous in the world as thieves. Their women are whores who don't even cover themselves when they walk in public. These Kochi have no honour, and they have no shame."

Wasif and Asadullah Amin stood in the back of the crowd, unnoticed, as the man continued talking. Faizal slipped around the crowd and disappeared inside the chai khana.

"They will run as soon we strike," said the shaggy young man. "Their whores will be collecting water and firewood by the river right now. If we move quickly, we can surprise them and take their women and everything that they have stolen on their travels. We will have our land back, and we will be rich!"

The men of the village began to shout enouragment to each other, gaining courage from their numbers as well as from the words of Jan Farooq's man. Their shouts added to the list of crimes that the Kochi were known for.

"They steal from everyone they meet!"

"They're not really even Muslims!"

"And don't forget that they have used the evil eye to make our children sick!"

Wasif began to push to the front of the crowd to speak to them and talk them out of attacking the Kochi, but before he could begin, the first ranks began to stride down toward the river. The bulk of the crowd swayed forward and soon followed.

"Wait, wait!" cried Wasif, but no one paid any attention. Soon, only he and his brother still stood beside the highway. The crowd had surged down into the fields that led to the river.

"We need to get the Mullah," said Asadullah Amin.

Wasif unslung his rifle. "I can deal with this on my own."

"How?" said Asadullah Amin. "By shooting everyone? No one will listen to you."

"I'll make them listen," said Wasif, before turning away from his brother and walking quickly after the crowd. Asadullah Amin hesitated for a moment, having always followed his brother, but then he turned around and started to run back up the hill to the madrassa.

Across the river, the Kochi men could be seen standing in a loose line along the bank. Every one of them carried some sort of weapon: a few were armed with kalashes, while others held older rifles and shotguns. Their black tents and their flocks, which they had hurried back from the river, dotted the landscape behind the grim-faced nomads. The village men exchanged nervous looks as they faced the Kochi across the water. They remembered that Jan Farooq's man had told them that defeating the Kochi would be easy. None of them dared contradict him now.

Gol Kochi stood in the centre of the line of his people. He scanned the line of villagers for the Mullah, but did not see him. Instead, he shouted across the river at all the villagers, "Go back to your houses! You cannot take what belongs to no one!"

The village men did not respond. They stood uneasily at the edge of the river, none of them wishing to be the first to advance against the better armed Kochi. Even Jan Farooq's man, accustomed as he was to fighting, did not scramble down past the grassy edge of the riverbank.

Wasif moved near him and spoke loudly so that all could hear his words. "There is nothing to be gained from fighting these people." The villagers ignored him, but their enthusiasm for the fight was already dampened by the sight of the waiting Kochi. They fell silent and stood or crouched where they were, watching the far side of the river warily. Not one stepped forward or back.

Wasif went from man to man, speaking to every one of them that he knew. No one would return his gaze, or answer his arguments, except one old man who carried a wooden hoe over his shoulder.

"Go home, boy. This is no business of yours, and no place for a beardless scholar."

Wasif turned from the man and walked a few paces back toward the highway, hiding his frustration as best he could. He squatted facing away from the line of men, gathering control of his thoughts and emotions as he tried to compose a new argument.

The lengthening stillness was broken by a sudden sharp crump from behind the tents, followed by the sound of painful bleating. Every man ducked instinctively at the sound. Sheep went running in all directions, scattering away from the explosion somewhere in the pasture behind the tents.

None of the Kochi men left the staggered line along the riverbed, knowing they must remain between their tents and the villagers. Not knowing what the explosion signified, but assuming some subterfuge of the villagers, first one Kochi took a shot at the villagers facing them across the river, and then another. A slow but steady fire began from the Kochi men, ricochets sounding along the opposite bank.

The village men scattered at the sound of the first shots. With little cover along the riverbed, they retreated back to the mud walls of their fields, hiding wherever they could. Wasif scampered away, as well, and lay behind a low wall, peering around the corner. He could no longer see any of the Kochi men, but he could hear the crackle of their shots continue at a slackened pace, few targets remaining for them to shoot at. He lay where he was, unsure of what to do next.

The pace of the firing slackened and then stopped. Both groups of men remained in hiding on opposite sides of the river.

"What foolishness is this?"

The Mullah's voice carried a great distance as he strode toward the river, trailed by Asadullah Amin, Umar, Rashid, and Isa. All of them carried their kalashes at the ready, except for the Mullah, whose hands were empty. Wasif reluctantly stood up to face him as he approached.

"The men of the village planned to attack the Kochi —"

The Mullah's eyes drilled straight into Wasif. "And what did you plan?"

"Only to stop them," said Wasif.

"And why am I only hearing of this after shots have been fired?"

"Forgive me, Ma'alim," said Wasif, his face contorted with emotion. "I didn't want you to be disturbed for a minor matter."

The Mullah walked past Wasif dismissively. "Peace in this village is not a minor matter." Wasif dropped his gaze in shame and fell in behind the others.

The Mullah stood at full height at the edge of the river, cupped his hands around his mouth, and shouted, "Gol Kochi! Must this continue?"

Across the river, Gol Kochi stood up from behind a small knot of grass where he had been lying. He held a short rifle in one hand and waved with the other. "Mullah, it is not we who started this."

The Mullah turned around and began to shout at the village men, still hiding in the fields. "Stand up! Stand up and let them see you walking back toward the road. All of you!" The men stood up slowly, avoiding the Mullah's glare as they slunk away. Jan Farooq's man was nowhere to be seen, having slipped away as soon as the village men had begun to scatter. Soon it was only the Mullah and his men who remained standing on the village side of the riverbank. He waved them back to the village as well, and followed as they walked slowly up to the highway. A few Kochi could now be seen standing along the opposite bank, watching their retreat.

When the Mullah reached the road, Jan Farooq was already there. The village men had gathered around his dusty SUV and were describing what had transpired. Jan Farooq stood by the hood and greeted each man in turn, starting with the eldest and the richest. The shaggy man who had instigated the confrontation sat in the back seat and said nothing. When Jan Farooq spotted the Mullah, he stepped toward him and gave him a quick embrace. The two men exchanged a long series of greetings and remained standing, looking intently at each other.

"It seems that things have gotten out of hand here," said Jan Farooq.

"I arrived to find the same thing."

"We must hold a jirga then, and quickly," said Jan Farooq. "Can you ask the Kochi for a truce?"

The Mullah signalled his agreement. "It is our way," he said.

The Mullah waded slowly across the shallow river, followed by Asadullah Amin and Wasif. Both boys had rifles slung behind their backs. Gol Kochi and two other nomads were waiting for them outside his tent. The other Kochi were nowhere to be seen, though the Mullah knew that they were nearby and watching. Laid out on the ground in front of the tent were four bloody sheep carcasses, badly mangled and barely recognizable.

Gol Kochi's mood was hard to read. "Salaam, Mullah." He gestured at the boys. "Are these your sons?"

The Mullah winced. "They are the closest thing to sons that I have left. The eldest is called Wasif, and his brother is Asadullah Amin."

The two boys shifted their feet uncomfortably as the Kochi men eyed them closely.

"Strong looking boys," said Gol Kochi.

"Mash'allah," replied the Mullah.

"Alas, I have no sons. But I have a nephew who brings me joy nonetheless." He gestured at a smooth-faced boy squatting behind the men. He pointed next at the sheep. "These must have stepped on a mine on the edge of a water hole on the other side of our camp."

The Mullah briefly eyed the carcasses. "Unfortunately, there are many such things left from the Russian times."

The old Kochi's eyes twinkled slightly. "Yes. Do you mean in the ground or in the homes of farmers?"

The Mullah looked directly at Gol Kochi. "If someone has planted that mine intending to harm you, that man will be punished."

225

Gol Kochi held his gaze, unblinking. "If? Did you not see what happened here? They intend to drive us off this land."

"And so we need a truce," said the Mullah, "so that a jirga can be held. To find the guilty, and to punish them."

"Is that what you have come here to ask for?"

"This is our way. The only way, I believe, to end this conflict," said the Mullah.

"It should be a simple matter. We will take the blood price for the animals that have been killed."

The Mullah exhaled deeply. "It is not so simple. Your people are accused of casting the evil eye on a girl in the village. She has fallen ill."

Gol Kochi spat on the ground. "We are the ones who have been wronged. Not your people."

The Mullah raised his hands, empty palms turned toward the Kochi. "This is what will be discussed at the jirga. I can guarantee your safety, but nothing else."

Jan Farooq's men had hastily assembled their tent again, though this time it was near the chai khana and within sight of the black tents of the Kochi. It was more crowded than before, and the mood was darker. A few men from the village and a small group from the nomad camp stood outside the tent, feigning disinterest in the meeting, but in fact watching and ready to raise the alarm should there be any sign of treachery. It was hard to tell how many Kochi men there were in the camp across the river, but it was doubtful that all of them had come to sit in the jirga; some must have remained behind to guard their camp and their livestock.

Inside the tent the two sides sat in tight clusters along opposite walls, eyeing each other carefully.

In the centre of the two groups along the wall farthest from the door sat Jan Farooq, Gol Kochi, and the Mullah. Faizal and Lala Chai passed through both crowds, pouring cups of tea for which Jan Farooq had paid. The Mullah sat in silence.

When the majority of the men had assembled, Jan Farooq stood to speak. The Mullah began to stand, as well, but a gesture from Jan Farooq stopped him. "In the name of Allah, the Most Gracious, the Most Merciful," began Jan Farooq. "We are here to resolve this dispute between our peoples. There are three matters at hand. The first is the use of the pasturage across the river. The second is the death of the one of our children at the hands of black magic."

This announcement brought a gasp from the crowd. The people hadn't heard that the child had died. Jan Farooq raised his hands for silence. "The third is the loss of the Kochi animals." As Jan Farooq sat down, the village men voiced their disagreement that this last was a matter to discuss.

Gol Kochi stood, his eyes rimmed heavily with kohl and flashing angrily. "The only matter to be resolved is the loss of our animals. It is our way that a man's wealth is not measured in money but in livestock. The death of these sheep, whose bloodline is ancient, is like the loss of our gold. Indeed, it is like the death of our children." The Kochi men muttered their agreement, gazing darkly at the men of the village whom they blamed for the loss. Gol Kochi's voice became louder. "The death of your child is not our fault, and cannot be proven as such. And the safe and continued use of this pasture is an ancient right, proven in writing, which this jirga cannot reverse." At this statement, men began to shout in disagreement at each other across the tent.

The Mullah stood up quickly. "Our lives must be governed by one thing alone," he said, "and that is the law of God. The matters raised by Jan Farooq burn in men's hearts. But the only matter to be settled here is the loss of the sheep."

Jan Farooq scowled at him. "Why are you so quick to turn your back on your own people in favour of these nomads?"

"The firman carried by Gol Kochi is not open to question," said the Mullah. "And there is no proof of fault that can be given regarding the death of the child."

The village men made a low hissing sound to signal their disapproval. Jan Farooq looked from man to man with incredulity, seemingly at a loss for words. "Mullah, you mistake this for your court. We are governed here today by our own ways. The old ways. We will discuss whatever matters burn in men's hearts. And if we do not find justice through this jirga, then honour demands that blood must be spilled."

Gol Kochi spat. "It will be your blood, not ours."

The tent erupted again as men shouted over each other to be heard. Hours passed as the arguing continued, each man demanding the opportunity to restate the case in his own words, over and over. The Mullah sat quietly, his face dark, as the day passed uselessly in bickering and complaint.

It was nighttime before the meeting finally ended, nothing having been accomplished. Men from each community quickly left the tent, heading back to their homes, tired after a long and unproductive day. The air outside the tent was cool, and the Mullah stood and watched as the Kochi men walked together in a group back to their tents. The soft glow of fires could be seen leaking out from under their blackened doorways.

A group of farmers approached the Mullah as he stood watching the Kochi. Pahzman, at the head of the group, took the Mullah's hand in his own. He tried to greet him in familiar tones, wishing the Mullah good health and success, but the Mullah was too weary and disheartened to reply. Pahzman tried to kiss the Mullah's hand, as would a supplicant, but the Mullah pulled it back. Finally, Pahzman screwed up the courage to speak the words the others had asked him to speak. "Ma'alim," he said, "we have come with a request."

The Mullah merely grunted, eyes fixed on him, waiting.

"The guns that you have seized from us." Pahzman hesitated. "We wish to be able to protect our families. We wish for the guns to be returned."

Another man broke in. "There are not enough of you to protect us. We must protect ourselves, as well."

"More guns are not the solution to this problem," said the Mullah, regarding the farmers coldly. "Certainly not in the hands of those who cannot be trusted to keep the peace."

Pahzman ended the conversation quickly. "Thank you for everything you have done for us." He led the men away before anything more could be said.

Jan Farooq had been watching this exchange from a short distance away, and as the farmers left, he pulled the Mullah aside and took one of his hands in his own. "My friend, walk with me." The two men walked a short distance along the highway away from the others and stopped. "I believe that I can see how this can be resolved," said Jan Farooq.

"That is a wondrous thing," replied the Mullah. "This problem is a knot, tied tightly and with many strands."

Jan Farooq laughed. "There are only three things at the heart of every conflict. Land, women, or gold. This problem has all three at once."

"And so what is the solution?"

"That both sides agree that there is no fault with the other in regard to the death of the child or the sheep. And that we respect the rights to pasture their animals written in the firman, if the Kochi agree to move onward in their journey immediately."

The Mullah hesitated, confused. "Why would either group agree to this? It is a defeat for everyone."

"Because we will also agree to two more things," said Jan Farooq, his eyes twinkling. "The Kochi will return here when they move back from summer to winter pasture. We will hire their men to help with the harvest, and pay them in cash. They will also transport the crop to Pakistan, using the routes that only they know, and sell it on our behalf, returning again in the spring."

"They do not have enough camels to carry that much wheat."

Jan Farooq smiled. "Not wheat, Mullah, upym. They are planting poppies in the upper fields. Did no one tell you?"

The Mullah's face set into a hard mask. "The use of narcotics is haram."

"It is well known," said Jan Farooq, "that selling upym is permissible, as it is only used by kafirs. And there is nothing else that will grow in one season on the upper fields that is worth growing. We can replant the olives and the grapes, as well, but it will be years before they produce anything of value."

The Mullah dropped Jan Farooq's hand. "The benefits of this plan are a season away," he said. "What will keep both sides to the bargain?"

Jan Farooq took the Mullah's hand again and squeezed it. "Blood."

The Mullah shook his head. "Threats of violence will not solve this."

"The mingling, not the shedding, of blood," laughed Jan Farooq. "Two marriages. An exchange of brides. This will make the ties between the village and the Kochi unbreakable."

The Mullah considered this solution for a moment, but it did not feel like justice. "It still remains to convince the people of this idea. Especially the Kochi. They have the strongest claim for compensation."

"Do not shepherds guide their sheep?" asked Jan Farooq. "They will accept this solution, if we insist."

The Mullah had little more to say. "Insh'allah. Will you pray with us, Haji?"

Jan Farooq released the Mullah's hand with finality. "Later, my friend, later. I will return in the morning."

The Mullah watched him walk away, greeting other men as he went.

The men gathered again for the second day. Gol Kochi took the Mullah's hand as he led his people into the tent. "Let today be a day of peace."

"Mash'allah," said the Mullah. "God smiles on mercy and forgiveness, if men can find it in their hearts."

The old Kochi smiled. "Trust the shepherds, not the sheep, to find the way."

The men found seats under the shade of the tent, whose sides had been lifted to invite a cool breeze. The mood was no brighter than the day before, but the shouting had subsided, and instead earnest discussion passed back and forth between the two sides. Both Jan Farooq and Gol Kochi were silent, listening to the others speak. The arguments made were repetitious, but every man sought to be heard giving his opinion.

As the day wore on, Jan Farooq nodded to Pahzman, who had not yet spoken. Pahzman cleared his throat and began. "Much of this dispute could be settled by the payment of money, to the Kochi for their sheep, and to this village for the loss of the child." Men from both sides began to speak over him, neither group wishing to admit any guilt. Pahzman waved his hands to quiet the group enough for him to speak again. "And while this would end the conflict, it brings no benefit to our communities." Pahzman tried to continue, but he was quickly drowned out by the voices of others who disagreed.

Jan Farooq stood and raised his hands for silence, waiting for a moment as the men in the tent began to settle down. He gestured to Pahzman. "Finish what you began to say." Jan Farooq remained standing, still in control of the crowd.

Pahzman looked uncomfortable, but continued. "And so, instead, I propose something else: That we accept the rights of the Kochi to graze on the pastures by the river twice a year. And that neither side pay any compensation to the other. But that we pay the Kochi to help us bring in the harvest when they return in the fall, and that they bring our ... our harvest to market when they return to Pakistan. And to bind our peoples together, that there be two marriages, to mingle our blood."

With Jan Farooq gazing over them, no one spoke out immediately against these ideas. Muttered conversations arose between the men as they considered this solution. Before any other man took the opportunity to speak, Gol Kochi stood. "Our lives are a stream of conflict. When we arrive in our summer pastures in the Hazarajat, the conflict will be one hundred times more than we have experienced here. But there, against the Hazara, we will fight. Here, among other Pashtun, there is no need." There was grumbled agreement with this logic. "I have a daughter," said Gol Kochi, "a maiden, who is in need of a suitable husband. Mullah, have you a son?"

The Mullah looked at him, startled. "You know I do not."

"But your boys?"

Asadullah Amin and Wasif, seated in the back of the crowd, sat up straighter. Gol Kochi saw them and pointed. "Is it true what they say of your one boy? That he killed Tarak Sagwan himself?"

"It is true," said the Mullah. "Asadullah Amin earned his name by killing the bandit king. But his brother, Wasif, is older."

"The young lion would be a better match for my daughter, I think, and my heart is glad to join my family to your own," said Gol Kochi.

Both Wasif and Asadullah Amin turned red as the village men stared at them. Asadullah Amin kept his gaze low, seemingly fascinated by a stain on the carpet, but Wasif quickly stood and left the tent without a word. The Mullah did not argue against the suggestion and remained seated, so Gol Kochi continued. "Although I do not have a son, my nephew is dear to me and also needs a wife."

No one from the village offered his daughter. Jan Farooq craned his neck, looking around at the men, trying to find one who would meet his eye. Finally, he gave up and spoke to Pahzman. "I know that you have a daughter ready for marriage. Is she promised to anyone?"

Pahzman stuttered. "I have spoken to the Mullah."

Jan Farooq stopped him. "Spoken to is not promised to. I am sure that your daughter will be happy." Pahzman looked pained, but said nothing. Jan Farooq stood and raised Gol Kochi by both elbows to stand with him. The two men towered over the seated Mullah, hiding him from the view of the other men. "This agreement will end this conflict," said Jan Farooq, "and will make us all rich through trade. It will bind our communities together to make them both stronger. There is no better way."

Gol Kochi took Jan Farooq's hand and looked at his own people. "This valley will become a welcome rest on our journey between summer and winter pastures, and a source of strength to us. We must save our strength for the journey to come, and plan ahead for our own prosperity."

Both groups sensed that a deal had been struck; no one raised his voice in opposition. Both Jan Farooq and Gol Kochi looked at the faces of the men in each of their communities, their expressions making it clear that dissent was not welcome. After a few moments of silence, the two men embraced.

"It is agreed," said Jan Farooq.

The Mullah muttered to himself, within earshot of the two leaders. "This is not justice."

Jan Farooq ignored him. "Mullah, would you give a blessing on this agreement?"

The Mullah stood and looked between Jan Farooq and Gol Kochi. Both stared back, neither betraying any misgivings that they might have. The Mullah looked out at the crowd, reading the faces of the men gathered there, and seeing acceptance, he grudgingly began. "If we are all in agreement ..." He let the words hang in the air, but no one dared challenge the deal that had been made. The Mullah waited a moment longer, then moved forward to stand between Jan Farooq and Gol Kochi. He raised his hands as if in prayer, and spoke loudly, so that all could hear him.

"This dispute is now finished. Woe upon anyone who would seek to reopen it. Forgiveness is the crown of greatness. Now let us pray."

Jan Farooq and Gol Kochi nodded their assent. The men gathered together outside the tent to pray.

Pahzman sat stoically in front of the meagre food that had been laid out for his family's evening meal: naan, tea, and a small dish of pickled vegetables. Both his wife and his daughter were crying, but he tried his best to ignore them. He broke off a small piece of bread in his hand and wrapped it around a pickled carrot, chewing slowly to make the meal seem larger than it was.

"Why did you agree to this?" muttered his wife. "We will never see our only child again."

Pahzman turned angrily toward her. "What was I to do? Speak against Jan Farooq in front of the whole community?"

His wife took her hand off her daughter's shoulder and waved it at Pahzman. "What was the point of leaving our home? Abandoning everything we could not carry? Following this Mullah? All of this suffering was wasted, if now we give our daughter away to a pack of savages!"

Pahzman drew back his hand and held it up as if to strike her. "Enough, woman, enough!"

She ducked under his hand and scooped up the bowl of pickles, throwing it at Pahzman's face. The brine stung his eyes as he fell backwards to avoid her next attack.

"Your job is to protect us, not to sell us to the highest bidder," she said.

Pahzman didn't look at her or answer. He heard a glass smash against the wall near him, but still he didn't look up. When he spoke, his voice caught in his throat and he could barely force out the words. "I have tried," he said. "I have tried."

He heard his wife go back to comfort his daughter on the other side of the room. Pahzman wiped his eyes, which were filled with tears. "I will try."

CHAPTER 16

Umar and Rashid stood back, looking at the rough hole that they had just made in the wall surrounding the madrassa. They had emptied a room in one corner of the compound that had been used for storage, and had built two rough walls to isolate it from the rest of the madrassa. Rashid took an adze and began to smooth the edges of the hole.

"I'm not sure if we will find anyone who can make a door in time," said Umar.

"There is still one house nearby that has not been rented out by Jan Farooq," said Rashid. "We can borrow a door from there." He paused to run one hand over the mud wall that he was scraping.

Isa appeared in the rough doorway, holding a bucket. "I've cleaned it as best I can, but there is only so much I can do."

"We'll have to paint it all eventually," said Rashid, "though it's more important that it is private and secure."

"Do you think he will be surprised?" asked Isa.

"I doubt he has even thought far enough ahead to realize that he will need somewhere else to live," said Umar.

The two men continued their work, happily preparing a living space for Asadullah Amin and his bride.

The chai khana had been cleared out to host a small meeting. Jan Farooq, Pahzman, and the Mullah sat along one side of the carpeted platform while Gol Kochi and two other Kochi elders sat along the other. A simple meal of tea, naan, and kebabs sat half-eaten between them. Faizal and Lala Chai both refilled glasses of tea from their copper pots.

Jan Farooq picked at a piece of gristle caught between his teeth, his words mumbled through his fingers. "If the walwar and the jehez are of equal value, no money need change hands at all."

Gol Kochi nodded. "That is acceptable."

The Mullah shook his head. "That is true. But it is written in the Hadith that there must be a mahr. The groom must pay this to the bride herself."

"And so you will provide this money, Mullah?"

"Truthfully, I have no money other than that collected for zakat, which I will not use."

Gol Kochi patted the Mullah's arm. "When I married my first wife, I paid the mahr in goods. Tea, sugar, and cloth."

"Would two kalashes be a suitable payment to your daughter?" asked the Mullah.

"Yes," laughed Gol Kochi. He looked at the other Kochi sitting with them, who appeared bored by all the talk. "It is settled, then. And in truth, such a payment would suit her temperament, as well."

Pahzman had been keeping silent. When he spoke, his eyes looked from man to man as if seeking something to grasp onto. "I know why these marriages are important. But she is my only daughter, and the Kochi —"

The Mullah cut off his argument with a chop of his hand. "This is necessary for the community. Did we save her from Tarak Sagwan to become a spinster?"

Pahzman's eyes were downcast. "I understand. But —"

The Mullah's eyes flashed brightly. "Enough. It is done. Can you provide a jehez?"

Pahzman shook his head slowly. "Truly, I have nothing to give and no money to pay. And to marry my only daughter out of the bonds of our tribe, and to the Kochi —"

"The only bond worth discussing," said the Mullah, "and the bond that binds us, is Islam."

Jan Farooq cleared his throat and looked at Gol Kochi. "Perhaps one wedding is enough for the moment. Pahzman will have money at harvest time, and we can have this wedding when you return. She can remain promised to you until then."

Gol Kochi scratched at his beard and nodded. "This is acceptable to me. Our ways will be difficult for this girl, and having her join us as we return to winter pastures will be simpler."

Pahzman took Gol Kochi's hands in his own. "Thank you, Haji, thank you."

The Mullah looked between Jan Farooq and Gol Kochi, but could not detect any sign that this result had been preordained. "This is not what was decided at the jirga."

Jan Farooq waved a hand in the air between them. "This is a minor detail. Nothing more."

The Mullah sighed. "Then the girl will remain betrothed until the harvest, at which point she will be wed. If this is acceptable to everyone."

Jan Farooq stood up. "Thank you, Mullah. It is."

The discussion finished, the men departed. The Mullah sat alone in the empty chai khana, and even with time to think, he was unable to devise a better solution than that just agreed upon.

Faizal and Rashid sat with Asadullah Amin outside the madrassa. Lala Chai brought a pot of tea from the stove and poured a glass for everyone. Wasif sat sullenly nearby, part of the circle of conversation and yet ignoring it. Faizal's eyes were shining, and he patted Asadullah Amin on the shoulder. "And so, do you know what to expect?"

Asadullah Amin looked uncomfortable. "God will lead me." Faizal held his laughter, but only barely. "I have already read in the Sunnah and the Hadith what prayers a man must say over his bride on their wedding night."

Faizal burst out laughing, holding his sides tightly. Asadullah Amin turned red, as did Wasif. Rashid put a hand on Asadullah Amin's shoulder and spoke in a gentle tone. "My brother, ignore Faizal. In this case his ignorance shows itself. Let me explain what you must know, and that you have probably never heard." Rashid looked up at Wasif. "And you can listen, as well. You, too, will be a man soon, I am sure."

Wasif sat with them, but he did not listen to what Rashid had to say. His thoughts were focused on those last words: *You, too, will be a man soon.*

Every man in the village was gathered outside the madrassa. There was a festive atmosphere, and each wore the best clothes he could muster. Faizal had given Asadullah Amin a black vest with embroidery around the edges, which he wore over his shalwar kamiz. The Mullah had fashioned a turban for him from dark green cloth. The Mullah and his disciples wore the only clothes they owned.

A dark SUV struggled up the path to the madrassa, the dirt

track much wider now from the constant wear of feet than it had been only a few weeks ago. The vehicle pulled up beside the well, and Jan Farooq climbed out of the back seat. Sitting in the front seat was Nasir Khan. The Mullah moved to speak with them both. As he approached the vehicle, he saw through the window that Ghulam Zia was sitting behind the wheel.

"This is a surprise," said the Mullah.

"Mash'allah," said Nasir Khan, climbing down from the passenger seat.

The men embraced each other, one after the other, each reciting a long greeting. "I hope you are well. I hope that your house is strong. May you not be tired. I hope that your family is well. May you be strong. I hope that your livestock are well. May your health be ever good."

When the greetings were over, Nasir Khan held the Mullah by the shoulders and spoke loudly enough for everyone to hear. "Where is the young lion? I wanted to personally give him a wedding gift."

The Mullah gestured to Asadullah Amin, who seemed small in the crowd of grown men. He approached Nasir Khan, the rest of the crowd pressing in behind him to better hear what would be said. Nasir Khan made a show of appraising him, touching his arms and chest.

"A young lion indeed!" he declared. Nasir Khan pressed an envelope into Asadullah Amin's hand. "This is for you and your bride." Asadullah Amin accepted the gift wordlessly, unsure what to do as the centre of attention.

The Mullah stepped in to help him. "Many thanks, Haji Nasir. Your reputation for generosity is well founded."

"Many thanks," repeated Asadullah Amin.

Other men now took the opportunity to greet both Jan Farooq and Nasir Khan. Soon they became the centre of the knot of men by the madrassa, and Asadullah Amin had been pushed aside to stand quietly with the Mullah.

Two of the village men had fashioned drums from huge pots used for cooking rice, which they hung around their necks using knotted ropes made of colourful rags. They stood in front of Jan Farooq and began to beat a simple rhythm. The men around them started to clap their hands to the beat. Asadullah Amin was both pulled and pushed to the front of the crowd, hands slapping him on the shoulders as he was drawn forward. Once he was in position, flanked by Nasir Khan and the Mullah, the group started walking down to the river. Despite the jostling crowd, Ghulam Zia kept close behind his master.

Nasir Khan reached behind Asadullah Amin and took the Mullah's hand. "So, my friend, what new adventures have you had since the death of Tarak Sagwan?"

The Mullah's face was impassive. "Much has been accomplished, thanks to God," said the Mullah. "The number of religious students has grown, as has the village. And we have once again dug the old water channels to irrigate the fields."

"Is that all?" asked Nasir Khan with a smile. "No more fighting bandits?"

"I am a teacher," said the Mullah. "We look to live in peace. Nothing more."

Nasir Khan looked sideways at the Mullah, still smiling. "Indeed, peace is what our people need."

When they reached the river, they could see the Kochi gathered on the other side to greet them. Strung out in a ragged line in front of the tents were both men and women, their clothing bright and colourful. The women wore loose head scarves and stared at the village men, proud and unafraid.

The river was beginning to run faster and deeper, and the water was cool. Umar and Rashid rushed forward, lifting Asadullah

Amin onto their shoulders, to the cheers of the men, and carried him across the water. When they set him down on the opposite shore, their faces were flushed with exertion.

Gol Kochi stepped forward to greet him, nodding as well at the Mullah and Jan Farooq as they waded the river. "Asadullah Amin, welcome." He embraced him, smiling broadly. "Are you and your people ready to prove themselves?"

Asadullah Amin nodded, unsure what the old Kochi meant. He strained his neck to look behind the older man, trying to determine which girl was to be his bride. A few girls were in the crowd, but Asadullah Amin thought that he could see one whose clothes seemed finer than the others. She was tall, her hands and feet covered in henna, and she looked at him fiercely. When he caught her eye, Asadullah Amin quickly looked away.

Gol Kochi pointed off into the pasture behind the tents. Several hundred yards away, a tall stake had been driven into the ground. A clay pot, turned upside down, balanced on top of the stake. "Before we begin, my people propose a test of your shooting prowess!" Another Kochi man handed Asadullah Amin a long-barrelled jezail, heavily decorated with brass and mother-of-pearl. The weapon stood as tall as he did. Asadullah Amin held it awkwardly and uncertainly in both hands as he tried to keep his balance. Gol Kochi led him to the other side of the tents, with the mixed crowd of men following them.

The Kochi women gathered to one side to watch the shooting demonstration. Asadullah Amin stood out in front and held the jezail as tightly as he could. Gol Kochi cocked the hammer for him; it was already loaded. He was not sure how to aim the ancient weapon, and had trouble keeping the barrel from wobbling. When he fired, there was a tremendous crack and a cloud of smoke, but the clay pot still stood at the end of the stake. The round had gone wide of its mark. Gol Kochi smiled at the

Mullah, who was watching from nearby. "Will you try it next?" he asked. "We won't hand my daughter over to a village of men who can't protect themselves."

The Mullah took the jezail from Asadullah Amin and accepted the powder and shot offered him by one of the Kochi. The Mullah gave a rare smile. "I haven't fired at marks like this since I was a boy."

"My people are not tainted by modern ways," laughed Gol Kochi. "We are Pashtun in the same way as we have always been, generation to generation. Today is an important day, and we celebrate as did our grandfathers."

The Mullah knelt and tried to brace his arms on his knees. The jezail was heavy, even for him, and when he fired his shot went wide, as well. The crowd cheered for him regardless.

One by one the Mullah's disciples took the jezail and loaded it, taking their turn to fire at the clay pot. Lala Chai pushed his way to the front of the group, digging his fists into his hips as he waited for his chance.

"Give me that thing and I will show you all how to shoot," said Lala Chai. The crowd roared with amusement. Lala Chai spun around to face them with an expression of disdain that sent them into further peals of laughter. Lala Chai could barely hold the jezail at all, so Gol Kochi took pity and loaded the musket for him. When it was prepared, the boy lifted the musket into the air with all of his might, but when he fired, the musket jumped out of his hands and bruised his face badly. Even though the clay pot still sat defiantly on the top of the stake, the crowd cheered louder for him than for anyone else. They saw that the boy had spirit.

None of the others had any more luck than Lala Chai, though Kochi and village men alike clamoured for a chance to try their luck. When it seemed that everyone had tried to shoot the clay pot, leaving Gol Kochi unsure whom to ask to shoot next, Asadullah Amin interrupted him with a request. "Father-in-law, I wish to shoot again. But before I do, I want to borrow a camel from you."

Gol Kochi's face shone with delight at the boy's odd request. He waved at a Kochi man, who returned shortly leading a small camel from the dozen or so in their herd. He brought it to Asadullah Amin, who took the rope in one hand. The camel pulled away from him, baring its teeth, while the crowd watched, wondering what would happen next.

Asadullah Amin pulled the camel around in a circle until it stood where he wanted it. The camel sat down, ignoring him to pull at some grass from a nearby clump. Satisfied, Asadullah Amin took the jezail again and carefully loaded it as he had seen the others do before him. He knelt down beside the camel and laid the jezail across the camel's back. It snorted at him but did not seem to mind, and was soon pulling at the grass again with its brown teeth. Asadullah Amin steadied the weapon, trying to remember everything that the men had told him about shooting in the months since the bandit attack. Holding his breath, he squeezed the trigger.

The jezail fired and belched smoke, and the camel stood up suddenly, upending both the boy and the musket. Asadullah Amin could not see the target, but the sound of the crowd told him that he had struck it. Peering around the camel's legs, he saw that the pot was gone.

Gol Kochi led the camel out of the way and helped Asadullah Amin to his feet. Folded in his hands was a turban made of fine, dark blue cloth. "Asadullah Amin, here is your prize." He handed the turban to the boy, who took it gratefully in his hands. "And now let us bring you a second prize," said Gol Kochi. "My daughter."

He then waded carefully into the crowd of women and returned leading the tall girl forward to stand beside Asadullah

Amin. She didn't look at him, focusing her eyes entirely on a small spot on the ground in front of her. The Kochi women remained separate from the men, looking on from the side. All of the men gathered in behind the bride and groom, Nasir Khan standing closest to Asadullah Amin.

The Mullah looked around at the crowd of men, his back to the women, and raised his hands and spoke. His speech, sometimes stiff and halting, on this occasion flowed across his lips melodiously.

"In the name of Allah, the Beneficent, the Merciful. Praise be to Allah, Lord of the Worlds, the Beneficent, the Merciful. Master of the Day of Judgment, Thee alone we worship; Thee alone we ask for help. Show us the straight path, the path of those whom Thou hast favoured, not the path of those who earn Thine anger nor of those who go astray."

He then nodded toward Gol Kochi, who turned to Asadullah Amin. "I give you my daughter in marriage, in accordance with Islam, for the dowry agreed upon, with Allah as our best witness."

Asadullah Amin stumbled over his words, not looking at his bride. "I accept this girl in marriage, in accordance with Islam, with Allah as our best witness."

The Mullah looked into the crowd for Rashid. He and Umar came forward, each holding a kalash that had been carefully cleaned and polished. They handed the weapons one at a time to Asadullah Amin, who laid them at the girl's feet. The Mullah's voice was strong and clear. "The agreed-upon mahr has been paid." He looked at Gol Kochi. "Who does she name as her protector?"

Gol Kochi cleared his throat. "She names Haji Jan Farooq." The Mullah looked back at him sharply, his face clearly showing surprise.

Jan Farooq stepped forward from within the crowd to stand beside Nasir Khan. "Bismillah. I accept."

The Mullah raised his hands as if in prayer and said the names of the bride and groom three times. "Asadullah Amin. Mahtab Kochi. Asadullah Amin. Mahtab Kochi. Asadullah Amin. Mahtab Kochi. Allah bless you, and may He unite you in good."

As the Mullah finished, the ceremony ended and the crowd of men cheered again. The Kochi women ululated loudly behind the Mullah, their voices overpowering those of the men. Gol Kochi gestured toward a low pile of cushions and rugs set between two tents, and Asadullah Amin and Mahtab took their seats on the pillows while the crowd gathered to sit on long rows of carpets laid out in front of them. Village men hastened back across the river to collect food from their wives, who had remained behind the walls of their homes. The men carried large pots of qabuli pilau and stacks of naan back across the river and set them down at the end of each of the long carpets. The naan was passed hand to hand along the rows of men. The rice was spooned onto large platters, the first of which were set down in front of the bride and groom and the most senior of the guests. Once their food was in place, the simple wedding feast began.

The Kochi women sat a short distance away in a tight circle, with Mahtab's mother and her relatives in the middle of the group. All of the men, both villagers and Kochi, sat mixed together, though the most senior of both groups sat closest to Asadullah Amin. Neither he nor Mahtab looked at or spoke to each other. Asadullah Amin tried to ignore the ribald comments made by the men, while Mahtab kept her gaze fixed on a point in the far distance.

Gol Kochi squeezed in beside the Mullah, squaring himself off with the largest of the platters of food. He picked through the rice to find a piece of boiled meat buried inside, which he popped in his mouth with a satisfied sound. As he slowly chewed the tough chunk of mutton, he scooped up a handful of rice in the fingers of his right hand, pressing it with his thumb before sticking it in his mouth. He looked around to satisfy himself that all was as it should be before fixing his eyes on the Mullah. "Our thanks to you for this feast, my friend. It is not easy to feed so many in times like these."

"The thanks belong to Jan Farooq," said the Mullah. "He is the one who has paid for it."

Gol Kochi searched the Mullah's face. "Mash'allah. Jan Farooq is a generous man." The Mullah grunted in agreement, but seemed focused on the communal plate of rice in front of him. Gol Kochi's eyes wandered through the crowd to find Jan Farooq. He was at the far end of the group of seated men, speaking earnestly with some of the farmers who had become his tenants. Jan Farooq's face appeared very serious until he broke abruptly into a wide smile, quickly mirrored by the others. He left the farmers at the far end of the carpets and took his place again at the head of the feast. He nodded to Gol Kochi and the Mullah as he sat down in front of Asadullah Amin, reaching for a handful of rice as he did so.

The eldest men ate in silence while those farther down the lines of carpets watched. When they had eaten their fill, the platters were passed down to the next most senior men, who ate from what was left. In this manner, the food slowly made its way down to the youngest, poorest, and weakest members of the community.

Gol Kochi belched and drew himself up on his haunches. "We have prepared something special for today," he said to the Mullah before jumping to his feet. He disappeared behind the tents for a few minutes, out of sight of the crowd. The Mullah sat nervously, picking at his food, until Gol Kochi reappeared followed by two men, far apart, each leading a camel.

PHIL HALTON

The camels were not saddled, but had fine blankets over their backs and bridles covered in heavy brocade. Bells tied along the edges of their blankets tinkled as they swayed forward. The two men led them by short, heavy ropes, the camels' heads tossing angrily as they were pulled into a clear area near the wedding party.

Gol Kochi stood behind the camels and looked out at the crowd. His people all leaned forward in anticipation, knowing what was coming next. Gol Kochi waved his hand, and a third camel, a female, was walked over toward the pair. The men pulled the two camels together, striking them across the chest with wooden switches, still holding tightly to the ropes. As the camels came closer they suddenly charged, colliding with each other, fighting over the female in heat.

The Kochi began to shout, egging the animals on. The camels grunted and dripped white froth from their mouths as they bit at each other and pushed with their chests. Each tried to put its neck over the other, pushing downward, and they began to turn around in a tight circle, fighting for position. The two men who had been restraining them finally let go of the ropes. Suddenly freed, the camels spun like dervishes.

Asadullah Amin leaned over and spoke to the old Kochi man seated closest to him whose eyes where fixed on the fight. "How does one animal win?"

The man replied without looking. "They fight until one runs away or is forced onto its back."

Jan Farooq leaned over to the Mullah and spoke into his ear. "They are savages. But they are useful ones." The Mullah did not reply.

The camels both pushed hard, their legs straining to keep upright. The Kochi men cheered and shouted, while the villagers simply watched with amazement. White froth was smeared

248

across each camel's back as they pushed and bit at each other. The camels turned and spun, pressing hard against each other until one stopped suddenly and spun in the opposite direction, moving fast, like a wrestler. Its feint caught the other camel off balance, causing it to stagger, its legs splayed wide with one foot off the ground. The faster of the two camels kept pushing, rolling its neck over the other and using its chest like a ram, until it had pushed its opponent onto the ground. It did not stop there, though, as it quickly dropped down, rolling the other camel over onto its back.

A loud cheer went up from all the men. With the match decided, the Kochi handlers immediately began to pull the camels apart. Soon there were several men pulling on each rope and pushing the camels to separate them before one injured the other.

Gol Kochi stood once again in front of the group, his face flushed with excitement from the entertainment. He signalled again with his hands, and called out: "Asadullah Amin! Come here."

Asadullah Amin stood up and walked hesitantly to stand beside the older man, aware of the eyes that followed him as he walked past the long lines of seated men. A Kochi had been waiting for the signal to come forward, and when he did he carried a dhol with him and sat on a carpet hastily laid in the centre of the ground that had been churned up by the camels. He was joined by a young Kochi carrying a rebab, who sat next to him. The young nomad plucked a few strings, ensuring that his instrument was tuned. The musicians looked at Gol Kochi for the signal to begin.

"Everyone, let us watch as our young men dance the atan," said Gol Kochi. "Asadullah Amin, you too will dance." They were joined by two more young nomads, and Gol Kochi arranged them and Asadullah Amin with himself into a circle around the musicians. The drummer began a simple beat, using one hand on each end of the double-sided dhol. After the rhythm had been established, the other musician began to play his rebab, plucking quickly at the strings to make a lively melody.

The dancers began to move in step around the musicians. Asadullah Amin stumbled, following along as best he could, watching the others closely. The dancers continued to circle, arms high in the air, stepping and turning in unison. The dance steps repeated over and over, and Asadullah Amin soon found the rhythm. As the music continued and the drumbeat became louder, he forgot the eyes of the men who were watching him and just danced. He repeated the same steps, his feet moving repeatedly to the rhythm, until he began to dance with abandon, circling the musicians again and again.

When the music finally ended there was a cheer. Asadullah Amin blinked, realizing again where he was and looking around for his friends. "Rashid! Isa!" he shouted. "Come join us!"

Gol Kochi once again took a seat heavily beside the Mullah, his face covered in sweat. He smiled at the Mullah, who did not smile back. "A young man's game," said Gol Kochi. The Mullah snorted in return.

The drummer now began a heavy beat, cupping one hand to make a different, deeper sound. The crowd began to clap along, and the dancers began to sway to a beat that sounded like *dum-taka-dum-taka-dum-taka-dum*. Asadullah Amin left the circle and stepped between the rows of men to grab Isa by the hand. "Come, brother. You have always said what a good dancer you are. Show us." Isa did not move, and cast his eyes downward at the memory. He said nothing, sitting shamefaced and as still and heavy as a stone. Finally, Rashid grabbed him under the elbows and lifted him to his feet. "It will do you good, my friend. Dance just one song." Rashid pulled him into the circle, where they were joined by another Kochi man, making six dancers in all.

Isa stared down at his feet, but when the melody began again he started to dance. Stiffly at first, Isa danced with his eyes closed. Soon he was stepping in a lively pattern, turning and moving more fluidly than the others. When they tried to follow his movements, they realized that he wasn't dancing in any particular pattern, but was moving freely as he felt the music. Isa danced the atan like a man with no future, focused only on the moment. As dancers turned and spun, Isa left the circle to pick up the two kalashes that had been given to the bride as mahr, the only weapons visible at the wedding. He handed one rifle to Asadullah Amin and he held the other in one hand, dancing and spinning with it above his head. From somewhere in the Kochi's black tents, old swords were produced, with heavy chopping blades and long tassles tied to their grips. These were pushed into the hands of the other dancers, who whirled with the blades as the drum sped up, sounding now like *dumtakadumtakadumtakadum*.

The crowd of men was on its feet now and had pulled in closer to the dancers, forming an outer ring around them. Gol Kochi stood and pushed to the front of the crowd. Puffs of dust surrounded the dancers' feet as they stamped on the ground and spun. The Mullah remained sitting where he was, Umar sitting close behind. Jan Farooq was on his feet at the front of the crowd, leading the spectators in a slow and rhythmic clap. Nasir Khan stood close to him, his eyes bright as he watched.

Gol Kochi frowned as he walked back to where the Mullah sat. "What is amiss, my friend?" he asked. "Have we Pashtuns not danced the atan for a thousand years, perhaps more?"

"Music, dancing," said the Mullah, "perhaps I am simply no longer used to these things. That's all."

Gol Kochi continued to watch the dancing, but spoke to the Mullah. "Our young men live three-day lives. First they are children, then they are men, and then they die. Let them enjoy what they can, when they can."

The Mullah considered this as Asadullah Amin spun through his line of sight, dancing and holding the kalash over his head with the zeal of a hero. The Mullah watched, but said nothing more.

The wedding ended when the dancing was over. The Mullah had left hours before, making a sign for Umar to stay when he stood up to go.

The bride stood in the open space between her new family and her old. Her family carried her dowry chest, a tin box painted gaily in geometric designs, and placed it on the ground in front of her. Isa and Rashid produced a stretcher made from patus and long sticks, which they set down in front of the bride. Folded on it was a light blue cloth, which Rashid handed to Asadullah Amin. He shook it out, revealing its shape. He handed the light blue chador to Mahtab, who reluctantly put it over her uncovered head. Asadullah Amin spoke quietly to her. "This was my mother's. It will be better if you wear it in the village."

Gol Kochi stood mutely looking at his daughter's covered form for a long moment. He gestured to Asadullah Amin, and then stepped away from the girl. Asadullah Amin took her by the hand and led her to the stretcher, on which she sat. With the chador carefully arranged around her, no part of her could be seen except the edges of her hennaed feet, which her husband quickly covered with the chador. Isa and Rashid took up the front of the stretcher, and Umar and Faizal took the back. They raised the girl up on their shoulders and began to walk back toward the river. The village men lifted the dowry chest, which did not seem heavy, and fell in behind them.

The Kochi men and women formed a single group again, Gol Kochi watching as his daughter left to join her new family. The Kochi pulled weapons from their tents and fired into the air, shouting wildly as the wedding procession departed.

They crossed the shallow river with the bride in the lead, but as they approached the village the group began to break up as each man returned to his home. Jan Farooq and Nasir Khan had stayed behind to speak with Gol Kochi. By the time the procession had reached the pathway up to the madrassa, there were few men left to accompany it.

The men carrying the stretcher had struggled to carry the girl up the sloping path, but if she rode uneasily on her swaying perch she did not show it. She sat perfectly still under the chador, Asadullah Amin walking along beside her.

When they reached the new back door that had been built into the madrassa's compound, Asadullah Amin looked at his friends expectantly. They continued to hold the girl high, the stretcher resting on their shoulders. Faizal smiled a wicked grin and taunted Asadullah Amin gently. "Friend, would you like us to deliver your bride?"

"Of course," said Asadullah Amin. "What are you waiting for?"

"Have you considered how much work it was to climb this hill?" asked Rashid.

Wasif giggled at his brother. "You'll have to pay them if you want her."

Asadullah Amin held out his hands. "You know I have no money. And neither do any of you!"

"You might have thought of that before you hired us for this job!" said Faizal.

Asadullah Amin looked frustrated for a moment, before he realized that his friends were only teasing him. He laughed, and the others laughed, too. Their merriment was cut short, though, when Mahtab slipped off the stretcher, just as she might do from a horse or camel. She ducked past her husband and his friends without a word, and went inside the house.

The men looked at each other in amazement, and then began to laugh again, even louder than before.

"You have your work cut out for you," said Faizal. The others continued to laugh.

Asadullah Amin, not knowing what to do, lifted the nearly empty dowry chest with his skinny arms and followed her inside. Setting the chest down, he closed the wooden door behind himself and laid the wooden bar across it to hold it in place. He stepped through the curtained doorway into the tiny room that had been given to him to find Mahtab seated on the one piece of furniture that had been brought in for them, a rope bed. She had taken off the chador and had tossed it on the floor. She glared at Asadullah Amin, who had difficulty looking directly at her for fear that he would blush uncontrollably. She was the first girl from outside his family that had ever spoken to him directly.

She pointed at the chador. "I will not wear that again."

Asadullah Amin imagined how the other men of the village would look at him if his wife went uncovered. He felt his cheeks go red, and a catch in his throat. "You must wear a chador in the village."

"I will not," she said defiantly.

"It is a requirement of our faith," said Asadullah Amin haughtily.

"It is not and I will not!" she repeated.

"You will not mock Islam!" he said, picking the chador up from the floor and pulling it over Mahtab's head. She fought him, pushing at him with her hands and pulling at the cloth to get out from under it. As they wrestled, he heard his mother's chador rip. Without thinking, he drew back his hand and hit her across the side of the head. He hit her hard, so hard that his hand hurt. He hit her again, and a third time, until she stopped struggling. Finally, she pushed herself away from him, staying under the chador, huddled in the corner of the bed.

Asadullah Amin stood by the bed and looked at her, ashamed and uncertain. He thought that he heard her weeping, but was not sure. After a few moments, he took his patu and lay down on the floor to sleep as he had always done. He tried to ignore the sounds that his bride made from where she hunched on the bed.

Wasif lay on his side among the sleeping boys in the madrassa. Beside him was an empty space on the floor, something that never in his memory had there been before. He pressed his hands against his eyes, willing the tears back inside before any of the other boys saw him, trying to act like a man. He knew that from this point forward he would be alone.

CHAPTER 17

The interior of the madrassa was crowded with sleeping boys, both orphans and the sons of families in the village. Their numbers had grown to the point that there was hardly room to walk between them.

The Mullah sat in his usual spot, with the Quran on its stand beside him. He was unfocused and irritable, fidgeting and unable to concentrate. After a long sigh, he blew out his candle and lay down to sleep.

The night passed fitfully, and by dawn he still had not slept. He woke the boys for prayer, ushering them outside where their devotion could be seen by the entire village. Asadullah Amin and Wasif acted as shepherds, moving the boys out of the madrassa in a long stream. Standing outside, the Mullah looked across the valley that was beginning to turn green. The sight of the ploughed fields and the canal, filling with water from the river below, gave him a degree of contentment.

Umar had trudged up the hill from the checkpoint to join the boys in prayer. He quickly washed, using a bowl of water left out for him, and then climbed a short ladder to stand on a wider section of the compound wall. He cleared his throat and began to sing the adhan.

"Allah-u akbar! Allah-u akbar!"

These first words drew men out of the surrounding houses, all recently occupied by families beholden to Jan Farooq. The community gathered in long rows by the water pump to pray.

"I bear witness that there is no God but Allah!" called Umar. "I bear witness that Muhammad is the Messenger of Allah! Hasten to worship! Hasten to success! Allah-u akbar! There is no God but Allah!"

Men and boys lined up behind the Mullah and at his signal began to pray.

On the path carved up the side of the hill, an old man stood leaning heavily on his stick as he walked. Tied to it were a few bells and a heavy cloth, inside of which were bundled the tools of his trade. He wiped a finger across the lenses of his thick glasses, clearing off a layer of dust, and looked around. He had heard the adhan, but he was in no shape to rush up the hill to pray. He looked up and down the hill again, and seeing no one close by to see him, decided not to bother to pray by himself. Instead, he continued to trudge up the path.

By the time he reached the top, all the people who had gathered to pray had finished and had returned to their homes. The man walked through the village, through the alleys between the houses, his stick tinkling gently as he went. At the edge of the houses, he continued, crossing the fields toward the graveyard. When he reached it, he found a shady spot to seat himself by the makeshift shrine to the dead girl, and carefully untied his cloth, laying it flat in front of him. He stacked a few well-thumbed prayer books off to one side of the cloth and took a seat beside them. On the other side of the cloth he laid out a number of small items: metal bowls, necklaces with cylinders to hold charms, chunks of incense, and small bottles of coloured inks. He adjusted the ballpoint pen that was clipped to the breast pocket of his chapan, and took a long strand of prayer beads from his pocket in his right hand. His fingers clicked the beads absent-mindedly as he waited.

It was not long before he was spotted by one of the residents of the village, and word spread from house to house that a holy man was in the graveyard. Soon, one of the farmers, who had recently moved to the upper village, led a woman wearing a chador to meet with him.

"Asalaam aleikum," said the farmer respectfully.

"Wa aleikum salaam," said the man. "I hope you are well. I hope that your house is strong. I hope that your family is well. May your health be ever good." The ritual greetings finished, he waited for the farmer to speak.

"Are you the magician of whom I have heard travellers speak?" asked the farmer.

The man seemed to nod, and adjusted his glasses to peer closely at the farmer. "I am Mullah Shafiq. What troubles you?"

The farmer sat down on the ground in front of the magician, his wife seated just behind him. Mullah Shafiq held out his right hand. The farmer took it in both of his own, and pressed his lips against the back of the man's knuckles. When he spoke, it was with a tinge of fear in his voice. "Recently, a girl died in this village from the evil eye," said the farmer.

Mullah Shafiq picked up one of his shabby prayer books and kissed it. "Powerful magic requires powerful protection," he said.

The farmer looked sideways at his wife before speaking. "When we moved into our house, it had been abandoned for many years. Everything of value had been stolen long ago, but my wife found this." The farmer handed a hard ball of dough the size of a marble to the holy man.

Mullah Shafiq rolled the ball around in his palm, and sniffed at it. Taking it between two fingers, he crushed it into his cupped hand. Inside the ball of dried dough was a small piece of paper. The magician let the bits of dough fall to the ground, and carefully unfolded the paper. It was old, and stained with red. Drawn on the paper was an esoteric pattern composed of a grid inside a diamond. In each part of the grid was scribbled writing in a language the farmer did not recognize and could not read. Mullah Shafiq held up the paper so that they could see it, causing the couple to gasp in fear. "Is it some kind of curse that has been put upon the house?" asked the farmer.

Mullah Shafiq ignored him and studied the paper closely. Finally satisfied with his studies, he placed it into a tiny copper bowl that was among the many things spread out on the blanket. He added a few other scraps of paper from inside the cover of one of his books, and held the bowl cupped in his right hand as he spoke a prayer aloud. "Remove the harm, Allah, O Lord of mankind. You are the Healer. There is no healing but Yours, a healing that leaves no disease behind."

He then produced a match from under his coat, which he struck and lit in a single flowing motion, setting the paper in the bowl on fire. It burned quickly, twisting as it curled into ash, until it had withered into nothingness.

"This was not a curse upon the house," said Mullah Shafiq authoritatively, "but a ta'wiz inviting a djinn to live there."

"Inviting a djinn into our house?" repeated the farmer in shock.

The magician nodded. "When the house was built, the natural home of a djinn must have been disturbed. They likely tried magic first to banish it, but if it was too powerful, they may have tried the opposite, and made it welcome instead."

"But what will we do now? Isn't our protection gone?"

"I suspect that the charm was losing its power in any case," said Mullah Shafiq. "Have you noticed things going missing? Objects broken? Fights between your animals or children?"

The woman reached a hand out from under her chador, and pulled on her husband's elbow. He leaned back to listen to her speak. Her voice was soft but urgent. After listening for a moment, he turned back to Mullah Shafiq. "We do not wish to live with this djinn in our house. Can you help us?"

Mullah Shafiq took off his glasses and wiped the lenses with the corner of his chapan. He seemed to be deep in thought. "I have banished djinn before with great success. But judging by the magic used in this ta'wiz, the one we are concerned with is very powerful. I will have to gather some rare things to crush into the ink …"

The farmer's face was distraught. "Anything, Mullah, anything that you can do to help us."

"And so it will cost money," continued Mullah Shafiq. "As much as four thousand rupees, maybe more. I will only know once I have gathered my materials."

The farmer glanced at his wife before speaking. "You shall have it, Mullah. Thank you."

Mullah Shafiq stood and began to bundle his books into his strip of cloth. "I will start right away." Before long, his belongings were packed up and he was making his way through the village and back to the path leading down to the highway.

The farmer remained squatting beside his wife, looking out over the fields. He had a tear of frustration in his eye, which he hastily wiped away with his sleeve. His wife spoke in a low tone, although they were alone. "How will we find that much money?" she asked. "Can we ask Jan Farooq to loan us more?"

The farmer did not look at her when he spoke. "I will find it. Now, go home."

He turned his back on her, his face red with shame at the thought of having to borrow so much money. The woman rose up and quickly made the short journey back to her home, not looking back at her husband once. She knew that his shame was only made worse by her seeing it.

The farmer gathered himself together and regained his calm. When he was ready, he walked the short distance to the entrance of the madrassa and dusted off his dirty shalwar kamiz. Taking a deep breath, he ducked under the arch of the doorway to enter the madrassa's courtyard.

The boys were playing raucously in the yard, watched over by the Mullah, who sat in the shade and clicked a strand of prayer beads between the fingers of his right hand. He noticed the farmer enter the compound, but did not rise to greet him. The farmer walked up to stand beside him and waited, holding his prayer cap in both hands, his nervousness twisting it into a tight roll. The Mullah finally turned from his thoughts to look at him. "Salaam."

"Wa aleikum salaam, Haji," replied the farmer.

The men recited a short litany of greetings to each other, the farmer stumbling over his words as he did so. When they were done, the silence lengthened for a few moments as the farmer worked up the courage to speak. "I have a request," said the farmer, "though it is a difficult one for me to ask."

The Mullah's face was impassive as he waited for the man to continue.

"I have need of zakat for my family. I am not a beggar, but a misfortune has befallen us."

The Mullah's face softened almost imperceptibly when he asked, "What has happened?"

"There is a djinn living in my house," said the farmer. "I need four thousand rupees to pay for the ta'wiz —"

Before the man could finish, the Mullah interrupted him. "What nonsense is this?"

The farmer looked at him pleadingly. "Mullah Shafiq has promised to help us, but the material for his charm is expensive."

The Mullah's jaw stiffened. "This 'mullah,'" he said, "Shafiq. Before promising to help, did he also tell you that you had a djinn in the first place?"

The farmer hesitated. "Well, yes, but we found a ball of dough —"

The Mullah chopped his hand through the air to cut the man off. "Buying ta'wiz is forbidden by the Quran."

"But Mullah, djinn are mentioned in the Quran —"

"Which also says that you are to put your faith in the hands of God, and no other. This man who tells you that he can bring blessings onto your house is a liar. To believe in his power is shirk. It is to disbelieve in the power of God alone!"

The farmer's face fell as the Mullah's tirade washed over him. The Mullah jabbed a finger at him. "Where is this 'mullah' now?"

The farmer mutely pointed down the hill. The Mullah stood, leaving the farmer standing awkwardly, and left the madrassa at a trot. But by the time he reached the track leading down to the highway, the magician was nowhere to be seen. When he returned to the madrassa, the farmer had also disappeared, though the boys continued to play noisily in the yard. The Mullah spied Wasif in one corner, talking to a small clutch of boys, and he shouted at him in a way that made all the boys stop what they were doing and turn toward him.

"Enough of this idle foolishness. Take these boys inside and practise their recitation."

"Yes, Ma'alim," replied Wasif, quickly shooing the boys past their teacher and into the school building. The Mullah took his seat again under a sheet strung up for shade along the edge of the courtyard. He seethed with rage at the wickedness that was taking hold just outside of his own walls. From inside the madrassa he could hear the boys practising, holy words streaming in unison from their lips. The sound calmed him slightly.

The Mullah closed his eyes and recited the words from memory along with the boys, feeling himself slipping comfortably into the familiar flow of the poetry of the Quran. Perhaps an hour had passed when he heard the courtyard door open and close, followed by footsteps and Umar's voice, cautiously interrupting his thoughts. "I have brought the men that we discussed."

The Mullah blinked his eyes open, seeing Umar still standing halfway across the yard. He waved him closer, composing himself again while pouring a glass of cold tea from a copper pot that sat beside him in the shade.

Umar turned and waved for the men to come through the doorway, and a dozen of them stepped through and approached the Mullah, squatting down in two rows in front of him. "These are the volunteers," said Umar.

The Mullah stood up and eyed each of them closely. He approached the first man, older than the rest, and squatted down in front of him to better look at him. The man was shabbily dressed but had a broad and powerful chest, and his hands and feet were heavily callused from hard work. He and the Mullah greeted each other, mouthing the ritual words as each appraised the other. When they had finished speaking, the volunteer reached out to take the Mullah's hand, prepared to kiss it in supplication. The Mullah pulled his hand away, refusing the gesture of deference, holding his hands behind his back. The older man defiantly looked the Mullah straight in the eye, his gaze unwavering.

"Why are you volunteering to join us?" asked the Mullah.

The man's voice and expression were sullen. "I am hungry," he said. "And I need somewhere safe to sleep."

"What kind of work can you do?" asked the Mullah.

"I can do anything you ask," said the man.

The Mullah handed him a piece of paper from his pocket on which were written a few notes. "What does this say?" he asked.

The man did not look at the paper, instead letting the wind blow it off of his hand and across the yard. "I came for work," he said, "not to be tested."

The other men began to show signs of restlessness as the exchange between the Mullah and the older man continued.

"Well, then," said the Mullah. "First, lead us in prayer."

The man pointed a finger at the Mullah as he spoke. "Enough of this. We know who we are. And you know what we are. We are not scholars or saints. We know what you need. Give us guns, and we will fight for you. We will fight anyone you want."

The other men nodded and mumbled in agreement. A skinny young man with long hair in the back row spoke up. "Feed us, house us, and pay us, and we will be yours to command."

The Mullah turned his back on the men and took his seat again in the shade. He poured himself another glass of tea and slowly placed the pot back on the edge of his small carpet. When he spoke, he did not look at the men in front of him at all, but instead addressed Umar. "They are all welcome to study here at the madrassa with the boys, if they wish to learn. If they prefer, we will help them find jobs here in the village. And while they are travellers in need, I will feed and house them from the zakat. But we have no need of their help otherwise."

The older man remained squatting in his place and looked at the Mullah for a long time. When the Mullah did not acknowledge him, he turned his head slightly to one side and spat on the ground. Finally, he stood and left, the other men following him out of the compound.

Umar watched them go and turned to the Mullah with a look of exasperation. "Twenty new families have arrived this week, and there are at least a dozen new shops set up along the road."

"Mash'allah," said the Mullah.

"We need help," pleaded Umar. "Those men could have protected the village."

The Mullah poured a second glass of tea and handed it to Umar. Umar accepted it graciously but did not drink, waiting for the Mullah to continue, fighting to conceal his frustration. The Mullah held up a finger as he spoke to him. "Righteousness is the citadel against all harm. Accepting those men into our circle would bring more danger than they would repel."

"If not them, then who?" asked Umar. "Where will we find an army of righteous men?"

The Mullah raised his hand, gesturing for silence. The boys in the madrassa could be heard again, the sound of their voices rising over the whistle of the dry wind between the houses. As they recited the Quran in unison, their voices rang out, strong and pure.

Umar knew what the Mullah wanted him to hear, but looked pensive. The Mullah leaned in toward him, placing a hand on his arm. "Umar, how old were you when your father first took you to fight the Russians?"

The checkpoint no longer stood isolated on the roadway by the chai khana, but was now surrounded on all sides by market stalls and tiny houses. Whereas the villages of old were set back the distance of a rifle shot from the roads, with houses clustered together to be more defensible, the new structures clung to the highway like a lifeline. Inside the low stone wall, Asadullah Amin and Wasif stood facing Rashid, each one carrying his kalash. Isa stood watch nearby, gazing up the road.

"How much ammunition do you have?" asked Rashid.

Asadullah Amin looked sheepish. Wasif's voice was bitter when he responded. "Only a few rounds each. Umar never gave us any more than that."

"But we know that an empty gun makes two people afraid," said Asadullah Amin.

Rashid smiled and handed each of them a fully loaded magazine from the stack that was kept at the checkpoint. "We'll stay here, while you two do a circuit up the road and around the village."

They changed the magazines on their rifles and cocked them as they had been shown, putting their old magazines aside. Newly emboldened, they walked together up the road and through the little market. It was not long before they were accosted by a group of young boys from the village. They were a motley bunch, each carrying a stick that he held like a rifle. They quickly gathered in a knot around the brothers.

"Take us with you!" pestered one of the young boys.

"We can help protect the village!" said another.

Wasif gave the younger boys a contemptuous look before ignoring them and continuing to patrol up the roadway. Asadullah Amin gave them a small smile, and drew his hand sharply back and forth through the air in what what he thought was a martial gesture to tell them to form a line behind him. The young boys quickly fell into line, following Asadullah Amin as he walked through the market.

At the far end of the row of simple stalls that had sprung up along the highway, a man was beginning to construct a new shop. His stall was built from skinny branches lashed together with strips of cloth to make a frame. The sides were covered with flattened cardboard boxes, with a piece of tarpaulin for a roof. What caught the boys' attention, though, were the posters that the man had begun to pin to the cardboard. Neither Wasif nor Asadullah Amin had ever seen anything like them. Each poster featured a woman, dressed in little more than silks and sequins. Their bodies were curved, their hands held up as if caught in the middle of some seductive dance. Never in their lives had either of the brothers seen women who looked like this.

Wasif walked up to the shopkeeper as he fastened the posters to the outside of his stall, and kicked at a box of cassettes and CDs on the ground at the man's feet. "What are you selling here?" demanded Wasif.

The shopkeeper didn't turn around to look at them, speaking through a closed mouth, pins clenched in his teeth. "Things that people will buy. Come back later when I'm open for business."

Wasif waved his hand at Asadullah Amin and the young boys to call them forward. "You won't be opening for business," he said. Wasif grabbed onto one of the slender poles holding up the front of the stall. "Get the other side," he said to his brother. Asadullah Amin grabbed the support opposite his brother. "No one will have the chance to buy your filth," Wasif said.

The shopkeeper turned toward them just as the boys pulled on the two poles and pushed the rickety stall over on top of him. The thin frame snapped as it collapsed, ripping the cardboard sides and tearing the posters. The man was still tangled in the tarpaulin as Wasif and Asadullah Amin pulled one of his boxes out from under the debris. They spilled the contents out on the ground, and Wasif brought the butt of his rifle down hard on a stack of CDs. They shattered into fragments that spread across the roadway, looking like the wreckage of a broken mirror. Asadullah Amin and the others joined in, pulling out more boxes of goods and smashing them to bits.

While they continued destroying the goods, the shopkeeper managed to crawl out from under the debris that had been his stand. His voice shook as he grabbed at Wasif's shirt. "Enough! You're nothing but child bandits!"

Wasif tried to twist out of the way, but the man managed to get a fistful of his shirt and held him fast. The shopkeeper lifted him off the ground and shook him hard before dropping him and slapping him across the face. Wasif, his eyes screwed tightly shut, dropped his rifle on the ground with a clatter while the man continued to assault him.

Asadullah Amin raised up his kalash and aimed at the man, shouting, "Take your hands off my brother!" The man ignored him. The young boys pelted the man ineffectively with rocks from close range, but he held his grip on Wasif. A crowd gathered quickly and pressed in closely around the commotion. Asadullah Amin felt as if the temperature had risen by a few degrees in only a few short minutes. The shopkeeper shouted at Wasif as he slapped him: "You will pay for everything you have broken!"

Asadullah Amin poked the shopkeeper with the muzzle of his rifle, pressing it hard into the man's back. His eyes closed involuntarily when he heard a sudden burst of automatic fire. When he opened his eyes again, he saw that he had not fired. It was Rashid, holding his rifle over his head in one hand, pushing to the front of the crowd as he fired bursts of warning shots. Isa was beside him, using his rifle in both hands to push the crowd back from the wreckage of the stall. The shopkeeper still held onto Wasif's shirt but turned to look at the men, his face a mask of rage. "They destroyed my shop!"

Asadullah Amin shouted back at him: "We don't want your vulgar things here!"

Rashid moved close to the shopkeeper and placed a hand on his chest. The man let go of Wasif, who scrambled on the ground to find his rifle. He grabbed it and stood, bringing it up almost vertically, muzzle pointing up under the man's chin.

Rashid's voice was calm when he spoke. "You are welcome to own a shop here, friend, but not one that corrupts society or that is against Islam. Everyone is safe here under the rule of Islam."

Asadullah Amin pulled a piece of a poster out of the wreckage, which he held up to the crowd. It showed the cleavage of a Bollywood star. "But this is not Islam!"

"Death to kafirs!" shouted someone in the crowd.

"Allah-u akbar!" shouted another.

The crowd pushed the shopkeeper away as it moved in and began to destroy what little remained of the shop. Rashid and the others stood back and let them finish what the boys had started.

Mullah Shafiq pushed twigs into a small fire that he had lit near the back of a shallow shepherd's cave set in the hillside. The orange glow could barely be seen from the highway or from the village in the valley below.

Shafiq adjusted the bundle of clothes that he used as a makeshift bed, and tried to find a position in which he could sleep while lying on the stony ground. As he got comfortable he took off his glasses, putting them carefully in a pocket of his chapan. He could see perfectly well without them.

The cave was primitive, but suited his purpose. Let the villagers think that he was an ascetic. A mysterious magician. And until he had money again, he had little choice in terms of accommodation.

His small pot of water had begun to boil. Shafiq threw a handful of tea leaves into the pot and wiped a metal cup with the tails of his coat. It had been a long time since he had had sugar for his tea. *Soon enough*, he thought.

Reclining on his side, he chewed on a piece of naan that he had taken as payment for blessing a young child with an eye infection. It was not much, but it was all the boy's parents could afford. *A warm fire on a cold night is better than a delicious meal*, he thought. And as Mullah Shafiq knew well, eating something was always preferable to eating nothing at all.

He dipped his cup into the pot of tea, holding it with his fingertips and blowing to cool it. He adjusted his posture, leaning against the side of the cave, sipping at the tea as he thought about the farmer and the problem that he had promised to solve. What wondrous ingredients would he claim to have found to make a ta'wiz powerful enough to banish a djinn? His mind quickly switched to thinking instead about how he would spend the money that he earned from doing so.

CHAPTER 18

Inside the chai khana, the Mullah sat in the centre of a crowd of village men, who filled the raised platforms and packed the room. As he looked from face to face, he realized that more often than before, he did not recognize the men. The village was growing at a rapid pace, and more and more travellers were using the chai khana as well. Discussion went back and forth among the men, although very little was being agreed upon. Rashid sat in the back of the room, outside of the tight circle around the Mullah. The Mullah sat silently between Umar and Asadullah Amin, listening to each of the speakers in turn. Lala Chai passed among the men, pouring tea into their cups from his long-spouted teapot. One of the villagers, a short man with a bushy beard and hair that stuck out from his face like a lion's mane, spoke louder than the rest, his voice carrying over the din of the others as he came to dominate the room.

"Of course it is good to grant mercy," said the villager, "but now that murderer is back out there somewhere. The safety of our people must be the first consideration."

PHIL HALTON

Umar quickly rebuked the man. "Mercy stems directly from God," he said. "Who are you to say that it is second best?"

"What of justice?" asked the villager. "For the murderer and his victims, but also for the whole community?"

"Justice and mercy are not exclusive. This man will now follow a straight path, insh'allah," said Rashid.

"And if not," added Umar, "justice will find him as surely as a raindrop runs to the river."

Another villager who had been silent now spoke up. "We have spoken of justice, protection, and piety. All important things. All things that have been recently brought to the village. But there are other things that we need, as well."

"Many things," said another man nervously.

Umar gave him a skeptical look. "What are these 'many things' that you speak of?"

The village men looked at each other, each hoping that some other would make the request for the group. Finally, the man with the lion's-mane beard spoke for them all. "The growing season has been good, so we have some crops to sell. There are also things we need to buy."

Umar held up his empty hands. "Unfortunately, we have little money to give, my friend. What we have collected is for the madrassa."

"Haji," said the man, "we don't need charity. We need help getting our goods to the market in Kandahar and back."

"There are too many tolls to be paid," said the man. "Travelling alone, each of us would have nothing left."

Rashid spoke up again from the back of the room. "I know what you are asking of us. But who will pay for our fuel? And perhaps our ammunition, as well?"

"We will do what is right, as you have always done," the villager replied.

"What is right is not always clear," said Umar.

Rashid stood up and moved to stand beside the bokhari stove around which the platforms formed a rough circle. "There are a dozen checkpoints from here to Kandahar," he said, gesturing down the highway. "Not one of which will let us pass easily if we have goods they want to steal. We may bring more trouble onto our heads than we solve by fighting with them."

"But we cannot stay trapped in this valley forever," said the villager.

"Better to live in the valley than die on the highway," replied Rashid.

The men were silent for a moment before the villager turned to the Mullah. "Haji Mullah, with no disrespect to the opinions of the others, what do you think?"

When the Mullah spoke, there was complete silence from the others in the room. "You have all spoken of many things. But all are tied to one idea. The idea is that of a strong community. The murderer's trial and its outcome are but a grain of sand in the desert compared to the work that is ahead of us. There are more sinners to be dealt with. The justice of God must extend across all within our community."

The crowd murmured their agreement.

"We have had men try to set up under our protection to peddle music and filth. These are the things that distract others from the correct path. What we build here must not allow such things to take root. Small allowances made now will bear ill fruit in the future."

"Not if we pull out these evils at the root," said Umar.

"Insh'allah," added Asadullah Amin.

"The murderer who was tried for his crimes atop the hill was granted mercy," continued the Mullah. "This is good and just, and pleasing to God. But that the murders occurred in the first place is an example of what happens when we are lax."

"It is a sad state of affairs," said the lion-bearded man, "when even fathers cannot protect their daughters against wickedness."

The Mullah nodded and raised a single finger above his head, pointing upward. "Which is why we must take matters into our hands, insh'allah."

The crowd listened eagerly, and the Mullah stood to address them.

"From now on, any woman not wearing the chador in public will be respectfully escorted back to her family home."

"And what then?" asked a man in the back of the crowd.

"Then her father or husband will be punished for failing in his duty. This is the law," said Asadullah Amin.

The Mullah smiled at him and looked around at the faces of the villagers. "Asadullah Amin is correct. Does anyone doubt that this is as it was in the time of the Prophet?"

The Mullah looked around at the assembled men, but no one spoke against him.

Wasif and Isa stood together at the checkpoint. Wasif gripped his kalash tightly in both hands and held it across his thin chest. Around him stood or crouched a crowd of young boys, many from the madrassa, including Lala Chai. The boldest of the boys begged them to see his rifle.

"Please show us how to use a kalash," asked the tallest of the young boys.

"We wish to become mujahideen like you," said another.

"We are old enough to fight, just show us," added the tallest boy.

"You're no better than us," said Lala Chai.

Wasif waved them away, pacing a circle around the outside of the low stone wall and pushing the boys back. "Give us room," he said. "This is not a game. We are here to protect the village, not to entertain children."

"I'm no child," said Lala Chai, "and I can protect the village as well as either of you."

The boys' disappointment was evident in their expressions, but ignoring Wasif they now turned their attention to Isa instead.

"Sing a song for us," asked the tallest boy.

"Or recite a poem. Something funny," said another.

Some of the boys snickered at the memory of Isa's previous performances, which had been bawdy and loud. Isa looked sadly at the boys, his eyes deeply set in his face, and shook his head. "I don't remember any of those songs," he mumbled.

The boys continued to demand that Isa perform for them, but he remained silent, finally turning away. Wasif climbed on top of the low stone wall, facing the boys, and waved his arms at them for silence. "I will recite a poem for you," he said.

Isa looked at him curiously and the boys shuffled around to stand in front of him in silence. Wasif cleared his throat and began to speak in a measured, almost musical, cadence.

"Be cautious, enemy, our hearth is dear to us. It is our
    love, it is our soul.
Many tyrants of the time have made assaults upon us here.
Many invaders have been put to shame here, struggling in
    vain.
Many have gone away from here in distress.
It is our love, it is our soul.

"It is an abode of tigers, adversaries cannot live in here.
It is a garden of nightingales, crows cannot come in here.
It is a dwelling place of honour, it is a place of pride.
It is our love, it is our soul.

"Young men have always laid down their heads for its
    freedom.
Many brave men have sacrificed their lives for its sake.
All the plains and all the mountains are coloured with
    their blood.
The sacred land of the Afghans.

"It is our love, it is our soul."

Wasif blinked self-consciously as he finished his poem. The
boys, who had listened in silence, began to clap and clamour even
louder for Wasif to teach them how to fire a kalash. "You can't
tell us about brave men and sacrifices and refuse to show us how
to shoot," said the tallest boy.

"You have to give us a chance now," said Lala Chai.

Finally, Wasif relented. "Enough. Watch and I will show you
how to shoot." He looked around at the boys, trying to harden
his face into a mask. "And how to kill."

He picked up a few empty cans that had been thrown to
the side of the road by the checkpoint and carefully counted
fifty paces away from the road and up the path that led to the
madrassa. When he reached a point that he decided was far
enough away, he placed the cans in a stack on top of a large
rock. Walking back, he saw Isa get into position to shoot,
with a tight knot of boys crowding together to squat down
behind him.

Isa readied the rifle and leaned in. Aiming carefully, he
squeezed off a few quick shots. One of the cans disappeared
as the sound of the shots echoed across the valley.

"Mash'allah!" said the tallest boy. People in the shops lining
the roadside came out to look at the source of the shooting, but
no one tried to interfere.

Wasif stepped up next, deliberately placing his feet just less than shoulder-width apart and sliding his left hand back and forth on the forestock of the rifle until he found the perfect position. Rashid's instructions on how to shoot ran through his mind as he checked off each thing that he had been told. He braced his elbows tight to his body, and once he was ready to fire, he held his breath. The boys behind him watched silently.

His first shot sent a can spinning away into the distance. He fired twice more and the remaining two cans went flying. The young boys cheered. Wasif smiled at them and turned around to give Isa a playful slap on the back. Isa ignored him and walked up the path to set up the cans again. Wasif turned to the boys. "Who's first?" he asked.

At the sound of gunfire outside the chai khana, the Mullah stood and moved to the door. Pushing aside the blanket that kept out the dust, he looked up and down the highway to find the source of the shooting. Seeing the large group of boys clustered around the checkpoint, with one of them aiming a kalash unsteadily into the distance, he strode down the road toward them, his prayer beads swinging wildly from one fist. Umar followed close behind him.

"Is this what religious study has become?" asked the Mullah loudly as he approached.

The boys froze in place, saying nothing. When the boy holding the rifle saw the Mullah looking at him, he lowered its butt to the ground, holding it uneasily around the barrel with one hand. Isa turned back from his mission to set up the cans again. Wasif, supporting a rifle for a young boy who could not hold it himself, looked up at the Mullah and stammered a reply. "We did not seek them out. They came here themselves."

Umar hurried to walk beside the Mullah. "Perhaps it is good that Wasif and Isa are teaching them what they know. Let there be no doubt that how to carry the sword of Islam is a suitable subject of study."

The Mullah looked at Umar, a reply forming in his mind, but then he merely grunted and said nothing further. He walked past the checkpoint and began to ascend the pathway to the madrassa. As he passed Isa, he turned and spoke to the boys, all still frozen in place. "I am returning to the madrassa. When I arrive, I expect that all of you who are students will be seated and fully engaged in your studies." The boys hesitated for a moment, but then raced pell-mell past him up the hill, led by Lala Chai, anxious not to disappoint.

The Mullah paused to let the boys stream past him and then began to walk up the hill, his strides long but slow. Umar kept pace beside him, with Wasif trailing close behind.

"I am losing focus on the madrassa. On what is important," said the Mullah.

"The madrassa does not exist in isolation," said Umar. "We need you to be involved in the community, as well. We need you to protect the madrassa from the world outside."

The Mullah shook his head. "My place is at the head of the class. Teaching the boys to live good lives will build a new world." He continued up the trail, now worn into a deep zigzag rut that wound around the rocks and scrub that dotted the hillside. As his conviction grew again, his pace quickened, until Umar was out of breath trying to keep up.

"And what of the villagers' request that we open a road to Kandahar so they can get to market?" panted Umar.

"All things in their time," said the Mullah. With a gesture of his hand, he indicated that the rest of the climb would be in silence.

Mullah Shafiq sat on his patu in the shade of the madrassa wall facing the cemetery across the fields. The ragged flags affixed to long sticks that marked some of the graves hung limply in the hot air. The farmer whose home was cursed by a djinn squatted in front of him, with his wife seated behind him. Sweat had soaked through the fabric of her chador wherever it touched her body.

Mullah Shafiq held up a vial of brownish mud between two fingers, turning it in the sunlight. "I have prepared the ink to be used in your ta'wiz, my friend. It took me quite some time and effort to find the ingredients."

"Are you certain that this charm will work?" asked the farmer anxiously.

"I have done this many times," said Mullah Shafiq confidently. "Although, based on the charm that you brought me, your djinn is one of the most powerful I have ever seen. You are lucky that you brought this problem to me in time."

A hand reached out from under the chador and tugged at the corner of the farmer's kamiz. He leaned back to listen to his wife, who whispered harshly at him. When she was finished, he turned back to Mullah Shafiq. "Are you certain that this will not only banish this djinn, but prevent it from returning?" he asked.

Mullah Shafiq pulled his glasses out of his pocket and cleaned the dusty lenses with the corner of his chapan while thinking. He perched them on his nose before replying. "My friend, if you doubt my powers, then you need not employ my services. I can use the magic in this ink to help others." He took the vial and slipped it into a pocket deep inside his chapan, and sat looking expectantly at his customer.

The woman's hand reached out suddenly again to touch her husband, but the man ignored her. "No, Haji Mullah, no. We do not doubt you. We beg you to help us."

Mullah Shafiq nodded, and pulled a sheaf of paper slips from within the pages of his Quran. He set them down on his patu, placing a rock on top to hold them in place. "I am ready to begin writing out the ta'wiz for you. But first, you must show me your commitment." Mullah Shafiq held out a small silver plate, black with tarnish.

The man pulled a folded wad of bills out of the breast pocket of his kamiz and placed it on the plate. Mullah Shafiq measured the thickness of the wad with his eyes, and once satisfied, said a few words of blessing over the payment. He set the plate aside, and picked up a heavy brass fountain pen from the holy trinkets arranged around him on the patu.

As he began to fill the pen with muddy ink from the vial, the Mullah appeared at the edge of the village. The Mullah stopped, his eyes fixing immediately on Shafiq. "Wasif, see to the boys in the madrassa." When Wasif hesitated, the Mullah's voice became harsher. "Now," he said. Wasif skirted Mullah Shafiq and his customers, keeping his eyes fixed on the doorway of the madrassa as he went past them.

The farmer jumped to his feet. His voice was strained, and the words tumbled out so fast that they were hard to understand. "Haji Mullah, we did not know what else to do. No one but Mullah Shafiq has said he could help us. This djinn is a plague upon our household."

"Silence!" said the Mullah as he strode toward the magician. The farmer continued to mumble his explanation, but the Mullah ignored the man and addressed Mullah Shafiq instead. "Take your heresy and your blasphemy and begone, sinner!"

Mullah Shafiq remained seated, looking up at the Mullah through his thick glasses. He gave the Mullah a look of pure disdain. "I'll not take orders from a pederast so holy as to live with a harem of orphan boys."

The door to the madrassa crashed open, shaking on its hinges. From inside, Wasif came running, wielding his brother's cricket bat over his head like a sword. He shouted as he ran: "Allah-u akbar!" He swung the bat with all his might, aiming at Mullah Shafiq's head. The old man raised his arms over his face and ducked, and the bat struck the mud wall of the compound over his head and shattered. Wasif was left with the stump of the bat in one hand, his arms aching from the impact.

Mullah Shafiq sprawled on his patu, surprised by the sudden attack. He lunged for the money sitting on the tarnished plate, but Wasif swung the handle of the bat, forcing him to duck again. Mullah Shafiq was on his feet before Wasif lunged at him a third time.

He backed away from Wasif, who was flanked by the Mullah and Umar, stumbling before turning and running. Wasif threw what was left of the bat at Mullah Shafiq's retreating back, missing him narrowly. They watched as the old charlatan disappeared out of sight at the far edge of the village fields.

Wasif scooped up the money from the ground and held it up to the Mullah with a smile. "He must have left this as his zakat."

Umar smiled. "You will be a ghazi yet, my young friend." He embraced Wasif tightly, kissing him on each cheek. When he had finished, Wasif looked to the Mullah, who was ignoring him. The farmer and his wife were still crouched down by the magician's patu.

"And what shall I do with you?" demanded the Mullah.

The farmer held up his hands in supplication, while his wife squatted against the wall nearby, her features unseen under her chador. The farmer averted his eyes, and this time he spoke softly and slowly. "Haji Mullah, thank you for saving us from that evil man."

The Mullah glared at him. "I had already warned you about his tricks. And yet here I find you dealing with him."

Sweat appeared on the farmer's brow, dripping into his eyes and making him blink over and over. "I did not doubt you," he said. "I swear it. But we did not know what to do."

"It is simple," said the Mullah. "You must do what is right. According to the Quran and the Hadith."

The village man stumbled over his words again. "Of course, Mullah, of course. But —"

"What, man?" said Umar. "Spit it out."

"About the djinn …" said the farmer. "What are we to do? I have money to pay you if only you could banish this creature from our home."

Before Umar could reply, the Mullah grabbed the man by the ear and dragged him along the ground to the centre of the open space. Then he propelled him forward with a violent shove, the farmer's knees skidding across the ground. The woman screamed as her husband tumbled but she did not move. The Mullah spoke in a roar. "Do you understand nothing that I have said to you?"

The farmer rolled over onto his back, raising his hands to defend himself. "Mercy, Mullah, mercy! I want only to be protected from evil."

"Get out of my sight!" shouted the Mullah. "I do not perform magic tricks! And you defile the Holy Quran and all it contains by believing that I do!"

The farmer quickly got to his feet, and, without looking back, ran the short distance to his home. His wife scuttled along the wall, keeping out of reach of the Mullah and the others, until she, too, turned and ran. The Mullah heard the sound of their door slamming closed and a heavy bar being placed against it to barricade it shut.

The Mullah looked around at the others, wild-eyed and angry, before striding into the madrassa alone.

Wasif let out a long breath, unaware that he had even been holding it. Umar put a hand on his shoulder and gave it a reassuring squeeze before following the Mullah into the madrassa. Wasif stayed outside for a moment before gingerly stepping through the doorway behind them.

Mullah Shafiq stumbled through the scrub. He had lost one sandal, and his bare foot was covered in blood. He leaned heavily on a stick that he had found, using it as a crutch. He briefly considered stopping to rest, but with no blanket to sleep in or food to eat there was little point, so he kept moving.

The day's light began to fade as he worked his way down a spill of rocks and debris toward some easier ground. By this time, his bloody foot was caked in dust and throbbed dully. As he stepped over a large bramble, he slipped, his ankle rolling out from underneath him as a loose rock shifted under his foot. Swaying quickly to stay upright, he lost his balance, tumbling down to the ground and rolling through the debris and dust before coming to a stop at the bottom of the hill. As he fell, his turban caught on the branches of a low bush and was pulled from his head, leaving his hair a long and unkempt mess in the dust.

He lay on his back, stunned, his unfocused stare searching the hill above him. The sky was already grey and turning quickly to night before he stood up again, shaking the dust and gravel out of the corners of his chapan. He looked up the treacherous slope to where his turban still hung from a branch, mostly unravelled and looking like the dirty rag that it was. He thought better of trying to climb back up to retrieve it, and so, putting his one sandal back on his foot, he began to walk again.

In the far distance he thought that he could see a dim smear of light. That would be Kandahar. *Where the gullible congregate, there will be opportunities,* he thought. And somewhere between that light and here, he knew, was the grand house of Nasir Khan, patron of learned men.

That pretentious mullah might have made a beggar of me, he thought. *But he should know that as you sow, so shall you reap.*

CHAPTER 19

The sun beat down on the highway cutting through the valley, causing the faded grey asphalt to shine dully. The Mullah and the others were crowded under the meagre shade of the ZIL beside the checkpoint, squatting and facing the dushka. Rashid stood beside it, holding the feed cover open with one hand and pointing at the mechanism inside. "This feed block revolves," he said, "pulling the belt through as it fires. The bullet on the bottom of the block is the one that fires."

Umar craned his neck to see it more closely.

"This little strip of metal is what pulls the belt off as it rotates," continued Rashid. "This is where it is most likely to jam. This needs to be kept clean and lightly oiled." He wiped the belt stripper with a cloth, and showed them the oil and dust that was crusted onto it. "This is one of the most reliable machine guns there is — if you keep this part of the mechanism very clean. Now let me show you the rest."

Rashid's hands moved over the gun with confidence. He pulled the trigger and slowly let the bolt come forward, restraining it with his other hand. He then moved around to the front of the gun and pulled the gas piston tube as far forward as it would come, and then unscrewed it until it came off in his hand. He lay this down to the left of the gun, on top of the ring of rocks. Rashid continued to fieldstrip the gun, naming each part and laying it in order beside the others.

"Who can put the gun back together again?" asked Rashid, looking up. Standing behind the group was a young stranger who had been listening quietly. When Rashid stared at him, the stranger nodded slightly and then spoke.

"Asalaam aleikum," the stranger said respectfully, his hand over his heart.

The Mullah recognized the stranger as Nasir Khan's nephew before the others did, and placed his own hand over his heart as he spoke. "Wa aleikum salaam."

The nephew quickly launched into a litany of greetings. "I hope you are well. I hope that your house is strong. May you not be tired. I hope that your family is well. May you be strong. I hope that your livestock are well. May your health be ever good."

When he had finished, the Mullah waited impassively.

"Haji Mullah, again I bring a message to you. My uncle continues to hear of the success of this village, and wishes to speak with you again. I can take you to his home."

"Of course I will come to speak with Nasir Khan," said the Mullah.

The nephew gestured to a pickup truck parked a short distance down the roadway, intermingled with other vehicles in the market. The Mullah saw that standing beside it, watching them, was Nasir Khan's man Ghulam Zia. "We can leave immediately, if you are ready," said the nephew.

The Mullah nodded and headed toward the truck, Umar, Rashid, and Isa following him. He paused to embrace Ghulam Zia as he approached. "Brother Ghulam, I trust that you are well?"

"Well enough," said Ghulam Zia.

"And I trust that it is no trouble for two of my men to accompany me?" asked the Mullah.

Ghulam Zia eyed Isa and Rashid, who each dangled a kalash loosely in his hand. "As you wish," he said with a shrug.

Rashid and Isa climbed into the bed of the pickup truck and took seats leaning against the rear of the cab, as Umar remained standing nearby. Ghulam Zia sat behind the wheel, and Nasir Khan's nephew took the middle seat. As the Mullah walked around to the passenger side, Umar tugged at his sleeve and spoke quickly into his ear. "I am saddened to say it, but I don't believe that Nasir Khan is to be trusted."

The Mullah turned and put his hands on Umar's shoulders. "He is a great man, involved in a great many things. Talking is our way — and at worst, one learns to be good by watching those who are not."

The nephew leaned over and opened the passenger-side door for the Mullah, who shook his head and closed the door firmly. "I will be more comfortable in the back."

The Mullah climbed into the back of the truck and took a seat between the others. Isa banged on the side of the truck with the flat of his hand, and the truck started rolling forward slowly through the market. Umar watched until it disappeared up the road, his face knotted with concern.

The truck raced down the highway for some time before reaching a point distinguishable only to Ghulam Zia, who pulled the truck off road and continued driving cross-country, a plume of dust rising high in the air behind the vehicle. The Mullah pulled the tails of his turban across his face and closed his eyes as the dust storm kicked up by the truck enveloped them. Shattered vehicles, the discarded remains of the Russian occupation, littered the countryside, reminding him of bad times. Soon, the dust was so thick that it obscured the world around them, leaving him to think.

After several hours they turned back onto another road, although this one was in worse shape than even the highway through the checkpoint. The pavement was badly cracked and buckled, and the cracks had filled with dirt and dust blown by the wind, giving it almost the appearance of being striped. It led toward a low, stony rise that dominated the surrounding countryside, at one end of which was perched an old walled compound.

A Russian tank was parked outside the compound. Its dull green paint was chipped all over and peppered with spots of rust. Its gun pointed menacingly down the road that led to the compound gate. As the truck approached the compound, armed men opened the gates and waved them through. The gates were closed again as soon as the truck was swallowed up inside.

Nasir Khan stood inside the gate to greet them as they arrived. He was dressed in a perfectly white shalwar kamiz and a bright turban. As the Mullah climbed out of the back of the truck, caked in dust, Nasir Khan stepped forward to embrace him. The men spoke their greetings into each other's ears as Nasir Khan held the embrace tightly. The ritual words finished, he pulled back from the Mullah and looked him in the eye.

"Welcome, Haji. Welcome to my home."

The Mullah grunted his reply.

"And how was your journey?" asked Nasir Khan.

"Uneventful," said the Mullah brusquely. "Of what do you wish to speak?"

"So quick to business!" smiled Nasir Khan, barely concealing his irritation. "It's unlike you, Mullah. Come inside and I will explain."

The Mullah turned to Rashid and Isa. "Wait here."

Nasir Khan clapped his hands to alert his servants. "Food and water will be brought for your friends." He then led the Mullah inside.

The interior of the house was filled with heavy wooden furniture, ornately carved with traditional designs. Nasir Khan led the Mullah to a room whose walls were lined with bookshelves. A massive wooden desk, covered in papers, dominated the open space in the library. Nasir Khan took a seat in a Western-style armchair with overstuffed pillows, and gestured for the Mullah to sit opposite him. The Mullah sank uncomfortably into his chair, shifting back and forth until he finally settled into a cross-legged position.

"Haji Mullah," said Nasir Khan, "I think that I have misunderstood you from the start."

The Mullah frowned. "I am not a complicated man," he said.

"No?" asked Nasir Khan. "Is it every day that we hear of mullahs who accept orphan boys into their madrassas, then arm them and send them to attack bandits?"

The Mullah dismissed this idea with a wave of his hand. "You are a powerful man. A Khan. Why do you allow these bandits to exist? Why did you not come to the jirga and speak against Tarak Sagwan?"

"The jirga was not persuaded by your arguments," said Nasir Khan, "and neither am I. I do not wish violence to fall upon any member of our tribe."

The Mullah twisted the end of his kamiz in his hands absentmindedly. "But is it violence," he asked, "when it is sanctioned by the tribe, or is it simply justice?"

"And what if it is only sanctioned by you?" replied Nasir Khan.

"I have no such pretensions," said the Mullah. "We merely defended ourselves."

A servant entered the room silently, carrying a small bowl of raisins and another of nuts on a silver tray. He did not look at either man as he went about his work, but the Mullah and Nasir Khan remained silent while the servant was in the room. He poured out glasses of tea for each man before disappearing deeper into the house.

When they were alone, the Mullah began again. "We are merely doing what is right."

"There is no need to be coy, my friend," said Nasir Khan. "Even if the tribe did not have the stomach for it, Tarak needed to be dealt with."

The Mullah was surprised. "Then why not do so yourself?"

"It was not the time," said Nasir Khan.

"But you are a famous ghazi," exclaimed the Mullah. "You should have no fear of bandits."

Nasir Khan smiled. "Stories grow with time. But I have learned about your past as well, your exploits as a mujahid, fighting with Nek Muhammad."

"That was in another lifetime, truly. I am a different man now," said the Mullah.

Nasir Khan held up his glass of tea. "No man truly changes from the shape in which he is first moulded. Men are like the glass, not the tea. No matter what is poured in, this is its shape. I believed you when you said that you wanted to retreat from the world, to simply run a madrassa."

The Mullah leaned forward, looking directly into Nasir Khan's eyes. "I do."

Nasir Khan returned his stare. "Your deeds speak louder than your words."

The Mullah shifted uncomfortably in the chair, but said nothing.

Nasir Khan smiled to break the tension and scooped a handful of nuts from the bowl. "Here is the truth," he said. "Tarak Sagwan owed allegiance to me. When you killed Tarak Sagwan,

I wanted you to replace him. But I didn't make the offer because I thought you would refuse."

The Mullah was stunned. "You wanted me to replace him?"

"He was a very useful man to me," explained Nasir Khan. "He was unpleasant, to be sure. He couldn't read and had little to talk about. But he fought the Russians, as did you and I. And he was good at many things."

The Mullah sat forward in his chair, still processing what he had heard. "He worked for you?"

Nasir Khan ignored the Mullah's incredulity and continued. "As could you. I've seen your initiative, your leadership. I have many commanders working for me, but none as able as you."

"Is not the leader of bandits just a bandit himself?" asked the Mullah.

Nasir Khan scowled and hesitated before responding. "I admit that Tarak, and others, have sometimes been excessive. One shears the wool, one does not slaughter the sheep unless he plans to have nothing in the next season. But don't forget that these men have earned some reward for their years of fighting in the tanzims. Mullah, together we can end the worst of the violence. Work with me, and not only will we control the district, we'll soon control the province."

"To what end?" asked the Mullah.

"I am a practical man," said Nasir Khan, smiling broadly. "But we could make enough money to expand your madrassa, if you like. Or to build mosques in every village. We would do well together, you and I."

Nasir Khan sat back and sipped his tea, waiting for a response. The Mullah left his glass untouched and said nothing, deep in thought.

The Mullah climbed into the back of the pickup truck again, and wrapped the tails of his turban tightly around his face in anticipation of the dust. Nasir Khan had followed him out to the courtyard, still smiling. "Consider my offer carefully, my friend," said Nasir Khan. "I do wish to work with you, but I will not make the offer twice."

The Mullah nodded and waved a hand in farewell as the truck pulled forward and out of the gate. As the compound doors were being pulled shut behind the truck, a boy in a sequined black vest approached Nasir Khan from across the compound. The boy smiled up at Nasir Khan as the man laid a protective hand on his shoulders.

Isa, Rashid, and the Mullah climbed down from the back of the truck after their return journey, pausing to beat the dust out of their clothing with their hands. Nasir Khan's nephew got out of the truck to shake the Mullah's hand. "Farewell, Haji. I hope that your business with my uncle went well."

The Mullah grasped his hand and nodded before turning toward the chai khana, leading Isa and Rashid inside. As he stepped through the doorway, he was met by Umar, who took him by the hands, warm words of greeting spilling out in a long stream. The Mullah looked weary but repeated the words back to him. Umar briefly greeted the other two men, as well, before turning back to the Mullah. "There is something we must discuss," he said.

The Mullah was irritable, stepping around Umar as he spoke. "Can I first wash the dust from my throat?"

"Jan Farooq was here looking for you," said Umar.

"Serious business, then," said the Mullah. "Nothing that I would start without tea."

The Mullah stood by the samovar while some new boy who had replaced Lala Chai drew a glass of tea from it. It came out scalding hot. He held the rim of the glass with his fingertips while he took sips of it, rolling the tea around in his mouth to cool it. He had not finished half of the small glass when Jan Farooq stepped into the room.

"Mullah! I have found you at last," said Jan Farooq, embracing the Mullah, who held his glass of tea at his side while they spoke the ritual words of greeting to each other. The Mullah's manner was considerably cooler than Jan Farooq's, but if the visitor noticed he said nothing about it.

When their greetings were finished, Jan Farooq took one of the Mullah's hands in his own. "I have come to ask if you would come hunting with me today," he asked.

The Mullah was surprised. "This is why you have been looking for me?"

"For no other," said Jan Farooq. "Hunting is the sport of the amirs. And it would be good to have time to talk, as well."

The Mullah hesitated, unsure. Jan Farooq gripped one of his shoulders and squeezed his hand. "Bring a few of your men with you if you wish. There is room in my truck for one or two more."

"I haven't hunted since I was a boy," said the Mullah.

"Then bring your boys instead of your men," replied Jan Farooq. "We will live today as our grandfathers did." He smiled and gave emphasis to his next words. "We shall *live* the Pashtunwali."

The Mullah finally relented. He finished his tea and followed Jan Farooq outside to where his SUV was parked. The Mullah saw that Isa and Rashid were on duty at the checkpoint, speaking with Asadullah Amin and Wasif.

The Mullah called them over to him. "Jan Farooq has asked that I join him hunting today. I want both of you to come with us." He looked over to Rashid and Isa. "I leave you two in charge here at the checkpoint."

Rashid nodded. "Of course."

Asadullah Amin and Wasif came over to the SUV, both carrying their rifles. Jan Farooq looked as if he would say something, but changed his mind. He laughed again instead, sizing them up. "And so a young man and a boy! Asadullah Amin, this is your chance to become a great hunter, as well — if you have any energy left over now that you have a wife," he said, laughing at his own joke and looking around at the others. Asadullah Amin blushed deep red, but the others were silent. Jan Farooq climbed into the front passenger seat of the SUV, speaking to them without looking. "Get in."

They all sat in the rear seat, the Mullah behind Jan Farooq. When the driver started the engine, the radio began to play music loudly, the latest Bollywood love song. Jan Farooq hummed along tunelessly, ignoring the obvious discomfort of his passengers. The SUV weaved around people walking through the market that had spread out around the checkpoint, driving slowly until they reached the open highway. The driver then accelerated, heading farther up the valley to the north.

Jan Farooq turned down the stereo so that he could be heard, and turned around to speak to Wasif and Asadullah Amin. "This is the way the Kochi went, heading to the Hazarajat. It is an ancient route that they take, leading them far to the north." Neither of them said anything in reply, but Jan Farooq continued. "In a way, I envy them. They live a natural life, like our forefathers."

Jan Farooq turned back around and they drove on in silence. No one spoke to the Mullah, who was brooding, watching moodily as the countryside passed by. After half an hour or so, the SUV pulled over to the side of the road. Trickling down the mountainside was a seasonal stream that cut a shallow channel down to the bottom of the valley. In a desolate landscape, the banks of the stream stood out, green with life.

Jan Farooq climbed out of the car and waited for the others by the side of the road. His driver went to the back of the SUV, digging around among a mess of cargo until returning with a heavy net folded and draped over his shoulders.

The Mullah was surprised. "No shotguns?"

"We will show these two how we hunted when we were youth ourselves," said Jan Farooq.

The Mullah gave a rare smile. "Wasif, Asadullah Amin. It is true. Hunting small birds with a shotgun only makes sense if you don't intend to eat them. This is how we hunted when I was a boy and our supper depended on it."

The little hunting party set out to walk along the near bank of the stream, Jan Farooq in the lead, followed by his driver with the net. They moved slowly, listening. Before long, they came across a stand of thick brush from which came the sound of birds. The driver unfolded the net, finding the weights tied to each of the corners. He held one corner, while Jan Farooq and the Mullah took hold of the other three between them. Wasif and Asadullah Amin stood back, watching in wonder.

The men quietly stalked up to the brush. On a signal from Jan Farooq they threw the net over top, quickly draping it over the entire bush, and pulled down hard. Their sudden movement and noise spooked the birds hiding inside, who tried to scatter. As they burst out of the bush and into the net, they quickly became ensnared, their heads and limbs trapped in the mesh.

With one hand Jan Farooq grasped one of the birds that was struggling to get free, reaching under the net to grasp it with his other hand. Once he had it firmly in his grasp, he pulled it out from under the net and wrung its neck all in one swift movement, handing it to his driver. One by one they plucked each of the captive birds from the net, collecting six in all.

"A fine haul for the first cast of the day," said Jan Farooq.

The Mullah seemed pleased, as well, though lost in thought. Asadullah Amin and Wasif were anxious to try their hand at casting the net, and so Jan Farooq handed it to them to carry. The hunting party stalked along the stream until they found another bush that seemed full of birds. Wasif and Asadullah Amin spread the net out between them and carefully approached the bush. As they dashed forward to stretch the heavy net over top of it, they managed to snag the mesh on a branch instead. As Wasif tried to pull the net over the bush, birds fled out the other side, settling farther up the stream and making a racket to warn their fellows. He looked sheepish.

"You ruined it for us!" said Asadullah Amin.

Jan Farooq laughed. "Not as easy as it looks!"

They all worked together to trap a few more birds along the near side of the stream. The Mullah rarely spoke of his early life, but this day he described how he and his brothers would net birds to feed their family. Jan Farooq took an interest in Asadullah Amin, showing him how to pull birds out from under the net without accidentally setting them free, and also how to snap their necks so that they died instantly.

When they finally reached the end of the brush along the stream, they trapped one last bird in a small bush. Jan Farooq urged Asadullah Amin to reach in and seize it. The boy emerged holding it firmly in both hands. The bird looked around wildly, but was held fast in the boy's grip. Wasif came over to look at it, stroking the bird's head to calm it. It began to coo gently.

Wasif looked at the Mullah pleadingly. "May we keep this one?"

The Mullah scowled. "We have no time for such frivolous things. Do you not recall how often we have gone hungry? This bird is for the pot." He gave Wasif a severe look and gestured at the bird. Wasif took it from his brother, stroking its feathers gently to calm it again as it was passed from boy to boy. He looked up at the Mullah, pleading again, but the Mullah was firm. When Wasif continued to hesitate, Asadullah Amin reached over and wrung the bird's neck. The Mullah turned away and began to walk back toward the SUV.

Jan Farooq watched the Mullah walk down to the road and spoke to the others. "Come, that is enough for today."

"What about the other side of the river?" asked Asadullah Amin.

Jan Farooq laughed. "As every bandit king knows, my young friend, if you kill all the pigeons today there will be nothing to eat tomorrow."

The hunting party followed the Mullah back to the SUV, the driver carrying the net draped over his shoulders again, and a heavy bag full of birds. Wasif hung back, gently carrying the last bird that they had caught. The Mullah said nothing as the others climbed into the vehicle, nor as the driver turned it around to return to the village.

After a short time, Jan Farooq turned around in his seat and addressed the Mullah. "Can I speak freely in front of them?" He gestured to Asadullah Amin and Wasif.

"They are like sons to me," said the Mullah. "You may say anything you wish."

"I know of the offer that Nasir Khan made to you today."

"And?"

"It is a very generous offer he has made. I suggest that you accept."

"Is this Nasir Khan making his offer twice? He said that he would not," replied the Mullah.

Jan Farooq laughed. "He won't. I've come on my own to urge you to accept it. Peace is what this country needs." He slapped a hand on his driver's shoulder. "It will make every one of us rich men."

The Mullah was circumspect. "Can Nasir Khan be trusted to keep his word?"

"Maybe so," said Jan Farooq. "He can certainly be trusted to do what is best for himself, no?"

The Mullah grimaced. "Is that what we now expect from 'good' men? Have we fallen that far?"

"You are the only man I know who speaks about good men and bad men," said Jan Farooq. "When Nasir Khan speaks, it is about survival. If you were paying attention, you would know that there is little else to be concerned about in times like these."

The Mullah shook his head. "I am not sure that I agree with him."

Jan Farooq smiled. "And so perhaps we need to have a different conversation."

The Mullah looked at him, waiting.

"Many of my men from the Russian times still follow me," said Jan Farooq. "We control this road from here to Maiwand. Everywhere except for your village. Nasir Khan's other commanders control the road all the way from there to the outskirts of Kandahar City, where we butt against Ustaz Abdul Haleem's men."

The Mullah said nothing, watching Jan Farooq closely.

"Working together, we could defeat both Nasir Khan and Ustaz Abdul, tax all the trade from here to Quetta, and become rich men, both of us. And why not? Are we not the mujahideen who defeated the Russians? Do we not deserve the sweet fruits of this life?"

The Mullah looked out the window, seemingly deep in thought. Jan Farooq pressed onward.

"If you don't believe in Nasir Khan, believe in yourself. Why not ally with me instead? We have known each other for many years, spilt blood together. It is only right that we be partners in this."

Wasif and Asadullah Amin listened with disbelief. "Go on," said the Mullah, causing the boys to look sharply at him.

Jan Farooq turned farther in his seat to face the Mullah, and used his hands for emphasis. His eyes twinkled as he spoke. "Together, we can carve up the district without him. Perhaps I can even lure him out from his home, and then you can do what you wish with him."

The Mullah's face was impassive. "You would do that for me?"

Jan Farooq laughed, glancing at his driver for support. "Of course! For my tribe, for my cousins, for my brothers, and for myself. Nasir Khan lives in a fortress. Why fight him head-on if we don't have to?"

The Mullah let out a long breath. "You are right, Jan Farooq."

Jan Farooq smiled and clapped the Mullah on the knee. "I knew you would see it my way. And so — you and I as brothers against Nasir Khan?"

The Mullah spoke in an even tone, but his eyes shone brightly as he did. "You are right that he has a strong fortress. But it is like a castle made of butter. In a cold, dark night, the castle stands, imposing and strong. But in the light of day, in the light of Islam, it melts in the sun and is no more powerful than a puddle of ghee."

Jan Farooq scowled and turned around to face forward again. "Would that life were as simple as you make it," he said.

They drove the rest of the journey in silence.

When they reached the village again, the SUV drove through the market and turned off the road, slowly picking its way up the track to the madrassa. The day was fading into evening and there was no one moving about outside of their homes. The SUV pulled up by the water pump and they all clambered out. Jan Farooq embraced the Mullah swiftly, though without much enthusiasm. The driver brought the bag of dead birds around from the back of the truck. He handed it to the Mullah.

Jan Farooq waved his hand at him. "You can keep them all. To feed the orphans."

"Your generosity is appreciated," said the Mullah. He handed the bag to Asadullah Amin, who could barely lift it. "Take this inside the madrassa," he said, "and then return to your wife."

Jan Farooq gave Asadullah Amin an embrace, as well. "Don't forget, Asadullah, that now you are a man. You have killed a bandit king. You are married. Soon you will have children of your own, and you will be the father of a dozen sons."

"Yes, Jan Farooq," said Asadullah Amin.

The Mullah spoke to Wasif. "Go down to the checkpoint and send Umar up to the madrassa. He should know how to dress these birds."

Jan Farooq gestured to the SUV. "Get in, Wasif. I will take you there, as I am driving back down to the highway."

Wasif looked to the Mullah for assurance, who merely nodded at him. After he had clambered into the back of the truck, he realized that he was still holding the last dead pigeon. He put it on the floor by his feet, trying to ignore it.

Jan Farooq reached out the window to take the Mullah's hand. "Think about Nasir Khan's offer," he said. "And about what refusing it might mean for you. Think also of my offer." He looked around at the houses surrounding the madrassa. "Your quiet life here cannot continue uninterrupted forever."

The Mullah's face was impassive as he watched them leave. Wasif sat quietly in the back of the SUV, ignored by Jan Farooq. When they reached the highway, the SUV stopped in front of the checkpoint. Jan Farooq snapped at the driver. "Wait here. I am going to speak to a man in the chai khana."

The driver lit a cigarette, blowing smoke at Wasif. "Off with you, boy," he said.

Wasif fumbled with the door handle until it opened, stepping out into the road. He looked down at the dead pigeon on the floor of the truck, but left it there and closed the door. When he turned to walk toward the checkpoint, he saw Umar, who greeted him warmly.

"The great hunter returns!"

Umar looked at him curiously, holding him by the shoulders, but Wasif simply looked away and said nothing.

"Are you sick?" asked Umar.

Wasif shook his head.

"I have had my doubts about Jan Farooq all along," said Umar. "Your face says much of what must have been discussed."

Wasif didn't look at Umar, but simply passed on his message. "The Mullah wishes to speak to you. He is at the madrassa."

Umar looked as if he wanted to say something more, but did not. He handed his rifle to Wasif, briefly pulling back the cocking handle to show him that a round was chambered.

"Rashid and Isa are eating in the chai khana," he said. "Stay here for now, and go eat when they come back."

Wasif took the rifle and sat on the low stone wall, looking down the road. Umar watched him for a moment, but knowing how impatient the Mullah could be, he hurried up the well-worn path to the madrassa.

Wasif sat alone, with tears in his eyes. His hands gripped the rifle tightly, twisting and wearing the wooden grips.

CHAPTER 20

Jan Farooq walked back from the chai khana to his SUV without glancing at Wasif. The sun was low in the sky, leaving much of the village and market in the darkness of shadows. The tail lights of Jan Farooq's truck lit up as the driver, seeing him approach, started the engine.

Wasif called out, his voice cracking as he did. "Haji, have you started your journey home? Do you no longer wish to enjoy our hospitality?"

Jan Farooq merely waved a hand at the boy without looking and climbed into the SUV. He rolled the window down and lit a cigarette.

Wasif set his kalash down on the rocks that had been stacked around their position on the road and stood behind the dushka. He pulled on the cocking lever, but the bolt was already to the rear — the gun was ready. Wasif tried not to think too much about the details of what he knew he must do. The most dangerous of evil men were the tempters, who led good men astray.

He slipped the index fingers of both hands around the gun's large trigger and pulled. The dushka shuddered in its mount, the vibration passing up Wasif's arms and into his chest. The deep thump of the gun was entirely unlike the sharp crack of a kalash.

The noise of the gun startled Wasif enough that he gripped it more tightly, firing a longer burst than he had intended. The empty casings that the gun spewed out were the size of fat pencils and soon a small pile of them lay smoking on the ground beside him. The SUV had started to drive away before he fired, but it had quickly rolled to a stop in the middle of the road, smoke rising from its shattered engine block. Nothing moved inside the truck. Its tail lights burned red in the grey of the evening light.

Men were running out of the chai khana and looking up the street toward the dushka from stalls all along the roadway ahead. Before anyone could stop him, Wasif took his kalash and approached the SUV, peering through the shattered back window.

Inside the truck, both the driver and Jan Farooq were a broken mess. The front windshield was blown out and the inside of the truck dripped with gore. Wasif was still staring at his handiwork when Isa and Rashid grabbed him by the elbows.

"What have you done?" demanded Rashid.

Wasif smiled and pushed out his chest. "Only the will of God, brother."

Rashid hit him with an open hand, hard across the face. The blow staggered Wasif, leaving a drop of blood hanging from the corner of his lip. Rashid's voice was tight. "You fool. Do you think that this will go unpunished?"

Wasif was in tears but he managed to choke out his words: "As my brother was punished for killing Tarak Sagwan?"

Rashid shook his head. A crowd had gathered around the SUV, bodies pressing against each other to look inside. Pahzman stood at the edge of the crowd, his eyes riveted on Wasif. Rashid pulled the boy by the arm, dragging him away from the crowd and back toward the dushka. He quickly grabbed the essential things that couldn't be left unattended, a few cardboard boxes of ammunition and three hand grenades, stuffing them into the fold of his patu.

Isa watched the crowd growing around the SUV nervously. "We need to leave," he said.

Rashid, lost in thought, didn't answer, instead finishing what he was doing with a methodical slowness. He took Wasif by the hand and led him up the path toward the madrassa.

Partway up the hill they were met by Umar and the Mullah, who were hurrying down to the highway. "What was that shooting?" asked Umar.

Wasif answered before Rashid. "I killed Jan Farooq," he said proudly. "He was nothing but a bandit in disguise."

Umar's mouth hung open in surprise, but the Mullah regarded Wasif coolly. "Did he attack you? Threaten you?"

"No, Mullah," said Wasif. "But he threatened all of us. He could not be trusted! I only did what had to be done. What any righteous man would do."

The Mullah looked down toward the roadway. There was still a crowd around the SUV, but no one had yet pursued them up the hill. "There will have to be a reckoning," said the Mullah.

"Perhaps a blood price could be paid," offered Umar.

Wasif was shaking with frustration. "But this was not murder," he said. "Are we not opposed to evil men?"

The Mullah put a hand on Wasif's shoulder. "It is not always so simple."

"It is simple when you say it, Ma'alim."

The Mullah sighed deeply, in a way that Wasif had never heard before. He began to walk back up the hill, his stride weary.

"Isa, go back down to the chai khana and have Faizal bring up food and tea for all of us," said Umar. He looked to the Mullah. "In the morning we will call for a jirga. We can resolve this."

The Mullah kept walking. "We will reap what has been sown," he said.

Isa led Faizal and his helper back to the top of the hill, each carrying some of the meal of bread, clear soup, and tea. The village surrounding the madrassa was dark and quiet, as the people remained shuttered in their homes. The madrassa was dark, as well.

Umar met them as they began to walk through the village, speaking in a low tone. "The Mullah has told us all to gather in the ruined garden rather than the madrassa."

Isa hesitated. "Why there?" he asked.

Umar shrugged. "It is his wish. He has moved all the boys from the madrassa, as well. Only Asadullah Amin and his bride remain locked in their side of the compound."

Faizal looked up at the sky. "It is a warm night to be outside, at least."

As the men stood together, Lala Chai took the copper pot from Faizal's helper and poured out short glasses of tea and handed one to each of them. None of the men spoke as they drank the tea, each privately wondering what would happen next. Umar looked up to judge the weather, but clouds obscured the stars and sky completely. The night around him was pitch-black.

Umar quickly tipped the last of the tea into his mouth and handed the empty glass back to the young boy who had come with Faizal. "Go to the madrassa with this tea," said Umar. "The Mullah is still there. Offer him a glass, and tell him that we are all gathering together here."

The boy hesitated, uncertain. Lala Chai snatched the glass from him imperiously. "This idiot doesn't even know where that is," he said. With a stack of glasses in one hand and the tea in the other, he moved off through the houses toward the madrassa, swinging the teapot as he went.

When he arrived at the madrassa, he found it was empty, save for the Mullah, who sat alone in the classroom, his patu wrapped around his shoulders. A candle stub burned low beside him and the Quran rested lightly in his hands. He did not look up as Lala Chai entered the room, nor when a glass of hot tea was held in front of him.

"I have been asked to bring you tea," said Lala Chai. "This is almost the last of it. Do you want me to make another pot?"

"No, I am fine," said the Mullah, looking up. "I simply needed some time alone."

"I will leave you then, Ma'alim. Everyone is gathered in the garden, as you asked."

When the Mullah didn't respond, Lala Chai hesitated. "Ma'alim, everyone is frightened, though none will say it to you."

The Mullah looked up at him, blinking in the half-light, and smiled. "I shall join them, then," he said. He stood and led the boy out of the madrassa and into the night. The Mullah and Lala Chai clasped hands as they walked across the village to the ruined garden. Perched on the edge of the village, it was nothing more than low stone walls and the stumps of trees and bushes. In the centre was a large round stone that had once been the base of an olive press. Gathered in the remains of the garden were all the boys from the madrassa, as well as the Mullah's followers.

He raised his hands as he entered. "A blessing upon you all."

Wasif burst from where he was sitting and knelt in front of the Mullah. "I am sorry, so sorry, for what I have done. Please forgive me."

The Mullah lifted Wasif up, and spoke to everyone. "To forgive you I would first have to blame you. There is but one judge, and I am not He."

"Even still," said Rashid, "this is a problem. Others will judge, and will ask for blood." He gestured toward Wasif. "His blood, and likely ours as well."

The Mullah put an arm around Wasif protectively. "Do any of you truly blame him for what he has done?"

Rashid shook his head. "It was murder."

The Mullah interrupted. "It was justice. Jan Farooq was a thief, a liar, and a sinner." He smiled at Wasif. "It was premature," he said. "Surprising, even. But justice nonetheless."

"Mullah, what would you have us do?" asked Umar.

"My friends," replied the Mullah, "for now I ask only that you watch over me. I will pray for guidance. This is a quiet place, well suited to concentration."

"But what will we do about Jan Farooq?" asked Rashid.

"Leave tomorrow for tomorrow. For now, we are in the hands of God."

Rashid looked unsatisfied, but said nothing further. The men and boys slowly dispersed, arranging themselves to sleep in the garden. Each found a comfortable spot among the low walls and rocks that made up the ruins, disappearing from sight as they found places to sleep. The night air was warm, and any other night the setting would be well suited for rest.

Wasif held his kalash in both hands, posturing for the young boys. "I will stand the first watch," he said. He then strode off to stand at the edge of the garden, looking away from the others and into the night.

The Mullah observed all of this quietly, taking a seat on the round stone in the centre of the garden, his face a mask. Umar came to him and asked quietly, "Are you all right?"

The Mullah sighed. "Truthfully, my soul is heavy with its burden. But having you and the others stand watch over me lightens the load, if only a little."

Umar nodded and moved a short distance away, laying out his patu on a flat piece of earth. He lay down, turning several times before he was comfortable, and tried to sleep.

The Mullah sat alone in the centre of the garden, with the Quran on its low stand and a kalash beside him. A candle burned down to a stub flickered nearby. The night was still and quiet, and the others around him all slept. Wasif sat propped up against the wall at the edge of the garden, kalash in his lap, snoring gently.

Eyes half-closed, the Mullah's face was tight with concentration. "Father of all, the Exceedingly Compassionate, the Controller, the Majestic: I see what You wish me to do. But there are others better suited to the task. If this burden may be lifted, let it be so. Not as I will it, but as Your servant, as You do."

The Mullah began to repeat a phrase in whispers, over and over again, in meditation.

"He is Allah, Who is One.

Allah, the eternal refuge, absolute.

He neither begets, nor is born.

Nor is there to Him any equivalent."

Lala Chai crept out of the garden where the others slept, the Mullah's own patu wrapped around his shoulders. He walked through the upper village, his footsteps breaking the stillness of the air. When he reached the madrassa, he went inside and stood at the front of the classroom. In his hands he held Asadullah Amin's cricket bat, which had lain forgotten in the courtyard.

The room was devoid of any furniture except carpets, but Lala Chai knew where the Mullah always sat. He positioned himself near that spot, imagining that he was in class. Tired, Lala Chai pulled the patu up around his shoulders, but he stayed upright, sitting facing the door, the bat across his knees. The rough wool rug, worn down by countless feet, seemed to be the most comfortable seat he had ever had. While the others slept in the garden, he would protect the classroom, just as Asadullah Amin had done before him.

Before long he was hunched over, asleep, feeling at home and safe, though alone in the empty madrassa.

CHAPTER 21

A single motorcycle threaded its way quietly up the hill toward the madrassa, leading two pickup trucks whose cargo beds carried a half-dozen armed men. None of the vehicles had turned on their headlights, so they drove slowly, weaving around rocks and dense brush. Driving the motorcycle was Ghulam Zia, a kalash slung across his back. Seated behind him, looking frightened, was Pahzman.

A few hundred yards from the village that surrounded the madrassa, the motorcycle pulled to a stop, with the trucks stopping close behind. Ghulam Zia leaned the bike on its kickstand and dismounted, pulling his weapon off his back with practised ease. He glared at Pahzman with a look of utter distaste. "Where is he?"

Pahzman kept his eyes low as he muttered an answer. "He always sleeps inside the madrassa, with the boys."

Ghulam Zia's men began to gather around him. "Do they post a guard?" asked Ghulam Zia.

"Perhaps at night. I don't really know," replied Pahzman.

At a signal from their leader, the men began to stalk slowly through the brush up to the top of the hill. As Ghulam Zia turned to follow them, Pahzman grabbed at his sleeve and held him back. "You haven't told me why he is being arrested. I told you he is not the murderer."

Ghulam Zia brushed Pahzman's hand off his arm with the barrel of his rifle. He leaned his face very close to Pahzman's, his voice low but full of contempt. "A man sleeps alone every night with forty young boys and you can't think of why Nasir Khan wants him arrested? We will arrest the boy, as well, but the Mullah is the root of the problem."

"But it was only the boy who has committed a crime. It was the boy that killed Jan Farooq."

Ghulam Zia pushed Pahzman away and began to move up the slope with long strides. "You were paid, fool. What do you care what happens now?"

Ghulam Zia and his men moved swiftly and quietly up the hill toward the madrassa, passing through the terraced fields surrounded by their low walls. They moved carefully, half of the group advancing at a time, until bound by bound they were among the houses that surrounded the madrassa. Ghulam Zia knew the way and so led the others to the dusty white building that housed the Mullah and his school. They spread out in front of the gate, some men watching the top of the wall while others looked either way down the narrow alley. Such was their skill that they had reached the outer gate without having made a sound.

Ghulam Zia gestured to one of the men, who pushed gently on the heavy wooden door. It was unlocked, and it swung slowly inward on its hinges. The man held it open while the others skipped inside to wait by the door to the classroom.

The man closest to the door held a hand grenade, his finger already tense against the safety ring. He looked to Ghulam Zia for a signal, ready to throw it into the room. Ghulam Zia paused when he saw the single pair of sandals on the ground in front

311

of the door, and he frowned. He placed a hand over the grenade and shook his head.

The Mullah sat perfectly still in intense concentration, his lips moving silently. The others were asleep around him. He opened his eyes at the sound of shuffling feet.

Standing in front of him on the other side of the garden was Ghulam Zia, holding Lala Chai by the scruff of the neck. Fanning out behind him were armed men whom the Mullah recognized from Nasir Khan's house. Pahzman stood nervously to one side.

Before the Mullah could speak, Ghulam Zia fired a short burst from his kalash into the air, waking everyone with a start. Rashid was on his feet in seconds, his rifle in his hands. Seeing the men, he kept it pointed low. Everyone else was frozen where they sat, not daring to raise themselves any farther.

Ghulam Zia's eyes were cold and opaque, addressing his words to no one in particular. "We have come to arrest the boy-murderer and the mullah who keeps the stable of bacha bereesh."

The boys and men had awoken with a start, and they peered back from the interior of the garden where the jumble of walls and the darkness partially concealed them. "One of them must be the boy you're looking for," said Pahzman.

Umar spat toward him. "Traitor."

Keeping an iron grip on Lala Chai, Ghulam Zia pulled a long knife from a sheath tucked into a sash tied around his waist. "Enough," he said. He pushed the knife up against Lala Chai's throat, the tip drawing a bead of blood. "Mullah, we are a lashkar. You and the boy-murderer are under arrest. You will be taken back to Nasir Khan to be tried for your crimes, as is our way. Come with us, and no harm will come to this one or the others."

Lala Chai struggled for a moment and then whimpered as Ghulam Zia's grip tightened further. All eyes were on the Mullah. The Mullah was still seated where he had been meditating. He ignored the armed men, and instead looked Lala Chai in the eye. The prayer beads clicked through his clenched fist at a furious pace, but otherwise he was still. He hesitated a long time, weighing his thoughts and looking at the boy. When Ghulam Zia saw his eyes soften, he knew that the Mullah would surrender; his grip on the boy's neck lessened imperceptibly.

The Mullah's voice was hoarse as he spoke. "And did not Ibrahim offer his own son Ismail in sacrifice?"

Before Ghulam Zia could respond with a further threat, the Mullah dove to one side and snatched his kalash up from where it lay on the flat stone. Ghulam Zia hesitated for a moment in surprise before pushing his dagger through Lala Chai's throat, tearing it horribly and ripping the flesh until the blade emerged from the other side of the boy's neck. The boy's shout was quickly stifled, turning to a ragged gurgle as a sea of blood washed over his chest and down his legs. Ghulam Zia's eyes widened, and his grip on the dagger tightened, as he saw the Mullah steady himself and swing his rifle barrel up to point straight at him.

The Mullah poured a long burst of fire through Lala Chai and into Ghulam Zia, driving them both to the ground. The bullets made a wet ripping sound as they tore through both bodies and thudded into the mud-brick wall behind them. The garden was suddenly alive with screams and firing. The young boys stayed hidden as best they could, while the others snatched up their guns and fired into the moonlit silhouettes of Nasir Khan's men from wherever they had been crouching. Only Faizal hid his face in his hands and cowered on the open ground.

Umar focused his first burst on Pahzman, whom he wounded badly in the leg, dropping him behind one of the low walls and out of sight. Rashid scampered backwards behind a jumble of stones and was firing fast, deliberate shots, aiming to take out the armed men one by one. Wasif held down the trigger of his weapon and raked a long burst across all of the men in front of him. The vicious gunfight lasted less than ten seconds. The ruins gave the Mullah's followers good cover, while the men standing exposed behind where Ghulam Zia had fallen were soon cut down by the Mullah's men, whom they could barely see.

The Mullah held up his hand and shouted: "Enough!" The only noises in the sudden silence were the moans of the dying and the whimpering of the young boys. The silence extended to the houses surrounding the garden and the madrassa and into the night beyond. No one ventured forth from his house. Every compound gate remained locked tight.

As Umar searched through the jumbled garden, he found two young boys dead, sprawled on their backs, hands clasped together. The remaining young boys from the madrassa had gathered together in the back of the garden, crouching behind each other. One had a minor wound in his leg, but the rest were uninjured.

"A miracle it wasn't worse," declared Umar as he checked on the boys and began to bandage the wounded one's leg.

Asadullah Amin came running into the garden breathing heavily, gripping his kalash in one hand and pulling his wife with the other. She wasn't wearing a chador, but over her shoulders and face she held the patu that she had been sleeping with, leaving a narrow gap for her eyes. Asadullah Amin and his young wife looked around in shock at the carnage that filled the front of the garden, but said nothing.

Rashid walked toward the heap of dead and dying men, firing a few shots from the hip when he saw movement. Umar left the boys to join him, working from the other side of the garden. He was about to fire when he suddenly stopped and instead reached into the pile of shattered bodies and pulled Pahzman to his feet. The man collapsed to his knees as he was yanked forward, one leg covered in blood. He wailed piteously and pleaded with his hands, crying: "Mercy!"

Umar knocked him down with a quick hit to the shoulder with the butt of his kalash. "Tell us, cousin, what were you doing here with these men?"

Pahzman rolled over onto his back and raised his hands in supplication. "I … I came to warn you —"

Umar leaned over and ground the barrel of his rifle into Pahzman's wounded leg. Pahzman howled and tried to roll away, but Umar kicked him and he rolled back into place. "Lies!" howled Umar.

Rashid sauntered slowly over to stand above Pahzman as well, taking a position by his head. "Don't lie, cousin, we can see that you were with Nasir Khan's men."

"No! They made me come with them," whimpered Pahzman.

Umar kicked him again. "They made you? With what? With money?"

Faizal held a wad of cloth over his ear, which bled profusely from a graze that left it looking ragged and torn. "To think that I once called you a friend," he said.

The Mullah ignored this discussion as if he were in a trance, walking past Pahzman to lift the broken body of Lala Chai from where he lay pinned under Ghulam Zia. The Mullah's shalwar kamiz quickly became soaked in blood, but he paid no attention. He carried the boy to the round, flat stone where he had been sitting, and lay him gently down, straightening his limbs and shutting his eyes with a gentle stroke of his hand.

The others watched the Mullah, expecting him to take charge and give direction. But he was entirely focused on the boy and lost in thought. Finally, Umar spoke to the Mullah in an urgent tone. "Mullah, there may be more of them coming. We need to leave. Now."

The Mullah gently pulled on Lala Chai's kamiz, straightening the bloody material from where it had gathered high above his waist. He gave no indication of having heard Umar speak, keeping his back turned and his focus on Lala Chai.

Umar stood behind him and placed a hand on his shoulder. "We need to find somewhere to hide, while we make a plan. We cannot stay here."

The Mullah looked up at him sharply. "Do you still believe that our plans mean anything? Have you lost your faith in God?"

Umar hesitated.

The Mullah straightened and turned to face the others. Covered in blood, his face a sheet of pain, he spoke in a low voice that was hard for them to hear. "Isn't it obvious, my friends?" he asked. "God is the Creator of all plans for all men. We must simply do what is right: that which is the will of God." His eyes pleaded with them to understand his words. "He has set us on a path that we must accept, no matter how difficult."

Pahzman still lay on the ground, moaning pitifully. He turned as best he could toward the Mullah, holding out his hands again. "I can help you! Nasir Khan has asked me for information about you. I can trick him. Lure him to you."

The Mullah smiled thinly at Pahzman. "You would do that for me?"

"Yes, Mullah. I am your servant."

Rashid saw the Mullah's expression change. "You do not become a pious man by betraying those for whom you betrayed us," said the Mullah. He looked up at his followers. "This man and his promises are worthless to us, even more so as the help of God is near."

The Mullah fixed his gaze on Rashid. "Is our cause just?"

Rashid nodded. "Yes. Of course."

The Mullah looked at the others. "Is he the only one who believes this? That our cause is just?"

"No, Ma'alim," said Asadullah Amin. "We all believe it."

"Is the cause of the enemy unjust?" asked the Mullah.

"It is," said Wasif, his voice loud enough to carry to the nearest houses.

The Mullah stepped up onto the flat stone, Lala Chai lying at his feet. "Then why should we be humble in our religion? For our cause?" His eyes shone brightly, and he began to roar. "We are the servants of God, we do not disobey Him, and so He will make us victorious."

Umar shouted: "Takbir!"

All of the others shouted back in unison: "Allah-u akbar!"

The Mullah gestured all around, at the village and the fields and the valley below. "Here, we have built the House of Peace. It is the House of God, and has room for all of His children."

Pahzman quietly rolled over and tried to get up onto his knees and elbows. Rashid, who felt the man move, kicked him and sent Pahzman rolling away in pain. Umar turned at the sound, his rifle in his hands. He tore off the empty magazine and snapped a fresh one in place. He cocked the rifle in a fluid gesture, stepping forward, and brought the rifle up to his shoulder. Umar fired one round into the back of Pahzman's head. The sharp crack of the rifle echoed across the village, and the impact drove the man's body forward to the ground with a dull thud. Dark blood pooled quickly in a circle around his smashed remains.

The Mullah watched this unfold impassively and then began to speak again. "Brothers!" he shouted. All eyes snapped back to him as he pointed down the valley toward Kandahar City. "We have built this House of Peace. But out there, all around us, until all men submit to the will of God, shall be the House of War."

"Takbir!" shouted Umar.

The men and boys shouted themselves hoarse, repeating the words over and over.

"Allah-u akbar!"

"Allah-u akbar!"

"Allah-u akbar!"

The convoy drove north along the road that cut through the valley, Rashid leading on the motorcycle. His eyes scanned the pastures on either side of the road for threats, but he saw nothing. The rest of the men and boys were packed into the back of the pickup trucks taken from Ghulam Zia, crouched low and huddled together against the cool night air. The Mullah refused a seat up front, instead sitting in the cargo bed with his back against the cab of the truck. He gripped the edge of the truck with one hand and with the other he steadied Lala Chai, who lay wrapped with the other two boys in a bloody shroud beside him.

PART THREE

PART THREE

CHAPTER 22

Rashid led the convoy off the highway. The motorcycle and the two trucks that followed began to roll slowly through the rough countryside. He picked the smoothest route he could, forcing them to drive a winding path around rocks and other obstacles. The grey morning light around them cast no shadows and gave little warmth.

The Mullah had not shifted from his seat beside Lala Chai throughout the journey, his hand resting lightly on the boy's shroud, which was thickly crusted with dust and blood. Around him sat his students, packed closely into the bed of the truck. The Mullah's eyes were wide open but unfocused as all the others dozed.

The bed of the second truck was also crowded with boys. Asadullah Amin sat beside his bride, holding the patu over her modestly. Wasif sat by himself, surrounded by boys, at the tail of the truck bed. Faizal had been dozing beside Asadullah Amin, but he woke as the truck turned off the road and began to bump across the rough ground. He turned and raised his head over the cab of the truck, craning his neck to see where they were going.

"I have been thinking," said Faizal to no one in particular. "I must speak to the Mullah. I have something that he needs to hear."

Wasif sneered at the older man. "Do you think that he is waiting for your advice? You heard him yourself. He is leading us to do the will of God! He doesn't need the help of a chaiwallah."

Faizal turned away from the others and closed his eyes again. "As I recall, it was good to be so young and so sure of oneself."

"I am not sure of myself," said Wasif. "But I am sure of this: There is no God but Allah, and Muhammad is the Messenger of Allah."

Faizal did not reply, and they rode on in silence. In time they came to a black felt tent pitched in the middle of a large field, surrounded by sheep. The vehicles stopped a respectful distance away and Rashid called out to the Kochi that he knew were inside. "Asalaam aleikum, cousins!"

A man stuck his head out of the tent flap. He sized up the visitors for a moment before standing up in front of the door of his home. In his hand was a rifle that looked old but well cared for. "Wa aleikum salaam." He said nothing further, watching and waiting.

Rashid called out again. "Do you have tea or food for visitors?"

"We are poor and have little, but what we have we will share."

Rashid looked at him doubtfully. The man stuck his head back in the tent for a moment, and shortly afterwards a boy came out from behind him, carrying a teapot and a stack of glasses. The man watched them carefully as the boy came over to Rashid.

"We are looking for Gol Kochi," said Rashid.

The man simply pointed farther up the valley. Rashid nodded and took the short glass of tea offered by the boy, drinking it with a quick flip of his hand. The others did the same as the boy offered glasses up to them, only the Mullah abstaining. When the pot was empty, the boy stood back. Rashid turned the motorcycle around and began riding to the north, the two trucks bouncing along behind him. They came to tent after tent, spread out over kilometres, each surrounded by livestock. In every case, they were pointed farther up the valley and into the foothills of the mountains surrounding the Hazarajat.

After a dozen stops and many glasses of tea, the convoy found a small cluster of Kochi camped together. Standing outside, as if waiting for them, was Gol Kochi. Rashid stopped a short distance away and looked back for the Mullah. Everyone else remained where they were seated, but the Mullah climbed down and walked past Rashid to greet the old Kochi.

"Asalaam aleikum," said the Mullah.

Gol Kochi embraced him tightly. "Wa aleikum salaam. I hope you are well. I hope that your house is strong. May you not be tired. May you be strong …" Gol Kochi broke the rhythm of the usual statements as his gaze lingered on the truckloads of boys behind the Mullah. "What tragedy causes this?"

"I will explain," said the Mullah. "But we come seeking nanawatai." The Mullah dropped down onto his knees with little ceremony, offering his kalash in one hand to Gol Kochi. Performed by anyone else, the gesture would have looked overly dramatic. The Mullah imbued it with quiet dignity.

Gol Kochi's eyes were fixed on the Mullah, but he did not move to accept the rifle or raise him up. He ran his fingers pensively through his hennaed beard. "And who do you need protection from?"

"Nasir Khan," said the Mullah flatly.

"And why not ask Jan Farooq for protection, and stay in your village?"

"One cannot ask an evil man for protection from evil men," said the Mullah.

Gol Kochi looked surprised. "I would not expect you to call Jan Farooq evil, my friend. What has changed?"

"Jan Farooq is dead."

Gol Kochi looked surprised for a moment, but then he controlled his expression. "You seem to have much to tell me, then." Gol Kochi reached out and took the kalash from the Mullah. He brought him to his feet and embraced him again before leading him back to his tent. "You know, Mullah, that we follow the old ways. Our fathers' ways. You have our protection simply by asking. But come, let us sit and talk. I suspect that there is a long story to be told."

As he glanced back, Gol Kochi's eyes caught sight of his daughter, huddled in the back of a truck with Asadullah Amin. He turned his eyes from her, avoiding the sin of looking at another man's wife. Asadullah Amin saw his glance and quickly pulled the patu back over her face, keeping her out of sight.

Gol Kochi's gait was heavy as he strode back to his tent, with the Mullah following closely behind.

Lala Chai's body was laid out on the tailgate of one of the pickup trucks, near the other two boys whose bodies had already been prepared. He was naked, with a clean white cloth laid modestly across his waist. Umar poured water over the body from a jug, while the Mullah gently washed him. The others crouched nearby, the boys from the madrassa huddled behind them. When they spoke, it was in hushed tones.

"We should attack him directly," whispered Wasif. "Quickly. Surprise *him* this time, and win."

Rashid shook his head. "There will be no surprising him. He will be waiting for us from now until this is finished."

"We simply have to wait until the Mullah tells us his plan," said Asadullah Amin dismissively. "Success comes from God alone, who in all things knows best."

"Are we even sure that there is a plan?" asked Faizal.

The Mullah ignored them, gently rocking the body onto its side and continuing to rub it with his cloth, moving it repeatedly in small circles. Umar poured water slowly for him as he worked.

"We are in the hands of God now," said Asadullah Amin. "I am not worried."

Rashid clucked in admonishment. "God favours the bold — and the clever. We need more than our faith."

The Mullah held a small bottle of perfume between his fingers and dripped it across Lala Chai's body, from his forehead down to his feet. He gently rubbed it into his skin, working his hands down the body with great care.

Faizal half turned toward the others so that he could look each man in the eye. "Perhaps Nasir Khan can be reasoned with. Or the Mullah can simply pay the blood price." He received nothing but blank looks. "Can we not even try to go back to how it was before?"

Isa spoke in such a low voice that no one heard him. "That's not possible. For any of us."

Umar and the Mullah wrapped Lala Chai in a white cloth, tying it off at the head and feet. The preparation of the body complete, the two men stood by the tailgate of the truck, Umar and the others watching the Mullah expectantly. The Mullah had turned away from them, looking at some point in the distance. The long silence grew uncomfortable, until the Mullah finally turned around to speak. His eyes were rimmed with red but he held his expression together tightly. The words caught in his throat, so he gestured to the others to help him lift Lala Chai onto their shoulders.

As they lifted the thin body of the boy, tears filled the deep creases in the Mullah's face. His voice was thick when he finally spoke. "Let us begin."

The Mullah sat beside a low fire in between the Kochi tents as the evening grew around him. The others sat in a circle centred on the fire, with the boys in a loose group around them. They had finished the last of the food given to them by Gol Kochi, which was eaten with little of the usual enthusiasm. A pot of tea sat untouched by the fire, empty glasses stacked beside it.

In one of the tents, all the Kochi men had gathered to speak. They had not asked the Mullah to join the jirga, although it was clear that the only topic of discussion would be the status of their guests.

After a long time with the crackle of the fire as the only sound, Umar broke the silence and spoke. "I still can't believe it. Nasir Khan is a traitor."

Rashid poked the fire with a stick. "I am sorry to say it, brother, but is it not right that they come to arrest a murderer?"

Wasif's face flushed hot. "He was an evil man! No better than a bandit!" Everyone looked away as he spoke. "No one tried to arrest my brother when he shot Tarak Sagwan!"

Asadullah Amin's voice had a tinge of venom. "That was different, Wasif, and you know it! Tarak broke into the madrassa. I had no choice."

"Jan Farooq was just as bad!" replied Wasif.

Umar interrupted them. "According to Islam, one instance was murder and one was not. But that does not mean that Nasir Khan has the jurisdiction to conduct a trial."

"If not a trial," said Rashid, "then a jirga. Wasif could admit his guilt and we could settle on a blood price with his family."

"Yes!" said Faizal. "We have money. We don't need to be fugitives."

"*If* they accept money," said Umar. "They may demand blood

instead. They may be forced to demand blood by men like Nasir Khan. And don't forget — they came to arrest the Mullah, as well."

"That charge was untrue. Everyone knows it," said Asadullah Amin.

"Then why would Nasir Khan try to arrest him?" asked Wasif.

"It was politics, for certain," said Rashid. "Or simply to get him out of the way while the other matter was settled."

"Nasir Khan cannot be trusted," said Umar. "He may have intended much more for the Mullah than you think."

"Then we are fugitives," said Rashid. "All of us. For as long as Nasir Khan wishes harm upon the Mullah."

Faizal's face betrayed his sense of exasperation. "This need not cause all of us to suffer. If there is to be a trial, it is not for all of us."

The others sat in silence, none replying to what Faizal had implied.

The Mullah had listened to everyone speak before he offered his own thoughts. "A trial is only necessary when there has been a sin, and the need for it remains until there is repentance."

Umar was shocked. "Mullah, you can't mean that. How have you sinned?"

The Mullah smiled. "This trial has been sent for all of our sins. Indeed, the state of our country is a trial for all the people, and for all of our sins."

"I don't understand," said Faizal.

"God will not change the condition of a people until they change what is in themselves that displeases him. When God intends misfortune for a people, there is no repelling it, only acceptance and change."

The others listened closely to his words.

"We thought that we did the bidding of God when we fought the Russians," said the Mullah. "Now every man who fought them, no matter how dishonourable, calls himself a mujahid. A ghazi. These same men now live how they please as reward for doing what they say was the work of God."

Umar was visibly upset. "But our cause was just. You know this in your heart."

"The cause was just," agreed the Mullah, "That is true. But our people, without the invaders to guide their actions, have fallen away from the path that is the will of God. We have the country that we deserve. And we ourselves have been given this trial for our sins."

"But, Mullah," said Asadullah Amin, "we are not sinners."

The Mullah smiled again. "We told ourselves that we led good lives, but we lived with many sinners. We heeded the words of men like Jan Farooq and Nasir Khan. We protected those who chose to lie and cheat. Our sins are many and great. And so God is testing us."

"And so how do we pass this test?" asked Umar.

The Mullah pointed at Wasif, who had been silent as the Mullah talked of sin. "This man, no longer a boy, saw the solution while the rest of us were blind. He chose to stab evil in the heart, not to live with it in our midst."

Wasif's cheeks reddened as he looked up at the Mullah. Umar turned and clapped him on the shoulder. "Wasif is no longer one of us. Instead we must welcome Jan Nasrollah, brother of Asadullah Amin." The others muttered their welcomes, as well, using the boy's new name.

The Mullah stood, lifting Wasif to his feet and embracing him. "Jan Nasrollah. Dearest Victory of God. This is a good name."

The men went back to sitting quietly by the fire, mostly gazing up at the stars. The young boys seated all around them were quiet as well, soaking in what had been discussed.

THIS SHALL BE *a* HOUSE *of* PEACE

After a time Faizal spoke. "Haji Mullah, forgive me for speaking again, but ... I know of something. Somewhere. From the Russian days — an arms cache. It belongs to Engineer Hekmatyar. It is far, near Spin Boldak. And it is guarded, I am sure, but ..."

Umar's look at Faizal was poisonous. "How long have you held on to this secret?"

Faizal was frightened by Umar's expression, but stammered out a reply: "I have not been hiding this information. My uncle told me of it many years ago. I only just remembered last night. Perhaps with more weapons ... well, we can protect ourselves at least."

"This hardly solves our problem," said Rashid dismissively. "Spin Boldak is far and driving there would be impossible. Surely Nasir Khan's men, and Jan Farooq's family, are looking for us on all the roads."

The Mullah held up a hand. "There is no straight answer here. The solution to our problem will itself be a problem." He leaned forward, his face glowing in the firelight. "Faizal, you have piqued my interest. Tell me more of what you know about this cache."

Faizal cleared his throat, and began to speak.

Early the following morning, the men and boys all lay wrapped in their patus, sleeping around the dying fire in the centre of the tents. Asadullah Amin had rigged a simple shelter from his patu in the back of one of the trucks, and slept there with his wife. The Mullah sat apart from the others, awake and looking out over the countryside.

Gol Kochi sat down beside the Mullah. "The jirga lasted late into the night," he said.

"I would not have thought there was much to discuss," replied the Mullah. "You offered us nanawatai shortly after we arrived."

Gol Kochi chuckled. "You know what it is, our way. Every man had his say. In the end, we agreed that the only thing to do was what had already been done — to offer you our protection."

The Mullah took Gol Kochi's hand in his own. "For this," he said, "you have my thanks. Truly."

Gol Kochi raised one eyebrow, his expression a warning. "But don't think that it is that easy. As is the custom, you may stay with us for as long as you wish. We will fight to defend you as if you were our own kin. That is our public decision."

"But privately?" asked the Mullah.

"The truth is that you bring many mouths with you, which is a concern. We will be moving again soon. One last push and we will be up and over the mountain passes and then into the Hazarajat."

"Is that all?"

Gol Kochi studied the grass at his feet. "We are also worried about the violence that will come to us once Nasir Khan finds out you are here." He looked up at the Mullah. "This violence will not stop until you are dead. Or more likely until we are all dead."

The Mullah sighed. "And so what would you have us do?"

"Publicly, you may stay with us forever," said Gol Kochi. "Privately, I ask that you leave. Asadullah Amin and the boy Wasif may both stay with us if you wish. I suspect that they are not the ones Nasir Khan really wants, in any case."

"The boy Wasif is now the man Jan Nasrollah," said the Mullah.

"No matter. He may stay. If there is to be a trial, I will endeavour to ensure that it is fair and that no blood is shed, you have my word."

"Is that all?"

Gol Kochi spat. "It is. Our grandfathers would cry to hear this decision, but it is so."

"Do you not agree with it?" asked the Mullah.

Gol Kochi's voice was heavy. "We are the Free People, but we are accustomed to being used. To being hated and chased away. You have dealt with us fairly and honestly, unlike others. Our children have married, although what will become of the second wedding that was promised?"

"The father is dead," said the Mullah, "but I do not know what will become of the girl."

"Even blood has been mingled already for the purpose," said Gol Kochi. "I have no quarrel with you or your people, who also follow the old ways."

The Mullah got up on his haunches, surveying the grassy land all around them. "I assume that you have men posted all around?"

"On a normal day, yes. Today, twice as many," said Gol Kochi.

"What if I told you that it was my intention to leave as soon as possible?"

"I would bless your journey and ask how you thought you would travel anywhere without being found."

"I have decided that I no longer wish to be the hunted. We will become the hunters."

Gol Kochi looked surprised. "Even still, easier said than done."

The Mullah entreated Gol Kochi: "Can you find us a Kamaz? One with a long cargo bed?"

"Is that all?" he asked.

"And we will need two dozen sheep. Maybe a few more."

"What will you do with these things?"

The Mullah looked at him earnestly. "You may keep these things when we are done. We just need them for a short time."

Gol Kochi pulled his fingers through his beard as he thought. "It is one thing for us to protect you in our homes. It is something else for us to help you attack Nasir Khan."

PHIL HALTON

"That is not what we ask of you. You need not be connected to this at all. But we need your help. As you say, they will be looking for us."

"Giving away our livestock is like giving away our children. It will be hard to convince the others."

The Mullah's mood turned. "You can take both of our trucks and the motorcycle as payment. To help with your grief."

Gol Kochi smiled. "That would be fine. We can likely find a Kamaz in a day or two."

"Can the boys from the madrassa stay with you until this is settled?"

Gol Kochi shook his head and spat. "Useless mouths. They are yours."

The Mullah pointed at them emphatically. "These boys are the future of our country."

Gol Kochi laughed dryly. "Your country, and your future, perhaps. The future is the enemy of those who live in the past as we do. We walk each journey from the high pastures to the low pastures as did our ancestors, except that we do it knowing it could be our last."

The Mullah nodded slowly, realizing that he had begun to ask for too much. "Will you take Asadullah Amin's wife? Where we will go is no place for a woman."

Gol Kochi looked past him at the truck. His eyes betrayed his true feelings even as he rejected the request. "She is no longer of our tribe. She is yours to care for."

"Let us not speak of custom now," said the Mullah, "but of mercy."

Gol Kochi hesitated, his fingers caught on a tangle in his long hennaed beard. "If only to keep her from being abandoned. Does her husband wish this?"

"He will say yes."

332

Gol Kochi did not smile or laugh this time. "Then she will be safe with us."

"We are agreed, then," said the Mullah.

CHAPTER 23

Dust swirled along the highway, chased up by the wheels of the Kamaz truck as it rolled along, bouncing roughly on the potholes. The back of the truck was filled with sheep and goats that complained loudly with every bump.

The truck began to slow as it approached a rockfall that narrowed the highway into a single lane. Armed men stood at the choke point, waving at the truck to stop. The brakes squealed as it slowed and lurched, halting just short of the rocks.

A fat bandit in a dirty shalwar kamiz climbed up onto the step by the driver's door, a kalash hanging loose from his hand. He blew cigarette smoke into the cab as he spoke. "What delights have you brought us?"

Two other bandits working with him circled the truck like scavenging birds, lifting the canvas flap to peer into the back. One called up to the front of the truck. "Sheep and goats, and a mountain of shit by the smell."

The two Kochi in the cab of the truck stayed very still. "We only want to pass through to market," said the driver. He gestured to the other Kochi, who pulled some money out of the pocket of his shirt. "Don't be foolish, brother. All of it," he said. The Kochi pulled more bills out of his pocket. The driver passed the wad of money out the window to the fat bandit. "This is all we have. For you, to feed those who protect this road from bandits."

The fat bandit laughed. "And we'll take a goat."

The driver held up his hands as if in surrender. "We want no trouble. Only to get to market to sell our livestock."

"In that case we'll take two," reasoned the bandit. "You'll be empty-handed when you come back."

The bandits at the back of the truck lifted two squealing goats and each slung one over his shoulders. The fat bandit stepped down and waved the truck onward. The truck belched black smoke as it rolled forward again.

The driver leaned over to watch the bandits recede in the distance through his mirrors. "Too many more fat greedy bastards like that one and we won't have a goat left by the time we get there."

The other Kochi reached through the broken back window and lifted the canvas a few inches. "Mullah," he said, "we're almost there."

Lying down under the feet of the remaining livestock, clutching their rifles, were the Mullah and the others.

After many hours of driving, the Kamaz rolled to a stop just behind the summit of a low hill. Somewhere along the side of the mountain beyond the hill was the border, an imaginary line on the map that had been long ignored by the Kochi. A small building sat perched partway up the slope, surrounded by thick mud walls.

The driver turned in his seat and lifted the canvas. "We are here."

The two Kochi climbed down out of the cab and went around to the rear of the cargo bed. Rashid and Isa had already climbed down, and they were helping all the boys down while jostling the remaining sheep and goats to keep them from falling out. In a few minutes, everyone stood at the back of the truck. Their clothing was soiled and their weapons were caked with dust and worse.

The Mullah walked a short distance to peer over the top of the hill that concealed the truck, and the other men followed him. Light streamed out from a crack along the bottom of the building's doorway, illuminating one half of the compound.

Rashid cupped his hands around his face to shade his eyes. "Is that it?"

Faizal strained to look, as well, and sounded hesitant. "Maybe. I've never actually been here before. The cache is at the foot of the mountain, where the trail north of Spin Boldak descends into the valley."

Rashid kept peering out at the house. "I don't know this area at all, but I think that is it. I can see a trail, and the Kochi say that we are near Spin Boldak."

"Is there nothing else around here?" asked Umar.

"There must be a reason for someone to be living there," said the Mullah. When he spoke, everyone else fell silent. He turned to the Kochi and spoke to them respectfully. "Will you stay while we make sure that this is the place?"

The driver didn't look at the Mullah when he replied. "Gol Kochi told us not to wait. To keep moving, and not be seen with you."

The Mullah expected as much. "Thank you for taking us this far. You are free to go."

The two Kochi placed their hands on their hearts as they bid farewell. They were soon back in the truck, which lurched forward and continued down toward the border crossing into Chaman. A cloud of dust rolled along the road behind the truck, briefly enveloping the Mullah and the others.

Without speaking a word, the Mullah began to walk into the hills, careful to keep below the crest so that he was concealed as he walked. The boys, exhausted and filthy, followed him in a ragged pack, with the men trailing behind.

Rashid, looking at the group, muttered to himself, "This is madness."

The house on the hillside was in poor repair and surrounded by junk. A motorcycle caked with dust and mud leaned against one wall beside an old bicycle whose handlebars were made of wood. An equally dirty man worked the handle on an old pump. The handle was broken, but had been spliced back together with a thick binding of string. A thin stream of brown water came out of the spout as he worked the handle, filling his bucket very slowly. The man shouted back at the house in frustration. "You said you fixed this pump! Unless we want to drink sludge, I will have to go down to the stream again!"

The man took the bucket from the ground and emptied out the muck. He picked up a rifle leaning against the wall and slung it over his back. Then he unlatched the metal door set in the thick wall, and left it open as he began the long walk down to the stream below.

As he walked along a thin path that cut through the underbrush, he saw two figures walking toward the house. He quickly realized that they were just young boys. He shouted at them but did not unsling his rifle. "Stop! What are you two doing out here?"

Asadullah Amin and Jan Nasrollah froze when they heard his voice. The man dropped the bucket but still left his rifle on his back as he moved quickly across the hill toward them. He was about to shout again when he was thrown to the ground by a hard tackle. His rifle was pinned under him, and before he could roll over, a scarf tied into a garrotte was slipped over his head and around his neck. It tightened until he stopped making noises.

Rashid kept one knee on his back, pulling the garrotte tight. He leaned down and spoke into the man's ear. "How many are you in the house?"

The man's eyes rolled wildly in his head, but he held up two fingers in response. Rashid kept pulling and tightening the garrotte until the man was still. He released the garrotte, and the man's lifeless body slumped heavily to the ground. He stood and signalled to the others, who quickly moved up the hill to the farmhouse.

Without wasting any time, the Mullah and his followers burst through the open door of the compound, weapons at the ready, just as Noor, the tall bandit, stepped out of the house, scratching himself. He froze when he saw the Mullah.

"You again!" shouted the Mullah.

The man tried to turn and run back into the house, but was quickly tackled by Rashid and Umar. Umar pinned him to the ground, shaking his head in disbelief. "You thought you'd never see us again."

Rashid leaned down close to his face. "It has been a long time since your trial, Noor. The Mullah will want to speak to you at length, I am sure." The boys crowded all around him in wide-eyed recognition.

Noor quivered as Umar held him to the ground. The Mullah stood over him, ignoring the bandit for the moment. He waved Isa and Rashid into the house, and waited as he listened to the noise they made violently searching the small building. Rashid appeared at the doorway, his eyes flashing as he looked straight at Faizal. "There's nothing but junk in here."

Faizal's hands twisted the ends of his kamiz. "I'm sure this is the right place."

Umar shook the bandit to get his attention. "Where is the cache?"

The bandit kept looking plaintively at the Mullah. His voice quavered as he spoke. "I don't know what you mean."

Umar let go of the bandit and picked up his kalash. The bandit tried to scramble backwards to get away from him, but Umar stepped in and butt-stroked him in the mouth as hard as he could, sending both blood and teeth flying across the yard. "Same question."

Noor spat blood and coughed. "You know me, Mullah. I will tell you the truth."

The Mullah did not look at him. "Speak and be quick about it."

The words came tumbling out of Noor. "This house belongs to Engineer Hekmatyar. We are paid to live here and guard it. But there is nothing here of value that I have ever seen."

Rashid looked down at him as he squirmed on the ground. "Then why guard it?"

Noor rolled over onto his hands and knees, letting out another stream of blood from his mouth. "It is not my place to question men like the Engineer." He spat. "He pays me, and I do as I am told."

Umar hit him with the butt of the kalash again, this time square in the back. Noor collapsed onto his chest, arms and legs giving out from under him.

"They say that the lands here belong to his uncle. We are guarding it because of that."

Rashid laughed. "He pays you to be here for his love of his uncle's land?"

Noor did not try to get up or to look at his attackers. "There is nothing here to steal, but take what you want and then go."

The Mullah walked around to look at Noor's face. "After our earlier experiences together, you think that we are here to rob you?"

Noor's eyes widened. "That's not what I meant, Haji ..."

The Mullah turned away in disgust, his fists clenched tightly. His voice was cold when he gave the next instruction. "Hang him by his feet."

The others hesitated for a short moment before carrying out the Mullah's wishes. Jan Nasrollah dug through the junk in the yard and found a long electrical cord. Umar and Rashid held Noor down as Jan Nasrollah tied the cord around his ankles and knotted it tightly. The loose end was thrown over a beam sticking out of the wall of the house, and all of them hoisted him up.

Umar looked down at Noor's face as he steadied him. "Where are the weapons?"

"There are no weapons but our own!" said Noor. "There is nothing! We do nothing wrong by being here! Mercy, Mullah, in the name of God have mercy!"

The Mullah ignored his pleas, and looked around the yard for a suitable tool. He put his rifle down and pulled the broken handle off the pump. Without warning, he swung the handle in a long arc that cracked against the bandit's leg. Noor screamed in pain. The Mullah swung again, hitting him lower on the leg. Swing after swing, the Mullah kept striking, never hitting the same spot twice. His voice was tight when he finally spoke.

"You would blaspheme while asking for mercy?" He hit him again just above the hip. "You were given mercy. You were given a second chance, bandit, which you squandered coming here."

The others formed a ring around the Mullah and his victim. They looked on in silence. Noor screamed and moaned as he was struck.

The Mullah gritted his teeth as he swung the handle. "Do you now feel what it is to be helpless? Frightened? In pain? What I do, I do in the name of your victims." Before long the Mullah's face was covered in a sheet of blood. Even still, he continued to swing at the bandit, again and again, as the others watched in silence.

The rising sun was a red smear in the haze across the horizon. The Mullah and his men performed their prayers, with the boys lined up behind them doing the same. As they bowed down, heads touching the ground, long shadows stretched out in front of them into the world. Noor's broken body had been cast out of the compound and lay in a heap under some brush nearby.

When the prayers were finished, Umar spoke quietly to the Mullah. "Do you wish for me to prepare him and the other for burial?"

The Mullah glanced at the corpse. "He was no Muslim. Leave him for the dogs."

Faizal had been listening. "Mullah, forgive me, but haven't you said yourself that all men are brothers? And that it is for God alone to judge?"

Umar pointed at the dead bandit. "Maybe so, but that man is an apostate. He deserves no help or mercy from us."

"I am not a scholar, as are you, Umar," said Faizal. "But Mullah, I thought that we are building a house of peace?"

The Mullah stared at Faizal, but spoke loud enough for everyone to hear. "Killing this man is not violence if it is the will of God. Then it is justice." He fixed his gaze directly on Faizal. "He was shown mercy and chose to reject Islam. He rejected the will of God. He is no better than a dog, and will be treated as a dog."

The Mullah turned and walked back into the compound, followed by all the others except Faizal, who remained by himself, looking out over the vast countryside around him. No matter where he looked, the body of Noor tugged at the corner of his field of view. Finally, after a long moment, Faizal followed the others inside, his lips pressed tightly together.

The men and boys spent the day washing their clothes and busying themselves with small tasks while they awaited direction from the Mullah. Soon, there were shalwar kamiz spread out to dry over almost all the brush that surrounded the house. The Mullah, however, withdrew from their company and spent the day in silent meditation in one corner of the farmhouse.

After the laundry was left to dry, the boys rushed out of the compound and into the surrounding fields, intent on using their freedom from the routine of the madrassa to play a game of cricket. They had made a ball from plastic bags retrieved from the garbage in the compound, and had a piece of firewood for their bat. Umar shooed them all back inside when he found that, instead of playing, they were gathered in a circle around Noor's body. He forced them to sit in rows in the shade of a wall and led them through recitation practice instead.

No one spoke of the missing cache as they waited for the Mullah to decide what must be done. When the men and boys prepared to sleep that evening, there was none of the usual banter. Everyone lay in silence, locked inside their thoughts.

Faizal and Rashid, each carrying a kalash, stood watch over the countryside from a small rise just outside the compound door. All around them was still.

Rashid yawned loudly, breaking the silence. Faizal stood close to him and spoke quietly. "What do you think we will do now?"

"You mean now that your arms cache has proven to be false?" asked Rashid.

Faizal's expression crumpled. "My story is not false."

"Oh, no?" Rashid mimed looking all around them. "Did I miss the piles of weapons and ammunition?"

"I only told the Mullah what my uncle told me," said Faizal.

"Umar thinks it convenient that your uncle is not here to explain himself."

"He is long dead."

"That's also convenient."

Faizal glared at him. "For whom?"

Rashid gave a shrug and said nothing more.

"You believe me, don't you?" asked Faizal.

Rashid looked him in the eye. "It is not what I do believe or don't believe that should concern you, Faizal."

"You mean the Mullah?"

"I mean that only God knows the truth in your heart."

Faizal turned away, hurt by the accusation. "I did not lie."

Rashid's voice softened a little. "As you say."

"I know that without the guns that we thought were here, we are lost."

Rashid shook his head. "Have you not been listening?"

"Do you mean that we will find victory if only we enact the will of God?" Faizal scoffed, "As if that were simple."

Rashid looked a bit less sure of himself, but no less serious. "Faizal, you know me well. I am a practical man. But this is not a topic to raise with the others."

Faizal continued in a mocking tone. "And why not? Are we no longer free to speak? Is that not our way?"

Rashid's voice was tight, and he spoke in a low voice. "We follow the Mullah. That is all we need to know for now."

Faizal shook his head. "This isn't what I had expected." He let the silence hang between them until, after a moment, he spoke again. "Rashid, you are a worldly man. You have seen much more of this earth than any of the rest of us. Do you think that we are on the righteous path?"

Rashid hesitated, but when he spoke his voice was firm. "All I know is that I have faith."

Faizal's smile was strained. "My faith is telling me something different than yours, perhaps."

Rashid said nothing.

The two men stood next to each other, scanning the ground in front of them, but seeing nothing. Rashid yawned again, and Faizal clapped him on the shoulder. "You are tired, brother," said Faizal. "Why not sleep for the first half of our shift while I stand guard. Then I will wake you, and you can cover the second half. We all need sleep, and there is no threat that requires us both to be awake."

Rashid considered this for a moment. "I suppose."

"I'm sure that our path will be more clear in the morning," said Faizal.

"We must trust the Mullah," said Rashid. "We have come too far to not finish the journey."

"Don't worry, my friend," smiled Faizal. "We will find our way."

Rashid looked at him intently. "Wake me at the first sign of anything."

"Of course."

Rashid went back into the compound, picking a spot close to the entrance on which to lie. The others were spread all around, preferring to sleep outside in the cool air. He wrapped his patu tightly around his head and shoulders, curling up on his side.

Within minutes, he was snoring gently.

CHAPTER 24

The sun was blazing hotly though still very low in the morning sky, when Rashid awoke with a start. He tore off the patu covering his head and looked around, blinking in the bright light. He was alone. He scooped his kalash up off of the ground and quickly searched throughout the compound to find Faizal.

He saw that the front gate was open and swung lazily in the morning breeze. Tire tracks led from where the old motorcycle had been leaning against the wall, out through the gate and beyond. Rashid stood at the doorway and looked out over the countryside. Not a single living thing was in sight. He stepped back inside, locked the gate, and just stood there for what felt to him like a very long time. As he turned around, he saw the Mullah standing in the courtyard, watching him.

"Is he gone?" asked the Mullah.

"I think so." Rashid hesitated before speaking again, "I have failed you. I let him go."

"It is for the best, Rashid. Letting nature take its course is not failure. Our journey is not for those who lack faith."

Rashid's face flushed hotly. "Mullah, he questioned the will of God ... whether we follow the will of God. I ... listened to him, and should have known what it meant, but I told no one."

The Mullah smiled and clapped Rashid on the shoulder. "And yet you are still here, and not with him. Wake the others. We have much to discuss."

Rashid only nodded, his throat still tight and dry, and did as he was asked. The Mullah sat in the shade of the compound wall and waited as each of the others was woken and joined him. Soon, they all sat in a circle around him, with the boys surrounding the men. They passed around pieces of stale bread that they had found in the farm building, dipping it in a can of condensed milk that was their only other food.

When the Mullah broke the news of Faizal's disappearance, the mood turned sour.

"Justice will find him, as sure as it will all of us," offered Umar.

Rashid stabbed his bread into the milk can. "Best that justice find him before I do."

Everyone but the Mullah laughed at this. He raised a hand for silence before speaking calmly. "God has set for us a straight path. We need not do anything except that which is His will to bring justice to all."

The others were silent. The Mullah looked around, but no one met his gaze directly. Finally, Umar spoke. "Mullah, we are all wondering the same thing. What will we do now?"

"Isn't it obvious, my friend?" said the Mullah. "We will do what is right — the will of God. He has set us on a path that we must accept, no matter how difficult."

Umar spoke again. "But, forgive me, what exactly are we to do? The path is not as clear to us as perhaps it is to you."

Rashid's voice was full of frustration. "I let Faizal betray us. It is my fault that we can no longer stay here."

Umar nodded. "Nasir Khan's men are numerous and well armed," he said. "We are tired and poorly equipped. We must do something, and quickly."

As the gravity of this fact sank in, all eyes turned to the Mullah again. He slowly stood and moved outside the circle to face everyone at once. "I am not tired. Indeed, I am refreshed." He lifted his arms up vigorously as if to show his energy. "I am refreshed by my complete submission to the will of God. We are not ill equipped. We ourselves, our bodies, are God's righteous sword. What better weapon than the heart of a righteous ghazi? You are right that we must leave this place. I know not yet where we will go. God will show us the path, if you are willing to walk it."

The men and boys sat stock-still, not looking directly at the Mullah, while letting his words sink in. A gust of wind blew a rolling stream of dust over them, obscuring the landscape around them, confining them for a few seconds inside the cloud. The Mullah continued speaking even as the others covered their mouths. "We must cease this discussion of what we will do next. We will be victorious, insh'allah. That is all we need to know or believe. Do you believe this with all your heart?"

As the dust rolled onward the Mullah reappeared before them all. He looked from person to person, saying each of their names so that they would look at him. He waited for a moment as each of them weighed the faith that resided in his own heart.

Umar stood up first. He walked over and knelt before the Mullah. "I place myself in the hands of God, and in your hands, as well. We will be victorious, insh'allah."

"It is God's will," answered the Mullah.

Jan Nasrollah and Asadullah Amin approached the Mullah together, each jostling to get ahead of the other. They spoke over each other, Jan Nasrollah's voice drowning out his brother's.

"Quiet," he said, "I am the eldest! Mullah, you are like our father. We are yours, and will be victorious, insh'allah."

"Insh'allah," repeated Asadullah Amin, with a vicious look at his brother.

The small boys began to crowd around the Mullah, each kneeling in turn as did Jan Nasrollah and Asadullah Amin. Their high voices were no less solemn than the others as they said the words: "Insh'allah, we will be victorious."

Rashid sat still, not looking at the others, deep in his own thoughts. Isa pushed himself to his feet with a hand on Rashid's shoulder and waded through the boys toward the Mullah. They parted for him, and he knelt down heavily. Isa's eyes shone dully. "Mullah, I have passed the point where I can claim to have led a good life. But a good death is to die performing a righteous deed. I will live as best as I can until then. Insh'allah, we will be victorious."

The Mullah took Isa by the shoulders, "It is God's will."

Rashid was the last to climb to his feet. He stood before the Mullah and looked him in the eye for a moment before dropping to his knees, saying only one word: "Insh'allah."

The Mullah raised Rashid to his feet again and embraced him tightly. "Insh'allah."

The sun was high overhead, and the Mullah's followers suffered in the heat. They carefully searched the compound, looking everywhere to find what might have made the farm worth guarding, their efforts made difficult by the high, scorching sun. Wrecked rope beds, empty cans, and rotten mattresses filled the empty space behind the building. Asadullah Amin picked through the garbage, piling it in one corner, while Isa and Jan Nasrollah worked together to move a pile of stones that might have concealed something. "Do you think that they buried it somewhere?" asked Jan Nasrollah.

"Do you see it lying around anywhere?" asked Asadullah Amin.

Rashid flipped over a stinking mattress that came apart in his hands. "I can't see that they did if it's the size that Faizal described."

Jan Nasrollah's tone was acidic. "We should never have believed a word that he said."

Rashid stopped and looked at him thoughtfully. "I don't think that he lied about the cache. His betrayal only came later."

Asadullah Amin tossed a broken wooden bed frame into the corner but added nothing to the conversation. Isa and Jan Nasrollah rolled a heavy stone together, pushing it against their growing pile. "Maybe they moved the cache," said Asadullah Amin.

"It sounded too big to be moved without someone noticing," said Rashid.

Jan Nasrollah stopped working and wiped his brow. "What if someone did notice, but they're not here to tell us?"

Rashid stopped working, as well. "Then we will soon know. There is little room to conceal anything here, and we have nearly turned over every stone. Literally."

Rashid hoped to get a smile or laugh from the two young men, but they just rolled their eyes before going back to their work. Isa did not look up, but worked as slowly now as he always did, his eyes dull and flat.

Jan Nasrollah heaved another stone to the edge of the compound. "Maybe we are just wasting our time here."

"Do you have a better idea of what to do, then?" asked Asadullah Amin.

Isa looked pale despite the heat. He wiped the sweat from his eyes and sat down heavily on the edge of an old rope bed that he had just uncovered from within a pile of garbage.

The bed collapsed with a crack, and Isa fell hard to the ground, disappearing from sight with a scream followed a few seconds later by a splash. Jan Nasrollah and Rashid stared at the hole in the ground that had opened up beneath him. Rashid moved to the edge of the hole and peered down. A square hole, cut into the mud and rock, plunged straight down into the earth, ending in a dark pool of brackish water. Deep handholds were cut into the sides of the well. Rashid quickly climbed into the hole and began to scramble down. Partway down, he let go of the wall and plunged into the water.

Rashid kept his eyes open, scanning underwater for Isa. He quickly found him and pulled him to the surface, legs kicking hard. Isa spat out a stream of water and dry-heaved as he came to the surface. Rashid held him carefully under one arm, holding onto the wall with the other. "You'll be all right, my friend."

The Mullah had come from inside the farm, alarmed by the noise, and had pushed the boys aside to peer down the hole that was illuminated by the midday sun. "It is a miracle," he said.

Rashid shouted up at him. "He will be all right."

"Can you bring him back up?" asked Umar.

"Send down a rope. He's not ready to climb just yet."

The boys all gathered behind the Mullah, wary of the deep hole. They chattered among themselves, alive with questions. "What is this hole?" they asked.

The Mullah turned to them, his voice again that of a schoolteacher. "This is a qanat."

Some of the boys tried the unfamiliar word.

"A qanat is a type of well," said the Mullah. "It draws water from the mountainside down to the valley farms. It is a long underground tunnel, with deep holes to access it along its length."

Umar addressed the boys, as well. "We mujahideen sometimes hid in them, or used them to travel in secret."

The Mullah held up a finger. "And to store things."

Asadullah Amin pulled a length of frayed rope from the wreckage in the corner. It was not nearly long enough to reach the bottom of the qanat, and so he tied it into a loop instead, which he draped over one shoulder. He struggled to find his footing as he began to lower himself over the lip of the hole.

"Help your brother," commanded the Mullah, and Jan Nasrollah grudgingly held out his hands.

Asadullah Amin climbed down the well, using the deep handholds cut into the rock. As he descended the shaft, he passed horizontal passages cut through the rock, too dark to peer into. He soon reached the bottom of the well, his feet just above Rashid's head. Isa was conscious and breathing normally, slumped against Rashid, who clung to the handholds concealed in the water. Asadullah Amin passed the loop of rope to Rashid, and climbed back up to the lowest horizontal chamber.

Rashid passed the rope under Isa's arms and the other end of the loop over one shoulder. He began to climb the side of the well. Isa followed him, supporting most of his own weight but held up by the rope linking him to Rashid should he fall. Asadullah Amin helped pull first Rashid and then Isa into the horizontal passage with a hand under each of their arms. As he did, he told each of them, "It is a miracle!"

They each gazed down the length of the deep chamber, their eyes adjusting to the dark. The passage was stacked with green military crates, crusted with mud and dust, extending into the darkness. On the floor were a few boards and a block and tackle.

Rashid brushed off one end of a box with his wet sleeve, reading the Cyrillic writing on the side. "It says that inside are ten kalashes." He gave a low whistle, looking at the others. "Ten kalashes times how many crates? A hundred?"

"And there are two more chambers that I passed as I climbed down," said Asadullah Amin.

They heard a shout from above, and tried to look up from the chamber. "What have you found?" asked the Mullah.

Asadullah Amin shouted up at the Mullah. "Quick! Come down quick! It is a miracle!"

The Mullah swiftly lowered himself over the rim of the hole, looking at Jan Nasrollah as he did. "Keep the boys up here away from the qanat."

When he reached the lower chamber, Rashid had already cracked open one of the crates of rifles. He pulled a kalash out from inside and smiled. "Still in packing grease."

The Mullah took it from him and turned it over in his hands, appreciating the pristine state that it was in. "What else?"

"I only looked down this chamber, but there seems to be a little of everything. Rifles, ammunition, mines, grenades. Anything you could ask for."

Asadullah Amin pulled another rifle from the crate. "Praise be to Allah!"

Rashid clapped him on the shoulder. "And thanks to Engineer Hekmatyar."

The Mullah turned to climb back up out of the well. "Rashid, you know well what kinds of things we need right away."

"Right away?" asked Rashid.

The Mullah disappeared up the shaft and back into the sunlight. "We must move quickly."

The boys took up the slack on the rope and began to haul the crate up out of the well. Inch by inch they pulled, until it swung unsteadily under the bed frame. Jan Nasrollah carefully pulled it to the side, gritting his teeth. "Let it down. Slowly, slowly."

The crate came to rest beside the entrance to the well. Jan Nasrollah quickly untied it and dragged it to the side with the other three crates they had already raised.

Rashid came climbing up out of the well. He clapped Jan Nasrollah on the shoulder as he passed him. His hand traced the outline of each crate that had been brought up and dragged off to the side, doing some mental calculations. He gave a satisfied grunt, and said, "Three more crates and we are done." He then went looking for the Mullah, whom he found seated in the shade of the wall around the front of the compound. "We have pulled almost everything that we need out of the well."

"Very good," said the Mullah. "How soon will we be ready?"

"By dark. We just have to break it down into individual loads."

"Mash'allah."

"If I knew more about our plans, I could —"

The Mullah waved off his concern with one hand. "All will become apparent once we are ready." The Mullah closed his eyes in meditation, dismissing Rashid and ending the conversation. Rashid returned to his task.

It was getting dark by the time the work was complete. Rashid laid out the weapons he had selected from the stores in the qanat and now began to assign them to each of the boys and men.

To each of the boys he handed a kalash from which most of the packing grease had been hastily wiped. The boys had occupied themselves filling magazines, and now each of them wore a simple set of pouches across his chest. "Make sure that your lifchikas are full, I want you to have six full magazines each."

He next selected two rocket-propelled grenade launchers off of the ground and handed them to Umar and Jan Nasrollah. He then helped them pull the ammunition carriers onto their backs.

"Three rounds each, including the one on the launcher already." Umar had been chatting quietly with Jan Nasrollah but fell silent when he felt the weight of the pack.

Rashid showed them how to carry the RPG tucked under one arm, the short sling over their shoulder taking up most of the weight. "You can fire it from here, too," he said.

A third backpack was handed to Isa, who buckled slightly under the weight. "The blocks of explosives in that pack are inert unless you use one of these." He held up a metal tube the size of a finger. "I'll hold on to the detonators for now."

Rashid turned to Asadullah Amin. "Little brother, I have something special for you." He wheeled a bicycle out from where it had been leaning on the wall. Two heavy ammunition crates were tied together by the handles with rope and sat hanging over the bicycle's frame. A pair of plastic water jugs were draped over the frame behind the crates. "This is much lighter to push than it would be to carry." Asadullah Amin took the handlebars and pushed it back and forth. With effort, he could move it.

Rashid picked up his own weapon, a kalash with a heavy drum magazine attached, and turned to the Mullah. "I have taken everything that I can imagine we will need from the qanat. Everything that we can carry, at least. We are ready, Mullah."

The Mullah shouldered his own pack. Its straps cut deeply into his broad shoulders, but he made no sign that he noticed. "We will cut off the head of the snake. We will finish this business with Nasir Khan directly, in his own home."

Looks of surprise crossed their faces, but no one spoke a word. The Mullah led the way out of the compound and into the countryside. He turned to Rashid as he stepped through the metal doorway. "You're sure it won't destroy it all?"

"Yes. It will just drop the entrances to the horizontal chambers."

"Good. Wait until we are all clear."

Rashid watched as each of them left the compound and walked along in single file behind the Mullah into the night. Once they were nearly a hundred yards away, he went back to the top of the qanat. A yellow detonation cord ran from where he had tied it to a broken bed frame down into the darkness of the well. Rashid pulled the pin from the detonator and turned the ring, letting it snap into place. The friction lit the cord, which burned down into the well.

Rashid left the compound at a light jog, well aware of how long the cord would burn. As he caught up to the column, the charges exploded with a deep thump. They all felt it in their chest as the sound wave washed over them. A plume of dust and smoke poured out of the well, obscuring their view of the building within the compound. Rashid stopped to admire his handiwork for a moment, and then he fell in with the others as they marched through the night.

CHAPTER 25

The Mullah lay on his back in what meagre shade he could create for himself. His patu, brown like the earth around him, sloped over him from the edge of the rock above, held down with small stones and earth. All around him lay his followers, concealed in a dry wadi where they waited through the heat of the day.

The Mullah's mouth was dry, his tongue thick. He pursed his cracked lips to speak, but did not, instead waving for Rashid to come to him from under the cover of his own patu.

Rashid saw the signal and scurried over to the Mullah, keeping low to the ground. He did not think that there was anyone who could see them, but he took no chances. He lay down next to the Mullah, his ear cocked to listen.

"How much water do we have left?" the Mullah whispered.

Rashid shook his head. His parched lips hurt as he spoke, although he barely moved them. "Very little."

The Mullah nodded. "Still, we will survive." The Mullah's eyes wandered to the end of the wadi. "Have another look over the rim of the wadi to make sure that there is no one who will disturb us."

Rashid moved off in a low crouch, his kalash hanging loosely from one hand. He moved to the edge of the wadi and stopped. Dropping down onto his belly, he crawled along the hot earth until he could just see the highway nearby.

A small collection of farms clustered around the junction of the highway and a small stream. At the edge of the village, rubble had been piled on the highway in a pattern that forced vehicles to slow down. Lying among the rubble were a half-dozen bandits, all seeking shade.

Rashid did not have binoculars, but his eyesight was keen. He pulled his patu over his head and shoulders to better conceal himself, and lay watching the highway for a long time. The bandits only roused themselves once, when a car appeared on the highway, but the car turned around without coming through the checkpoint at all. The bandits went back to their shade.

Rashid's mouth was hot and dry, so he popped a small, round pebble under his tongue. The pebble tricked his mouth into salivating and provided some small relief for a few minutes. He licked his lips, though he knew that it would not help for long.

A few villagers moved about in the fields surrounding the village, but Rashid did not see what he feared the most. The village was poor, and seemed to have no herds of animals. A shepherd might use the wadi to move his flock and would be sure to spot them. Satisfied that they were in no danger, Rashid slid backwards and returned to the Mullah.

"We should be safe."

The Mullah nodded and went back to his thoughts. Rashid waited a moment longer and then went back to his shady spot at the other end of the group. He placed his kalash on the ground and lay down in the thin shade of the wadi's walls. Jan Nasrollah and Asadullah Amin lay behind him, separated from him by a large rock.

"Any news?" asked Asadullah Amin.

Rashid shook his head. "We wait. The bandits in the village below aren't likely to come up here looking for us."

Jan Nasrollah scowled. "We should go and kill them. And all the rest of the bandits in this district."

Rashid smiled. "As the Mullah has said, we will cut the head off this snake instead of fighting it inch by inch."

"I am sick of walking. And hiding. I want to fight," said Jan Nasrollah.

Rashid gave him a wan smile. "You will have your chance, my friend. Of that, I have no doubt."

With nothing more to be said through parched lips, he and the boys tried to sleep as they waited for the sun to go down.

As night fell, Rashid moved down the line of men and boys lying in the wadi, warning them with a touch on the shoulder to get ready. The cooler night air was refreshing, though the thought of another night's march was not a pleasant one. The Mullah stood with his heavy rucksack on his back, waiting for Rashid.

"We will move along the top of the ridgeline," said the Mullah, gesturing with one finger. "We will stay far enough below the crest to remain unseen."

Rashid nodded. "If you lead them that way, I will take Asadullah Amin and the bicycle higher up to see if there is a spring. We need water."

The Mullah nodded in agreement, and without another word he turned and began to march. The others fell in behind him. Rashid watched them pass, one by one. Isa stared at the feet of the boy in front of him as he shuffled past. Umar forced a smile as he struggled along in line, but Rashid saw blood on his sandals from burst blisters.

As Asadullah Amin pushed his bicycle past Rashid, Rashid placed a hand on the young man's shoulder. "Wait here with me."

Jan Nasrollah hesitated, as well, but Rashid waved him back in line. As he passed, Asadullah Amin saw that some of the boys walking near his brother were empty-handed, but his brother had three rifles and a grenade launcher slung across his back. Jan Nasrollah hunched forward under the weight but said nothing. Asadullah Amin blushed as he remembered the many days, before they found the madrassa, that his brother had led him by the hand, looking for food and shelter.

The column struggled onward, the Mullah's long legs carrying him at a fast pace into the growing darkness of the night.

Once he was sure that the column was far enough away, Rashid turned to Asadullah Amin. "We are going to climb up there." He pointed farther up the slope. "I am hoping to find a spring that we can use to fill these jugs."

Asadullah Amin's expression betrayed his dark thoughts. He let out a deep sigh. "Truly, Rashid, I am not sure if I can push this bicycle up this hill."

Rashid handed his rifle to the boy and took the bicycle by the handlebars. "Follow me, then."

The pair headed up the dry wadi together. The air became cooler as they climbed, Rashid's eyes searching the area around them, never pausing as he marched. In time, he found what he was searching for: a small clump of brush, its leaves dark and very slightly fragrant.

They stopped beside the low brush, and Rashid looked closely at the branches. Small green buds hung from the ends of the lowest branches. He spoke while continuing to look intensely at the ground around them for more signs. "These bushes are drawing water up from somewhere."

Rashid quickly found an area that looked as if water had run over it in the past. A shallow channel had been cut through the earth, leading to a small notch in a dry rock face. Rashid knelt down in front of it and began to dig with his hands. He pulled out scoops of dry earth and round stones. "These stones are a good sign." He held one up to Asadullah Amin. "This was washed down from a stream somewhere above, perhaps a long time ago." He kept digging at the notch in the stones until he was suddenly rewarded.

There was no gush of water, but the soil around his hands began to darken. He dug a little more and a thin layer of water pooled at the base of his hole. He scooped a little out with his fingers and pressed it to his lips. It had a sharp, metallic taste, but he gestured to Asadullah Amin to try some and pressed more of the water to his own lips, as well.

Rashid and Asadullah Amin continued to dig until one of the jugs could fit into the hole, its lips pressed up against the soil where the water continued to slowly well up. Rashid stretched a piece of scarf over the mouth of the jug and let the water run into it through this simple filter. He pulled some more small rocks and debris out of the cut in the rock, and the water began to seep through the earth a little faster.

The jug was only three-quarters full when Rashid decided it was time to leave. Asadullah Amin complained. "This is barely enough water for everyone, Rashid. We should stay."

Rashid shook his head. "We have a hard walk ahead of us if we are going to catch up to the Mullah. If we lose him tonight, we might lose him for good."

Asadullah Amin pulled the jug out from the hole with both hands, grunting with the effort, and Rashid quickly filled the hole back in and scattered some dry brush over top to conceal their work. He carefully poured water from one jug into the other to balance the load, and hung both of them back on the frame of the bicycle, tied together with a short piece of string. He began to push it back the way that they had come while Asadullah Amin followed, carrying their rifles.

In the distance they could see the checkpoint on the road, lit up with an oil lamp. The bandits were seated together, likely playing cards or dice. Asadullah Amin watched them for a while as they walked, pondering in silence, before asking a question. "Rashid, do you think that there are men like that, making a living like that, all over the country?"

"Sadly, I know that that is the case."

Asadullah Amin was silent for a few minutes again. "Then ... are we no more than grains of sand fighting against the desert?"

Rashid said nothing, letting his footsteps punctuate his thoughts. "I have been like a grain of sand blown by the wind, dust collecting wherever it catches against something bigger than itself. But a strong wind can shape the dust and the sand. The Mullah is such a wind."

Asadullah Amin nodded, and they walked onward without speaking. The journey down the slope was much easier than the journey up had been. Rashid thought briefly of his own youth. Riding bicycles had been one of the few pleasures for teenagers where he'd lived, but that seemed like a thousand years ago now, or a dream. He shook his head to clear the thought out.

Farther down the slope there was more dry vegetation to conceal their movement. Rashid and Asadullah Amin moved quickly, trying to catch up to where they thought the Mullah would be. When the ground became flatter, Rashid handed the bicycle over to Asadullah Amin again, and took his own rifle in his hands. Cradling it in his arms, he moved smoothly along a track that he assumed the Mullah had taken before them.

Before they'd gone very far, Rashid paused again, looking intently at a low bed of leafy plants. He laid the bicycle down, careful not to spill the water, and squatted to examine the vegetation that grew beside the trail they walked along. He pulled a stalk out of the ground and handed it to Asadullah Amin. It was a little stiff from lack of water, but was long and leafy. "Eat this," he said. "Wild rhubarb."

Asadullah Amin took a tentative bite. It tasted tart, too much so, but it was also juicy. He finished the stalk off quickly. Red juices dripped down his chin, but he wiped them up with his finger and licked them off. He squatted down beside Rashid and pulled another stalk out of the ground for himself. Rashid had slung his rifle across his back and had pulled up the front of his shirt to make a basket. He filled it with as much rhubarb as he could find before they moved off again.

It took two more hours of hard walking to catch up to the Mullah and the others. The Mullah had stopped the group in a rough circle, ready to fight if it had not been Rashid and Asadullah Amin who approached. Nearby stood the shells of a few burnt-out buildings, the remains of a small village left jutting from the landscape like rotten teeth.

When the Mullah saw the bicycle reflected in the dull moonlight, he knew who it was. He stood up and waved briefly at the pair before squatting again behind cover.

As Rashid and Asadullah Amin approached the Mullah, he stood up and clutched Rashid in a bear hug. The Mullah spoke in a whisper, his lips cracked and dry. "Asalaam aleikum, my brother." His eyes twinkled as he said the familiar words. "May you not be tired. May you be strong. May your house and family prosper. May your health be ever good."

Rashid hugged him back. "We found water, but not much."

The Mullah squeezed him again. "Enough to share between us all right now?"

"Of course." Rashid handed the Mullah a stalk of rhubarb. "And we found this. Enough for everyone, as well."

"Praise be!"

Rashid and Asadullah Amin moved through the group, handing out the rhubarb and offering drinks from the jug. When they reached Jan Nasrollah, he was flat on his back, exhausted. Asadullah Amin held out a cup of water to him. "Drink, brother."

Jan Nasrollah barely lifted his head. "I don't need it. Give it to the others."

Rashid eyed him carefully. "Do as he says," he said.

When Asadullah Amin had moved farther down the line, Rashid offered his cup of water to the boy. "Take this. There is no shame in being thirsty." Jan Nasrollah opened his eyes and looked around before gulping down the water. He then took a piece of rhubarb, looking guilty as he chewed on the stalk.

"How much farther?" he asked.

"It is not far to Nasir Khan's," said Rashid.

"How far is not far?"

"We will be there tonight."

Jan Nasrollah smiled. "It will be a great fight," he said, "with much opportunity for glory. His men will not give up as easily as these others we have met."

Rashid smiled encouragingly. "We travel in the footsteps of greatness. This is the route that Alexander's army took."

"Who?" asked Jan Nasrollah.

"Iskander. Alexander the Great. He fought here thousands of years ago. Kandahar is named after him."

"Was he an Afghan?" asked Jan Nasrollah.

"No, a Greek."

"Then we would have beat him," said Jan Nasrollah.

Rashid laughed quietly. "Rest for a few more minutes, my friend. And then we march."

The first light of dawn began to glow below the horizon. The Mullah led the long line of his followers into a small gully where they could conceal themselves again during daylight. He stood in the centre of the group as they gathered. "We will stop here for the day."

Boys and men flung themselves down wherever they stood. Hands rubbed aching feet, and no one spoke. There was more shade and concealment here than the previous day, so no one needed to hang his patu as a shelter. Soon most of the group were asleep, not yet tormented by the full heat of the day.

Rashid squatted beside the Mullah, not yet ready to rest. "How close are we now?"

The Mullah thought for a moment. "No more than a few hours' walking."

"Do you want me to scout it out in daylight?"

The Mullah clapped Rashid on the shoulder. "You are a good man to have for a job like this, my friend. But we are too close to expose ourselves needlessly. I have seen it with my own eyes, as have you and Isa. We will be victorious —"

Rashid mouthed the final word. "Insh'allah."

The Mullah smiled. "Insh'allah. Now rest. I will take the first watch."

"Don't you need sleep, as well, Mullah?"

"I am refreshed by my complete submersion in the will of God. I will rest later."

Rashid was exhausted. He lay down beside the Mullah. Before long, like the others, he, too, was asleep.

The Mullah waited until the night sky was completely dark before waking the others. Everyone had slept for most of the day, and as they woke they looked at each other groggily. It took the Mullah several tries to get everyone on their feet, shaking them awake one at a time, careful not to make too much noise. He had Rashid check each of their weapons, making sure that nothing was forgotten, before he led them off into the night.

The Mullah led them in single file, taking a circuitous route behind a small crest that overlooked their destination. When he saw that their position was good, he signalled to the others to stop. He crawled up to the top of the crest and saw that Nasir Khan's home sat only four hundred yards away atop its hill like a squat fortress, with a few smaller houses scattered through the valley around it. He watched as the gates opened just wide enough for two guards with automatic rifles to slip out. Once they were through the door, it slammed shut and was barred with an audible rattle. One of the two guards carried a small parcel of food, the other a lit lantern. They walked over to the tank that guarded the hilltop, where two other men awaited them.

The new guards relieved the others, who had probably spent the day lounging in the shade of the tank. The guards who had been relieved walked sleepily to the gate and were admitted back into the compound. The other two climbed atop the tank and sat, looking out over the valley.

The Mullah watched them from his vantage point. Rashid had crawled forward to lie beside him, his eyes fixed on the compound. The others lay in various positions behind them, out of sight.

The Mullah spoke to Rashid and gestured at the rusted tracks and sprockets on the tank. "It looks like it has not moved in a very long time."

Rashid's expert eyes examined the tank. "I doubt that it can move. It is sagging on its tracks. It looks like it was dragged or pushed into position."

"So it is only the gun we need worry about. The plan that you suggested — are you sure you can do it?"

Rashid nodded. "Isa and I will have both guards' throats slit before they can raise the alarm. Even if it is immobile, we don't want to have to fight that tank if we don't have to."

The Mullah's eyes scanned the countryside for a covered approach to the tank, extending one finger to indicate the route that he saw. "You could crawl up alongside that jumble of rocks and gravel."

Rashid strained his neck to see what the Mullah meant. He could just pick out the ground that the Mullah's eyes had found. The night was dark, with clouds drifting across the moon. Once he was satisfied that he had seen the route, he asked, "Will you wait here with the others? You will be able to see us once we are close."

The Mullah's eyes searched the ground again. "No, this is a little too far. We will move around the slope and wait in a position over there." Rashid strained to look again. "We will be concealed as we wait for you, though more by darkness than anything else."

Rashid nodded. The position the Mullah had selected looked good. "Once the tank crew are dead, we will blow the doors. We will set the charges as you move closer. As soon as they go off, we will all charge in."

The Mullah nodded in agreement and clapped Rashid on the shoulder. Then he slid back down the slope and rolled over to face the others, Rashid squatting beside him. Umar sat nearby, his feet out of his sandals and both covered in blood. The Mullah glanced at Umar but said nothing, instead beckoning everyone to move closer to him. When they were ringed tightly around him he began to speak, his voice very low. "We will wait until just before dawn — when the guards are tired and thinking only of going to bed."

Rashid quickly sketched out the plan in the dust, scratching out lines with a stick and using stones to represent the compound gate and the tank. The dim moonlight cast a grey pall over the diagram on the ground. "Isa and I will eliminate the outside guards," said Rashid. "We will then place the charges on the doors. When they blow off, everyone will follow the Mullah into the compound. We must move room by room, working fast to keep them off balance."

He looked around at the others, their faces shining faintly in the moonlight. They looked tired and anxious.

The Mullah spoke to them softly, saying the words they needed to hear. "Our journey has been long. The struggle is not yet over. But by the dawn, we will be victorious, insh'allah, or we will sit at the feet of God."

The boys whispered a response in unison, "Allah-u akbar."

The Mullah whispered back, "Allah-u akbar."

Rashid moved to where Umar sat, his face a mask barely concealing his pain. He lifted from the ground the rocket-propelled grenade launcher that Umar had been carrying, unloaded it, and checked over the mechanism. "Do you remember what I showed you?" asked Rashid

"Of course," said Umar.

"And you?" asked Rashid.

Jan Nasrollah held up his grenade launcher, showing Rashid that he had already wiped down the firing mechanism. "I do."

Rashid smiled and spoke to everyone who could hear him, his voice barely above a whisper. "Then I suggest that you get some sleep. I will be the first sentry."

The men and boys all quietly took off their remaining gear and found positions where they could sleep. The cool night air was a blessing, and wrapped in their patus, they lay quietly. Isa moved to lie down next to where Rashid sat. His skin was grey and his eyes were glassy.

Rashid leaned over and spoke quietly in his ear. "There will always be times that you feel like this. Like you want the needle again. You fight this struggle every day. But you can win. I know, as I have done it. Am doing it now."

Isa looked at Rashid but said nothing. Rashid turned over and crawled a short distance away, peering over the crest and focusing his attention on the compound and the men sitting on top of the tank. Although they had the chance to sleep, none of the others, except the Mullah, closed their eyes. They lay thinking and waiting.

The Mullah slept deeply.

CHAPTER 26

The pre-dawn morning was dark, the moon having retreated behind a thick bank of clouds. The inky blackness concealed Isa and Rashid as they crept slowly through the underbrush toward Nasir Khan's fortress. Each carried a kalash tightly in his hands, and the canvas backpack that hung heavily on Isa's back was filled with explosives. His feet dragged in the dust as he walked, weighed down by his burden.

Rashid stopped frequently, Isa crouching close behind him, moving his shoulders impatiently to find a way to balance the weight on his back so that it did not hurt. When they paused, Rashid listened carefully for any sign that they had been seen or that Nasir Khan's men were patrolling. In this manner they moved slowly, from cover to cover, creeping closer.

Rashid stepped gingerly through a small patch of gravel and stopped to crouch behind a large, low rock. Behind him, Isa stumbled on the same gravel and slipped, rolling under the weight of his pack. As he fell, he gripped his rifle tightly, instinctively, and his finger squeezed the trigger when he hit the ground.

PHIL HALTON

A single shot went straight into the air and the sound carried sharply in all directions.

Rashid and Isa froze where they were, hoping not to be seen in the darkness. The tank crew lounging by their vehicle shot to their feet. In their haste to mount the vehicle, the driver knocked over their lantern, which smashed on the ground and went out. The other guard scrambled to the top of the turret and shouted at the compound, "Wake up! They're here!"

As Rashid watched, the two guards dropped into the tank, slamming the hatch closed over their heads. Seconds later the turret began to rotate slowly, as if cranked by hand, to point in the direction from which they had heard the shot.

Rashid and Isa hugged the earth as tightly as they could as firing started along the top of the compound wall, the chatter of kalashes filling the pre-dawn darkness with noise. The ground around them was sprayed with bullets, fired wildly but still deadly. A heavy machine gun started firing, as well, adding a deeper thump to the sound of the gunfire.

They expected us, thought Rashid. The sound of gunfire resonated in the pit of his stomach. Rashid saw in Isa's eyes that he was full of fear. Isa reached out and took Rashid's hand as they clung to the ground together.

A few hundred yards away, the Mullah and the others watched as the compound came alive like a nest of angry ants. There was a brief pause in the wild firing aimed at the sound of the shot, just long enough for Nasir Khan's voice to be heard. "You are outgunned, Mullah! You cannot fight my men and a tank! Surrender!"

The Mullah's followers froze, cowed by the surprising weight of fire coming from the compound and the failure of their plan. The boys all huddled together, wild-eyed, each pressing against one another in a tight clump. Some whimpered quietly at the tremendous noise of the gunfire, but most seemed to have been frightened into a state of silent shock. The Mullah looked at them for a moment, and then began to bark out orders to the others who had not yet frozen completely. "Fire the RPGs. We must hit the tank and machine gun from here."

Umar and Jan Nasrollah loaded the RPGs they had been carrying, sliding rockets into the end of the tubes. Once they were both loaded, Umar gave a nod to Jan Nasrollah, and they stood up in unison. Umar shouted as they fired the rockets. "Allah-u akbar!"

The rockets streaked up the hill toward their targets, but both went high, carrying on into the dark sky and exploding in the far distance. The Mullah slid along the ground toward them, keeping low. He spoke directly into their ears so that he could be heard over the deafening sound of the gunfire around them.

"Umar, look at the tank," said the Mullah. "Aim for the point between the turret and the hull." When Umar nodded that he understood, the Mullah turned and spoke to Jan Nasrollah. "Aim for the wall just below the gun."

Umar and Jan Nasrollah reloaded their launchers, the boy's fingers shaking as he tried to slide the round into the tube. Umar watched him as he fumbled before using one hand to steady the rocket and drive it home. Umar looked Jan Nasrollah in the eye and nodded. Once more they pushed themselves off the ground into a standing position, rockets balanced on their shoulders. As they stood, the ground around them was torn up by incoming fire, throwing dust and sparks into their faces. They pulled their triggers and dropped to the ground, not pausing to see where their shots would land. The rockets went wide, peeling off into the darkness again. The heavy machine gun at the edge of the compound wall began to rake back and forth around the source of the rocket fire. The bullets dug into the ground in front of the men, throwing up a bigger cloud of dust and a hail of stones that peppered them as they pressed themselves into the earth.

The Mullah slid backwards and raised himself into a half crouch, speaking now to the boys who cowered in a heap on the ground, clutching their kalashes. "Move up! Move up!" He grabbed one boy by the kamiz and lifted him onto his feet. He began to manhandle the other boys as he spoke. "When I give the signal, you must all fire at the edge of the compound wall. This will give Umar and Jan Nasrollah a chance to fire their rockets."

The boys looked at him mutely, but seemed to understand. Asadullah Amin crawled over to squat in the midst of the boys. From this position, he was just barely able to make out the outline of the tank in the darkness. The turret was still traversing slowly, and now the huge barrel of the gun was starting to elevate, as well. Asadullah Amin realized that soon it would be pointing in their direction.

Umar and Jan Nasrollah, having reloaded their launchers, looked to the Mullah for a signal. The Mullah held out a hand toward them like a symphony conductor. He shouted at the boys: "Stand! Stand and fire!" Asadullah Amin was the first on his feet, and the boys followed his example.

They stood like old men bent down as they faced into a sandstorm. The boys fired their kalashes at the compound, most with their eyes closed and triggers held down tightly. The sudden volume of fire surprised Nasir Khan's men, but not before two of the boys were cut down like wheat under a scythe. Asadullah Amin looked down at their shattered bodies. Rasul, the youngest boy in the madrassa, bled from a half a dozen holes in his chest. He lay on his back, his arms thrown over his head as if merely playing dead. The other boy fell closer to the firing line, but his face was no longer recognizable. Asadullah Amin did not take the time to look at the others in order to determine who it must be. He focused instead on firing his own kalash, mechanically changing magazines when it ran dry.

As the fire from the boys built, the Mullah waved his hand at Umar and Jan Nasrollah, who quickly stood, carefully aiming their rockets at their targets. The rockets streaked out through the night one after the other. Umar's rocket hit the ground in front of the tank, sending a spray of dirt and gravel up at the turret.

Jan Nasrollah's rocket hit the compound wall just below where the machine gun had been firing. Mud bricks shattered, spraying deadly shrapnel through the men who had been manning the machine gun. Their bodies toppled to the ground, and one of the metal compound doors now hung askew in its frame. The fire from the compound slackened off again.

"Allah-u akbar!" cried the Mullah.

After a moment, the shout went up from the boys, as well. "Allah-u akbar!"

Before they finished shouting, the Mullah was already on his feet and running toward the compound. Asadullah Amin was close behind him, shouting at the boys, "Up! Get up! With the Mullah! Allah-u akbar!"

Isa and Rashid were still firmly pressing their bodies against the earth, trying to use what little cover the rolling ground could give them. They were covered in clods of dirt sprayed over them by bullets that had struck all around. Hearing the firing slacken, Rashid lifted his head enough to turn and speak to Isa. "We need to pull back now. You move first. I'll cover you."

Isa hid his head behind his backpack, which he clutched with both hands. "But what about the tank?"

Rashid shook his head. "We'll have to find another way."

Isa looked Rashid in the eye and began to scramble to his feet. "Death in the company of friends is as a feast, my brother." He leapt up, but instead of retreating he ran forward toward the tank. Rashid pulled himself up into a crouch, and fired every round in his drum magazine in one very long burst at the top edge of the compound wall. His eyes followed Isa the whole time that his kalash shuddered in his hands.

By a miracle, Isa made it to the side of the tank unscathed. He swung himself up onto the hull over one of the tracks, fumbling the backpack as he did so. Rounds struck the side of the tank with metallic pings, forcing him to tuck himself into the seam of the turret and the body, pushing his face against the metal. When the firing paused for a moment, he rolled off the tank and onto the ground, recovering the backpack and hoisting it back up.

Isa pulled himself onto the tank again, sheltering the explosives with his body. He adjusted the backpack, pushing it firmly against the base of the turret, which continued to grind slowly around toward the Mullah and the others. His hands worked quickly, pulling a simple timer out of the bag, checking that the detonator cord was still firmly seated inside its metal body.

Rashid changed magazines and raised his weapon to fire again. Before he did, he heard a burst of fire from the compound wall. Bullets ripped through Isa and ricocheted off the hull underneath him. His body slumped over top of the charge that he had just set, blood seeping through the backpack. A second burst tore through his legs, spattering the side of the turret with blood.

Rashid began to climb to his feet, ready to charge toward the tank to set the explosives, when he saw that Isa's head had turned to face him. In his fingers was the timer, which he twisted to set for a short delay. Isa pulled the safety pin with what little strength he had. Isa's lips moved, wet with blood, but Rashid could not tell what he was saying.

Rashid whispered to himself, "None is worthy of worship except Allah."

With a thunderous crack and a billow of black smoke, the charge detonated against the weakest point in the tank. Isa was flung in a thousand directions at once. Smoke streamed out of the buckled hatches. The tank was no longer a threat to anyone.

Rashid could hear the cries of the Mullah and the boys as they charged up the slope behind him. Umar and Jan Nasrollah were behind them, herding the boys forward and firing over their heads. The boys were firing sporadically from the hip toward the top of the compound wall, but by now there was little resistance as they closed the short distance remaining to the wrecked gate.

The Mullah disappeared through the entrance first, but the boys hesitated. One metal door hung off of its hinges, blackened and twisted. Rashid rushed past the boys, shouting encouragement at them as he ran, Umar on his heels, and ducked through the doorway, stepping over the crumpled body of one of the machine gunners as he went. He heard his own voice crying out: "Takbir!"

Hearing his shout, the boys followed him into the fortress. "Allah-u akbar!"

They all fired madly at everything they saw, shouting takbirs as they went. Asadullah Amin watched them run, hearing the short bursts of fire as they reached each new room in the building. He turned in a different direction, walking cautiously along the outer perimeter of the compound, reasoning that Nasir Khan would be as far from the fighting as he could get. He reached a heavy door that was closed but not locked. He swung it open and listened. There was neither the sound of gunfire nor shouting from this section of the fortress, and so he stepped through the doorway and began to follow a long hallway that seemed to lead into a separate back compound.

While he could still hear the others charging madly from room to room behind him, he watched and listened before moving. He gripped his kalash in both hands, holding it out in front of him at the ready, letting the barrel turn corners and enter rooms before he did himself. Asadullah Amin rounded the final corner at the end of the passage to find himself in a small courtyard. In the corner were a huddle of women and very young children. Some of the women wore chadors, and the others hid their faces with their hands. The children tried to hide behind them or in the folds of their veils. The women and children all wailed piteously, hands stretched out, begging for mercy.

Asadullah Amin lowered the barrel of his rifle, and averted his eyes from the women. "Peace be upon you, sisters. We are not here for you."

The women and children began to wail again as the boy in the sequined vest pushed himself through the little group, holding a short-barrelled rifle in his hands. He briefly thought about shouting at Asadullah Amin, to draw attention to himself, and to the power that he held in his hands, but instead he just fired a series of short bursts.

Asadullah Amin was still looking away when the rounds ripped through his arms and chest. He turned as he fell, his mind detached, briefly noting the pockmarks that were appearing in the plaster of the wall behind him. He did not feel himself hit the ground and no longer heard the women or children over the sound of blood pulsing in his ears.

The boy growled like an animal as he saw Asadullah Amin drop to the floor in a widening pool of blood. The other children clutched at his legs and hid their faces in fear, but he ignored them, staring only at the destruction he had caused.

When Jan Nasrollah stepped into the courtyard, drawn by the firing and the shout, his eyes quickly skimmed over the boy in the sequined vest to his fallen brother, lying on the floor like a broken toy. As he ran toward his brother, he fired a long salvo of bullets from the hip, cutting across the boy and the women and children huddled around him. The boy's slight body was driven back against the wall, collapsing in a spray of blood. The women

376

and children fell on top of him, shattered by the gunfire.

"Allah-u akbar!" cried Jan Nasrollah from where he stood on the other side of the courtyard. When his rifle had run dry, he snapped a fresh magazine into place and fired again, into the boy in the sequined vest, into the bodies of the women, into the children, into everything.

"Allah-u akbar!"

When his rifle was empty for the last time and he had no more magazines left, he dropped the rifle and collapsed beside his brother. Cradling his brother's head in his lap, he sobbed. His head was full of all the words that he wanted to say, that he had not said in months, but his tongue was thick and the words stuck there. He tried to force them out between his lips.

"Amin."

There was a bubble of blood at his brother's lips, which may have moved ever so slightly. He strained his ears to listen.

"Wasif. Tell me a story."

CHAPTER 27

The Mullah moved cautiously through the guest house library where he had once met with Nasir Khan. The room was silent, though shots could be heard coming from the rest of the compound. The Mullah examined each room carefully, checking everywhere that a person could hide. Rounding a long, low couch, he stopped. Spread across the floor at his feet were bundles of rupees, each wrapped in a strip of paper and tied with string. There were dozens of these bundles, so many that walking across the floor here was difficult. All together they were a fortune. He reached down and picked up one packet of rupees, turning it over in his hands thoughtfully. His eyes strayed from the money to a battered tin trunk that was tucked up against the wall nearby.

The Mullah dropped the rupees as he moved toward the trunk, lightning quick. He flung open the lid with one hand, pointing the barrel of his kalash into it with the other. Crouched down inside of it on what stacks of money remained was Nasir Khan.

He shook with terror, hands clutched over his head, as he looked up at the Mullah. "Stop! Please! I am unarmed!"

The Mullah sneered. "Stop what? What do you think I am here to do?"

Nasir Khan took his hands from his head and stood up awkwardly, balancing on the uneven piles of money in the tin trunk. He held out his hands to the Mullah, begging. "I was right when I said that I underestimated you. For that, I am very sorry."

"Just for that?" asked the Mullah.

Nasir Khan slowly crouched down, grasping a bundle of money in each hand and holding them out to the Mullah. "Let me reframe my offer from before. I will work for you. Gladly."

The Mullah looked at him silently as Nasir Khan continued to speak.

"Together we can still run this district. Maybe even more. And we can both be rich men." As if to prove it, he held the money out again.

The Mullah grabbed him roughly by the shirt collar and dragged him out of the tin box. His feet dragged across the floor of the room as the Mullah pulled him along. "Let me ask the others what they think of your offer. Discussion is the way of our people, as you well know."

When the Mullah emerged from the compound, dawn had begun to break over the far hills, spreading light in jagged fingers through the mountaintops, slowly illuminating the dark landscape. He looked around for a moment, blinking. Black smoke poured from several places inside the compound. Outside of it, a gaggle of boys stood next to the blackened hull of the tank. Asadullah Amin and two other dead boys lay at their feet on a bedspread taken from inside.

Jan Nasrollah sat beside his brother, holding his hand tightly. With his other hand he clutched his kalash across his lap. Rashid stood over him, one hand on his shoulder. He chose his words carefully. "Jan Nasrollah, today you are truly a man. You will marry your brother's widow, as is right and proper."

Jan Nasrollah made no indication that he heard him.

Rashid climbed up onto the tank and peered down through an open hatch. "I thought as much. If there were any ammo inside this tank, it would have cooked off. There would be nothing left of it." He looked around at the others. "An unloaded weapon makes two people afraid."

No one responded to him. They stood close together, almost touching. They looked away from the bodies at their feet.

The Mullah dragged Nasir Khan by one arm through them, stopping in front of the tank. All eyes were fixed on him as he spoke. "This man has made us an offer. He will work for me and will make us all rich men. What do you think?"

Before anyone could respond, Umar appeared at the tangled gates dragging a wounded man. He shouted, "Mullah, wait. Look who I found. Another old friend." Umar held him up at the shoulders, but the man was so covered in blood as to be unrecognizable.

The injured man looked up, wiping blood from his eyes so that he could see the others. It was Faizal. He dropped to his knees on the spot, arms outstretched. "Please, forgive me, all of you."

The Mullah looked at him without pity. His grip on Nasir Khan tightened, and he forced him to his knees, as well.

"A trial! We deserve a trial," begged Faizal.

Umar hit Faizal across the back of the head with an open-handed blow, knocking the old man to the ground. He put a foot on his back, holding him in place. Faizal let out a cry as Umar's sandal pressed into his back. "When he was trusted, he betrayed us. When he spoke, he lied. When he made a promise, he broke it."

The Mullah pointed at both of their captives. "These men are not Muslims. We do not need to judge them. They will be judged by God Himself."

Without a word, the boys from the madrassa seized both Nasir Khan and Faizal and held them fast. Rashid took two sheets that had been retrieved from the house for Asadullah Amin's shroud and twisted each one into a cord, tying a simple loop at the end. He pulled one loop over each man's head.

Rashid directed the boys to first position Nasir Khan under the barrel of the tank. He struggled, wrenching his arms free from the boys' grip and pushing them away from him. Umar struck him across the face with the butt of his rifle, and Nasir Khan crumpled. The boys held him up, their small hands pushing him under the arms. Rashid took the loose end of the cord and threw it over the tank barrel. The boys let go of Nasir Khan to help Umar haul on the rope, lifting Nasir Khan about a foot off the ground. His feet kicked wildly as he tried to gain a footing. Rashid tied the cord off with a few quick turns around the barrel, and Nasir Khan's flailing quickly tightened the knot.

Umar pulled Faizal to his feet, the man crying and endeavouring to stay prone on the ground. Jan Nasrollah took one arm from Umar, and together they dragged him under the barrel of the tank, as well. Rashid took the free end of the cord and pulled it over the tank barrel. Together they hauled Faizal off his feet, and he, too, began to writhe back and forth, swinging into Nasir Khan.

Rashid tied off the cord and stood back. Both men and boys watched them suffer, without a word, until a few long minutes had passed, and the hanged men were still.

Umar stepped forward to cut the men down, but the Mullah raised a hand and motioned for him to stop. "Leave them. I want their bodies to be seen."

The Mullah's order was obeyed. Nasir Khan and Faizal twisted grotesquely in the breeze as the Mullah's companions set about searching the compound for weapons, money, and survivors.

As the sky continued to lighten, local men began to approach the compound. They gathered in front of the tank, eyeing the two hanged men. One man, with wide streaks of grey in his beard, spoke to the Mullah. "Is it true? Are you the one Nasir Khan has been seeking to kill?"

The Mullah ignored the old man, lost in his thoughts. Umar answered instead. "We are simple men who run a madrassa, nothing more."

The old man raised his hands. "Then God be praised, and may the children of all good people study at your madrassa."

The crowd of local men began to grow. Everyone in the surrounding villages came to see with their own eyes what had become of Nasir Khan. Umar greeted each man as they arrived, carefully ensuring that no one was missed. As their numbers grew, he approached the Mullah. "You should speak. They are all wondering about you, and will want to hear what you have to say."

The Mullah nodded, fingers untangling his beard as he collected his thoughts. He climbed onto the front of the tank, looking down over the hanged men. His voice was rich and loud when he finally spoke. "Peace be upon you all."

The men in the crowd murmured in reply, "And unto you."

"Cousins, I am here to ask for your help." The Mullah swung his arm around, pointing in all directions. "I am going to restore peace to our country. I will enforce the laws of God. I will make this country into what it once was — a land under Islam, and a house of peace."

Jan Nasrollah stood up from where he had been sitting beside his brother. "I want to help you."

Umar went to stand beside him. "You know that we all do."

The Mullah's expression was severe. "Even though it will be a struggle greater than any you have faced?"

Umar smiled. "Because of that. Mullah, you know that we are your students in all things."

One of the local men looked around at his neighbours and shouted: "It is the will of God!"

Someone in the crowd shouted: "Takbir!"

"Allah-u akbar!"

"Allah-u akbar!"

"Allah-u akbar!"

The crowd shouted until they were hoarse as the sun rose fully over the horizon, bathing the world in intense bright light.

EPILOGUE

Umar stood at the front of a classroom full of boys, who all looked at him attentively. He held a copy of the Quran reverently in his right hand. "All knowledge that is required by humankind is to be found in this book, praise God!"

In the classroom next door, Jan Nasrollah walked between boys seated in long rows, learning to write by copying passages of the Quran. "This is the Umm al-Kitab — the mother of all books. It contains the solution to every human problem, no matter how complex."

Rashid stood outside in a makeshift classroom of his own. He was surrounded by very young boys who hung off his every word as he held up a kalash and showed them how to disassemble it. "You are truly rich and blessed beyond belief."

Outside the madrassa, the Mullah stood wearing a new shalwar kamiz and turban, both jet black. The sound of the adhan was playing over loudspeakers affixed to a pole in the corner of the compound. As it finished, he clapped his hands together once. "Now, let us pray."

Hundreds of young boys came streaming out from the madrassa that had once been Nasir Khan's home, and from tents set up five deep all around it. The boys and their teachers all lined up behind the Mullah to pray. He looked out over them, his eyes searching. All looked at him in wonder, filled with faith and hope. Satisfied with his students, he focused on his heart, making his intentions pure. Raising his hands, he began. "Allah-u akbar."

His students repeated his words as they began to pray. "Allah-u akbar."

In Afghanistan, the word for students is *taliban*.

ACKNOWLEDGEMENTS

This novel would not have taken the shape that it has without the sharp minds and pencils of Scott Fraser and Cy Strom, to whom I am very grateful.

It might not have seen the light of day at all if not for the encouragement and example of my good friend, Matt Lennox.

My children, Lily and Leif, have been my biggest fans throughout this process and have been unwavering in their support, even when I had my own doubts.

And finally, thank you to all my friends in Afghanistan, who opened their lives and their world to me.

GLOSSARY

adhan – the call to prayer.

Allah – God.

Allah-u akbar – "God is great."

Allah yahaneek – "God bless you," used popularly as a positive exclamation.

amir – king.

asalaam aleikum – a typical greeting meaning "peace be upon you." The ritual reply is "wa aleikum salaam," meaning "and peace upon you, also." Sometimes abbreviated as "salaam," meaning "peace."

atan – a traditional Pashtun dance.

bacha bereesh – literally a beardless boy, specifically a young boy who dances and performs sexual favours for men.

bismillah – "In the name of Allah."

bokhari – a simple, round wood stove made of metal.

chador – a head-to-toe covering worn by women to maintain their modesty. Vision is allowed by a fabric "grill" over the eyes. Also known as a burka.

chai khana – a tea house that provides simple food and a place to sleep.

chaiwallah – someone who makes a living preparing tea.

chapan – a long-sleeved coat.

chars – hashish.

ʹchelam – a water pipe, used for smoking flavoured tobacco or chars.

Chyort poberi! – (Russian) "The Devil take you!"

daal – a simple stew made of boiled lentils, peas, or beans.

dahi – plain curd yoghurt.

dhikr – meditation.

dhol – a double-headed drum.

djinn – along with humans and angels, one of the three types of creatures who possess intelligence and free will according to the Quran. In popular belief, sometimes feared for causing mischief.

doshak – a long pillow used for sitting or sleeping on.

dushka – a DShK Russian heavy machine gun, also the Russian slang for "sweetie."

dushmen – enemy; used by the Russians to describe the mujahideen.

firman – a royal proclamation.

GAZ – a Soviet vehicle manufacturer, also used to refer to the trucks built by this manufacturer and brought to Afghanistan by the Russian army.

ghazi – the title given to a champion among Islamic warriors.

Hadith – the collected accounts of the deeds, teachings, and sayings of the prophet Muhammad (peace be upon him), used as a guide for behaviour.

haji – someone who has completed the hajj. May also be used as a respectful title for an elder person.

haram – forbidden by Islam.

Hazarajat – the traditional lands of the Hazara people. A mountainous area located in Central Afghanistan.

hibachi – a small, portable charcoal grill.

hujra – a community guest house, or the private area for guests within a home, that allows a Pashtun to practise melmastia without breaking purdah.

insh'allah – "If Allah wills it."

jangi spay – literally, "fighting dog." An Afghan or Kochi shepherd breed of dog.

jazak'allah – "May Allah reward you with goodness."

jehez – the money and property brought into a marriage by the bride, or sometimes paid to the groom's family by the bride's family.

jerib – a customary measurement of land, equal to approximately one half of an acre.

jezail – a handmade muzzle-loading musket, often with an intricately decorated stock and a curved butt. Typically found in Southwest and Central Asia.

jihad – internal or external struggle or striving, with a righteous aim.

jirga – a meeting of community members to resolve disputes or reach decisions through consensus. A key element of Pashtunwali.

kafir – an infidel or unbeliever.

kalash – a colloquial term for an AK-47 or AK-74 (Kalashnikov) automatic rifle.

Kamaz – a Soviet truck manufacturer, also used to refer to the trucks built by this manufacturer and brought to Afghanistan by the Russian army.

KHAD – the Soviet-era secret police in Afghanistan.

kishmesh khana – a building, often communally owned, used to dry grapes into raisins.

Kochi – a nomadic population.

lakh – the number 100,000.

lashkar – a posse formed by a community to protect itself or to enforce the decisions of a jirga.

lifchika – Russian slang for magazine pouches worn by soldiers across their chest (literally, a brassiere).

ma'alim – teacher.

madrassa – a school.

maharam – a male member of a female's family who escorts the female when she is outside of the house.

mahr – the payment made by a groom to his bride for her own use, as required by the Hadith.

mash'allah – literally, "God has willed it."

melmastia – hospitality, one of the key tenets of Pashtunwali.

mujahid – a person engaged in jihad. Often used to describe the guerillas who fought the Russian invasion of Afghanistan. The plural is "mujahideen."

naan – unleavened bread baked in a tandoor.

nanawatai – literally meaning "sanctuary," it is a key tenet of Pashtunwali that requires a person to protect another who requests it, even at great risk.

Pashtun – an eastern Iranian people, who believe themselves descended from the biblical tribe of Joseph. Subdivided into many tribes and clans.

Pashtunwali – the way and customs of the Pashtun people.

patu – a wool blanket.

pir – a saint or holy person, either living or dead.

poder – heroin.

powindah – people who subsist through herding animals.

purdah – the separation of the sexes within a society.

rebab – a traditional stringed instrument.

qabuli pilau – a traditional dish of rice, raisins, carrots, and spices.

qanat – a deep well that is connected by underground passages to collect water from high in the mountains and bring it down to the plains.

Quran – the holy book of Islam, believed to record the literal word of God as recited by the Prophet Muhammad (peace be upon him). Along with the Sunnah, it forms the primary source for Islamic theology.

salat – prayer.

salat al janazah – specific prayers used during funerals.

salat-e-isha – the fifth obligatory prayer of the day, conducted between dusk and dawn but often in the early evening.

shabnamah – literally, "night letter." A threatening letter, often posed publicly under cover of darkness.

shalwar kamiz – the loose pants (shalwar) and shirt (kamiz) worn ubiquitously in Afghanistan.

shirk – the sin of practising idolatry or polytheism.

shura – a meeting. Roughly synonymous with "jirga," though the implication is more religious than tribal.

spingiri – literally, "greybeard." An elder.

Sunnah – the orally transmitted record of the teachings and actions of the Prophet Muhammad (peace be upon him). Along with the Quran, it forms the primary source for Islamic theology.

takbir – the name given to the phrase "Allah-u akbar."

tandoor – a clay oven, often set into the ground.

tanzim – organization. The anti-Soviet mujahideen were organized into seven major parties or tanzims.

taslim – the concluding portion of a Muslim prayer: "May the peace and blessings of Allah be upon you."

ta'wiz – an amulet inscribed with holy verses worn to prevent the evil eye or to cure illnesses.

Timur-e Lang – often transliterated as Tamerlane, fourteenth-century Central Asian conqueror and founder of the Timurid dynasty.

tulee – a piece of opium roughly the size of an AK-47 bullet; enough to sustain a serious opium user for a day.

upym – opium.

ushr – a tax on agricultural produce sanctioned by Islam.

wa aleikum salaam – literally, "And peace upon you." The reply to the greeting of "asalaam aleikum."

walwar – the "bride price" paid by the groom's family to the bride's family to secure a marriage arrangement. Unlike the mahr, which is part of Islamic law, it is a cultural practice.

zakat – alms paid to benefit the needy. Paying zakat is one of the five obligations of a devout Muslim.

zebiba – literally, "raisin" in Arabic. Refers to a callus on the forehead caused by zealously performing salat.

ZIL – a Soviet truck manufacturer, also used to refer to the trucks built by this manufacturer and brought to Afghanistan by the Russian army.

More Great Fiction from Dundurn

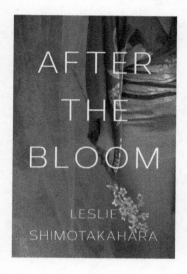

After the Bloom

Leslie Shimotakahara

A daughter's search for her mother reveals her family's past in a Japanese internment camp during the Second World War.

Lily Takemitsu goes missing from her home in Toronto one luminous summer morning in the mid-1980s. Her daughter, Rita, knows her mother has a history of dissociation and memory problems, which have led her to wander off before. But never has she stayed away so long. Unconvinced the police are taking the case seriously, Rita begins to carry out her own investigation. In the course of searching for her mom, she is forced to confront a labyrinth of secrets surrounding the family's internment at a camp in the California desert during the Second World War, their postwar immigration to Toronto, and the father she has never known.

Epic in scope, intimate in style, *After the Bloom* blurs between the present and the ever-present past, beautifully depicting one family's struggle to face the darker side of its history and find some form of redemption.

After the Bloom

Leslie Shimotakahara